D0457672

3-19-98

FINAL
SECONDS

FINAL

John Lutz and David August

SECONDS

KENSINGTON BOOKS
http://www.kensingtonbooks.com

KENSINGTON BOOKS are published by

Kensington Publishing Corp.
850 Third Avenue
New York, NY 10022

Library of Congress Card Catalog Number: 97-075929
ISBN 1-57566-259-0

First Kensington Hardcover Printing: April, 1998
10 9 8 7 6 5 4 3 2 1

Printed in the United States of America

PROLOGUE

For the kids at a New York City high school, a bomb scare is like an extra recess.

As the student body of H.S. 146 in Queens poured down the back steps and out into the schoolyard, there were a few hushed and frightened kids among them, but only a few. The small number of gangbangers, who probably knew something about the bomb, were keeping silent and watching the police warily. But the rest of the kids were glad to be out in the crisp autumn air. Mock brawls broke out. Skateboards clattered to the pavement. Caps were snatched from heads and games of keep-away began. Red-faced, shouting cops and security guards struggled to get the kids back in line and keep them moving to the far end of the schoolyard. Back toward the fence, away from the patrolling teachers, two boys were mooning the camera crew on the sidewalk. The crew had been sent by one of the local television stations, just in case the school blew up.

In addition to the blue-uniformed cops who were trying to keep order in the schoolyard, there were brown uniforms from the Traffic Division who were closing the street with sawhorses and yellow tape, and suits from the Detective Division, who were questioning a suspect near the steps of the building. So there were a lot of cops on the scene, and they were busy, but when the gray van inched between the sawhorses and rolled slowly up to the gates, all of them paused to take a look. It was a moment to be grateful you had the job you did—and not the job the cops in the van had come to do.

The gray van was an old and battered Ford Aerostar. It had the shield of the NYPD on the side, and above that the words BOMB SQUAD. It came to a stop and both doors opened.

Out of the driver's side jumped a wiry young man in his mid twenties. He had curly black hair, fair Irish skin, and handsome features. He was aware that people were staring at him. It showed in the studied nonchalance of his movements as he walked around the van and lifted the back door.

The man who'd gotten out of the passenger's side seemed oblivious to the attention. His hair was going gray at the temples and he had a sergeant's stripes on the sleeves of his uniform shirt. He stood well over six feet, with wide, sloping shoulders and a linebacker's neck. He had a broad face, with a lined brow and wide-set hazel eyes. It was the face of a craftsman or a musician—of someone who had learned the habits of deep concentration.

By the time he got around to the back of the van, the young man had his arms full of equipment. The sergeant picked up several cases and shut the door.

The young man went up to the Scene Control Officer, who was standing at the gate of the schoolyard. "EOD Team 6," he said, "Officer Fahey and Sergeant Harper. Want badge numbers?"

The cop shook his head and wrote down the names. He looked up from his clipboard as the sergeant walked by. "No kidding," he said to Fahey, "that's Harper?"

Fahey grinned. "That's him."

He hurried to catch up with Harper. They walked past a skinny Latino teenager with his hands cuffed behind him who was being questioned by detectives. This would be the kid in whose locker the "suspicious parcel"—as it was officially termed—had been found. Fahey and Harper didn't look at him. How the parcel had gotten in the kid's locker was the detectives' problem. Getting it out was theirs.

A school security guard was waiting for them at the door to the building. The last of the students were just coming out. As he led them upstairs to the second floor, Fahey questioned the guard. The parcel had been found during a routine search of the lockers for drugs. It had an unpleasant chemical smell. No one had touched it.

Harper listened to Fahey's easy banter with the guard, all the time eliciting information. Fahey liked to joke around and stay loose. Most bomb scares turned out to be false alarms. No need to get tense until you were sure you were up against the real thing, that was how Fahey saw it.

Harper liked Jimmy Fahey. He'd had him in training classes, and they'd been partners for six months. When you were partners in the Bomb Squad, you spent hours together in the ready room at the Sixth Precinct, waiting for the call to come in. You got to know each other very well. Jimmy Fahey was a good man. But Harper disagreed with him about this bantering stuff. Harper preferred to keep quiet in the last moments before facing a "suspicious parcel," emptying his mind of extraneous thoughts, sharpening his focus. It was better to assume the worst. Then you'd be ready for it.

Fahey was saying, "Or one time—this really drove us nuts—it was a fake bomb. Some kid's chemistry project. No explosives in it, but even under the fluoroscope we couldn't tell it was fake."

"This one's real," said the guard grimly. "You work in a high school these days, you learn a lot about ordnance."

Fahey got quiet after that. They were walking down a second-floor corridor. They reached a turning in the hallway and stopped. Harper and Fahey dropped their heavy equipment. The guard pointed down the line of lockers and said, "It's in 176." Then he turned to go.

"Hold it," Harper said.

Ignoring him, the guard started to walk away. He figured he'd done his job and he didn't want to linger around locker 176.

"*Stop*," Harper said, quietly but with emphasis.

The guard halted and turned. His expression was receptive. Harper pointed. Across from the lockers was a row of windows. Through them, he could see a brick office building on the other side of the street. People were moving around inside it. Traffic noise was drifting up from the street.

"Go to the Traffic Division guys. Tell whoever's in charge he better close that street and evacuate the building opposite. Right away. If the bomb blows, those windows'll turn into shrapnel."

"I'll tell him," said the guard, and went on his way.

Fahey was grinning. Harper said, "What?"

"So when do I learn that voice?"

"What voice?"

"The one that makes people do what you say."

Harper shrugged and bent down to open one of the cases.

"C'mon, Sarge," Fahey went on. "When you were down under Astor Place Station with a bomb and they handed you the phone and Mayor Koch was on the line, and you said he better shut down the goddamn Lexington Avenue line *now*—was that the voice you used?"

Not for the first time, Harper wondered who made up these stories about him. "I didn't say anything like that."

"Okay, but you used the voice—and he shut down the Lexington Avenue line."

Harper shrugged again. He was already struggling into his blast protection suit. Fahey grabbed the nylon pants from his own bag and started to climb into them. It was a special kind of nylon, heavy and stiff as chain mail, and intended to serve the same purpose.

Putting on the protective suit ought to have been reassuring. But it never had that effect on Harper. This was the last step. Once you fastened the final strap, you went to face the bomb. His heartbeat was growing more rapid and his insides were tightening up. With a conscious effort, he began breathing more deeply, slowing his movements.

Fahey straightened up with his helmet in his hands. His fair-skinned, Irish face was very pale now. He said, "Say, Sarge? Does this part ever get any easier?"

Harper shook his head.

"But after you've done it hundreds of times and come through, you must start to think—"

"You start to think the law of averages is going to catch up with you."

He'd blurted it out without considering, and it brought him up short. Now he tried to dismiss the thought from his mind.

Fahey was blinking at him in surprise. "But you could've stopped going out on calls years ago, couldn't you?"

"I did," said Harper. "Then came the budget cuts and personnel shortages. So I came back."

"They'll kick you upstairs for good pretty soon," Fahey said. "And you know what? I bet you'll mind plenty."

"No, I won't," said Harper, as he attached a Velcro strap on his wrist. "I like investigative work and training. I'll be happy when that's all I do."

"That right?"

Harper nodded. "It's every teacher's dream, teaching bomb disposal. Your class tends to pay attention."

Fahey grinned. "Well, if you really don't mind leaving the field, that's fine with me."

Harper looked at him, puzzled. "Why?"

" 'Cause I want to be the next you." The handsome youthful face wasn't smiling now. He meant it.

Embarrassed, Harper looked away. He bent down to pick up his helmet. "If that's what you want, I expect you'll get your chance. There are plenty of terrorists around." He lowered his helmet, a steel box with a glass faceplate, over his head. "Let's go, Jimmy."

They walked slowly, two moon-men in an empty corridor. Noises filtered up from the street, but the building itself was quiet. The door of locker 176 was standing ajar. Fahey carefully opened it all the way.

A big cardboard box rested on the bottom of the locker. The guard had been right about the chemical smell: gasoline, Harper thought, and something else, a smell he couldn't identify. But it was a bomb, all right. All his senses told him it was a bomb.

"Mind if I handle this one, Sarge?"

Behind the glass plate, Fahey's face was calm and alert. There was no trace of the nervousness of a few minutes ago.

"Go ahead, Jimmy."

Fahey went down on his haunches. The flaps at the top of the box weren't sealed, but he didn't take a chance on lifting them. You never went in the way a bomber would expect you to. He took the glass knife out of his tool kit. If the bomb had a magnetic detonator, a metal knife could set it off. Fahey made a slit in the side of the box.

He glanced at Harper, who nodded for him to go on. Using a cold light, he peered through the slit.

After a moment, he gave a breathy chuckle. "Well, Sarge, the first thing I see is the timer. It's a cheap alarm clock, and the hands are not moving. Repeat, *not* moving." He sat back on his heels and grinned up at Harper through his faceplate. "This baby hasn't been armed."

Harper blew out his breath in relief. His faceplate clouded over. He started to take off his helmet, then thought better of it. "What else can you see?"

Fahey went down on his knees and used the knife to lengthen and widen the slit. He probed with the light. "The timer's wired to a fifty-volt dry cell battery, which is wired to a stick of—it looks like gelignite. There's also a can of gas, straight from the service station. Strictly a high school kid's job."

"Okay." Now Harper took off his helmet. That first breath you drew after taking off the helmet always felt so deep and fresh. "Go down and tell the detectives." The fact that the timer hadn't been set indicated that the boy they had in custody was the bomber. It would be good news for the detectives, a chance for Fahey to rack up some points.

"Right, Sarge." Fahey rose to his feet and started to unbuckle his helmet.

"The bomb wagon should be there by now," Harper said, referring to the armored vehicle that would transport the bomb to the range for disassembly. "Bring up a containment chamber and we'll move the package right into it."

Harper glanced out the window and frowned. There were still people in the opposite building. And it sounded as if they hadn't closed the street yet. It didn't matter now, but still—he made a mental note to have a word with the Traffic Division guy when he got outside.

"Jimmy!" he called after Fahey, who was walking down the corridor. "Make sure they understand, they can't let anyone back in till we have the bomb out of the building, okay?"

"Okay," Fahey called without turning.

Harper tried to think if there was anything else, but nothing came to him. He was alone with the bomb. He squatted down and lifted the flaps. It was a crude, amateur job, as Fahey had said. The smells were stronger—the gasoline, and the other one he hadn't placed yet. When Harper saw the grease stains on the cardboard around the stick of gelignite, he realized what the smell was.

Oh no! he thought. *Oh Jesus!*

Turning his head he yelled, "Fahey!"

Fahey had reached the turn in the corridor where they had left their gear. He spun around.

"It's unstable. The gelignite."

Fahey took a step back toward him. Hesitated.

He didn't need an explanation. The explosive had been stored far too long in whatever warehouse the kid had stolen it from. It was chemically unstable. The kid was lucky it hadn't blown up on him.

Harper might not be so lucky.

He leaned closer. Now the sticky-sweet smell was even stronger, and he could see the beads of moisture on the tacky gray surface of the stick of gelignite.

"Will!" Fahey called out to him. "Get your helmet on!"

Christ—how could he forget that? Harper sat back and reached for the helmet.

"Get away from it," Fahey said. "They can bring up a robot to transfer it to the containment box."

Harper hesitated with the helmet in his hands. It would take hours to move the robot into position. "Jimmy, we have to get the stick away from the gasoline."

Fahey stood stock-still, fifty feet away. Slowly he began to shake his head. "Will, don't."

But there was no other way. To reach the gasoline can, he would have to move the stick. It was better just to pick up the stick. Harper secured the helmet and bent forward. He reached into the box. His hands were bare; he didn't have any gloves. His fingers closed on the stick. It felt clammy. He cut the wire that connected it to the battery and gently lifted it out. Then, very slowly, he rose to a standing position.

"Will, throw it!" Fahey yelled. "Just throw the goddamn thing as far as you can."

But it would go off for sure then. And the windows would blow out. And glass fragments would fly into the building opposite and down to the street below.

Harper stood there motionless, holding the stick of gelignite in the palm of his hand. He called, "Bring me the blanket."

Fahey looked down. The bulky blast suppression blanket lay folded at his feet. It would effectively smother the explosion of a single stick of gelignite. All they had to do was put the stick down on the floor and cover it with the blanket.

"Come on, Jimmy," Harper said.

But Fahey didn't move. He was still looking down. Harper held his breath. After a long moment, Fahey looked up—but not at Harper's face. He looked at the stick of gelignite in his outstretched hand.

He was paralyzed with fear. Five minutes ago Fahey had been able to go to work on the bomb, knowing that a mistake could mean his death. He'd been willing to bet his life on his skill. But this was different. The situation was out of his control now. Out of anyone's control. It was sheer chance whether he and Harper would survive the next few minutes.

Harper spoke just loudly enough to make himself heard. "Jimmy, I need you to bring me the blanket. Now."

Fahey wrested his gaze away from the gelignite. Stooping, he gathered the blanket in his arms. Then, with halting steps, he began to move down the corridor toward Harper.

For Christ's sake, run! Harper wanted to scream at him. But the kid was doing his best. The closer he got, the more clearly Harper could see the terror clenching his features. With his white face and unsteady steps, he was like an invalid who might collapse at any moment. But he kept coming.

The only sound in the corridor was the scrape of his shoes on the linoleum.

Harper stood absolutely still with the stick of gelignite in his hand. He tried not to look at it. If the stick went off, the helmet and armor plates should protect his head and torso, but what about his limbs? His right arm would be blown off, that was certain. Would the paramedics get to him before he bled to death?

He stopped himself from thinking. Fahey was getting close now. His eyes were locked on to Harper's. It was as if only the older man's steady gaze could pull him over the last few paces.

When he was close enough, Harper said, "That's good, Jimmy. Now just drop the blanket."

He allowed himself to think they were going to get out of this. He'd be seeing his wife Laura at home in a few hours. He'd feel like shouting for joy and throwing his arms around her, but he mustn't do that. He wouldn't want to have to explain to her how much danger he'd been in. All he'd say was that it had been a hairy job, but Jimmy had done fine.

Fahey stiffly opened his arms and the blanket fell. It lay at Harper's feet. Harper slowly sank down on one knee. With his free hand he lifted a fold of the blanket. He began to lower his right hand, taking care to keep it perfectly level. He was going to tuck the stick of gelignite in as gently as if it were his baby.

Harper almost made it.

That was the thought that was to haunt him in the months and years to come. He would never know what went wrong. Maybe he got overeager, moved his hand too quickly at the last second. Or maybe he hadn't made a mistake, and the gelignite was simply ready to blow.

There was a roar in his ears and Harper went tumbling and spinning to the floor.

Stunned, he stared at a splash of red on the wall. It was his blood. He felt no pain in his hand, only in his ears. He looked down at his arm, at the shredded nylon, the burned and blackened skin.

Fahey was kneeling beside him. "Oh God!" he said. "Hang on, Will! Just hang on!"

Slowly, disbelievingly, Harper raised his arm and stared at what had been his hand.

1

This was all new to him.

Will Harper exited the highway and coasted down the ramp to the stop sign. There was no one behind him, so he paused to look around. He'd never been in this part of the country before.

He was in northwest Florida, just outside Pensacola. The landscape was different from what he'd seen in other parts of Florida. He liked it. The road in front of him had curves and hills and was lined with tall pine trees. The occasional palm tree still surprised him. He switched off the air conditioner and rolled down the window. Then he grasped the gear stick and shifted into first.

To be exact, he didn't grasp it. He pinched it. Harper's grasping days were over, at least with his right hand. The little finger and ring finger were gone, along with the top joint of the middle finger. The surgeons had done their best with that hand: It worked, it didn't hurt anymore, and apart from the missing fingers it looked normal. Harper complained sometimes that because of the extensive skin grafts, the hair on the back of his hand and forearm had grown back in a strange pattern, but Laura said not to worry, no one would notice. This was true, Harper thought, because most people never got over staring at the fingers that weren't there. But he kept this thought to himself.

As he accelerated down the road, he took a quick look at his map.

It was only a couple more miles. Harper shifted his weight, a little nervously. He wasn't looking forward to the end of this trip. He didn't know what kind of reception he'd receive from Jimmy Fahey.

He and Fahey hadn't seen each other in the two and a half years since the explosion in the high school corridor. Harper was still in the hospital when he heard that Fahey had quit the NYPD and left the city. No one knew where he'd gone.

For the next few weeks, the operations and therapy were all Harper could cope with. After he got out of the hospital, though, he started to think about Fahey again. He wrote to him, explaining that he'd retired from the Department with full disability and pension and was recovering quickly. He wanted to know how Fahey was.

It was a short letter, but hard to write. There were so many things he wanted to say but couldn't put into words. And the physical act of writing was difficult for him. His right hand could still hold a pen, but the weak, wavering writing no longer looked like his own. Looking at the finished letter, he wondered about the effect his handwriting would have on Fahey. He copied the letter on a typewriter, laboriously hunting and pecking. Then he sent it in care of Fahey's parents. Almost a year passed, and he had supposed Fahey had never gotten the letter, or decided not to reply.

Then a postcard arrived from Pensacola. The hurried scrawl said that Fahey had a cushy job running security on a millionaire's estate. He was living in paradise and had plenty of leisure time. Harper ought to drop by if he was ever in the Panhandle. That was all it said.

Harper told his wife Laura that maybe he'd better leave well enough alone. She replied that this didn't look like "well enough" to her.

So when they came on vacation to visit her parents, who lived a few hours' drive north of Pensacola, he called the number on the postcard.

After Harper identified himself, Fahey said nothing for a long moment. Then he turned on the easy good humor that had always been his specialty. It would be great to see Will. The estate was fabulous and there were all sorts of fun things to do. Harper had put down the phone thinking the initial moment of shocked silence after he'd identified himself had been the only honest part of the conversation.

The pine trees gave way to a high wall overgrown with vines. This was the estate. Harper drove along it for several minutes before the gatehouse came into view. It was a low building in faded yellow stucco, with a sloping tile roof that projected over the drive. There was a permanent-looking painted sign at the mouth of the drive, red letters on a white background:

SOME THINGS HISS BEFORE THEY KILL
SOME THINGS RATTLE
SOME THINGS TICK
SOME THINGS ARE SILENT
WELCOME

The gates were open, so Harper, feeling less welcome than he had a minute ago, turned in. A guard in a khaki uniform was standing in the middle of the drive. He motioned for Harper to stop.

As the guard approached, Harper noticed the machine pistol strapped to his belt. It was an Ingram with a phenomenally rapid rate of fire, suitable for perforating brick walls or chopping down trees. The gun and the guard's expression both meant business. Harper wondered who this millionaire client of Fahey's was.

"Help you?"

"Yeah, I'm looking for Jimmy Fahey. My name's Harper."

The guard checked his clipboard. Evidently Harper's name was there, because he said, "Please park your vehicle on the apron over there. I'll take you up to the house in the golf cart."

Harper parked and walked back. The guard was already sitting behind the wheel of a yellow golf cart with a canvas sun shade. A second guard had taken over his post in the driveway. Through a window in the gatehouse, Harper could see other uniformed men. This was quite a setup Fahey was running, and Harper couldn't contain his curiosity any longer. As he got into the cart, he asked, "Who lives here, anyway?"

The guard blinked at the question, as if surprised that anyone could fail to know. "This is the estate of Mr. Rod Buckner."

"Oh," said Harper, suitably impressed, understanding the sign by the driveway now. Rod Buckner was a bestselling author of macho technothrillers. It seemed that every time Harper got on the subway, he saw somebody reading one of Buckner's thick paperbacks. There had been hit movie adaptations, too. Harper had seen one. It was about a gung ho CIA agent named Buck Reilly who was battling Iranian terrorists. Harper had liked it. He'd even bought Buckner's latest. But the first chapter took place on a submarine and had so much technical detail that Harper bogged down. He hoped he wouldn't be meeting Buckner today. He'd never met a novelist, but he figured the first question they'd ask you was whether you'd read their books. Harper wondered where Buckner got his ideas.

The driveway wound through beautifully landscaped grounds. They passed bank upon bank of azaleas, all blooming in brilliant and varied colors. Back home in New York, Harper reflected, the azaleas wouldn't bloom for another three months. Back home, in fact, it was probably sleeting right now. On that postcard Fahey had said he was living in paradise. Maybe he'd meant it. Maybe he'd put the past behind him. Maybe this mission of Harper's wasn't necessary.

Harper put the questions out of his mind. He'd have the answers soon enough.

There was a distant, muffled boom. It sounded like thunder. Harper looked at the sky. It was overcast, but he saw no sign of a storm.

"Sonic boom," the guard said, noticing his confusion. "We get a lot of 'em. There's a naval air station just down the road."

"Oh. Too bad. Must be a nuisance."

"No," said the guard. "Mr. Buckner likes sonic booms."

Harper looked over at him, to see if this was a joke, but the guard kept a stony face.

The house gradually came into view through the trees. It was a sprawling villa in a vaguely Mediterranean style. Like the gatehouse, it had buff stucco walls and a tile roof. On a circle of grass before the front door stood a flagpole flying the American flag. At its base, where another proud owner might have placed an ornamental bench or a lawn jockey, Rod Buckner had set up a slim white missile—a SAM of some sort, Harper guessed.

As they came around the bend in the drive, a figure emerged from an archway at the side of the house. It was Jimmy Fahey. His uniform of short-sleeved bush jacket, Sam Browne belt, and khaki shorts struck Harper as something you'd expect to see on a doorman at a resort hotel, but it was just as immaculate and crisply pressed as Fahey's NYPD blues used to be. He still liked to wear aviator shades, too. His mouth was smiling, but Harper wished he could see his eyes. He saw only his own reflection as he approached.

"Will, how you doing?"

"Just fine, Jimmy. You?"

"Fine."

Harper was only a few strides away. In a second they would shake hands. But Fahey hadn't even looked down at his hand yet, and at the last moment he turned away.

"Come meet my boss."

Harper had to walk quickly to catch up with him. "You mean Rod Buckner?"

The fixed smile faltered. Fahey looked crestfallen. "Oh, somebody told you. I wanted it to be a surprise. So how about that? Me working for Rod Buckner."

"Congratulations," Harper said, since Fahey seemed to want him to.

"Thanks. He's a great guy. Says he'll put me in a book sometime." Fahey was smiling again. "Of course, he'll probably bump me off."

The archway led to a patio shaded by mimosas. In the turquoise waters of a swimming pool, a couple of little girls were splashing and shouting. The novelist himself was sitting at a table under an umbrella. He had a laptop computer in front of him and was talking on a portable phone. As they approached, Harper was trying to remember the title of the novel whose first chapter he'd read.

Buckner put down the phone, which for some reason had two stubby, flexible antennae, and lit a cigarette.

"Rod," said Fahey, "like you to meet my old partner at the NYPD, Will Harper."

Harper didn't say anything. It always threw him a little, meeting in the flesh somebody he'd seen on television. Their very familiarity was jarring, somehow.

Buckner didn't speak either. He took a drag on his cigarette and studied Harper, who studied him back. The novelist was fiftyish and stocky, with a lined, jowly face. His eyes slitted as he exhaled, the way Duke Wayne's used to do. He too was wearing a safari jacket with cutoff sleeves, and a blue baseball cap with U.S.S. NIMITZ stenciled across it in gold. He put the cigarette in an ashtray and stood.

"It's Sergeant Harper, isn't it?" he said, in the gravelly voice that was as familiar as his face.

Harper nodded.

"It was you who disarmed that bomb under Madison Square Garden—what was it, six, seven years ago?"

"That was me." It had been seven years before, to be exact, and Harper had discovered just how exhilarating and fleeting fame could be. He was surprised that Buckner would remember.

"It was Egyptian fundamentalists, wasn't it, and they got 'em?"

"They got 'em."

Buckner hitched up his Bermuda shorts and put his hands on his hips. "I always wondered how come you didn't use a remote control vehicle?"

The question threw Harper for a moment.

"I mean, NYPD was deploying the Dollman EOD vehicle at the time, wasn't it? Or did you use the Morfax Marauder Mk XII?"

"We had a robot," Harper said, "but it wasn't working."

Buckner's brow furrowed. "Sabotage?"

"No. It just wasn't working."

"So you went in there yourself. How'd you disarm the bomb?"

"Cut the wires, pulled out the detonator."

Buckner's frown grew some more wrinkles. "How come you didn't use the BAS Developments BA93 Disruptor? It had just become available at the time. Used ultrasonic waves to neutralize a wide range of detonators. British Army had an eighty-seven percent success rate with it."

"Well," said Hipper, "I had the wire cutters right there."

Fahey stepped forward. "Excuse me, Rod, you mind if I take a little break now and show Will around?"

"Sure, Jim. Show him around. And while you're at it, talk him into staying the night." Buckner's eyes shifted back to Harper. "See you at breakfast, Sergeant. We'll talk more."

He sat down and picked up his cigarette. But as Fahey and Harper started to turn away he said, "Jim? What are you carrying today?"

Fahey glanced down at the covered holster on his hip. "SigSauer nine-millimeter."

Buckner nodded, like a wine waiter approving a customer's choice of vintage. "What load?"

"Standard full-jacketed rounds."

"We'll be going down to the beach club for drinks this evening." Buckner was looking at him, expecting something from him.

Fahey thought fast, just the way he used to in class at the NYPD, when Harper asked him a tough one. "I'll reload before we go, Rod. Soft points."

Again Buckner nodded his approval. "That'd be good, Jim. If you have to open up, you don't want the bullets penetrating, hitting innocent bystanders."

"No, sir."

Buckner went back to work on his laptop. Harper followed Fahey along the pool. One of the girls, who looked to be about eight, splashed Fahey's shoe as he went by. He gave her a mock glare and she giggled delightedly. They passed through the archway.

Another sonic boom sounded as they walked along the vast frontage of the house.

2

A lizard about a foot long stared at Harper from beneath a low palm frond, then retreated into cool shadow.

"You're gonna stay, aren't you?" Fahey said, walking slightly ahead of Harper. "I'll show you your room."

"I don't think so, Jimmy. We're flying out day after tomorrow and—"

"Oh, you've got to stay. Breakfast around here is something. Starts off with fresh-squeezed orange juice from our own grove—"

"Sorry."

"But Rod wants to talk to you. He'll probably tape-record you."

Harper could only shrug. He found Jimmy's eagerness to please Buckner a little sad. Of course, he knew how attractive fame was, and how some people were content to bask in a celebrity's reflected glory, but he would never have expected it of Jimmy Fahey.

"Not a bad little dump, is it?" Fahey said, gesturing at the house. "We can go in, if you want. Or we can go to my place. Rod gave me a little house of my own to stay in, around back. *He* calls it little, but it's bigger than the house I grew up in in Queens."

"This is some operation you're running here, Jimmy," Harper said. "Your people at the gatehouse seem to be on the ball."

Fahey looked over at him, gratified as always by his praise. "You don't know the half of it. We got video cameras covering every inch of the perimeter fence. Twenty-four-hour patrols of the grounds. Rod says if I want heat sensors, motion detectors, anything at all, whatever the cost, all I have to do is ask."

"Does Mr. Buckner really need all this stuff?"

Harper looked over at Fahey, but Fahey wouldn't meet his eye.

"He writes about dangerous people—the Iranians, the Cali cartels, Hezbollah—"

"You mean you've received threats?"

"No, but—" Suddenly Fahey's tanned, handsome face broke into the old, familiar grin. It was like a mask dropping. "The truth is, he's in no danger. Sometimes Rod thinks he's Buck Reilly of the CIA. In fact, most of the time he does. But if that's what it takes to get him in the mood to write those bestsellers, who's gonna knock it?"

Harper stopped and turned to face him. "Wait a minute. You mean, you have no threats to deal with?"

Fahey frowned. "Sure we got problems. Tourists, press photographers, autograph hounds—"

"And for that kind of nuisance you're running a state-of-the-art security system?"

"That's what Mr. Buckner's paying me to do," said Fahey stonily.

"You shouldn't be here, Jimmy. You should be a cop, not a rich man's toy."

The words leapt out, unplanned, but as soon as he said them, Harper realized this was what he'd come here to say.

Fahey's face was flushed under the tan, but he shook his head and kept his voice down, pretending not to be strongly affected. "You're gonna have to go somewhere else to sell that kind of stuff, Will. I've fallen into a sweet deal here. You have no idea what a great life a person like Rod lives. I've been with him to London, Hong Kong, Rio. First class all the way. I've met George Bush and Michelle Pfeiffer. And of course the admirals from the base down the road are over here all the time. They'd do anything for Rod. I've had a ride in an F-16. I've landed on an aircraft carrier."

"Jimmy, why the hell did you quit the NYPD?"

Fahey didn't answer. He put his hands on his hips and bowed his head and sighed. "I can't believe it. You came here to tell me to give up all this and go back to the NYPD?"

"Not necessarily," Harper said. "You could join a department down here, if you want."

"Give it up, Will, you're wasting your time."

"You're a good cop, Jimmy. A hell of an EOD expert. Leave this kind of job for when you retire."

Fahey was clearly struggling with his temper now. He looked away and said in a taut voice, "I'm not asking for your advice anymore."

"You should have asked for it before you quit the Department. I'd have told you to stay."

Fahey said nothing.

"The people who were criticizing you didn't know what the hell they were talking about."

Fahey held up a hand to stop him. Harper fell silent. He was struck by the pain on the younger man's face. "Cut it out, Will. I know you were making excuses for me from your hospital bed. Nobody believed 'em."

"I wasn't making excuses. I put the facts in my report, that's all. I told the truth. It wasn't your fault."

Abruptly, Fahey swung around and started to stride away. But he took only two steps and turned back. He whipped off his sunglasses. "I should've got to you quicker. I had the goddamn suppression blanket in my arms and all I had to do was *run*. You wouldn't have got hurt."

Harper stepped right up to him and looked him in the eye. As forcefully as he could, he said, "There's no way of knowing that. The explosive was unstable. Maybe my moving it set it off. Maybe the timing had nothing to do with it. We'll never know. So quit thinking about it."

Fahey's face twisted up. He started shaking his head again. "Quit thinking about it. What kind of sick joke is that? Can *you* stop thinking about it?"

Harper hesitated. Then he said, "No. And sometimes I get mad at you, Jimmy. But more often I get mad at myself. Because if I was gonna pick up a goddamn stick of gelignite that was gonna go off, why the hell couldn't I have picked it up in my *left* hand?"

Fahey stood frowning and blinking at him for a moment. "But that doesn't make any sense, Will, blaming yourself for that."

"Makes about as much sense as what you've been blaming yourself for."

They stood with their gazes locked for another long moment. Then Fahey turned and started to walk slowly, his hands in his pockets, his expression abstracted. Harper walked beside him, but didn't speak. He'd said his piece and now it was time for Jimmy to think.

Another sonic boom rumbled off beyond the clouds. They crunched over the crushed seashell drive and came to the lawn. Sprinklers were throwing long whips of water across it. An egret stepped out of their way, blasé as a New York pigeon. Harper watched the elegant white bird with pleasure. He'd come to try to lift a weight from Fahey's shoulders; he hadn't expected to feel such a sense of relief himself.

They'd come to Rod Buckner's SAM missile and flagpole. Old Glory was snapping in the breeze. Abruptly Fahey stopped and faced Harper.

"Say, Will. How do you shake hands now?"

Harper smiled. "Same as before."

He held out his right hand. Fahey looked at it for a long moment, then took it. He gripped it tightly.

"Thanks for coming, Will."

"You going to take my advice?"

"I didn't say that. I'll think about it."

"You'd really miss those admirals that much?"

"Nah. I'd miss Michelle Pfeiffer." Fahey looked back at the house. "I don't suppose you're much interested in a tour of Rod's manse. You want to go down to the beach?"

"Never mind, Jimmy. I know you have to get back to work."

"Actually I'm heading for the gatehouse. Want to ride along?"

They walked back to the front of the house, where a golf cart was parked. As they got in, Fahey said, "You look good, Will. I like the face-fuzz."

Harper touched his beard. It had come in dense and even, but all gray, which had surprised him. His hair was still mostly dark. "Perk of retirement."

"Is that okay? I mean—do you mind being retired?"

Harper hesitated. Before, he'd felt he owed Fahey honesty. Now, hearing the tension in the young man's voice, he knew he owed him a lie. Forcing a grin, he said, "You kidding? Retired at age forty-seven with full disability and pension? It's every cop's dream."

Fahey looked at him, then back at the road. If he doubted Harper, he decided not to say so. "I'll bet it's a sweet life. Plus you've got Laura. How is she?"

"Busy as always. She sends her regards."

For the rest of the drive they talked as easily as they used to in the old days. Fahey explained how different the Florida panhandle was from the rest of the state and how much he liked it.

As they drew to a stop under the overhanging roof of the gatehouse, the tall, grim guard whom Harper had spoken to before appeared in the doorway. He had a long, flat package in his hands.

"What is it, Kent?" Fahey said.

"Sorry, sir. Heard the cart and thought it was Mr. Buckner."

Fahey frowned. "What've you got there?"

"Latest edition of *Jane's Guide to the Ships of the World's Navies.* Mr. Buckner's coming down for it."

"*He's* coming down for it," Fahey said to Harper, rolling his eyes. "Rod's a stickler for security procedures unless they get in his way. Then he says the hell with them."

Kent's eyes widened in surprise. Harper guessed Fahey didn't usually talk about his employer in that tone. Harper took it as a hopeful sign. Maybe Fahey was already thinking he wasn't long for this job.

"You know the drill, Kent," Fahey went on. "We examine all parcels and then we take them up to the house. Mr. Buckner does *not* come down for them."

"Sure, but—"

Fahey walked over and took the package. "Has this been fluoroscoped yet?"

"Sure. I mean, Alvarez must have done it. It was on the counter with the other packages."

"Who called Mr. Buckner and told him it had arrived?"

"Not me," said Kent, who by now was stiff and red-faced. "But everybody knows Mr. Buckner's always in a hurry to get the latest *Jane's.*"

Fahey gave the package back. "Take it in and fluoroscope it."

"But Mr. Buckner'll be here any minute."

"I'll deal with him. Go."

Kent went back into the gate house. Fahey turned to Harper. "Sorry, Will, but you better leave. Rod's gonna be pissed. And rich people don't like to have strangers around when they cuss out the servants."

Harper smiled. Fahey's discontent sounded sweet to his ears. He'd be willing to bet that by the end of the week the kid would be writing off for police department applications. He said, "Stay in touch, Jimmy."

"I will."

They shook hands again, and Harper crossed the drive to his car and got in. As he pulled away he waved out the window, but Fahey didn't see. A green Land Rover was drawing to a stop under the overhang, and Rod Buckner was leaning out.

Harper went through the gates and turned onto the road.

He was just shifting into third gear when there was a flash behind him. The reflection off his driving mirrors was as dazzling as lightning at night. The roar of the explosion deafened him. Suddenly there was cloth against his face and he could see nothing. Instinctively he stamped on the brakes. The shock wave had rocked the car so violently the air bag had deployed. Even as he realized this the bag emptied, collapsing onto his knees.

The car had come to a stop now. His ears were ringing painfully. Otherwise, he seemed to be all right. The car's windshield was gone, blown out completely, along with the other windows. Blue-tinted nuggets of safety glass filled his lap and the passenger seat. Something hit the roof over his head. Harper couldn't hear the impact—couldn't hear anything—but it was hard enough to rock the whole car again. Something else struck the hood and bounced off, leaving a big dent. It was a roof tile. They were coming down like giant hailstones. There was nothing to do except fold his arms over his head and hope.

Harper was lucky. None of the tiles fell through the windshield frame. He fumbled the door open and stood shakily, looking around. Roof tiles were scattered all over the road. A car coming the other way was slowing to a halt. The driver gaped at him.

Turning, Harper looked at the gatehouse. Flames were licking through the windows, but the walls still stood. The roof was gone. What hadn't blown out over the road must have collapsed into the building. The sloping projection that had formed the overhang had fallen to the driveway. In the smoke and rubble there was no sign of the Land Rover. It had been buried in debris. Along with Rod Buckner, Harper realized numbly.

Along with Jimmy Fahey.

3

Rodman's Neck, in the northeast corner of the Bronx, was a penin-
sula jutting into Long Island Sound. It was as out-of-the-way a
place as you could find in the crowded city, and this was where New
York cops came to perform tasks that called for some room: small arms
practice, dog training, and bomb disassembly.

Harper hadn't been back to Rodman's Neck since he'd left the Department. It hadn't changed. It still struck him as the quietest place in
New York. There was the popping of small-arms fire on the range, and
the barking of dogs in their pens, but the wind seemed to lift these
sharp little noises and blow them out to sea.

He walked along the road. Ahead of him was a guard kiosk and a
high chain-link fence. Beyond it he could see only a plain of wintry
tan grass and gray sky. This was the way to the bunkers. Many times
Harper had ridden out there in a bomb wagon, with a bomb he'd
disarmed somewhere or other in the five boroughs and was taking to
the bunkers for disassembly. On bleak days like this, he used to feel
as if he were going to the end of the earth. He'd wonder if he'd be
coming back.

Thinking about it now, Harper didn't mind one bit that he'd never
have to go out there again, never have to take apart another bomb.

But his mood changed as soon as he turned and started walking back to the complex of aging Quonset huts that housed the Bomb Squad. He'd put in eighteen years on the Squad and he missed this place. Regret about his premature retirement stabbed at him. He'd liked teaching, and he'd liked advising the detectives on the Homicide and Terrorism squads about how to catch bombers. But that was all over now.

Entering the building, he glanced at the bulletin board. There was the usual collection of official Department and ATF notices, mixed up with announcements of birthday booze-ups and used cars for sale. And there was the usual caustic smell of coffee gradually burning down to bitter sludge. Harper thought of several doors he'd like to knock on. But he marched straight past them to the end of the corridor. He was going to the office of a man he'd disliked more than anyone else on the Squad—its commander, Captain Nathan Brand.

Harper had telephoned Brand's secretary for an appointment. He'd been surprised when she'd told him Brand could see him right away, and at Rodman's Neck. When he wasn't attending antiterrorism seminars in European capitals, Brand could usually be found at the Bomb Squad's other office, in the Sixth Precinct. The Sixth was located in Greenwich Village, which put Brand within steps of a number of good restaurants, and within a mile of the top brass at One Police Plaza. As Harper knocked on the door, he reminded himself not to get carried away by his contempt for Brand. The captain was good at what he did. He'd certainly been able to outmaneuver Harper, as he had eight years ago, when Harper should have been the one promoted to lieutenant. Brand had gotten the advancement instead, and Harper was sure he'd done it by spreading a rumor about Harper's involvement with a prostitute who was a police informer for Narcotics. There had been a lingering animosity between the two men ever since.

"Come in," Brand said, rising from behind his desk, smiling. He was a lean man in his fifties, with a gleaming bald dome, and bushy white sideburns. "Hello, Harper, you're looking good. Retirement agrees with you."

"Thanks for seeing me, Captain. How's it going?"

"Oh, not too bad. The Fortunato case is a problem, though. I suppose you've read about it."

Harper nodded. Domenic Fortunato, a six-year-old Queens boy, had been killed in a fire in his parents' garage. He'd been playing with fireworks. His father, a sergeant in the NYPD, had obtained them illegally. The rumor was that they had come from here on Rodman's Neck.

Harper asked Brand, "Do they know for sure yet whether the fireworks came out of our dump?"

"No. But the Internal Affairs guys keep bugging me."

"I guess you can't blame them. The dump is the most likely source." Selling fireworks to individuals is illegal in New York City, but people were always trying to do it. When they got caught, the confiscated fireworks ended up in a dump on Rodman's Neck. At any time there were crates of firecrackers and Roman candles in the dump. From time to time, things disappeared. Policemen and their friends and relatives liked flashes and bangs as much as anybody. Harper'd never had anything to do with it. He'd seen too many kids lose eyes or fingers. He knew how quickly explosives could become unstable in storage.

"No," said Brand, "you can't blame IAD. But you don't like to have them around."

He continued to stand and look at Harper. But he had his reading glasses in one hand while the other was in his pocket. He wasn't going to shake hands. Harper'd noticed before that Brand was squeamish about his injury, and wondered if he could somehow turn that to his advantage. With Brand, you had to think that way.

"Matter of fact, Harper, I was expecting you to call," Brand said.

"You know why I'm here?"

"Yes. Fahey." Brand's face became grave. "You and I were his superior officers. Sure, he wasn't in the NYPD anymore, but we're interested in seeing his killer caught."

As they took seats, Harper reflected that so far this was going the way of his past meetings with the captain. Brand always told you what you wanted to hear. Then you had to figure out how much of it he meant.

"I've seen you quoted a number of times in media coverage of the case," Harper said.

Brand gave a satisfied smile.

"You told the *Times* Fahey was one of your best men. Said you regretted the circumstances of his departure."

"Yes. That was a good piece the *Times* ran, I thought."

"Then you told the San Francisco *Chronicle* that Fahey was kind of a fuckup and no loss."

Brand frowned. "Now, I didn't say—"

But then he broke off. Tossing his glasses onto the desk top, he folded his arms and grinned at Harper with genuine amusement. "You're something else, Harper. But you're right. Why should we even pretend we can stand each other?"

"It's not worth the effort," Harper agreed. "So what's this crap you're giving the *Chronicle*?"

"You never understood reporters, Harper, that was your problem. I wasn't talking to this *Chronicle* guy for more than two minutes before I figured him out. His angle was, what if Buck Reilly had been protecting his creator? Would he have been able to save him? So naturally, with that angle, the reporter's got to make Fahey the goat. He was gonna do that anyway. If I didn't give him what he wanted, I wouldn't have gotten quoted."

"Sure, I understand. If Jimmy had wanted people to take his death seriously, he shouldn't have gotten killed along with a celebrity."

Brand narrowed his eyes, studying Harper. "You're really worked up about this, aren't you? I couldn't believe it when I heard you'd gone down there to see him. Why you, of all people, would have any tender feelings for Jimmy Fahey is beyond me."

Harper didn't reply. It was no use arguing ancient history with Brand. He said, "It's been more than three weeks since the bombing. There hasn't been any real news about the investigation in a long time. What the hell's going on?"

Brand leaned back in his chair. He was amused again. "This is really tough for you, isn't it, Harper? I mean coming here today. You always thought I spent too much time going to meetings, keeping up my contacts, schmoozing. And now you have to come to me for information. You know I've got the inside stuff. You know you can't get it anywhere else."

"And you're the man Winona Ryder dreams of, Captain. Anything else I have to say?"

Brand savored his amusement in silence for another moment, then said, "The investigation isn't going well. They haven't been able to develop a suspect. In fact, they're still shopping for a theory."

Harper had hoped the Florida cops were finding leads they weren't revealing to the media. He clenched his fists in frustration. Then he remembered to do as Laura kept telling him: take a deep breath, let it out, relax his fists. She worried about his heart. He said, "What about the theory that it was some drug cartel or terrorist group who hit Buckner?"

"That got going because Buckner used to say he wasn't afraid to make the enemies of America his enemies. Stuff like that. To sell books. But the CIA and FBI think it's bullshit. They won't go near the case. They're leaving it to the Florida State Police and the ATF."

"So what have they got? What can they say about the bomber?"

"He's not a terrorist operative, but he's a pro. No question about that. He's had training of some kind. Maybe been in the military."

Harper frowned. He was always skeptical when investigators arrived at that conclusion. He said, "Anybody can make a bomb these days. I don't have to tell you that. You can get step-by-step instructions in a book, or over the Internet. You can legally buy most of the components—"

Brand shook his head. "This guy understands blasts—how explosions work. And he did his research before he made his plan."

Nodding, Harper said, "He must have spent a long time in the woods opposite the estate with his binoculars and insect repellent, studying Jimmy's personnel and their routines."

"More than that." Brand hesitated, then went on. "Here's something hasn't been released yet. If you leak it, you didn't get it from me. Somewhere or other—probably in the Pensacola City Engineer's office, but we can't confirm that—our guy did research on the construction of that gatehouse."

"Oh?"

"When Buckner bought the estate, he replaced the gatehouse roof. Put in the new one to project out over the drive, give a sort of classy porte cochere effect. The rest of the gatehouse dates back to the fifties, when the estate was built. The guy who built it was worried about hurricanes, so he made everything strong. The gatehouse has only a few narrow windows. And there was cinder block under the stucco."

Harper began to understand. He said grimly, "And the bomber found all this out?"

"He must have. He knew those strong walls would channel the

blast upward and collapse the roof. It didn't matter whether Buckner was inside the gatehouse or in his car under the overhang, he was a goner."

Harper said, "The way it actually happened, a guard almost gave the package to Buckner. I was thinking, if he'd done so, the bomber could've detonated it after Buckner drove away, so only Buckner would've been killed."

"That wasn't the plan. The plan was to take out the whole gatehouse and everybody in or near it."

So the bastard had meant to kill Fahey and the others all along. Why? Another wave of helpless anger swept over Harper. He breathed deeply and relaxed his fists. He said, "That call to Buckner telling him the book he wanted was at the gatehouse—"

"They don't have a recording, unfortunately. But the maid heard Buckner take it. Came in over the intercom, she said, like calls from the gatehouse always did."

"The intercom? How did the bomber patch into that?"

"They don't know. Apparently there are a number of ways it can be done, assuming you have the equipment and expertise. One thing we know, it wasn't an inside job. Everyone who was in the gatehouse was killed. The entire day shift, except for two guys who were out patrolling the grounds. The Florida cops are satisfied they're clean."

"It was a radio-controlled detonator?"

Brand nodded.

The bomber had been out there watching, and had pressed the button at exactly the right moment. "That tells us something about him," said Harper.

"He wanted to be absolutely sure the bomb went off at the right moment."

"My guess is he wanted to see it, too," Harper murmured, "wanted to watch it go off." He looked up at Brand. "So they've dropped the foreign terrorist theory. What's the popular theory now?"

"Our guy's a pro, like I said."

"So who's he supposed to be working for?"

"Someone close to home. The Florida cops've found plenty of people with a grudge against Buckner. His ex-wife, for one. His ex-publisher for another. It was a small publisher that brought out his first book, made a big hit of it. For the next book, Buckner went to a big New

York publisher. The small publisher went belly-up last year, and he bears a grudge. And one guy the cops especially like is this druggie producer out in Hollywood who claims Buckner stole the idea for his third bestseller from him."

"So they're going to trash Buckner pretty thoroughly. Should be fun for the media."

"You don't buy it, Harper? So what's *your* theory?"

"I'm not big on theories. You know the way I used to work. I wish I could see the bomb reconstruction, if they've made one. And I'd like to see whatever fragments have survived."

"That's right, you always were a hardware guy. Well, let's see what I can do for you." Swiveling his chair around, he turned to the filing cabinets. "I may have some pictures here."

The phone rang while he was searching. It was unusual for Brand's phone to have been silent for so long. In previous meetings in this office, Harper had spent most of the time waiting while Brand talked on the phone. This was someone named Charlie, and Brand was delighted to hear from him, or at least said he was. As he talked, though, he fished a manila folder out of the drawer. He dropped it on the desk in front of Harper.

In calling Harper a hardware guy, Brand was referring to the work Harper used to do with the detectives who were trying to catch a bomber. By analyzing the fragments of the bomb and reconstructing it, Harper was able to tell them a lot about the person they were looking for.

He opened the folder and skimmed through the forensic technician's report. Then he turned to the photographs of the twisted bits of metal that had been recovered from the rubble of the gatehouse. Absorbed, he blocked out all traces of Brand's phone conversation until Brand said, "So what've you got?"

He'd hung up. Harper, preoccupied, said, "Have you got a magnifying glass?" Brand reached in a drawer and handed one over.

The bomb was a pipe bomb. The explosive had been packed into a length of iron pipe inside the cardboard box, in order to concentrate the explosion and make it more powerful. Harper held up a photograph of a surviving fragment of pipe. "There's a C on here."

"A what?"

"The letter C. Here, near the left edge."

Brand took the magnifying glass and photo. "Oh, yeah. Well, it looks like a C. So what?"

"The bomber inscribed it into the metal."

"Harper, c'mon. This is a fragment of exploded bomb. They found it buried a foot deep in debris. Along the way it picked up a scratch."

"I don't think so. I think the bomber put it there."

"Why? You think it's his initial? We should be looking for a guy named Chris? Or Calvin?" Brand picked up the lab report. "The forensic guys in the Florida State Police and the ATF have both been over this fragment. You think they wouldn't have picked up on this if it was significant?"

Harper dropped the photos on the desk. "I'd like to have a look at the fragments themselves."

Brand shook his head, smiling. "That I can't do for you."

"Then pass on what I said the next time you're schmoozing and making contacts." Brand was still avoiding his eye. "Captain, this isn't the first time I've asked you to pass something on. And you've always ended up looking good."

"This time I'd look like a jerk." Brand shuffled the prints into order and slid them back into the folder.

Harper's instincts told him not to let this go. "Come on, Brand. What's the worst that can happen? You get embarrassed. What's that compared to the chance of catching Fahey's killer?"

Brand didn't answer. He swiveled and put the photos back in the file.

Harper waited for him to face front, then said, "Well?"

"Harper, go home to your lovely wife." Brand smiled, not quite meeting his eye. "You're retired, with a full pension and benefits. You're on a paid vacation for life. It's every cop's dream."

Abruptly Harper lost control. He'd borne the festering resentment about his departure from the Squad for a long time. But his frustration and sorrow over Fahey's murder were too much for him. "Don't act like you did me any favors, Brand. You forced me out. You just had to make it look good because the media were watching."

Uncharacteristically, Brand seemed to welcome the confrontation. He leaned back in his chair, smiling. "Yeah, that's right, Harper. If the

Post hadn't been calling you *Martyr Cop*, I'd have kicked you out to starve in the gutter."

"There's no reason I couldn't have come back to work."

"Here? On the Squad?" Brand's amusement deepened. "We all know the NYPD's an equal-opportunity employer. Open to both sexes, all races, every sexual orientation. But Harper, there's no room on the Bomb Squad for the digitally challenged."

A surge of anger nearly lifted Harper to his feet. But he stayed put and let it pass. Knowing it would annoy Brand, he smiled. "Cute line, Captain. But I was almost out of bomb disposal anyway. You know that. I could've done training and investigation. You didn't have to retire me."

"Harper, don't you understand? It wasn't me. It was the Squad."

Harper felt as if he'd been kicked hard just below the breastbone. For a moment he couldn't recover his breath to answer. Then he said, "Don't give me that. It was you. The people I worked with wanted me to come back."

"Of course, I'm not saying it was anything personal, Will. People like you. They feel sorry as hell about what happened to you. But your luck ran out. That's why people don't want you around. You're unlucky, and they're afraid of catching it."

Harper sat there, incapable of replying. He could almost feel Brand's words burning into his memory.

"I can't have a guy whose fingers have been blown off hanging around here," Brand said. "I especially can't have him training the new guys. You know what the young macho types around here say, don't you? You remember, Will?"

Harper did remember. He knew what was coming, but there was nothing to do except sit there.

"They say the big bomb is nothing to fear," Brand went on. "You make a mistake and it blows you out of existence, you never know what hit you. No, it's the crummy little bomb you got to be afraid of. The one that goes off and leaves you to live out your life blind, or disfigured, or crippled. That's the worst thing."

"I know," Harper murmured. "I remember saying that myself. But I was a young stupid kid then. It's better to be alive."

Brand smiled and raised both hands. His cuff links glittered. "So we're back where we started from. You got a great life. Do what retired people do. Take up golf. Move to Arizona. Whatever."

The phone rang again. Brand picked it up. "Ben!" he shouted into the mouthpiece. "Great to hear from you."

Harper stood and walked out of the office. He got away from Rodman's Neck as quickly as he could.

4

Will and Laura Harper lived in an 1880s brownstone near Prospect Park in Brooklyn. It was a spacious town house on a good block, and the only reason it was within financial reach of a cop and a nurse was that it needed help. This was realtorese for hundreds of hours of backbreaking labor.

The Harpers weren't deterred. They drew up a detailed seven-year plan to turn the place from shambles to showplace. Laura had boundless energy, and Harper had always enjoyed working with his hands.

Six months after they bought the house, Harper had his "accident." That was what they'd come to call it. Laura put the house on the market, assuming they would have to move back to an apartment.

But when Harper came home from the hospital, he took down the FOR SALE sign. He'd decided to use the renovation work as a continuation of his physical therapy.

It was agony at first. Even the most routine tasks seemed impossible. He spent a week mashing his fingers before he learned how to hammer in a nail. By a slow, frustrating process of trial and error, he found out which jobs he could still do with his right hand. Others he learned how to do with his left. The hardest part was admitting to himself that there were some jobs he couldn't do without help. His skill and confidence slowly returned and his pace picked up. He'd gotten well ahead of schedule on the seven-year plan.

But in the month since he'd returned from Florida—the month since Jimmy Fahey had died—he hadn't been able to get any work done at all. There didn't seem to be any point. The original plan had been to rehab the place and sell it for a small fortune. Then Laura would take early retirement and they'd travel or maybe buy a little place in the country. Now, though, this sounded to Harper like the every-cop's-dream retirement Captain Brand had recommended to him. It made him feel bitter. Made his life seem futile.

It was ten-thirty at night and Harper was lying in bed, staring at the TV and waiting for the news to come on. More and more lately, the Buckner case wouldn't get on the news at all. Either there were no developments, or viewers were losing interest. But Harper was watching anyway.

He was lying on top of the coverlet, fully clothed. The only light in the room was the flickering blue glow of the television. He didn't want to see the parquet floor, which needed cleaning and polishing, or the stained-glass fanlight over the door, which needed to have several panes replaced.

The program, a talk show about men who'd slept with women who employed them, didn't hold his attention. He kept glancing at his watch. Laura was late. Only a few minutes, but she was definitely late. These days she was *always* late.

He pulled himself upright, trying to shake off the feeling of annoyance. He knew it was petty, unfair. Before, when he'd had a busy life of his own, he'd never noticed Laura's unpunctuality. Only now, when time moved so slowly for him, did it bother him.

They'd only been married three years. For Harper it was his second marriage. The first had been a disaster. Like a lot of ambitious young cops, he'd put his job before his family and paid the price. His wife had left him and moved to Oregon, taking the infant daughter he'd never gotten a chance to know. He still ached over that. For the next fifteen years he was wary, determined not to repeat his mistake. Then he met Laura.

She was forty when they met, and she'd never been married. He couldn't stop wondering at his luck, and at the blindness of other men. Laura was lovely and vibrant. She had a sly sense of humor and a wide variety of interests. Every time Harper tried to describe her to someone, he ended up sounding like the ideal personals ad. He'd often asked her why she hadn't married before, and never got a straight answer. The one he liked most was that since she had a good job and a close family, she wasn't about to settle for just any man.

He heard the key in the lock and then her bright "Hel-*lo!*"

"I'm upstairs," Harper called. With an effort, he held back from checking his watch to see how late she was. He was determined to shake off this rotten mood. Or at least to hide it from her.

He heard her quick light step on the stairs. Living in a New York row house, you did a lot of climbing, but that never seemed to bother Laura, even at the end of a long day. Where did she get all that energy?

She appeared in the doorway, taking off her raincoat. Underneath, she was wearing her white nurse's uniform. That meant she'd hurried: She preferred to change before leaving the hospital. She was a small, slender woman with dark curly hair. Her bright blue eyes seemed almost too large for her face, her smile too broad. "What a day," she said. "Dr. Lautenberg was doing a triple bypass. We were in there for eight hours. Thank God the guy pulled through."

Harper was glad he hadn't complained that she was a few minutes late. She sat on the edge of the bed and kissed him. "So. How was your day?"

"All right." He figured if he was going to cheer up, he'd better pick another topic for conversation. "You have a lot of phone messages."

"Oh, Will, I've told you before you don't have to pick up. Let the machine take them."

I have nothing else to do. He angrily shoved the self-pitying musing away. He said, "Jan called. She said the Shorewalkers are hiking Sheepshead Bay on Saturday and do you want to come. Then Bernie called to remind you you've got soup kitchen duty tomorrow evening. And Toni from the Metropolitan Opera Guild says do you want to do a walk-on in *Aida*, Saturday matinee."

Laura's expressive face responded to each of these messages. At the final one she burst into a grin. "*Aida!* That's really fun, I did that last year. They've got about a hundred people on stage, so nobody ever notices you, but it's great. I hope I get to be a Nubian slave. Wear a gold bikini and feathers in my hair. With luck, I may get to wrap myself in a snake."

By now she was on her feet, indicating the costume to him with gestures. Since she was still in her nurse's uniform, it was hard to imagine. She stopped and said, "All right. What's with the look?"

"Nothing. Just that you're the only person I know who really takes advantage of living in New York. Everybody else is so tired they can hardly get the laundry done."

She gave him a sly look. "Uh-huh. I've heard this before. The truth is, you figured with all these activities of mine, I was just a poor lonely spinster trying to keep busy. You thought as soon as I had a man of my own, I'd drop all that stuff and stay home."

Harper shook his head. "No. I knew I wasn't marrying a beer-fetcher. And I was glad. I was away so much, I didn't want to think of you sitting at home bored."

The change in her expression told him he'd betrayed himself with those last words. *He* was the one sitting at home bored. His cheerful act wasn't going to work. She sat down on the edge of the bed and looked at him sympathetically.

"Do you have to do that?" said Harper irritably. "I feel like a patient."

Ignoring this, she took his hand. The maimed one. It was the one she always chose to hold. "Oh, Will, I know you can't help thinking about Jimmy. It's terrible what happened to him. But at least you got to see him before he died. To set things right between you. Isn't that some comfort? There's no reason for you to feel guilty."

"I don't feel guilty. The son of a bitch who killed him is the one who's guilty, and I want them to nail his ass. Only it's not happening."

Frowning, she turned to look at the television. "Was there any—"

"No, there's nothing new. Count on Brand to have the inside dope. The reporters keep digging up more dirt on what a ruthless sleaze Buckner was, and why people would've wanted to kill him, but the investigation's going nowhere. I think they're going to let this bastard get away."

She let go of his hand and straightened up. "I'm sorry, Will. I don't know what to say."

Harper blew out his breath, hoping some of his useless pent-up anger would go with it. He reached out to touch Laura's hair. "I'm sorry too."

She stood up and went to the closet, unzipping her uniform. "Well, I'd better let Toni know I'm interested in *Aida*. If you don't mind me being away on Saturday?"

"No, go ahead."

"What time is it?"

He glanced at his watch. "Eleven-fifteen."

"Oh, that's too late. I'll wake her kid."

"You could send her e-mail."

"Good idea."

She walked across the room to the computer and turned it on. Harper went back to watching the news. This was a dismal scene, he thought, the two of them on opposite sides of the dark bedroom, communing with their cathode-ray tubes. He had to do something about Fahey; he couldn't stand this feeling of helplessness. For the hundredth time, he thought about calling an acquaintance in the ATF and telling him about the C on the bomb fragment. But he was doubtful, not having the photograph in front of him. Probably Brand was right. It was just a scratch.

The modem made sighing and burbling noises as it connected with their computer network.

"Will?"

"What?"

"You've got an e-mail message."

That was strange. Harper never received e-mail. He came around and bent over her shoulder. There was the message, glowing in green letters on the black screen.

Harper,

Hope you remember me. Sorry about your friend. I have some ideas about that case. Want to come see me? We could talk about it.

Harold Addleman

"Well, well," Harper murmured.

"Do you know this guy?"

He nodded. His heart was beating faster, but he warned himself not to build too much on this. "FBI. Behavioral Sciences Unit."

"Behavioral—you mean he's one of those profiler guys?"

"Yes."

"The ones you see quoted in the papers, saying things like, 'the perpetrator is a thirty-two-year-old divorced Presbyterian male who breeds corgis and wears women's underwear?' "

"That's right."

"When I listen to those guys on TV I can't make up my mind if they're crazy or brilliant."

"That's how I felt working with Addleman," said Harper. "I decided maybe he's both. He's an odd one, lives in his own intense world." Harper straightened up from the screen and stretched. It was difficult to stay calm. His mind was popping with speculations about what Addleman might have gotten hold of.

"Were you and he close?"

"It's hard to say. We worked together on a bombing case six or seven years ago. Never caught the guy, but Addleman and I sort of hit it off. He's an odd combination of mercurial and methodical. I was the plodder, exploring the usual avenues, and Addleman roamed the side streets."

"You sound like the Odd Couple."

"We were that way, I guess. But our methods somehow meshed. Together we made a hell of a team. I knew it, and by the time the investigation ended, I think Addleman knew it. Of course, he'd never say so. He's grudging with his compliments, even to himself. Not that he doesn't think he's brilliant. . . ."

Laura smiled. "Oscar gets dinner done in time but burns the roast. Felix uses what's left and makes stew."

"Something like that," Harper said. "Except that we got along better than Oscar and Felix, and we respected each other because we're both methodical in our own fields."

"This is great, Will, isn't it? He wants to talk to you about the case. The FBI wants your help."

He shook his head. "I don't know. If it was an official approach, this isn't the way they'd do it. I wish Addleman had given me a phone number."

"Obviously he expects you to reply by e-mail."

Harper didn't like that. He was too impatient. He wanted to get hold of Addleman and make him answer questions, right away. He crossed the room to his dresser and pulled his address book out of the top drawer. Riffling through it, he sat down on the bed next to the phone on the night table.

"What are you going to do?" called Laura from the computer.

"Call the Bureau."

"But it's eleven-fifteen at night."

"The Bureau never sleeps."

They were awake, but they weren't inclined to be helpful. He called the Behavioral Sciences Unit in Quantico, where Addleman had worked. They told him Addleman was no longer with the Bureau. They had no other information at this time.

"He's left the FBI," Harper told Laura. "But that's not surprising. Profilers are hot right now. A lot of them are getting hired away by private security companies. Some of 'em even end up as consultants in Hollywood. Addleman's a unique and brilliant guy. He'd be in demand."

Harper called Addleman's home number. It wasn't in service. He tried directory assistance, and didn't give up until he'd covered all the area codes around Washington.

"No luck?" Laura said. "Why don't I just reply that you accept his invitation and ask him when and where?"

Harper nodded. He'd simply have to contain his impatience for a while and do it Addleman's way. "Go ahead."

Laura smiled, and her fingers flew over the keys.

Harper watched them. When he was in a low mood it would give him a twinge to watch someone touch-type, or play piano, or perform any of the other little tasks that called for ten fingers. But watching Laura's hands now didn't bother him.

It made him realize just how much better he was feeling. He knew he shouldn't build too much on this message, but he couldn't help it. He had hope again, and what a difference it made.

He sat back on the bed so that he could watch Laura more comfortably. The computer chair was one of those ergonomic models in which you knelt on one pad and rested your backside against another. She'd told him she liked it because it reminded her of the "lazy-kneeling" posture she used to adopt as a girl at St. Roch's Church—at least, until the nuns caught her.

The posture might be the same, but she didn't look like a Catholic schoolgirl now. She was wearing nothing but a bra and panties. Harper moved slightly so that he could get a better view of the white bra strap that crossed her arched back. That lean and muscled back. That white-clad, jutting bottom.

Funny about being married. The two of you could be moving around the bedroom or bathroom and you'd be totally oblivious to your wife's body, and the next minute the focus would shift and you'd be achingly aware of it.

She moved the mouse to select from a window, and the message disappeared from the screen. "It's off. Bet you hear from him by tomorrow morning."

She swung around, smiling. The smile grew broader when she saw the look in his eye. Turning off the computer, she got up and came toward him. Her hands moved behind her back to undo the bra strap.

Harper didn't fall asleep after the lovemaking. He lay still on his back until Laura's breathing deepened and became even. Then, very quietly, he got out of bed and padded barefoot over to the computer. He turned the screen away so the light wouldn't wake her, and switched it on.

Addleman's reply was there when he logged on, brief and to the point. He'd expect Harper anytime in the afternoon. His address was in Philadelphia.

He didn't mention that he was no longer with the Bureau, no doubt figuring that by this time Harper already knew. He would also know Harper was eager to travel to Philadelphia to see him.

Harper smiled with anticipation. Addleman was always a jump or two ahead.

Or three.

5

When he read the taxi driver outside the Philadelphia train station the address Addleman had given him, the driver glanced at him in some alarm. Twenty minutes later, Harper knew why.

The former FBI profiler lived in a slum that looked tough enough to scare even a veteran New York cop. Some of the old brick apartment buildings were burned-out shells. In others, half the windows were boarded up or covered with steel plates. Three teenage boys with shaved heads and matching black T-shirts stood near the corner and stared at the taxi as it pulled to the curb. Harper stayed inside while he paid the driver. As soon as he got out, the taxi sped away.

Eccentric as Addleman had been when Harper had known him, he'd lived the conventional life of a middle-rung government employee, with a ranch-style house in the Virginia suburbs, a wife, and two teenage sons. Twins, if Harper remembered correctly. What the hell had happened to him?

The hair on the nape of Harper's neck rose as he walked up onto the cracked concrete stoop of Addleman's building and entered a grafitti-covered vestibule that held the stench of stale urine. Discarded crack vials crunched beneath his soles as he moved to the bank of blackened brass mailboxes. Yes, Addleman's name was there. Apartment 3E. He began climbing the narrow and squeaking wooden stairs, glad to be moving away from the odorous vestibule.

The third floor was little better. Only a dim light came through the grimy windows. The window at the end of the hall let in more light than the others because its wooden frame didn't contain any glass. The floor and the wall beneath the sill were stained from rain and probably snow that had blown in.

Harper found apartment 3E and knocked on its door.

He heard movement inside the apartment, but no one came to the door. Below him in the building, a woman yelled something unintelligible at someone named Rico. Rico yelled something unintelligible back at her.

Harper knocked again, hard, noticing that Addleman's door wasn't like the apartment doors across the hall. This one was a solid-core exterior door equipped with a new-looking heavy dead bolt lock.

Hardware snicked inside the lock as Harper stood looking at it. A chain rattled. The door opened about an inch. A cool blue eye with loose flesh under it peered out.

"Hello, Addleman," Harper said.

The door opened wider to reveal a small, stooped man in pleated brown pinstriped suitpants and a white shirt with the sleeves rolled up above the elbows. Odd Couple Felix was gone. Addleman's clothes were wrinkled, and he looked much older than he had last time Harper had seen him. He had a deeply lined forehead and narrow, pained features beneath a sharp black widow's peak. "Good to see you again, Harper. Come on in."

Harper entered. Addleman locked the door. Then he turned and stood facing Harper, his arms hanging at his sides. Harper put out his right hand. Addleman's eyebrows rose fractionally as he took it and Harper realized that he'd just taken part in a little experiment. Addleman wanted to know if he'd offer the injured hand, or the left one. Now he was filing the result away in his behavioral scientist's brain. Harper remembered this was something he'd had to get used to with Addleman; you might be his friend and colleague, but you were also, in a sense, his lab rat.

Glancing about the apartment, Harper was pleasantly surprised. Though cheaply furnished, it was clean and warm. The walls were bare except for one photograph, which showed two young men in caps and gowns grasping their diplomas. The sons. No picture of the wife, Harper noticed

"Want a cigarette? Something to drink?"

"No, thanks."

Addleman got out a crumpled pack of cigarettes from his pants pocket and held it up. "You mind?"

Harper figured it was Addleman's apartment. "No, go ahead and smoke."

Addleman indicated the sofa. "Sit down for a minute. You have some questions you want to ask before we get started."

He smiled thinly and Harper smiled back. There were questions all right.

"Why did you leave the Bureau?"

"They fired me."

"I'm sorry," said Harper. "You were one of the best."

Addleman shrugged. "The Bureau correctly perceived that I wasn't any use to them as long as I was drunk off my ass practically all the time."

Harper nodded. When they'd been on the case together six years before, every long workday had ended in a bar, where Addleman drank hard. Harper wasn't entirely surprised that the drinking had gotten out of hand. He said, "Didn't they offer a rehab program?"

Addleman made a face and a gesture, batting the idea away. "What for? So I could learn about the underlying forces that were compelling me to behave in this self-destructive fashion? Fuck that. I've got a Ph.D. in psychology myself, Harper. I could analyze my own case. Problem was, I didn't give a shit."

Harper waited while Addleman smoked.

Eventually, he went on. "The people you work with, the agents and supervisors—most of 'em don't believe in the scientific basis of profiling. So if you don't come through for them, they treat you like some kind of con artist. I had a couple big cases where I didn't come through. Started keeping a vodka bottle in my desk. There were problems at home, too. If you don't mind, I'll skip that part."

"Sure. Sorry to make you talk about this."

He shrugged his rounded shoulders. "I don't mind. It's kind of interesting to look back on, now that I've survived it."

"You did survive it," Harper said. "You turned things around. That took some doing."

"Nothing original," said Addleman. "AA. The twelve steps. There are still a lot of times when I want a drink. I just don't have one."

"You're not working for anyone now?"

"I don't think I'm . . . sturdy enough to go out in the world yet. I've got a small pension and a small inheritance I can live on." Addleman smiled. "My rent's not too high."

"But you must miss doing what you're good at," said Harper. This was a point on which he felt he could speak with authority.

"Oh, I'm still doing what I'm good at."

Harper looked at him questioningly.

"I read about cases and I speculate. Can't help doing that." Addleman leaned forward and stubbed out his cigarette in the ashtray. "I've stumbled onto something now that I think I have to act on. That's why I asked you to come down. I need your help to get taken seriously."

"You've got a line on the bomber who killed Buckner. And Fahey."

"Oh, he'd killed other people, before he blew up Buckner's gatehouse. And he may kill a lot more before he's through."

The weary certainty of Addleman's tone chilled Harper. He said nothing.

"You look uneasy, Harper," Addleman went on. "Like you're wondering if you oughta get up and walk out of this apartment now."

"No, I—"

Addleman held up a hand to stop him. "If you want to leave, go ahead. You don't have to explain. When we worked together I had an office and a title and a government salary. Now everything's changed. If you're thinking I'm some kind of demented alkey—well, what I have to tell you isn't gonna change your mind. It's very weird stuff, Harper. Very dark."

Harper shook his head. "I don't hold it against you, what you've been through. I don't have an office or title anymore, either. But—"

He broke off, hesitating.

"Go ahead. Let's get it all out in the open." Addleman was trying to stay absolutely still and keep his face impassive. But he was pale and his lips were trembling. Harper realized how vulnerable he was. It had taken a lot of courage for him to face Harper and describe his breakdown. It took courage now to await Harper's judgment.

Harper chose his words with care. "What I'm uneasy about—it doesn't have anything to do with your breakdown."

Addleman looked puzzled. "What is it then?"

"When we were hunting that bomber six years ago, the one we never caught—"

"He committed suicide," Addleman put in. "I'm sure of it. He's not walking around anymore."

"That guy was so twisted, so cold and cruel, that I—I didn't even recognize him as a human being. But you were able to think yourself right into his head. You could almost *become* him."

Addleman had been leaning forward in a tense half crouch. Now he sat back and put his hands on his knees. He was smiling slightly. "I see. So what you're worried about isn't that I'm wrong. You're worried that I may be right."

"Yes. I guess that's it."

Addleman stood up. His smile had grown broader. It was the old, mordant smile Harper remembered all too well.

"Good," he said. "That's an appropriate frame of mind for you to be in. Let's go."

Harper rose and followed him down a short hall and into a doorway.

Every inch of the apartment's bedroom had been usurped by file cabinets, shelves of books and software, and card tables bearing papers, floppy disks, CDs, and software manuals. A door—possibly the original apartment door—was laid over a pair of two-drawer steel file cabinets to create a vast table supporting a computer and its appendages.

It was some computer. It had a CD drive, three types of disk drives, and the biggest color monitor Harper had ever seen. It was connected to three-foot-high stereo speakers, a modem, a printer, and a scanner.

"Quite a setup," said Harper.

Addleman sat down in the desk chair. He looked pleased, almost smug. "I lost my taste for going places and meeting people," he said. "So I stopped doing it. Now everything comes to me. And I mean *everything*. The Louvre is on line now, did you know that? And the New York Philharmonic. And all the country's great libraries, of course."

He pointed to a lens that was built into the casing of the monitor. "That's a video camera. My AA sponsor has one on his computer too. So we can see each other when we talk."

He swiveled around to face Harper. "More to the point, I can access all the information I need for my work."

"You can get into the NCIC? Into police files?"

"Haven't you noticed, Harper? Half the cop cars you see have computers in them. These days case files are routinely entered into online data bases. And if it's on a data base, I can usually figure a way to make it show up here." He tapped the glass screen of his monitor.

Harper picked his way among the piles of books and papers on the floor to a straight wooden chair. He removed books from its seat and turned it to face Addleman.

"Oh, sorry," the profiler said. "My social graces are a little rusty."

Harper sat down. He couldn't be patient any longer. He said, "You've found a previous bombing that was the work of the guy who killed Fahey?"

Addleman nodded. "Two of them."

"Then you've got something the Florida police don't have."

Addleman smiled and took out a roll of peppermints. He popped one in his mouth. Probably he didn't smoke in here because it was bad for the computer.

"How could they have missed this?" Harper went on. "You mean there've been other recent bombings in the same area—"

"Not in the same area. And not recent. These go back years."

"So it's the same kind of bomb?"

"They're all pipe bombs."

"That doesn't tell you anything. It's a common type. What else is similar about them?"

"Nothing, as far as I can see."

Harper frowned, puzzled. "I don't get it, then. Where's your thread? Your common factor?"

"The victims," Addleman said.

"What about them?"

"All celebrities. Our guy kills the rich and famous."

Harper sat back so quickly that the chair creaked under him. He was thinking maybe he should have left the apartment when Addleman gave him the chance. "You're saying there's a serial killer targeting celebrities, and no one's noticed it but you? Come on! When a famous person dies it's a high-profile case. Cops and media are all over it—"

Addleman was nodding. "Yeah. Like what's happening now in the Buckner case. And all the attention isn't solving it, is it?"

Harper had no comeback to that. He said, "All right. I'm listening. Tell me about your cases."

"The first case I've definitely linked to this bomber took place five years ago. The victim was Tim Sothern."

He looked at Harper, who looked blankly back.

"Don't remember him? He was the Number Ten ranked tennis player in the world. But famous way beyond tennis."

"I do seem to remember him now. Blond guy, big smile. Advertised some kind of high-energy drink on television."

"Right. He'd do endorsements and commercials for anything. And he was good-looking and personable, so he was much in demand. You couldn't turn on the TV without seeing him."

A vague television image of a blond and laughing Sothern was emerging from Harper's memory: Sothern and another player were volleying to each other while standing in the backseats of two sports cars, roaring down a desert highway. "He got blown up in some mall, didn't he?"

"Not just any mall. The Mall of America, up in Minnesota. He was doing a personal appearance in a sporting goods store. He opened a box he was expecting to contain a pair of tennis shoes. But it was a pipe bomb. It blew his right arm off at the shoulder. He died of shock and loss of blood."

Harper nodded grimly. "Any other casualties?"

"Few cuts and bruises."

"That's lucky. I bet the store was packed."

"Yes. The bomber made some kind of mistake, so the blast wasn't as powerful as it might have been. You'll see when you read the report. Next time, he didn't make that mistake."

"When was the next time?"

"A little over a year ago. Susan Burton Wylie."

"This one I remember. The U.S. Congresswoman who was assassinated in Mexico. They thought it was some drug gang."

"It wasn't. Remember anything about Wylie herself?"

Harper considered and shook his head.

"She was a freshman member. Her campaign created quite a stir. She ran as a typical working mom who wasn't going to be just another politician. Very strong populist and feminist."

"But she was on a junket when she died, wasn't she?"

"Yeah, well, they all do that. Some lobbyists get together and put up money for a few congresspeople to go to a resort for a winter weekend. The catch is the lobbyists get to go along and talk to them. They usually call it a seminar or symposium, but basically it's a junket. So they're in Cozumel, in Representative Wylie's suite, and a bomb goes off. Two lobbyists and a staff person died along with Wylie, and the other eight people in the room were badly injured."

"I read a story about the investigation," Harper said. "Very big deal. The FBI and the Mexican National Police swapping charges about the lack of progress."

"They still haven't gotten anywhere."

"They haven't made the link to the Sothern case, you mean."

Addleman nodded.

Harper hesitated, then said, "You know, operating in a foreign country, going after a congressperson who must've had pretty fair security— that's a hell of a lot more difficult than blowing up a tennis player in a mall."

"Yes," said Addleman. "And going after Rod Buckner on his own heavily guarded estate was even more difficult. Our guy seeks out challenges. He's constantly striving to improve."

Addleman's voice was soft and mild. He had the faraway look in his eye that Harper remembered from working with him before. A drop of sweat was trickling down Harper's spine. It felt as cold and heavy as a bowling ball rolling down a gutter.

He straightened up in the uncomfortable chair. "But there's no connection, Addleman. A tennis star, a left-wing congresswoman, a right-wing novelist. They were famous, sure, but why would your guy choose to go after these three people?"

"What makes you think there has to be a connection?"

"I don't get you."

"See, Harper, this is why no one else understands that these three bombings were the work of one man. We're all dazzled by celebrities. They do such important, exciting things. Their faults and virtues are larger than life. When a famous person gets killed, we figure it's because of something he did, or it's something about him personally. But with this bomber, suppose it's not personal?"

"I still don't follow."

Addleman's upper lip tightened with impatience. Harper was being a dull student. "Say you've got a serial killer who's murdering prostitutes. Would you assume it's because he's got something personal against each prostitute?"

"No. It's because he has a problem with sex."

"Right. So our bomber has a problem with fame."

"He's a psycho, you think."

Addleman nodded. "Smart, patient, methodical, totally crazy."

"What's he got against fame?"

"I don't know yet. Not enough data."

"Look, Addleman—Harold, I'm sorry, but it doesn't seem to me that you have anything here."

"I don't have any evidence. I admit that. That's what I need you for."

"I don't see where you've even got a reasonable theory."

Addleman surged out of the chair, his fists clenched. His blue eyes looked hard as glass. "Damn it, Harper! Can't you see the pattern? He's done the same thing three times and you can't see it?"

Harper could only shrug.

The profiler was very agitated. He obviously would have liked to pace, but there was no room. So he sat down again. Glaring at Harper as he spoke, he raised his forefinger to emphasize his point. "One: Sothern. Athlete and product endorser. The bomber gets him in a sports store surrounded by his fans. Tried to get the fans too."

Addleman raised a second finger. "Two: Wylie. Washington outsider and famous woman of the people. The bomber gets her in a resort hotel surrounded by lobbyists."

The third finger went up. "Three: Buckner. A writer who claims to know all about high-tech weapons and security. The bomber gets him in his own security center, surrounded by his own guards."

"You mean he wanted to humiliate the celebrities, in addition to killing them."

"No, it's more than that." Addleman was wagging his head vigorously. "It's not only celebrities he hates. It's the people who indulge them, pay court to them, crave being associated with them. He's not just out to kill celebrities. He wants the people who kiss their asses to die with them."

Harper was nodding slowly. He didn't say anything.

After a long moment, Addleman said, "No disrespect meant to your friend. Sorry if I got a little overexcited there."

Harper hardly heard this. He was turning over in his mind all that Addleman had told him. "If you're right," he said, "this guy is only going to get more and more dangerous."

"Yes," Addleman replied. "He's got a pretty broad definition of celebrity ass-kisser. I mean, those people in the mall, they were buying Tim Sothern shirts in hopes it would give them a Tim Sothern backhand. In the bomber's book, that's enough to get you a death sentence. Maybe he thinks just buying a ticket is enough, too. Maybe he'll target a concert by Garth Brooks, or Nine Inch Nails, or the Three Tenors."

"He could kill hundreds," said Harper softly. "Maybe thousands."

"Of course, we can't know where he's going. Or where he came from. But the part of the arc that we *can* see is definitely trending upward. Each person he kills is more famous than the last. The bomb is more sophisticated and powerful. More people are killed or wounded. And every time, he chooses to go up against tougher security. It's like he's practicing. Preparing for the Big One. Whatever it is."

Another bead of sweat trickled down Harper's back. Outside, a car went slowly by. Its radio was playing a rap song so loudly the apartment windows vibrated in time with the rumble of the bass. Harper thought about Addleman, a battered and lonely man, scanning his computer screen in his slum apartment. Was it possible he'd picked up on a serial killer the entire vast web of law enforcement had missed?

Addleman caught his eye and guessed at his thoughts. "Well, Harper? Am I right? Or did I dream this up to keep me from thinking about how much I want a drink?"

Harper gave him the only answer he could. "I don't know. You've scared me. No question about that. But I'm not much for theories. I'd have to look at the files, the lab reports—"

Addleman pointed to a stack of printouts resting on the floor. "There they are. You can take 'em with you."

"Exactly what do you want me to do?"

"Well, like I said, I haven't got any proof. Nothing the FBI would consider proof, anyway. Analyzing bomb fragments and crime scenes to find out about the bomber—that was what you were brilliant at. If anybody can come up with physical evidence linking these three crimes, it's you. Then we'll go have a talk with my former employers and see if we can convince them."

Harper took a deep breath and let it out. "Okay. I'll take the files."

"That's all I ask." Addleman gave his quick, sardonic smile. "Well, no, that's not all. I'm also going to have to ask you not to take too long getting back to me."

"I'll get right on it. If this bomber's for real, if he's the one who killed Jimmy Fahey, I want him bad."

"There's more to it than that." Addleman straightened up and looked down at his hands. "Remember, while you're working, the bomber's working too."

Harper felt the old tension begin to gnaw at his insides. "Seems to me your bomber leaves a long time between his attacks."

"So far. But we can't count on that. What we do know is that he's a meticulous planner and preparer. He's working on his next attack right now."

Harper nodded and went over to the stack of printouts. By the time he rose with the papers under his arm, Addleman was standing in the hall, at a safe distance from his beloved computer, lighting a cigarette. Harper observed the expression of relief on his face with the first deep inhalation. Almost everyone had at least one vice that could be a destructive compulsion: tobacco, booze, food, sex.

Bombs.

6

At the side of a quiet road in western Missouri, not far from Interstate 44, a man was pacing next to his parked car. He was waiting
for someone. He paced methodically, six steps out and six back. There
was a puddle in his path which he avoided with the same side step
each time. At the conclusion of each circuit, he glanced at his watch.
Evidently he was the sort of man who liked to keep track of how long
he was being kept waiting.

He was a tall man in his early forties. The afternoon was dim and
damp, and he was wearing the raincoat of a city businessman: knee-
length, tan, the front buttons covered by a fly. He had it buttoned up
to the collar, but he wasn't wearing a hat. His lank brown hair had
receded, leaving a vast expanse of pale, deeply furrowed forehead. His
dense, dark eyebrows, growing together over his nose, seemed to divide
his face in half, with his features scrunched together in the lower half.
The eyes were deep-set and, in the dim light, seemingly colorless. They
could have been blue, hazel, or gray. The nose was short and straight,
the mouth wide and thin-lipped. His chin was receding into his neck,
the way a middle-aged man's will.

The place where the man was waiting had been well-chosen—a
rectangle of pitted and rutted concrete on which a service station or
convenience store must once have stood, though no trace of the building

remained. It was only a few yards from the road, but dense thickets screened it from passing traffic. Not that this mattered, for there was hardly any traffic, and dusk was closing in fast. In the other direction, Interstate 44 could be seen in the distance, one band of white lights and another of red, snaking over a hill. The rush and shuffle of speeding cars could be clearly heard over the sound of water dripping from tree limbs.

The quiet was broken by the roar of an approaching car. The man checked his watch one final time and lowered it with a look of cold satisfaction. Putting his hands in his raincoat pockets, he turned to face the road.

An old, rust-pitted Camaro came bucking and swaying over the potholed concrete to stop next to the waiting man's nondescript sedan. Apparently the door no longer worked, because the driver hoisted himself out through the window.

This man was bad news, and he wanted everybody to know it. He was wearing a sleeveless T-shirt, grimy jeans, and sharp-toed cowboy boots. He had a fat stomach, but his shoulders and arms were thickly muscled, the muscles adorned with tattoos. There were heavy, jagged rings on all four fingers of his left hand. His long black hair hadn't been washed in a long time. It was parted in the middle, revealing a pale scar running down his forehead to his right cheek. The lid of the right eye had never healed, and the eye was bloodshot. The man had the habit of blinking frequently.

"Hey, how you doing?" he said, as he advanced on the older man. "I'm Steve. Who're you?"

"I'm—Leonard's friend."

"I know *that*. If Leonard hadn't sent you, you wouldn't be here. What's your first name?"

The older man hesitated. "Leonard didn't say anything about—"

"Look, I just need something to call you. Make something up. Or I will." Steve stepped closer to the older man, sizing him up. What he saw made him grin, showing bad teeth. "How 'bout I call you Klingon? Like them geeks in *Star Trek*. You got the forehead for it. Plus, you look real tough."

The man frowned. He said quickly, "Call me Anthony."

"Yeah? I bet that's your real name, too. Right?" Steve's grin was wider and nastier now. He obviously took pride in his ability to goad people into making mistakes.

Anthony said, "You're seventeen minutes late."

The grin vanished from Steve's face, to be replaced by a look of bewilderment. A reedy middle-aged straight citizen like Anthony ought to be trying very hard to keep him in a good mood.

But Anthony went on, "I told Leonard, if either party is even a minute early or late, the deal's off."

Steve stood blinking at him. "Hey, man, don't give me a hard time. I'm here now and I got your stuff. What happened was, I got pulled over and—"

"Pulled over? By a cop?"

"It was just a speeding ticket, and anyway I talked my way out of it."

"You were speeding?" Anthony said. "With what you had in the car, you were speeding?"

"I was trying to get here on time. Jesus Christ! What's with you, pal? You think you're my fucking dad or something?" Steve wiped his nose on one beefy forearm. As he lowered it he flexed his fingers and the line of rings glittered.

Anthony stared at him for a while with undisguised contempt, then said, "All right. I'm willing to go ahead with the deal."

"Yeah? Well, maybe I'm not." Steve's legs were braced and his fists were clenched at his sides. His whole muscular frame was vibrating. He kept quiet for a long moment, but his face was working. He was turning what Anthony had said to him over and over in his mind, and liking it less each time. Finally he said, "How do I know you're not a Fed?"

"Leonard vouched for me. Look, if you don't go through with this deal, Leonard will never set anything up with you again."

"I gotta be careful," Steve said. "That heap you're driving looks like it's right out of the motor pool. You dress like a Fed. And you're a tight-assed bastard like a Fed."

"You don't really think I'm an undercover agent," said Anthony in a weary tone. "Let's get this over with. Show me the stuff and I'll give you your money."

Steve stepped right up to Anthony. The older man held his ground, his arms hanging at his sides and his face blank. Steve grinned and bent forward, as if speaking into a microphone under Anthony's coat. "What stuff? What money? I don't know what you're talking about."

"You're wasting—"

"I'm gonna search you, Anthony."

The older man's high forehead wrinkled with disgust. "That won't do you any good. I haven't got the money on me."

"I'm not looking for the money. I'm looking for a wire."

"That's ridiculous. Will you—"

Steve grabbed him by the shoulders and roughly spun him around and pushed him. Anthony had to throw out his arms and catch himself against the roof of his car. Steve patted him down roughly but sloppily, with no real effort to be thorough. It was obvious that he didn't really think Anthony was a Fed. He just wanted to lay hands on him, push him around. Show him who was boss.

"Nothing," said Steve, as if disappointed, backing away. "Say, where you keep your wallet?"

Anthony turned around, lowering his arms. He hadn't resisted the frisking, but it didn't seem to have intimidated him either. "The money for you isn't in my wallet. It's well hidden. If you want it, show me the stuff."

"I'm not trying to steal your money. I want to know who the fuck you are. 'Cause everything about you is wrong, pal."

"Leonard—"

"Shut up!" Steve turned his head to look at the car. "I bet your wallet's in the glove compartment."

"It isn't."

For the first time there was a trace of apprehension in the older man's voice. Steve picked up on it and grinned. "Sure it is. Straight citizen like you isn't gonna go out driving without his license. You're scared you might end up in jail. Never been in jail, have you, Anthony?"

"Please don't search the car," said Anthony. It didn't sound like a plea, though. It sounded like a warning.

Steve's head reared back. He stared at Anthony, blinking rapidly. Then he backpedaled until he reached the driver's door of his Camaro. Keeping his eyes on Anthony, he reached inside through the window.

His hand came out holding a heavy, long-barreled revolver. "Now we're gonna see what's in your car."

"I told you, there's nothing."

Steve stepped over to Anthony's car and reached for the passenger door handle. Then he hesitated. The hand dropped.

"Come over here."

Anthony approached. His hands were still hanging limply at his sides.

Steve said, "Get in the car, open the glove compartment door, and take out whatever's in there."

Anthony did as he was told. Steve kept the gun trained on him as he sat down in the car. His hand emerged from the glove compartment holding a folded piece of paper. "This is all," he said. "You can come and look for yourself, the glove compartment's empty. I left my wallet and license behind."

Anthony was holding the folded piece of paper to his chest protectively. Steve noticed. "What is that?"

"Nothing. Just a calendar."

"Let's see it."

Anthony hesitated.

"Listen, I've had about enough from you, Mr. Tight-Ass. I want to see that piece of paper and I got the gun, so don't fuck with me."

Anthony slowly extended his hand through the open car door and Steve snatched the paper from him.

"Now put both your hands on the dashboard where I can see 'em. And don't move."

Anthony obeyed. He let out his breath in a long sigh.

Steve was unfolding the calendar on the hood of the car.

"You see," Anthony said, "it's just a calendar."

"No, not just a calendar." Steve sounded amused, mocking. "You put a lot of work into this, didn't you? You're crossing off the days. That why you brought this along with you, so you wouldn't miss crossing off today? I bet you have to wait till exactly midnight and then you make your X. I knew a guy like that once. Course, he had an excuse, he was in prison. But you're just a tight-ass."

Anthony didn't reply.

"Is this really April sixth already?" said Steve. "I thought it was the fourth, but no, it's Tuesday, so I guess you're right."

He ran his finger down the page. Anthony watched, his face impassive.

"Hey, you wrote little numbers in each square. You're counting off days, aren't you? Sixteen . . . fifteen . . . fourteen." His finger ran down toward the bottom of the page. "Three, two, one, and here's the big day, April twenty-second. All colored in red. So what happens on April twenty-second?"

Anthony said, "An event."

"Oh, yeah? That when you're gonna use the stuff I'm selling you?"

Anthony didn't answer, but Steve didn't seem to mind. He was grinning through the windshield at the older man, enjoying his humiliation. Anthony continued looking at the calendar. The raindrops on the hood were soaking into the paper and the ink was smudging and running.

"Hey, we're not done, are we? I see we're counting down again." Steve flipped the page over. "What is this? You cut the page off on May fifteenth."

Anthony said, "It doesn't matter what happens after May fifteenth."

Steve was grinning and shaking his head. Without noticing, he'd lowered the gun so that it was no longer pointing at Anthony. He said, "So May fifteenth, you figure that's the Grand Calypso, right?"

"What?"

"The Grand Calypso. The end of the world. Behold the seas shall smoke, and the Beast with four eyes and six dicks shall come forth, leading the armies of Satan or the United Nations or whoever. And you're gonna be there to take 'em on in the last battle."

Anthony sat there patiently, with his eyes downcast and his hands on the dashboard. "Can we get on with it?"

"Sure, sure. I just wanted to know who I was dealing with, and now I do. Straight citizen on the outside, total nutso on the inside."

He held out the calendar, which was now damp and ink-stained. Anthony slowly lifted one hand from the dashboard, took it, and put it away.

"Get out of the car," Steve said.

Anthony complied. He stood motionless while Steve backed away to his own car and reached inside. He brought out a cardboard box, the same size as a shoebox. The sides were grease-stained, like a fast-food container.

He slapped it down hard on the trunk of Anthony's car, watching Anthony with a grin, as if he expected this to make him jump. It didn't.

Anthony looked out at the road. No cars were coming. He opened the box. Inside was what looked like a large lump of wet clay.

"There you go," said Steve. "C-4, prime U.S. Army Special Forces plastic explosive."

"I was expecting more," said Anthony. He used the same dry, demanding tone he'd used when complaining about Steve's lateness. It was as if the search and the confrontation over the map hadn't happened.

"You got twenty ounces there, for Christ's sake. You got any idea how powerful that stuff is? This is enough to blow down a couple of good-size buildings. You remember Pan Am 103? The airliner the rag-heads brought down over Scotland? They did that with a bomb stuffed in a minicassette player. Ten inches by seven. You've got four times as much here."

"That was Semtex, not C-4," said Anthony.

"Same thing, basically," Steve said. Anthony's comment had surprised him. He looked sideways at him. "You know something about explosives?"

Anthony was still looking down at the grayish lump in the box. He said, "Yes. I haven't worked with plastique before, though."

"This is great shit, man. You can roll it like dough, mold it like putty, or fold it like paper. And it's damn near undetectable by security equipment." Steve had shifted into salesman mode, now that his wares were on display. He seemed to have forgotten the confrontation of a few minutes before in his enthusiasm.

"Taggants?" asked Anthony.

Steve gave him another sideways look. Taggants were chemical markers that made it possible for investigators to trace the explosive used in a bombing back to its manufacturer. Steve said, "Hey, Anthony. You really do know what you're talking about, don't you? I thought I finally had you figured. You were one of those nutcases with an AK-47 under the bed and a six-month supply of canned food in the basement. I figured you wanted the C-4 just to make you feel like a bad dude. But that ain't you, is it?"

"Taggants?" said Anthony again.

Steve rolled his eyes and sighed. "This is manufactured exclusively for the military. There are no taggants. That's one thing makes it better than Semtex. They got different laws in Europe, where Semtex is manufactured."

Anthony said, "Where did you get this?"

"It was stolen from an Army base. I'm not gonna tell you which one."

"Tell me when."

Steve was growing irritated again. It was plain on his face, but Anthony wasn't looking at him. "Don't worry about it. They won't know it's missing till the next war breaks out and they go looking for it."

"I need to know that it's stable," said Anthony testily. "You can see for yourself, it's sweating." He pointed to the grease stains on the box.

"C-4 always does that. It's not unstable. It's U.S. Army issue. The stuff the Special Forces guys train with. Now, you want it or not?"

Anthony considered, then shrugged. "You never know till you run some tests anyway," he murmured, more to himself than to Steve. He put the lid back on the box. "I'll get you your money." He picked up the box and started to turn away.

"Put the box down," said Steve. He backed away a few steps, raising his gun. He was blinking rapidly, nervously.

Anthony put the C-4 down on the trunk of his car. "You don't need that," he said.

"Look. I don't know who you are or what the fuck you're planning. I don't want to know. All I want is my money."

"Then let me give it to you."

Steve's face was a mask of wariness. He dropped into a shooter's stance, knees bent, both arms out, with the left hand cradling the gun hand.

"You give me a real bad feeling, pal, you know that? Don't do anything till I tell you, and then do it slow. I mean that. Be real careful or you're going to get yourself shot."

"You've already searched me. You know I'm not armed." There was no trace of fear, or any other emotion, in Anthony's voice.

"Where's the money?"

Anthony made a small gesture with his hand. "Right here in the wheel well."

"The wheel well. Now that's a real smart place to hide it. Christ, it prob'ly fell off by now. Or got soaking wet."

"No. It's in a special carrier I made myself. It's fine. I'll tell you exactly where it is, if you want to get it yourself."

"No way. I want you to get it for me."

Anthony knelt by the side of his car. He moved slowly and carefully. Steve continued to keep the pistol trained on him as he reached in behind the wheel. There was a metallic scrape, as of something sliding off a bracket.

"Freeze!" Steve yelled, and Anthony froze.

"Now you're gonna bring your hands out of there real slow," Steve said. "*Real* slow."

When he was finished speaking, he took a step to his left, so he wouldn't be standing where Anthony had last seen him. He was blinking more rapidly than ever.

Very slowly, Anthony drew a small metal box into the light where Steve could see it. It was spattered with mud.

"Okay." Steve relaxed a little. "Get up."

Anthony rose and held out the hand with the box in it.

"You take out the cash."

Anthony slid the lid of the box down, a fraction of an inch at a time. With the same deliberation he lifted out the thick stack of bills.

Steve was just close enough to make out the features of Ulysses S. Grant on the top bill. He grinned, for the first time in several minutes. "Put the money down on the roof of the car and back away."

Anthony obeyed.

"Farther back."

Anthony took two more steps. He was now standing in the center of the bare concrete apron. Once again his arms hung at his sides.

Steve came forward. Shifting the gun to his left hand he picked up the money in his right. His grinning mouth turned down. "Shit! I knew it. This is wet."

"No," Anthony said. "The container is watertight."

"It's *wet*. Oh, Christ, it's sticky too. You jerk off on this or what?"

He laid the gun down on the roof within easy reach and grasped the paper band that held the money. He kept his eyes on Anthony, who remained motionless. Or seemed to. In fact, he made one move too small for Steve to see: He closed his eyes.

As Steve tore the paper it made a *pop!* like a child's Christmas cracker. There was a flash as the money and Steve's hands caught fire.

Steve screamed. His gun fell to the concrete. Instinctively he tried to put out the flames by tucking his hands under his arms. His shirt caught fire. His screams redoubled as he sank to his knees and toppled over.

Anthony was watching. His expression didn't change. Unhurriedly he reached into his pocket and took out a handkerchief, which he used to wipe off the napalm that had stuck to his own hands as he passed the money to Steve. Then he dropped the handkerchief and advanced. He bent to pick up the gun. Steve was shrieking and rolling around on the concrete in paroxysms of agony. Anthony, standing over him, took a long time lining up the shot. He fired once. The bullet cut off Steve's scream and he was still.

Anthony slid the gun into his raincoat pocket. He stood listening for a moment, but it was just as quiet now as it had been before Steve arrived. The only sounds were traffic on the distant highway and water dripping from the trees.

Anthony went to his car and took out a whisk broom and a small dustpan. Bending down, he shuffled back and forth over the concrete around the body, brushing up ashes and charred flakes of paper, which were all that was left of the wad he'd handed Steve. It was just white paper, in fact: Only the top and bottom bills had been real. There was a nauseating smell of burned fabric and roasted flesh, but it didn't seem to bother Anthony. He kept on brushing until he had every last flake.

Carrying the full dustpan carefully, he brought it back to his car and put it inside. Then he picked up his handkerchief. A last look around assured him he was leaving nothing behind except for Steve's car and Steve himself.

He took the box of C-4 off the trunk lid and got in the car, where he put it on the passenger-side floor. Then he started the car, switched on the headlights, and bumped back onto the road.

As he drove, the sky darkened and the rain began again. He switched on his headlights and wipers. The big green reflective sign for Interstate 44 came up. But Anthony pulled onto the shoulder before reaching the entrance ramp.

Leaning back, he shut his eyes and kneaded his forehead. Then he sat forward and reached into the glove compartment for the calendar. He frowned to see the smears and runs, but the numbers he'd written in were still legible.

With an X that filled the box, Anthony crossed off today, April 6.

There were now fifteen days to go until April 22, the date he'd blocked in in red. Thirty-nine days to go until May 15, the last date on the calendar.

Anthony didn't wait until midnight to cross off a day. Steve had been wrong about that.

7

The second week of April brought springlike weather to the Northeast. The Harpers opened their windows wide for the first time
since October. Mild breezes wafted into the house the usual sounds of
a Brooklyn night: boomboxes, sirens, and car alarms.

None of the noises reached Will Harper. He was absorbed in rereading
the file on the Wylie case. The dining room, in which he was sitting,
was a high-ceilinged, wainscoted room that was going to need a lot of
work to return it to its original Victorian elegance. The parquet floors
were dull and stained and there were gaping holes in the walls, through
which you could see laths and wiring. But the room did have a table,
a stout cherrywood piece long enough to seat ten. And table space was
what Harper needed.

Piled on either side of him were the bulky files on the Sothern and
Wylie cases which Addleman had given him. There was also other
information Addleman had sent him since then, via computer. Only
the slow speed of Harper's modem had put a limit on how much data
the eager Addleman could transmit. Then there were Harper's own
heavy technical manuals, some of them still bearing their PROPERTY OF
NYPD stencils. And finally there were the models Harper had built:
reconstructions of the bombs, based on what he'd read in the files, and
models that looked like miniature stage sets, representing the rooms

where the bombs had gone off. Some of them were shattered and blackened. He'd blown them up with firecrackers in the back garden as he experimented with the effects of blast.

He looked up to see Laura standing in the doorway, wearing old surgical scrubs, her favorite lounging outfit. He hadn't heard the door open. To judge from her expression, she must have just said something to him, and he hadn't heard that, either.

"Sorry," he said. "What is it?"

"I might as well be speaking Tagalog, for all the effect it has on you. You scrawl notes to yourself and leave them all over the apartment. You get up in the middle of the night to pace and mutter. You leave your keys in the front door and the milk on the kitchen counter." She grinned at him. "Oh, Will, it's great to see you like this again."

"It is?"

"You're excited about what you're doing. You're all the way alive again."

"I'm frustrated, if you want to know the truth." Pushing back from the table, he stretched his arms above his head. He'd been working for several hours straight and there were kinks in his back.

"Anything I can do to help?"

"Well, maybe there is."

She sat down across from him. They hadn't yet found chairs to match their splendid table; for the present, they were using a few rickety deck chairs.

Harper opened the Wylie file and took out a photo, which he placed in front of Laura. It was a close view of a portion of the pipe bomb, blackened and misshapen from the explosion. "Do you see anything there? On the surface of the pipe, I mean."

He handed her a magnifying glass and she peered through it, frowning. "It's hard to tell. This photo's a little grainy."

He nodded. "Addleman downloaded it from the NCIC computer. Even with a top-of-the-line modem and color printer, it's not as good as the original photo."

"Well, I don't see anything, Will. Sorry."

He sighed, unsurprised but still disappointed. "See that mark, right in the center of the picture? If that was a letter of the alphabet, which letter would it be?"

Laura picked up the photo and experimented with the magnifying glass, moving it closer and then farther away. Finally she said, "*E*."

He nodded morosely. "Yeah. It looks like an *E* to me, too. I was hoping for a *C*."

She put down the magnifying glass and photo. "Why?"

"Brand showed me a picture of a fragment of the Buckner bomb."

"And there was a *C* on it?"

"I thought so. Brand didn't."

"Well, if Captain Brand doesn't see it, maybe it's significant," said Laura, smiling. "How about the other bomb?"

"The Sothern bomb? No, I couldn't see anything on that one."

"Maybe he's spelling out *celebrity bomber*, a letter on each bomb, not in any particular order."

"Possible, but not likely. We call him the Celebrity Bomber, but for all we know he thinks of himself as the Fame Blaster or some such thing. Or maybe he doesn't have a name for himself."

"Still, it's possible."

Harper nodded but said nothing.

She picked up the photo again. "And why would he put a *C* on each bomb? You think it's his initial?"

"I don't know. But it would be a common factor." Harper was getting stiff from sitting for so long. He got up and started to pace. "Something that would prove the three bombs were the work of the same person. But I haven't found anything to indicate that so far."

"You think Addleman's wrong, then? There is no Celebrity Bomber?"

Harper paused in his pacing and looked at her. "No, Addleman's right. The guy's for real. He's out there."

For a long moment, Laura stared back at him without saying anything. Finally she murmured, "I see. Well, if you're convinced, how come you can't prove it?"

Harper returned to his chair. "Maybe it'll help if I talk this all out. You mind listening?"

She shook her head and leaned forward, watching him expectantly. He reached into the Sothern file. "Can you stand a gory crime scene photo?"

"I'm a nurse, remember?"

He placed the photograph on the table between them. The Racquets Etc. sporting goods store in the Mall of America looked as if it had been picked up by a giant hand and given a hard shake. Clothing and other merchandise that had been on the shelves was lying in mounds on the floor. Wall hooks on which racquets had been displayed were empty. Windows had been blown out. In the center of the wall-to-wall carpeting was a large red stain.

"Is that where your fatality was standing?"

"Tim Sothern, the tennis player. Yes. His right arm was blown off at the shoulder."

"How awful."

"He was opening a box he thought contained a pair of tennis shoes. Actually, it contained a pipe bomb."

"That's a length of iron pipe stuffed with explosive?"

"Right. All three bombs were pipe bombs, but nobody will be impressed with that as a common factor. It would be like saying because three murders were committed with revolvers, must be the same guy who committed them."

"I see. Nothing special about the pipe bomb in the Sothern case?"

"The pipe must have come out of a junkyard somewhere. But the bomber had beaten out the dents and sanded off the rust."

Laura frowned. "Why?"

"We don't know. But he's a guy who doesn't mind taking trouble. The explosive was match heads and black powder. He got the powder from shotgun shells."

"You'd have to pry apart an awful lot of shotgun shells, wouldn't you?"

"Hundreds. His detonator was homemade. Like nothing I've ever seen before. I couldn't exactly reconstruct it, but basically when the flaps of the box were opened, a hinge drove a nail into a blasting cap. Kind of a Rube Goldberg device."

"But obviously it worked," said Laura, glancing at the bloodstain in the photo.

"Yes, but not as well as he'd hoped. The idea with a pipe bomb is that the explosive is so tightly compressed, it blows the pipe to pieces. The pieces act as shrapnel." Harper looked again at the photo. "That store was full of people who'd come to see Sothern. They would have been cut to pieces. But the bomber only got Sothern himself."

"What did the bomber do wrong?"

"He didn't plug one end of the pipe tightly enough. So most of the force of the explosion went out that end. It was enough to finish Sothern. But I imagine our bomber wasn't happy, after all the work he'd put in."

Harper returned the photo to the Sothern file and reached for the Wylie file. "Next case."

He laid down a crime scene photo in front of Laura.

"Oh my God," she murmured.

The store in Minnesota had still been recognizable as a store. But the hotel suite in Cozumel was nothing but a scene of horrific violence. The windows had been blown out and the steel railing on the balcony beyond had been twisted out of shape. Interior walls were reduced to a few spars of wood and piles of plaster. Heavy pieces of furniture had been upended or blown across the room. The blast had even flayed sections of wallpaper off the wall, revealing plaster pockmarked from the impacts of shrapnel. And blood was everywhere.

Laura stared at the photo for a long moment, then turned it over. She said somberly, "I suppose you're going to tell me that this is what happens when you do a pipe bomb right."

"Yes," said Harper. "If the other was a do-it-yourselfer, this one was state-of-the-art. A new length of pipe, straight from the plumber's supply store. Cast iron, which gives you shrapnel with a nice, sharp edge. The explosive was a mixture of ammonium nitrate and aluminum powder. Not difficult to get hold of the ingredients, but tricky to blend them right. This guy did. The detonator was electrical, attached to a timer. All very slick."

"And I assume the bomb was sealed tight at both ends.The bomber made no mistakes?"

"No mistakes.".

"And the Buckner bomb—"

"Different kind of pipe, different explosive, different detonator. And all of them much more sophisticated than the Wylie bomb."

"I see your problem." Laura frowned and folded her arms. "So why is this 'common factor' you keep talking about so important?"

"Bombers don't experiment, as a rule. They hit on a design that works and stick with it. They want to spend as little time as possible putting the bomb together."

"Reasonably enough. Less chance of blowing yourself up that way."

"This one is different. He doesn't care how long it takes. Doesn't follow the usual procedures. He's making it all up out of his head, and he does it differently every time. The common factor is that there is no common factor."

Leaning forward, Harper picked up the Sothern file again. "You know what was the clincher? Convinced me it was the same guy? It's that he learns from his mistakes."

Harper opened the file and took out the picture of the bulging, twisted pipe bomb. "Remember, he didn't fasten the one end tightly enough on this bomb. Well, on the Wylie bomb he took no chances. He welded the caps on."

"Wait—you mean he used a welding torch on a pipe full of high explosive?"

"The guy is very confident about his workmanship. Also, of course, he's insane."

"And did he do the same with the Buckner bomb?"

"No, damn it! He bought the pipe prethreaded and screwed the caps onto it." Harper slapped the file shut and sat back. "So if Addleman and I take this to some FBI guy with a master's degree in forensic science and no imagination, he's going to say, 'You've got three bombs of widely varying degrees of sophistication and that means three different bombers.' I'll say it's one guy who's getting better and more dangerous all the time, and he'll say that's just my theory."

Laura's eyes widened combatively. Twenty years of working with doctors had expunged every trace of diffidence from her own character, and she hated it when Harper was modest. "Just your theory? Your theory *counts*. Because of who you are, what you've accomplished."

Harper shrugged. "It would be different if I was going to NYPD detectives. Guys I've cracked cases for in the past. With them, my opinion counts. But the Feebs are different." Harper slumped in his chair and wearily surveyed the cluttered table.

After a moment, Laura said, "Will? I think you should call Addleman."

"Why? I haven't got anything we can take to the Bureau."

"Just to tell him you believe him. From what you've told me about Addleman, that'll mean a great deal to him. Besides, two minds are better than one."

"Even if they're deluded?"

She gazed evenly at him. She loathed self-pity as much as he did. "Don't piss me off, Will."

He thought he'd better not. "Okay, I'll make the call."

She smiled. Much better.

8

Laura was right.

After Harper finished talking, there was a moment of silence so long he wondered if Addleman was still on the other end of the line.

Finally, Addleman spoke. "Thank God, Will. I admit, there were times when I wondered if I was crazy. But you've proved me right."

"No, I haven't," Harper said. "Maybe there are two of us who are crazy."

"Come on, Will! You've shown that what I said is true. This guy's varying methodology, constantly improving, setting new challenges for himself, and meeting them. The son of a bitch is practicing, for Christ's sake! He's building up to something really big. The Bureau's *got* to listen to us."

"Without a common factor other than celebrities, they won't listen."

Addleman subsided. For a moment, there was no sound over the line except his excited breathing. "So what do you think? It's impossible? There is no common factor?"

Harper thought for a while. He said, "There has to be. In some way or other, our guy's put his stamp on all three bombs. I haven't seen it yet, but that's because I don't know him well enough yet."

"Explain," said Addleman tersely.

"I think the problem is, I'm working from pictures and lab reports.

When I was with the NYPD, I worked with the actual bomb fragments. I handled the same pieces the bomber had handled. That was how I figured out how his mind worked. I know it's kind of weird, but—"

"Not at all. It sounds like something I'd do."

This didn't set Harper's mind at rest. "We're going to have to get access to one of the bombs. The Sothern one, ideally. It's the most intact. You know anybody in the Minnesota State Police Crime Lab?"

Addleman thought a moment and said, "No. But I must know someone who knows someone there."

"Or maybe I do. Tomorrow, let's start working the phones."

At nine the next morning, Harper started placing calls to old friends in various branches of law enforcement. It didn't surprise him that no one was in to take his call; working cops were notoriously hard to reach. He left messages.

But when lunchtime came around and the phone hadn't rung, he began to worry. He placed second calls. This time he caught several people at their desks. They were apologetic about not returning his call. They were even sorrier they couldn't help him. No one was interested in why he wanted to see bomb fragments. In fact, it was clear to Harper that they wanted to get him off the line as quickly as possible.

Finally a fellow pensioned-off cop, Al Thomas, who owed Harper, told him what the problem was.

"You heard of the Domenic Fortunato case, Will?"

Harper remembered the six-year-old Queens boy who'd died in a blaze caused by fireworks his father, a police sergeant, had obtained illegally. He said, "Yes, I know the case. Captain Brand said he was worried about it, last time I talked to him."

"Well, he's a lot more worried now."

"You mean the fireworks came from the Bomb Squad dump on Rodman's Neck?"

"Yeah. Apparently that's what Sergeant Fortunato is telling IAD now."

"But what's all this got to do with me?"

Thomas hesitated.

Harper's stomach muscles grew taut. With an effort, he kept his voice level. "Is Fortunato saying he got the fireworks from me?"

Thomas sighed. "The rumor is, there's pressure being put on him to make him say that."

"But I never met the guy. Never heard of him till this case came up."

"Sure, Will. But it's a question of what he can be made to say. The poor guy's in terrible shape. You can imagine how guilty he feels about his son's death. And IAD is really working him over. So far, all he's saying is that he obtained the fireworks years ago and he can't remember who his contact was. But they keep running names by him. Yours, most often. Yours every day, in fact, the way I hear it."

Harper gripped the phone. His heart was pounding with anger, but he could still think calmly. He was fairly sure who'd suggested his name to IAD: Captain Brand. The captain and Harper had their longtime grudge, and their last meeting had been none too friendly. Besides, Harper, being both well-known and out of the Department, would suit Brand's purposes perfectly.

"They need a scapegoat," Harper said.

"You think that's it?"

"Sure it is. They want to contain the damage. They don't want the Fortunato case turning into a wider inquiry. The problem is, Al, people are always pilfering fireworks from the dump at Rodman's Neck. And it isn't just John Q. Patrolman, wanting some sparklers for his kid's birthday. It's the Borough President, wanting to liven up his fundraising picnic. It's the D.A., having a Fourth of July party at his country place. People on the Squad tell me they've gotten calls from Gracie Mansion. From Albany, even."

"Yeah, I see the problem," Thomas said. "A lot of higher-ups would rather see your head roll than theirs. But Will, this is just rumors so far. Fortunato hasn't named you. It may not go any farther."

Harper thanked Thomas and hung up the phone. It had already gone too far, he thought. Even if Harper was never charged, even if his name never went out to the media, the rumors were already getting around, staining his good name at the worst possible time. From now on, he would have a whiff of corruption about him. Some would even go so far as to consider him a sort of accesory in the killing of a child.

In the afternoon, he called the Minnesota State Police direct. Out there they hadn't heard the rumors about him. They explained that the Sothern bombing was still an open case, so of course an outsider couldn't be permitted to handle the fragments. Evidence might be contaminated. The chain of custody might be broken. They were sorry, but—

Laura was working late, so Harper ate dinner alone in the kitchen and then went back into the dining room to go over the files again. He didn't expect a call from Addleman. The ex-profiler's contacts had probably treated him just as contemptuously as Harper's had. They were two of a kind, he and Addleman. Hard-luck guys. Losers.

The rickety chair squeaked under Harper as he sat down. He surveyed the piles of paper and open books and the laboriously constructed models on the table. There was no point in going back to work now. He was tired, and the three beers he'd drunk before dinner to take the sting out of the day weren't helping his mental acuity.

Still, he reached for the Sothern file and took out the photographs of the bomb. He'd found a C on the Buckner bomb, and an E on the Wylie bomb. But on this, the most nearly intact of the bombs, he hadn't been able to find either letter. That kept nagging at him. What did it mean?

Probably that the C and E were just scratches, and Harper's imagination had run away from him.

Putting away the thought, he reached for a picture of the pipe. He spent the next ten minutes going over it with the magnifying glass, but once again he saw no C or E, no scratch that looked like any letter of the alphabet, in fact.

The reproductions weren't as sharp as they should have been. If only he could see the actual bomb fragments—

No point thinking about that, either.

He put down the glass and straightened up, massaging his aching neck. The end of the pipe which had blown out was torn and twisted, but the other end was mostly intact. It was easy to see the bomber's crude fastening method: He'd drilled two sets of holes through pipe and cap, and then put screws through at right angles, one just above the other, and fastened them with nuts.

Harper rummaged through photographs and came up with one of the screws they'd recovered. It was the lower screw, the slightly thicker one. The other hadn't been found.

He studied the side view and saw nothing. Then he looked at the head-view. It was blown up to two or three times life-size. He could see the cross-shaped Phillips head groove.

And placed neatly in one quadrant was a tiny letter A.

Harper gave a wordless shout of surprise and excitement. Why hadn't he seen this before? The answer was, because he hadn't expected to see a letter on a screw head; the others had been on the pipes. But what was it doing there?

"C, E, A," said Harper to himself. He got up from the table and walked around it, muttering the letters over and over. On the sixth lap, he stopped and picked up the photo of the pipe. He looked at the screw holes, one slightly smaller than the other.

Suddenly, he understood.

"They're assembly instructions," he said to Addleman over the phone.

"What?"

"That's why they're all different letters. They're not his initials, they're not some kind of message to the world, they're just assembly instructions."

"Slow down, Will. Take it from the top. And remember, I'm not mechanically minded."

"Okay. He's got two screws that he uses to fasten the cap to the pipe. One's thicker than the other, and goes in holes that are lower down. So he puts a little A, on it, just to remind himself. If we had the other screw, it would say B. I'm sure of that."

"Wait a minute. Why does he need assembly instructions? He puts the bomb together, and that's it. Why the hell should he take it apart and put it back together?"

"He has to," Harper said. "He's obsessive."

"What?"

"This guy builds bombs the way other people practice on the piano or play chess. He loves it. Can't get enough of it. That's why he's getting so damned good. It's his passion, building them, disassembling them, putting them back together. He can't leave a bomb alone. It's his compulsion." Harper didn't say why he was so sure he knew that about this bomber, how he understood him because, in a way, bombs were his compulsion, too.

Addleman gave a wheezing chuckle. It was the first time Harper had heard him laugh. "So this is it, right, Will? The breakthrough. The common factor."

"Yes. This'll prove it. Now I know what to look for. All I have to do is examine the other bomb fragments and I bet I'll find letters all over them."

"The Bureau can unlock all those doors for you," said Addleman. "I think it's time for you to go down to the J. Edgar Hoover Building and present our case."

"Me?" said Harper. "It's time for *us* to go."

Addleman was silent for a moment. "I told you, I'm not much for going places and meeting people anymore. Especially my former employers."

"Forget it, Addleman. You're coming with me."

Another pause. When Addleman spoke again, his voice was smaller. "How about this? I told you, I've got a video camera rigged to my computer. You have a computer at your end, and I pop up on the screen. I'm as good as there."

"This isn't *The NewsHour With Jim Lehrer*, Addleman," Harper said firmly. "You're going to be there. I don't know much about the Bureau. You used to work there. I need you."

Addleman sighed. "Yeah, you probably do. Okay, stay in tomorrow morning. I'll call you as soon as I've got the meeting set up."

"Sounds like you already know who we're going to talk to."

"Yeah. Somebody I've worked with before. Her name is Frances Wilson."

"She's good?"

"Not only good, she's unusual."

9

There was no portrait of J. Edgar Hoover in Special Agent Wilson's office.

It was otherwise a typical senior agent's office, small, but with a good view of Pennsylvania Avenue. In the distance, the Washington Monument could be seen poking into the overcast sky. There was a desk with a comfortable chair behind it and two less comfortable chairs in front. Harper and Addleman were sitting in these chairs, waiting for Agent Wilson to come in. Harper was spending the time studying the wall on which her awards, commendations, and official portraits were displayed. The current FBI Director was there, and the Attorney General, and the President—but not J. Edgar.

There was no one in the Bureau more open to an unconventional approach than Frances Wilson, Addleman had said. No matter how high she rose, she'd always be an outsider because she was a black woman. It hadn't been toeing the line and kissing ass that had put her where she was now. She'd always shown guts, originality, a willingness to confront her superiors—all the qualities Harper and Addleman were going to need in an ally.

On the train ride down from Philadelphia, the two men had prepared their presentation carefully. Harper would deliver it. Addleman said he was too nervous. He'd shaved so close that his cheeks looked raw, and he was wearing a suit and tie. The shirt collar looked too tight for him. Smoking was not allowed in the J. Edgar Hoover Building, so he was chewing peppermints. Harper could smell their spicy scent.

The door opened and Frances Wilson came in. She greeted her old colleague Addleman with affection, and that gave Harper a moment to study her.

She was wearing the female version of standard Federal rig: a pleated white blouse and a navy blue suit of a boxy, broad-shouldered cut, with a skirt that was longer than fashionable. She was tall, five-eight or five-nine, with dark-brown skin, a broad nose, and high cheekbones. Her eyes were dark, almost black, and deeply set. She hadn't straightened or colored her hair; there were threads of gray above her ears. Harper guessed she was in her late thirties.

He didn't get any further in his scrutiny before she turned and looked at him. It was the quick, comprehensive once-over of a trained cop. She'd be able to describe Harper right down to the color of his eyes and the mole on his neck, should that ever become necessary.

"Hello, Mr. Harper," she said. "I've heard a lot about you."

Harper tried to lighten the moment. "You can't believe everything Addleman says."

"I heard about you long before Addleman." She didn't elaborate, but stepped forward with a cool smile and put out her left hand.

It annoyed Harper when people did that, though he supposed they thought they were sparing him an awkward moment. He shook left-handed with Frances Wilson, then they took their seats.

There were no papers on the desk except for a fresh yellow legal pad. Wilson drew it toward her and said, "So. What have you got for me?"

Addleman looked at Harper, who swallowed hard and said, "We think we have a line on the bomber who killed Congresswoman Wylie in Mexico last year."

Addleman had advised him to lead with this. Inability to solve the Wylie case was a thorn in the Bureau's side. And Frances Wilson was definitely interested. She looked at Harper and said, "Go on."

So Harper did. Starting with Sothern, he laid out the three cases and everything he and Addleman knew about the bomber. At first, Wilson listened in perfect stillness, her eyes dark and glittering in a face that might have been carved out of wood. But as Harper got deeper into his presentation she began to take notes. When he finished, she went on writing for some time. The scratching of the pen sounded loud in the quiet room.

Finally Addleman couldn't stand it any longer. He burst out, "Frances, what do you think? You going to take the case or not?"

She put the pen down and turned to face him. "Of course we'll check this out, Hal." She smiled. "You wouldn't believe the kind of wacky leads we've followed on the Wylie case. What you've given us here—"

"Frances, this is a lot bigger than Wylie. Weren't you listening? I think this bomber's got the potential to turn into the worst mass murderer we've ever seen."

"Hal, I know you. And I assure you I'm taking you seriously. Now, what steps are you recommending we take?"

The two men exchanged an uneasy glance. In their own minds, they'd built this up into the climactic meeting. Either Agent Wilson would be shocked and alarmed by what they said and commit totally to the case, or she'd laugh in their faces. Now it seemed neither would happen. Instead the gray and treacherous middle path was opening before them.

Addleman leaned forward and spoke with as much emphasis as he could muster. "We think it's imperative that the Bureau move on three fronts immediately. First, we need to go through unsolved bombing cases—not necessarily homicides. I'm talking about all bombing cases, all over the country. We'll start, say, twenty years ago, and go up to the time of the Sothern killing. I know it's an intimidating job, and it's going to call for a lot of agents, but I feel sure our perp didn't start with Sothern. He's been honing his skills for a long time. We look hard enough and we'll find earlier bombings, when he was making more mistakes, and that'll give us a line on him."

Frances Wilson was writing on her legal pad. She didn't look up. "And your second recommendation?"

With another glance at Harper, Addleman resumed. "This is going to call for a lot of agents too, but it may be the quickest way to get a lead. We should start looking into thefts of explosives from quarries, construction sights, and military bases."

"Especially military bases," Harper put in. "As I said, this bomber uses more sophisticated explosives each time. He might be trying to get hold of a plastic explosive right now."

"And your final recommendation?"

"This is the cheap and easy one," said Addleman with a smile. "Send Harper out to Minnesota and down to Florida to examine the bombs, or what's left of them. Send him to Mexico too, if you can work things out with the cops down there. Send one of your own lab guys with him, if you want. But he can tell a lot from looking at the actual bombs."

"Seems to me he's been able to tell a lot just by looking at the photos," said Wilson. But her dry tone told Harper he wasn't being complimented. His stomach seemed to drop as he wondered if she'd believed anything he'd told her.

"Look," he said, "it isn't really necessary for me to go. Just send your own expert."

"We'll do better than that," said Wilson. "We'll arrange to have the fragments brought here, for a thorough workup in our labs."

Addleman gave a harsh, astonished laugh. "You're going to go through channels and arrange for a formal transfer of custody? Even on the Mexican bomb? Frances, that'll take weeks!"

She shrugged her heavily padded blue shoulders. "You're building up an awful lot on these letters Harper saw in the photos—the 'assembly instructions.' I have to see for myself and have the opinion of my experts before I write my report."

"Before you write your report!" Addleman was perched on the edge of his seat, his hands clenched into fists. "So what's going to be happening in the meantime, with the old bombing cases and the thefts from military bases? *Nothing?*"

Wilson put out a level hand in a placating gesture. Her nails were cut short but beautifully manicured. "As you said yourself, both those projects are going to call for a lot of agents. The decision to assign them is going to have to go up to the Assistant Deputy Director. Maybe even higher."

"Fine." Addleman got to his feet. "Where's his office? We'll go in with you."

Wilson leaned back in her chair and looked up at him. "Hal, the question is, am *I* willing to go in with *you?* And at this stage, I'm afraid the answer's no."

So there it was. Now they knew. Addleman sank into his chair and sat looking at the floor.

Harper said, "Agent Wilson."

She turned to look at him. She had a faint smile on her face. "Mr. Harper?"

"Let's take the next flight to St. Paul. Just you and me. You've got the clout to get us into the Minnesota State Police Crime Lab. I'll show you the bomb fragments. You'll see what I'm talking about."

"That's what I've heard about you, Harper. You never let bureaucratic procedures stand between you and a bomber—or between you and a buck."

"And what does that mean?" Addleman said, puzzled.

"My former commander, Captain Brand, started a smear campaign against me," Harper said, "and it obviously worked on Agent Wilson."

"You wanted to make a few bucks on the side, and a little boy got killed," said Agent Wilson. "That's what I hear."

"You've heard a pack of lies," Harper shot back.

"I can vouch for Harper," Addleman said.

"That's the only reason I even let him in the office."

"Can we get back to the point?" Harper said to Agent Wilson. "What's your gut reaction to what we've told you?"

She gave him a long look. Her dark eyes glittered. She said, "I've been a cop long enough to know gut reactions aren't necessarily right."

"You mean, you don't know what you think till you ask your superiors. That's it." Addleman was smiling without humor, blinking rapidly behind his glasses. "You didn't used to be this way, Frances. You used to hate the whole Bureau mind-set. You didn't mind making waves."

Wilson rose from her desk. Turning her back on them, she looked through the window at the busy traffic on Pennsylvania Avenue. "I know what's coming," she said. "So let's skip it, Hal, okay?"

"No. I want Harper to know you're not as chickenshit as you look to him right now."

Wilson didn't respond, didn't even turn.

"Frances started out in a Southern field office," Addleman began. "The guys hung a sign over her desk that said, FEMALE GORILLA. Such wit. When she complained to the SAC, he made 'em take down the sign, and they put up a new one that said FEMALE GORILLA IN HEAT. That was it for the SAC, he didn't want to make his guys mad. He told her to ignore the harassment and eventually it would stop. It didn't, of course. So Frances had to fight the SAC as well as the comedians. Had to take her case all the way to Washington. For months she had to work with guys who were trying to sabotage her career at every turn. Who wouldn't have minded much if she got shot on a stakeout. But in the end, she won. The SAC got busted down a rank, and the comedians got transferred to Idaho."

Addleman shook his head and said with disgust, "That's the way Frances used to be."

Wilson spoke without turning. She wouldn't let them see her face, but her hushed, shaken voice showed that hearing the story had moved her. "I've been dealing with jerks like that since I was in first grade. That kind of blatant, juvenile crap I know how to fight."

She turned to look at Addleman, who wouldn't meet her eye. "But it's different at this level, Hal. You don't have the confrontations. Nobody even says an impolite word to you. But if they don't feel completely comfortable putting the big cases in your hands . . . well, that's it. Nothing happens to you except your career stalls out and everybody else blows right by you."

Addleman kept avoiding her eye, so she turned to Harper. "There's nobody above me in this organization who's my color and my sex. So they have a hard time feeling comfortable with me. I'm trying to make it easier for them. So I don't go with my gut instincts. I don't make risky moves before I test the waters. I think long and hard and take one step at a time."

"I understand that," said Harper evenly. "But the bomber might not give you all the time you need."

She raised her eyebrows. "You've just been telling me how he plans and prepares, takes a long time between his crimes—"

"Damn it, Frances, we don't have a schedule for him." Addleman's face was bright red. Unbuttoning his collar he yanked his tie loose. "It was years between the first bombing and the second. Months between the second and third. Maybe it's only going to be weeks before the next one. Hell, he's had six weeks already. He may be lining up his next target right now."

Standing, Addleman faced her squarely. "What's going to happen to your all-important career if he strikes again while you're still working on your goddamn report?"

She looked from one to the other with glittering eyes. "I don't think either of you gentlemen is in a position to give me career advice."

She was right about that. Within five minutes, they'd been politely but firmly ushered out and were on the street.

"You okay?" Harper asked.

He and Addleman were at Union Station, on the platform beside Addleman's train. It was loading now and due to leave in a few minutes, but Addleman didn't want to board. He preferred to walk up and down in the drizzle, smoking. He'd been lighting one cigarette off the end of the last since they'd left the Hoover Building. Harper was damp down to his undershirt. He had a reservation on the Metroliner, leaving in fifteen minutes. He didn't know now why he'd thought it necessary to pay extra for the express train. He must have thought that after the meeting with Wilson, events would start moving fast and his time would be short.

"Am I okay?" Addleman smiled sourly as he repeated the question. "What you mean is, do I want a drink?"

Harper nodded. No point in avoiding it, he was worried about Addleman.

"Yeah, of course I want one. Hell, I want ten or twelve." He laughed, barking out a cloud of smoke. "Gimps. We're a couple of gimps, Harper. You're a physical gimp and I'm a mental one. Just the kind of people to develop this delusion that there's a serial killer out there bombing celebrities. Time to snap out of that now and rejoin the real world, don't you think?"

Harper looked sideways at him.

"Frances weighed the odds, like the bureaucrat she's become," Addleman went on. "Sure, she'll drop a few letters in the file, to cover her ass in case the bomber's for real. But she's ninety-nine percent sure we're delusional. And she's got a set of FBI creds and a government-issue sidearm. She's got an office with her name on the door. So she must be right. Right?"

"Wrong," said Harper. "The bomber's out there."

Addleman grinned, showing his yellowish uneven teeth. He threw away the cigarette. But he wasn't ready to board the train yet. "All right," he said. "That's what I think too. So I'll skip the ten drinks and let's figure out what the hell we do next."

"Well," said Harper slowly. "Some of those case files you sent me on old, unsolved bombings, I haven't had time to look at yet. When I get home I'll start going over them. Maybe one of them will turn out to be the work of our guy. . . ."

His voice trailed off and he looked at Addleman.

"Sure," Addleman said with forced brightness. "And I can start monitoring the NCIC computers, looking for reports of theft of explosives. Anything recent, I'll—"

Breaking off abruptly, Addleman lowered his head. His hair was wet and the pallid skin of his scalp showed through. "Who are we kidding, Will? We're two middle-aged guys and we don't have a set of creds between us. We can't possibly do on our own the kinds of things we were hoping the Bureau would do. We'd be searching the haystack for the needle, straw by straw."

Harper nodded. "We'll have to think of another approach. Somebody's going to get killed and we know it. We can't just let it happen."

They continued walking along the platform. The loudspeakers were warning of the imminent departure of the Philadelphia train, but neither man paid any attention.

Addleman stopped short and turned to face Harper. "Only one thing to do," he said. "We'll have to steal a march on the bomber. We'll figure out who the next target is going to be and we'll warn him. Or her."

"But how—"

"Yeah," Addleman went on, carried away by his inspiration, "it's going to be somebody rich and famous, we know that much. Somebody with clout. We warn 'em that they're next, and they'll know how to shake up the media, get some action out of the Bureau."

"Addleman, how are we going to guess who's next?"

"We know it's going to be a bigger celebrity than Rod Buckner."

"You're still talking about hundreds of people. How do we narrow it down? You said yourself, the bomber has no connection to his victims. He has nothing personal against them. He just wants to destroy celebrities, along with the people who kiss their asses."

"Is that what I said?" Addleman grinned. "Man, I sure know how to make it tough on myself, don't I?"

They were now the only ones on the platform. The intercom was making the final departure announcement and the conductors were picking up their stepping blocks and climbing into the train.

"Jeez, I gotta go. I'll call you tomorrow." Addleman started running to get on board.

"Addleman—"

"Don't worry," he called without turning. "I do my best thinking on trains."

On this particular night, the earth probably offered no better vantage point on the stars than this field in the middle of Barber County, Kansas. There was nothing to mar the beauty of the night sky. The nearest town was miles away, so there were no blurs of man-made light on the horizon, and the stars could be seen all the way down to the edge of the earth. The moon was a thin sliver and there were no clouds. The vast blackness glittered with innumerable stars—some bright as jewels, some so tiny and faint they were barely visible.

The man who'd said his name was Anthony—and whose full name was Anthony Edward Markman—was lying on his back in the grass, looking up. His high, deeply lined brow was as clear as it could ever be, and his eyes, their pupils dilated, looked wide and innocent as a child's. As his rapt gaze moved from star to star, his lips occasionally moved, forming a word, but no sound emerged. The only sound was the wind.

Markman's wristwatch alarm began to beep. Compunction gripped his features, furrows creased his brow, and he looked like his usual self. Silencing the alarm, he got to his feet.

He strode over to his car and opened the door. It wasn't the nondescript sedan he'd driven to meet Steve, but a red Toyota Land Cruiser. He would have needed the off-road vehicle to get to the middle of this field.

A flat metal box, like a tackle box, was resting on the passenger seat. He opened it. The top tray was divided into four compartments, which he'd neatly labeled A through D. Each compartment held a small lump of the plastic explosive he'd bought from Steve. They were all shaped differently. Markman was here, in this remote place, to carry out the tests he'd mentioned to Steve. Before he'd killed him.

He took the lump from box A, which was shaped into a ball not quite as large as a golf ball. Then he started walking across the field toward a line of cottonwood trees. From them came the silvery chirruping of tree frogs.

The cottonwoods lined a small stream, and on its bank was a derelict car that had been there so long cattails had grown up through it. Their furry heads drooped out the open windows. Frowning with distaste, Markman knelt in the mud beside the car. Taking a simple timer-detonator from his pocket, he set it and plugged the wire into the ball of C-4. The ticking of the timer could be heard, a sharp, urgent sound, but Markman didn't hurry. He went down on his stomach and placed the explosive under the car. Then he got up and walked away, plucking his wet, muddy shirt away from his body.

He was counting paces out loud, and when he reached a hundred, he turned. For a few moments there was no sound but the singing of the tree frogs. Then came the roar of the explosion and the blinding flash. Markman stood with his eyes and mouth wide open. The power of the explosion produced by the tiny ball of C-4 astonished him.

When the darkness returned, he stood blinking and grinning for several moments.

Then he went back to the riverbank to inspect the damage. The tree frogs were silent now, and the only sound was the faint rush and gurgle of the stream. He drew a flashlight from his pocket and aimed it at the car. The explosion had almost broken it in half. The roof was gone and the passenger seat had been blown into the stream. The wheels and parts of the chassis were strewn all over the bank and field. Markman spent some minutes playing his light around, shaking his head and chuckling with disbelief. Evidently he was satisfied with his purchase.

He walked back to the Land Cruiser. Climbing into the passenger seat, he switched on the light and picked up a clipboard. At the top of the page he wrote A. Then he recorded the results of the test in a small, neat hand. When he was finished, he put the clipboard away and reached into the glove compartment.

He'd made a fresh copy of his calendar, which had gotten wet and blurred when Steve examined it. The copy was exact, with all the numbers and markings as before.

Anthony crossed off today's date, April 10.

There were now twelve days to go to the date he'd marked off in red, April 22, and thirty-five days to go to the last date on the calendar.

May 15.

10

Harper had almost been expecting a message from Addleman to be waiting when he got home from Washington on Friday night. But there wasn't one, and Saturday passed without a call. He waited and worried, telling himself that Addleman would call when he was ready.

Finally, early Sunday morning, the phone rang.

"Harper?"

The voice was muted and drawn. Harper asked, "Are you okay?"

Addleman roused himself to waspishness. "What, you still worried I'm hitting the booze? Well, I'm not. But I was up all night, trying to think myself into our pal's head."

Harper felt a coolness on the nape of his neck. When he'd been working with Addleman years ago, some of their eeriest talks had started this way. He asked, "Did you get there?"

"At least part way, I think. Want to hear about it?"

Harper was standing in the front hall of his house. He picked up the phone from the table and sat down on the steps with it. "Go ahead."

"What's the bomber like? Let's start with what we know for sure."

"Well, he has to be a pretty methodical guy."

"Is he ever. His personality type . . . well, I'll skip the technical terms. Our guy is a control freak. He never goes grocery shopping without a list. He changes the oil in his car every three thousand miles. I mean, he'd rather *walk* than go over three thousand miles. He has no favorite shirt; he wears 'em in strict rotation. He keeps a running balance in his checkbook, or has a computer program to do it."

"Uh-huh," said Harper. He'd listened to speculations like this from Addleman and other profilers before. A lot of the time they turned out to be wrong. But sometimes they were uncannily accurate.

"What day is this, Harper?"

"Sunday."

"No, what date?"

"Uh, April tenth."

"No, it's the eleventh. That's a mistake the bomber would never make. He always knows the date. And every day he makes up a schedule. Even if he's not seeing anybody else, he'll keep to the schedule himself. Noon to one-thirty, work on stamp collection. Three to three-fifteen, take a shit. He wears a wristwatch with an alarm, and when that alarm beeps he hops off the can."

"You may be right, but where does this get us?"

"Patterns. Our guy has to follow a pattern. He *needs* a pattern to hold himself together. Otherwise he'll fly off in a million pieces, because he's a very sick cookie."

"I'm not sure what you mean by a pattern."

"I'm not sure either." Addleman was silent. Harper could picture him leaning forward in his intensity, gesturing to a blank wall in front of him. "Okay, so the celebrities mean nothing to him as individuals. That doesn't mean he's picking them at random. That would be too scary for a guy like this. He's deeply repressed, scared of his own impulses. He's got to have a sense of structure to reassure himself." Addleman paused. "This sound like bullshit to you?"

"No, I wouldn't say that, but I don't see—"

"It's okay. I'm used to dealing with the squareheads at the Bureau. You're not bad by comparison."

"Thanks," said Harper dryly.

"Let's try another approach. What's the guy doing? He's exploding celebrities. Popping them like balloons. And when they go, they take with them some of the people who've indulged them, or bought into them in some way, or supported them."

"Right."

"He doesn't just hate celebrities. He's mad at the rest of us for making them celebrities. He wants to send us a message. So how come he doesn't go public? Why doesn't he call the media and claim responsibility for his bombings?"

"Because the cops will start chasing him. His targets will be more wary. Everything will get tougher for him."

"Exactly!" said Addleman. He was almost breathless with excitement. "He doesn't want any interference now. He's building up to the finale, this—this big, terrible bombing of . . . whatever it's going to be! *Then* he'll go public."

"You think he has it all planned out already," said Harper.

"He's had it planned out for a long time. That's the whole idea, the mainspring of his personality. There's a pattern, and he's going to complete it. He's got to complete it."

"But what kind of pattern—"

"Jeez, Harper, what do you want from me?" said Addleman impatiently. "I don't know. If I knew what was important to this guy I'd at least have a starting point, but I don't. I'm gonna start by feeding some numbers into the computer. Dates of the three bombings. Latitudes and longitudes where they took place. The birthdays of the victims. This isn't going to be easy. The pattern won't be something that would readily occur to a sane mind. But if we keep at it, we're going to find a big red arrow pointing at the next victim. Sane or not, the bomber won't deviate from his pattern. He likes things neat."

"Do you want me to come down?"

"Soon as you can, Will."

Harper didn't know how much help he could be. He didn't have as much confidence in this new approach as Addleman did. But he said, "I'll catch the next train."

As he put the phone back on the table, he was wondering how Laura would take his abrupt departure. Probably she wouldn't mind. She'd been supportive of his efforts on the case all along. When he'd returned from Washington the day before yesterday and told her the disappointing news, she'd damned the Bureau up and down for its obtuseness. Her indignation had warmed him, done a lot to banish his own glum mood. She'd be pleased to hear that he and Addleman weren't going to take the Bureau's verdict lying down.

He called her name up the stairwell. The muffled "in here," coming through the pocket doors behind him, was a surprise. He hadn't thought she'd come down yet this morning. He walked to the doors and opened them.

She was standing with her back to him. Her hair was bound up in a red kerchief and she was wearing one of her oldest sets of surgical scrubs. The thin, worn green cloth clung to her trim figure. He was still appreciating the view when she turned, smiling, and flung out her arms.

"Surprise!"

He looked around the room. The front parlor was the largest room in the house, and it had been in bad shape. Harper had put in several weeks here, sanding woodwork and patching walls. But lately Laura had been at work. The wood floor was covered with canvas, and the mantelpiece and window and door frames had newspaper protecting them. A ladder leaned against the wall, and beside it were brushes, rollers, and cans of paint.

"When did you do all this?" he asked.

"While you were in Washington. An operation canceled and I had the day off."

"I didn't realize—I didn't even look in here yesterday."

"I don't blame you. After all the work you've put into this room, you must be sick of it. But all it needs now is paint. With the two of us working, we should be able to finish today. How about it?"

Harper said nothing.

"What is it?"

"I have to go to Philadelphia. I'm sorry."

"Philadelphia? You mean Addleman?"

Harper nodded. It was only as he opened his mouth to explain that he realized he hadn't told her about his last talk with Addleman on the train platform in Washington. Why hadn't he done so? Maybe it was because Addleman's idea of identifying the bomber's next victim had seemed so vague and tentative to him, not worth mentioning yet.

Or maybe he hadn't told her because he sensed she wouldn't want to hear it.

He began to explain. As he talked, she knelt next to an open paint can and began to stir it. Characteristically, she was intending to go ahead on the job without him. But as he continued to talk, she left the wooden stirrer standing upright in the paint and sat back on her haunches. She wasn't looking at him as he spoke, but he noticed the stiffening of her facial muscles. It made him apprehensive and he finished lamely.

"I see," she said. "And when you figure out who the next victim is going to be, what are you going to do about it?"

"We haven't really gotten that far. We don't know if we will be able to figure it out. Of course we'll warn him. Or her. How strongly we put the warning depends on how sure we are he—or she—is the one."

"You say *we*. But you'll be the one to go see this person. Of course you will. You could barely pry Addleman out of his lair to go to the Bureau."

"I suppose it'll be me. I hadn't really thought that far—"

"You're going to find someone who's sitting on a bull's eye, and you're going to sit on it with him."

"*What?*"

Laura abruptly stood up. "You'll be the one who spotted the threat to this celebrity. So he'll make you his bodyguard. And when the bomber strikes, you'll get killed along with him—just like Fahey."

Harper stared at her in astonishment. The abruptness of her switch from being supportive to fearful puzzled him.

She looked straight back at him. Her eyes were dry, but she was trembling slightly. "You have to try to understand this. When your hand was injured, a part of me was glad. It meant I'd never have to worry about you dying on the job again."

"And you *don't* have to worry."

"Like I said, you'll be on a bull's-eye again. I didn't count on that."

He said, "That'll never happen. For one thing, anyone as rich and famous as this person's bound to be is going to have plenty of security people of his own. He won't need me. If he believes me—if I can convince him—then obviously he'll take precautions to avoid the bomber. He won't offer himself as a target."

She ducked her head, squeezing her eyes shut, as if she found it physically painful to listen to his words. "Will, don't go any further with this thing. Drop it right here. While there's still time."

"I can't get over this. You encouraged me before. What's changed?"

"I was all for you going to the Bureau. I think you're right. But the shitheads wouldn't listen to you. Let it be on their heads when something else happens. You did your best. Now drop it. Before it's too late."

Her fear for him was so strong he could almost sense it as a presence in the room. Try as he might to explain it away, it rattled him. Made him angry, the way fear often did. Instead of reassuring his wife, he reproached her. "Do you think this is just some little project, something to keep me busy, and I can bag it anytime I want? Laura, this is for real. The bomber's out there. Lives are at stake. Maybe a lot of lives."

Suddenly the tears were flooding her eyes, running down her cheeks. He stared at one as it dangled quivering from her chin, then dropped to make a dark spot on her shirt.

"Haven't you saved enough lives?" she said brokenly. "This shouldn't be your problem anymore."

He put out his hand, but hesitated to touch her. "Laura—listen to me—you're upset out of all proportion. I'm not running into any kind of danger. I'm going to Philadelphia to talk to Addleman. That's all it is, for now. That's all it may ever be."

She angrily brushed away her tears with both hands. "Damn it, Will! Don't patronize me. Don't pretend you're not going over the line. You couldn't convince the people who should be going after this bomber to do it, so you're going after him yourself. I know what's happening, even if you don't."

She could control her voice, but the tears were still running from her eyes. Turning away from him, she started blindly across the room. Her left foot kicked over the open can and paint sloshed onto the canvas. Harper rushed to set it upright. Laura didn't seem to notice what had happened. She crossed the room to the ladder and sat down on a lower rung. Undoing the kerchief from her hair, she used it to wipe her eyes and nose. She swallowed several times. When she spoke again, she was calm and self-possessed.

"Well, I can't say you didn't warn me going in. Remember that night four days before the wedding? You tried to talk me out of marrying you."

He smiled. "I was never so glad to lose an argument."

She didn't return the smile. "You told me there'd be nights of waiting for the phone to ring."

"Yes."

She looked at his maimed hand. "And the phone did ring. Only it was in the middle of a busy day. They got me out of the operating room and this voice said there'd been an explosion and you were down. I didn't understand. For about thirty seconds I thought you were dead. I remember those thirty seconds well."

"Laura, if we can figure out who's next on this madman's list, I've got to try to warn him. You can see that."

She sighed heavily. "Yes. I can see that."

"Either he'll believe me or he won't, and that'll be the end of it. He's not going to offer me some bodyguarding job. If he does, I won't take it. I promise you."

Her face wore a wry and miserable expression he'd never seen before. Standing up, she said, "Don't make any promises, okay? I remember what you're like when you're working a case, even if you don't. You become obsessed. That won't change. It's your pattern."

She left the room without looking at him again. He listened to her footsteps going up the creaking stairs. Then he picked up the lid and placed it back on the paint can.

He liked things neat.

Addleman had sounded so keyed up on the phone that Harper assumed he hadn't slept since their appointment at FBI Headquarters. He expected to find him bleary-eyed and unshaven. But when Addleman opened the door of his apartment to Harper, he was as carefully groomed as he had been on Harper's first visit, the black hair combed back from the widow's peak, the jaw smoothly shaven, the white shirt neatly pressed, though threadbare at the cuffs. His black wingtips were polished to a gloss Harper hadn't seen since the last cop funeral he'd attended.

"Come in, Will." He smiled to show Harper he was glad to see him.

"Any progress yet?"

Addleman's mouth set. After a moment, he said, "It won't go like that. Don't expect steady progress. It'll seem hopeless and then suddenly we'll make a breakthrough. Come along."

Harper followed him on a zigzag path across the living room. Almost every square foot of floor space was taken up with books and stacks of paper. Some of them reached as high as Harper's waist. Addleman explained, with a wave of his hand, "I've been downloading information from the 'net."

They went into Addleman's workroom. There were two other computers on the big desk with the computer Harper had seen before.

One, an older model, consisted of a monochrome monitor atop a big, heavy cpu. The other was a laptop. All of them were displaying WORK-ING messages on their screens and emitting humming and whirring noises.

Addleman pointed at his original computer and explained what it was doing. "I've programmed that one with bios of all three victims. It's doing word searches now to try to ferret out common denominators. Maybe their families drove Fords when they were kids. Or they had an Airedale once. Something as trivial as that could be the common factor."

"Any luck?"

"No matches so far." He pointed at the old computer. "That one's working on their birth dates. Factoring the numbers. Scrambling the letters in the months to see if it comes up with anything."

Harper had an inspiration. "Would it be able to check if any of them were born on dates that were significant in history?"

Addleman gave him a melancholy look. "That was the first thing I tried. No luck." He pointed at the laptop. "That one's working on their names."

"Find anything yet?"

"It's gotten some amusing anagrams for Rod Buckner." Addleman took out a cigarette but, mindful as ever of the well-being of his computers, he didn't light it. "Let me show you what you can do."

They returned to the living room. Addleman waved him to an overstuffed chair by the window, which was almost completely surrounded by stacks of printout. He took the top few pages off one of them. "Here's what I was working on just now."

Harper riffled through the pages. "Birth dates of the Popes?"

"I'm looking for some clue to the timing of the bomber's attacks. The second date is when each pope was raised to the papacy. Wylie was killed on the hundredth anniversary of the elevation of Pius X, but that's all I've got so far."

Harper scanned the long column of dates. Behind the middle of his forehead, he could feel a headache begin to throb.

Addleman was holding up another page. "I've got the ecclesiastical calendar here, for when you get finished with the Popes."

"Ecclesiastical calendar?"

Addleman nodded. "Feast days of the saints. I had a case once where this guy was killing three prostitutes a year—one on the feast day of each saint he'd been named after. He figured that without his patron saint looking after him, it wasn't safe to do murder." Addleman smiled reminiscently. "I interviewed the guy for five days when we caught him. Fascinating mind."

"So you're assuming the bomber's Catholic?"

"Oh no." Addleman pointed at the nearest tower of printout. "You'll find the birth dates and coronation dates of all the British monarchs in there. And the emperors of Ancient Rome. And China. And the dates of decisive battles of both World Wars as well as the Napoleonic wars. There's no telling what our guy considers important."

"True." Harper was daunted by the extent of the task Addleman wanted him to undertake. It seemed impossible. And futile. "He may be irreligious, you know. And totally ignorant of history."

Addleman nodded. "That's why I've got game schedules of the NFL, ABA, and the National and American Leagues in there, too."

"Uh-huh. What do you expect me to do with those?"

"Use your imagination, Harper. And when you get through with all that, we've got some calendars over here—Hebrew, Indian, Chinese, Aztec. I'll be writing a program for my next computer search. Give me a shout if you find anything."

"Okay," said Harper . With a sigh, he sank down in the chair and began studying the birth dates of the Popes.

For the rest of the day and into the evening the two men worked. The ache behind his brow grew to occupy Harper's entire head. He found no plausible system in the dates, and Addleman found no common factor linking the victims.

At nine, they broke for a meal. From the stack of frozen dinners in the freezer, Addleman chose Salisbury steak, Harper pork chops. Since every inch of table space in the apartment was covered with papers, they ate in the armchairs in the living room.

Munching on thawed succotash, Harper remembered that yesterday Laura had found the first asparagus of the year at the farmer's market in Grand Army Plaza. She'd told him she planned to have it tonight, with new potatoes and lamb. Harper wondered if she'd gone ahead and made the meal for herself alone. Probably. Otherwise the asparagus would go bad, and Laura hated waste.

Harper didn't realize how long the silence had been going on until Addleman broke it. "Anything the matter?"

"No, nothing. The pork chops are good." Which they were—at least, compared to the vegetables.

"Thinking about your wife? I guess she feels you're getting too deeply involved in this case."

The all-too-accurate probing annoyed Harper. He looked down at his half-eaten dinner. "Your psychological training makes it possible for you to read minds?"

"Not my training. Personal experience." Addleman was chuckling dryly. "Some experiences I wish I'd never had."

Harper didn't want to talk about it. Putting the tray aside, he got up and turned to look out the window. Behind Addleman's building was a vacant lot, and on the other side of it, facing a busy street, stood a KFC outlet. There was a long line of cars at the drive-through. The neighborhood being what it was, the restaurant and its lot were brightly floodlit. It almost hurt Harper's eyes. He raised them to the sky. The night was clear, but here in the middle of the city he couldn't see any stars, only a quarter moon high in the east.

"I suppose you've checked whether the timing of the bomber's attacks has anything to do with the phases of the moon," he said.

"Yes. No connection." Addleman paused and then went on. "I did download some stuff from the National Observatory that we ought to take a look at sometime."

"Oh?"

"I was thinking we ought to consider the possibility that our man is interested in stars."

Harper didn't have to turn around to see if Addleman was smiling. He could hear it in the voice. "Stars like celebrities?" Harper asked. "You think the bomber has a weakness for bad puns, too?"

"We all make puns, whether we mean to or not. And the ones we make unconsciously tell the most about us. That's basic psychology. Read your Freud."

"Don't think I'll read him right now, if you don't mind." Harper still had the headache. Massaging his brow, he turned away from the starless sky. "Mind if I use your phone, Addleman? It's late. I'd better arrange for a hotel room and a cab."

Addleman blinked up at him. "You'll never get a cab to come down here this time of night. I was assuming you'd stay here. We can get another couple of hours' work in, then get started first thing in the morning."

Harper wagged his head, smiling ruefully. "Don't you ever sleep?"

"Not much." Addleman thought for a moment and added, "I don't think the bomber does, either."

When he lifted his head from the pillow in the morning, Harper found that his headache was still in place. Though Addleman's sofa bed was comfortable, he had slept badly. The window shades did not keep out the glare from the KFC, which seemed to stay open most of the night. And the noise was continuous. Harper's Brooklyn neighborhood was far from quiet, but the noise was nothing compared to this street. The parties and quarrels went on all night, punctuated by wailing sirens and occasional gunshots.

He found Addleman at his desk. Coffee and cigarettes appeared to be his idea of breakfast, so there was nothing to delay Harper from returning to his chair and his lists and calendars. He'd forgotten their talk about the stars last night and did not ask Addleman for the data from the National Observatory. He worked all morning on the pro sports schedules and found nothing.

By noon, the apartment seemed stuffy. Outside it must be getting warm, unusually warm for the middle of April. Harper raised the window behind him, sat down again and returned to work.

"Welcome to KFC, may I take your order?" The words, spoken through the intercom at the drive-through window, came to Harper with surprising clarity. It was one loud intercom. Either that, or the wind was blowing in his direction.

After a few seconds, the delicious smell of frying chicken began to fill Harper's nostrils. It was the wind, all right.

"Welcome to KFC, may I take your order?" said the clerk to the next car in line.

Harper tossed aside his list of Roman emperors and stood up. He paced across the room, placing his feet carefully among the piles of paper. He felt useless—*was* useless. Playing mind-ticklers with an insane killer was Addleman's game, one he was brilliant at. But Harper had no talent for it. He wasn't going to find anything among these lists and schedules, no matter how long he looked.

Putting his hands on his hips, he turned in a slow circle, surveying the room full of paper. There had to be a more useful way to occupy his time.

12

Addleman didn't emerge from the computer room until it was almost nightfall. The long, hot day had taken its toll on his neat appearance. His jaw was stubbled, his eyes red-rimmed. Strands of black hair trailed over his forehead. He'd taken off his shirt, revealing an undershirt, one of the old-fashioned kind, with skinny straps. Harper was surprised to see how muscular his chest and shoulders were. Addleman's stoop-shouldered posture made him appear hollow-chested. But he had hidden strengths.

He looked first at the chair by the window where he had left Harper. He was surprised to see it empty.

"Over here," Harper said. He was sitting across the room, on the floor, beside stacks of plastic folders that reached almost as high as his head.

"What are you doing?" Addleman demanded testily.

Harper raised the file in his lap. "I found these old casefiles you downloaded from the NCIC—"

"That's ancient history, Harper, that won't do us any good now. I thought I told you to concentrate on the timing of the attacks."

Harper smiled. "Harold, you can't program me like one of your computers."

Addleman smiled back. He gave a shrug. "Sorry."

"It's okay."

"But I still think you're wasting your time. Those are old cases I downloaded when I was first trying to find out if there even was a serial bomber targeting celebrities. But you've got the rejects there. They didn't fit my criteria. Buckner, Wylie, and Sothern were the only three I could be sure of."

"We know more about his bomb construction methods now. Or I do. There's a chance I can spot his handiwork. And if we could find an earlier strike by him, it would give us more data. We'd have a better chance of figuring out his pattern."

"Any luck yet?"

Harper shook his head. "Some possibles, but none I can say for sure is him."

Addleman grunted. "That's the kind of job that can only be done by the Bureau." He glanced around the room. "Christ, what I'd give for twenty or thirty keen young agents. For a few hours on one of the Bureau's Cray supercomputers."

Harper didn't comment. They'd failed to interest Frances Wilson. There was no point in talking about the Bureau anymore. He said, "You had any luck?"

"I discovered Wylie had three sevens in her Social Security number. So did Sothern. Amazing, huh? Can you imagine the odds against that? I thought it had to be significant."

"And Buckner?"

"No sevens at all. Another promising theory bites the dust." Addleman combed his errant hairs back into place with his hand. "You want to break for dinner?"

Harper had been waiting for that suggestion for hours. He said, "Tell you what, Addleman. Let's go over to the KFC."

"The KFC?" Brilliant floodlight from the restaurant was pouring in the back windows, illuminating half the apartment, but Addleman sounded puzzled, as if he had never noticed the KFC before, had perhaps never heard of chickens themselves.

"Why not? It won't hurt us to get out of here for a while."

The suggestion seemed to agitate him. "But we can't go to the drive-through window. We haven't got a car."

"True," said Harper, smiling. "So let's go in. Let's even eat there."

But Addleman plunged his hands deep into his pockets, his chin sunk to his chest and his shoulders bowed. It was as if an icy gale, rather than a balmy chicken-scented breeze, was blowing through the window. Harper had forgotten what a confirmed recluse the former profiler had become. "Why go all the way over there when I've got a freezer full of TV dinners? You can take your choice. Me, I'm going to have the Salisbury steak."

He'd had the Salisbury steak last night. But if he didn't remember, there was no point in reminding him. Harper sighed deeply. It seemed that the two of them were going to remain locked up in this apartment until they figured out the bomber's pattern—or until the bomber struck again. That seemed to be how Addleman saw it, and Harper didn't have a better idea.

Harper lifted the pile of case folders out of his lap so that he could rise. Underneath them was something he'd been working on earlier. It was a map of North America, on which he'd X'd in the sites of the bomber's three known attacks. Looking at the map now, he was struck by something he hadn't noticed before.

He said, "Pensacola is due north of Cozumel."

"What?"

Harper held up the map. "You can draw a straight vertical line from the place where Wylie was killed to the place where Buckner was killed."

Addleman looked from the map to Harper's face and back again, not understanding. "I guess you can. So what?"

Harper wasn't sure himself what he was getting at. He was working this out as he went along. "So, suppose the bomber is drawing a vertical line on purpose?"

"No. Minnesota, where Sothern bought it, is way off to the west— I mean, to the left."

Harper shook his head. "You don't understand. What I'm saying is, maybe we've been asking ourselves the wrong questions."

"How do you mean?"

"We want to know who the next victim's going to be. We want to know when the attack's going to take place. But maybe *who* and *when* are the wrong questions. Maybe we should be asking *where?*"

Addleman gave him a noncommittal stare. "Go on."

"We've been saying all along that this guy's trying to complete a pattern. Well, suppose he's literally drawing the pattern on the map?

With each killing he puts a dot on the map, and when he makes this final attack he's building up to, the drawing will be finished."

"Yes, but a drawing of what?" said Addleman impatiently. "This is all very ingenious, Harper, but it doesn't get us anywhere. We've still got the problem that we don't know anything about what's important to our guy. What obsesses him—apart from bombs and celebrities, of course."

Harper was looking down at the map—the vertical line from Cozumel to Pensacola, the slanting line from Pensacola to the Twin Cities area. "It could be part of the letter Y," he said.

"Great. So we're looking for someone named Yakov. Or Yogi. Or Yoda." Addleman laughed hopelessly and shook his head. "It could be his initial, or his girlfriend's initial. Or the first digit of his phone number. But you don't know any of these things, so how are you going to figure out the pattern? We haven't got that kind of information on the guy, not even his favorite color or his astrological sign."

"Astrological sign," Harper repeated. He didn't know why the words struck him. They reminded him of something, but he couldn't remember what.

"No. Forget about that." Addleman stood up straight and held up one finger, like a stern reproving teacher. "I was kidding. An interest in astrology would be totally inconsistent with his profile."

"It would?"

"One thing I do know about him is he's not a New Age type. This guy is not warm, he's not open, he's not touchy-feely. Technology is his thing. He identifies himself with inventors and engineers. He'd look on astrology as superstition. Wouldn't get near it. What are you getting at, anyway?"

Harper had remembered by now. "You were saying last night he might be interested in the stars."

"Oh, sure. Astronomy, Harper, not astrology. That would be consistent with his profile. Our guy is very systematic, and this is the biggest system of all. Astronomers make calculations involving millions of years, billions of miles, and yet they can tell us—well, exactly when a particular comet is going to pass by earth, for instance. I was speculating that the killer's attacks might be timed to some comet—something like that."

Harper slowly shook his head. He tapped the paper in his lap. "I don't think so. I think he's drawing a constellation on the map."

"A constellation?"

"Each star is a spot where he's blown up a celebrity. When he's through killing, he'll have the whole constellation."

Addleman laughed again. "You're keen on this aren't you? You know how crazy it is?"

"Crazy enough for our bomber," Harper replied.

Addleman took a deep breath and exhaled slowly. Digging his cigarettes out of a pants pocket, he lit one. As he shook out the match he said, "You know how many constellations there are?"

Harper shook his head.

"Eighty-eight, recognized by the International Astronomical Union." Addleman took a puff and blew out a thin stream of smoke. "Too bad for you this guy *isn't* into astrology. Then you'd only have twelve to worry about."

"I'll look at all eighty-eight," said Harper.

"Okay. I don't buy this theory, but as long as you're not asking me to invest any computer time in it, you can go ahead." He turned and leaned down, to rummage through a stack of large reference books. "Here we go. Astronomical atlas. Have fun."

He handed the atlas to Harper and went into the kitchen to microwave his Salisbury steak.

Harper bent over the book and went to work.

13

It was long past midnight when Harper rapped on Addleman's office door and went in.

The room was warm and stuffy. Addleman could have let in cool, fresh night air, but he didn't seem to notice. None of the city sounds could be heard in here, only the humming and whirring of computers. All three monitor screens glowed brightly in the dim light. Addleman was sitting at the keyboard of the old computer, tapping keys with his right hand. His left elbow was on the desk and his other hand supported his head. He looked exhausted. He turned to gaze blearily at Harper. "What is it? Think you found something?"

"Yes." Harper's voice was even, but his heart was pounding. He was so full of energy and confidence that he felt as if it were a bright morning and he'd had a full night's sleep. But he kept a lid on his excitement. All that he'd found out in the last few hours seemed to hold together, but Addleman might find a flaw in his reasoning and blow it apart.

Tapping a final key, Addleman swiveled his chair away from the screen. "So what have you got?"

Harper wheeled the spare chair over to the desk. He sat down next to Addleman and put the books and folders he'd brought with him next to the computer. Addleman looked at the one on top and said,

"Oh, astronomy," in a bored voice. Their dinnertime conversation had slipped his mind. He was going to be a hard sell.

Harper began. "The constellation is Aquila."

"Really?" Addleman replied. "The eagle. Maybe our guy is a super-patriot, you think?"

"I have no idea what significance Aquila has for him," said Harper. "But it *is* Aquila. It works out."

"Show me."

Harper opened the astronomy book to the illustration of Aquila. There were eight white dots on the black page, and drawn over them was the outline of an eagle seen from above, its wings spread in flight.

"You have to hand it to those ancient Greeks, don't you," said Addleman. "Eight stars and they get an entire bird out of it."

Ignoring the comment, Harper took a piece of onionskin typing paper from the book. "I've redrawn the eight stars to the same scale as the map of North America. Now watch what happens."

He laid the thin page over the atlas. The dots that represented the eagle's lower wing fell on Cozumel and Pensacola. The upper dot just missed Bloomfield, Minnesota—the location of the Mall of America, where Tim Sothern had been killed.

Folding his arms, Addleman hunched over the desk. After studying paper and atlas for a moment, he chuckled softly. "So you made it work. But with only three stars. You try this with any other constellations?"

"With the other eighty-seven."

"And?"

Harper shrugged. "You can work the same trick with five other constellations. You can approximately make it work with another dozen or so."

"So what are you doing in here, Harper? Why are you bothering me with this?"

Harper said, "Tailfeathers, Addleman."

"What?"

"Look at the three close-set stars representing the eagle's tail."

"Oh, I get it. You figure if you're right, he's going to strike next at—" Addleman flattened the page against the map with his fingers so that he could read through it "—Dodge City, Kansas? What celebrity is he going to kill in Dodge City? Wyatt Earp's already dead."

Harper shook his head. "Earl Walker, Jr. A car dealer. He did his own TV ads and was known throughout the state."

Addleman raised his head and looked at Harper. "Was?"

"He was blown up in 1981." Harper picked a case folder out of his stack and dropped it in front of Addleman.

Addleman seemed to have a hard time taking his eyes off Harper's. A nerve had been touched. He was wide awake now. Eventually he opened the folder and looked down at it. "Oh yeah. I remember this case. I eliminated it from consideration because the killer used a letter bomb."

"You shouldn't have. It looks like one of his, and maybe he never used a letter bomb again. The report said the bomb was made of ordinary materials you could have found in any junkyard, but that it had been assembled with great care." Harper tapped the file. "This is the Celebrity Bomber's first attack."

"But 1981, Harper? You think it's the same guy? There's more than a ten-year gap until you get to the Sothern killing."

"No, there isn't."

Addleman gave Harper another long stare. Then he bent over, squinting through the paper at the map. "Tulsa, Oklahoma?"

"June Lamont, weather girl on the local NBC affiliate. Killed by a car bomb in 1985." Harper dropped the case folder on top of the Walker file.

Addleman opened it. He turned the pages very slowly. He seemed a little dazed. "I don't remember this one. I guess I thought a local weather girl didn't really count as a celebrity."

"She wouldn't now. But our guy was just getting started."

Addleman pushed the two files away. He leaned over the map again. "I suppose you found another bombing in . . . Fort Smith, Arkansas?"

Harper nodded. "1987. The Christian Rock singer Ann Taylor Graham. She was in town for a concert. Rented a boat and went out on the lake. The boat blew up. Two members of her band and her producer were killed with her."

"I think I remember that," Addleman said. "There was a big scandal, wasn't there? She was having an affair with this record producer and he had Mob connections and it was assumed to be a Mob hit?"

"That's what the media were saying, but no one was ever arrested."

Addleman pushed away from the desk. Leaning back in the chair, he rubbed his face. "Three attacks I didn't know about. Six more deaths. I don't want to believe it, Harper, but I have to. It can't be coincidence."

"No," Harper replied, "it can't."

"Aquila." Addleman wagged his head wonderingly. "Who'd believe this nut could get so hung up on a constellation? And why that one? This is very interesting. It opens up all sorts of new avenues for speculation on his mental pathology. For instance—"

"The warning," Harper interrupted.

Addleman blinked at him.

"We have to figure out who the next victim is going to be and warn him. Beat the bomber to him."

"Oh, right. Well, that should be easy enough. Our guy has been moving from left to right and from top to bottom. Just the behavior you would expect from an obsessive-compulsive. So the next attack will take place in—" He bent over the map.

Harper decided to save him the trouble. "The next star falls on southeastern Indiana. Pretty much in the middle of nowhere. That's the one part of this I haven't been able to figure out. How's the bomber going to find a celebrity there, someone bigger than his last victim? Who've they got in southeastern Indiana who's more famous than Rod Buckner?"

"I don't know. Maybe some Hollywood stars are shooting a movie on location there. Or one of the Indiana Senators has a campaign swing planned. We'll have to check the media. What's the nearest town?" Addleman was still squinting through the paper.

"Place called Elmhart. Never heard of it."

Addleman laughed.

"What is it?"

"Never heard of Elmhart? It's easy to see you don't listen to talk radio much."

Harper looked at him blankly. It was true; he wasn't a regular listener.

Addleman made him wait a while. The last few minutes had been hard on his pride. He was glad that now he was a step ahead of Harper again.

"Well, come on," said Harper impatiently.

Addleman inhaled, straightened up, and said loudly, "The voice of the people, the friend of the common man, coming to you live from the heartland of the real America—"

"Of course!" Harper said. "Speed Rogers!" He'd completely forgotten that the bombastic right-wing radio commentator broadcast from Elmhart, Indiana.

"I haven't listened to the show for a while myself. Rogers may be a bit past his peak."

"I was never a fan," said Harper.

Addleman raised his eyebrows. "Hope that won't stop you from trying to save his life."

"No. Rogers is just the man we need to get some action out of the Bureau. Rich, powerful in the media, well-connected in the Republican Party. We convince him that he's in danger from the bomber and he'll get things moving."

Addleman nodded. "Let's hope he can live up to his name. Things are going to have to move fast."

Harper nodded. "The bomber's farther along in his career than we thought. After Elmhart, there's only one star left in the Aquila constellation."

"The big one," Addleman said. "The one he's been building up to from the beginning. So where do you figure it's going to happen?"

Harper didn't tell him this time. Didn't have to.

Addleman's finger traced a straight line east from Elmhart to the star that represented the eagle's head. He didn't have to read the name of the city to know. They should have guessed it long ago.

"So," he said. "Washington, D.C. The bomber saved the juiciest target for last. He's been looking forward to it for a long time."

Harper folded his hands and looked at them. "He'll never get there. He'll never even get to Elmhart, Indiana."

"Not if we can stop him, Will."

"We can stop him," Harper said. "We will stop him."

14

The following afternoon, Harper was sitting in Speed Rogers's waiting room. He'd been there long enough to wonder if he'd be able to get up out of the sofa.

The first calls he and Addleman had made were to find out where the radio host was. They learned he was on the east coast, doing television shows from New York and Washington. His regular radio program from Elmhart was scheduled to resume on April 22—the day after tomorrow.

So they had a little time. The bomber's weakness was his rigidity, Addleman said. The pattern required him to kill Rogers in Elmhart. As long as Rogers stayed away from Elmhart, he was safe. Harper caught the first morning train from Philadelphia to New York, and was now waiting to deliver this message to Rogers in person.

Though Rogers excoriated the liberal media establishment tirelessly on the air, his own office was located in the very heart of it, on Sixth Avenue, in midtown Manhattan.

The decor was a surprise, too. The way the talk show host rambled on about Middle American values, Harper would've expected to find rocking chairs, gingham curtains, Norman Rockwell prints. But this reception room was all dark wood, stainless steel, and smoked glass. The magnificent Persian carpets looked like the real thing, and brand new, too, indicating that Rogers, like his hero Ronald Reagan, had traded with the Ayatollahs. All the furniture was low and sleek. If the brown leather and stainless steel couch Harper was sitting in had been raked back any more sharply, he'd have been looking up at his knees.

The young black woman sitting at the reception console had been another surprise; Harper could only assume that she'd been the most qualified applicant, since Rogers bitterly opposed affirmative action.

Entering the office two hours before, Harper had approached her carefully. He didn't want to be misunderstood, and treated as a nutcase. So he showed the card that identified him as a retired sergeant in the NYPD, and quietly explained that he had uncovered information that led him to fear that Rogers's life was in danger.

The receptionist wasn't alarmed. She didn't even seem surprised. Over the intercom she paged someone named Courtney, then explained to Harper that Courtney was in charge of death threats this month.

Courtney turned out to be a young woman with a thick mane of blond hair. She was wearing a man's oversize shirt and tight jeans. Again, she wasn't what Harper expected. The callers who spoke to Rogers on the air were mostly groveling sycophants who agreed with everything he said, even when he was insulting them. Harper would've thought that anyone who worked for Rogers would have to be a pale and trembling yes-man. But Courtney had a breezy, casual manner and spoke of Speed with tolerant affection, as if he were an eccentric uncle. Her mind was needle-sharp, though. In her small cubicle, she heard Harper out at length, taking notes and asking acute questions. But it was impossible to tell what she made of the story. At the end she merely asked him to wait.

So Harper returned to the reception room, where he and a number of other people who were waiting for their appointments had no choice but to watch Speed Rogers on a huge television set placed directly across from the couch. He was accusing a Democratic Senator of the grossest financial and sexual improprieties, and damning hypocritical liberal establishment reporters for failing to investigate him. The program was being broadcast live, from a studio somewhere in Manhattan, so Harper resigned himself to waiting a long time before he got to see Rogers.

He was a little nervous about the interview. Rogers might be an egotistical blowhard, but he never seemed to have any trouble making up his mind. If he believed Harper, he would take quick, decisive action. If he didn't, Harper might well be treated to the sarcasm and insults for which Rogers was famous.

Harper kept glancing at the phone on the table beside him. Laura was just across town, at New York University Hospital. He was thinking about calling her, but he kept putting it off. He wanted to see how his meeting would go. He'd told Laura that once he delivered his warning to the bomber's next target, he'd feel that his job was done, whether the man believed him or not. Now he was hoping that when he called Laura he'd be able to say he'd done just as he promised, and was on his way home.

A door opened and Courtney came out. She was smiling and her hair bounced on her shoulders as she approached him with long-legged strides. "We're ready for you now, Will."

Harper stared at her and then at the screen, where Speed Rogers was still raging about the perfidious senator. "What—? Who—?" Harper asked.

"The whole staff. A special meeting's been called to hear you."

"What do you mean by *staff*, exactly?"

"Oh, we've all got job titles—writer, producer, researcher—but basically what we do is make Speed Rogers Speed Rogers." Smiling, she nodded at the television screen. "You don't think he dreams up all these ideas on his own, do you?"

Harper hadn't thought about it. He shrugged and said, "Lead the way."

Scrambling out of the low-slung sofa, he followed Courtney's blond head through the door and down a narrow, busy corridor. They came to a set of double doors which were standing open. She motioned Harper through.

It was a small meeting room. The windows gave a view of other midtown towers, with the green of Central Park showing through the gaps between them. Rogers's show was playing on a TV set in the corner, but the volume had been muted. Eight or ten young people, casually but expensively dressed, were lounging around a long table. None of them paid the slightest attention to Harper. Some were reading newspapers or magazines. Others had their feet up on the table and were chatting with each other, or making phone calls. A few were tapping keys on laptop computers. Despite their casual attitudes, they gave off a buzz of nervous energy. Harper felt as if he were standing next to a humming power line.

By now he'd seen enough of Speed Rogers's operation that he wasn't surprised to discover that the famed right-winger's staffers didn't look like Mormon missionaries. These were media people who'd graduated from the best universities and come to New York seeking fame and fortune. Rogers would have hired the most imaginative people. He'd be confident they would adapt themselves to his politics.

Harper wasn't at all sure these were the people he should be talking to.

Courtney urged him forward with a hand on his shoulder, toward the head of the table, where a dark-haired woman was rising to her feet. "Naomi Glidden, this is Will Harper."

She was a thin woman with a narrow face. Her brown eyes were large and her smile was very broad; there seemed to be genuine friendliness in it, though Harper couldn't be sure. She had long, crinkled black hair tucked into a rather ragged bun at the back of her head, and was wearing the kind of glasses that were now in fashion: flimsy-looking ones with tiny oval lenses, such as you saw people wearing in old newsreels. Harper couldn't guess her age. The long hours and ceaseless pressure of media jobs aged people prematurely. Then they got plastic surgery, because it was important for them to look young. Naomi Glidden had no wrinkles or bags, but you could tell somehow that the days of carefree youth were far behind her.

"Will, pleased to meet you. Thank you for bringing this to us."

It seemed a strange way to talk about a death threat. Harper said, "I was hoping I could speak to Speed Rogers personally."

"Everyone does," she replied wearily. "I can't commit to anything at this stage. Sorry."

"All right. Can I talk to his Security Chief?"

"Not necessary. I'll be sending him e-mail as soon as this meeting's over. Chief Clifford's a very able man, by the way. Our security is fully capable of dealing with any threat to Speed."

"This is a different kind of threat," said Harper.

"That's exactly what we want to talk about."

She waved him to the seat at her left hand. Then she addressed the table. "So. The Celebrity Bomber. What do we think of this?"

"Let's go with it," said a young man halfway down the table. He had thick brown hair, glistening with styling mousse. His skinny frame was enveloped in an unstructured jacket, as if he were trying to emulate the bulk of his boss. He wasn't wearing one of the loud vests that were Rogers's trademark, though. "We put Will on the show as soon as possible—Wednesday, if we can clear the schedule."

"Now, wait," Harper said, "I have no intention of—"

Naomi laid her hand on his forearm. "At this stage of the meeting, Will, we're just throwing out ideas. We don't allow any negativity. Go on, Stuart."

Stuart continued. "Just picture it. Speed interviewing a former hero of the NYPD about a threat to his own life. Can you imagine the calls we'll get? Speed's fans will be outraged. They'll rally to his defense, light up the switchboard. Remember when Howard Stern attacked Speed? That brought in five thousand calls in the first ten minutes of the show. And that was just dirty words. For a threat to Speed's life—"

"From the same nut who killed Rod Buckner," Courtney put in. "This pathetic loser has silenced one of America's strongest voices for national pride and a strong defense and gotten away with it. Now he's threatening—"

Harper leaned forward. "Excuse me, but I think you're all going off on a tangent here. For one thing, the bomber isn't political. He also killed Congresswoman Wylie, remember."

"That was more than a year ago," shrugged Courtney. "Everybody's forgotten her. But Rod Buckner is Number six on the *Times* paperback bestseller list this week. We should definitely go with the Buckner tie-in."

There were murmurs of agreement around the table.

Harper turned to Naomi. "I'm not sure what I'm doing here. Do you believe me? Do you understand that Rogers's life really is in danger?"

Before she could reply, an Asian man spoke up from the end of the table. He was the only one in a suit, and it was obviously tailor-made and had plenty of silk in its dark blue material. "All right, let's talk about that. Suppose Will is wrong."

"Go ahead, Howard, suppose," Stuart invited.

Howard politely introduced himself to Harper. His last name was Woo. Pushing his glasses up on his nose, he returned his attention to the room at large and continued: "Worst case scenario: Suppose we go public with the threat. Weeks pass. Nobody tries to kill Speed. What would happen?"

"A *Saturday Night Live* sketch," said a young black man. There were murmurs of agreement. "Probably more than one. They might even start doing a count—'Speed Rogers is still not dead.' The way Chevy Chase did with Generalissimo Francisco Franco."

A silence fell over the table as everyone contemplated this prospect.

Finally, Stuart spoke. "I say Speed can handle it. Say a week passes and no attack is made, okay. Speed says it was all a hoax. Like the time back in ninety-two when he announced he'd changed his mind and was voting for Clinton. Remember how many calls—"

Harper smacked the table with his open hand. It was the maimed one. He raised it high, and it got everyone's attention. The room fell silent.

"A bomb did this," Harper said. He looked around at the young faces. "You have to understand, what we're talking about is for real. Your boss's life is at stake. Or that's what I think, anyway. If you're not going to take seriously what I have to say, you should let me talk to him. You owe him at least that much."

He sat back, lowering his arm. The staffers looked somber now. They exchanged glances. Then Stuart spoke up, "Sorry, Will. No offense meant. But Speed gets a threat from some crackpot or other every day."

"This isn't just another crackpot. He's killed twenty-two people already. Your boss could be Number twenty-three."

He'd turned as he'd spoken. At the end he was addressing Naomi directly.

She frowned. "We have to deal with all of the ramifications, Will. We have to foresee all the ways in which Speed's words and actions can be perceived. He has millions of people tuning in to him every day—confused, frustrated people, looking to him to focus and direct their anger. A threat to Speed Rogers matters not just to him but to the whole country. Before I make such a thing public, before I let you on the show, I have to—"

"I'm not trying to get on the show. That's what I've been trying to tell you. And you don't have to make the threat public." Harper was amazed at the affects of fame, at the unreal world these people lived in. Speed Rogers must be completely insulated from the real world and its everyday concerns. His staff didn't even want to tell him about a possible attempt on his life.

Naomi turned her head to one side, puzzled. He could hear surprised muttering behind him. "What I'm advising is that Speed Rogers should place some calls to his friends in Washington. People who can nudge the FBI into taking the bomber case seriously. Other than that, all he has to do is stay out of Elmhart."

"Stay out of Elmhart?" she repeated. The muttering behind Harper grew louder.

"The bomber's a careful planner who can't adapt to change. His pattern calls for him to make his next attack in Elmhart. If Rogers doesn't go there, the bomber can only wait. Just keep your boss out of Elmhart, and he's safe."

Naomi was staring at him through the tiny oval lenses of her glasses. "And where would you have him broadcast from?"

Harper shrugged. "New York, Washington."

"But surely you've heard the program. Speed signs on saying he's broadcasting from the heartland of the real America. Now he's going to announce that he's not safe there?"

"Let him broadcast from Kansas, Ohio—anywhere but Elmhart, Indiana."

"Elmhart is Speed's hometown. Now he can't go home again, and we're not going to explain why?" She was shaking her head emphatically. "You have no idea of the repercussions."

Harper sighed. "You're right. How Speed's actions are perceived isn't my problem. I'm just trying to keep him in one piece. You have to let me speak to him."

Naomi shook her head even more vigorously. The bun of hair above the nape of her neck was in danger of coming undone.

"It's his life," Harper said. "It ought to be his decision."

This seemed to get to Naomi. At least she stopped shaking her head and looked at Harper for a long moment. Then she turned away from him and announced, "I think we're done here, people. Thank you."

The young staffers were surprised. It took them a while to clear the room. Naomi opened her PowerBook, tapped keys, and read the screen.

"I can get you five minutes with Speed," she said. "But no more."

"Okay," replied Harper.

"One o'clock tomorrow," she said. "His house in Elmhart."

"Elmhart?" Harper was incredulous. "But I'm trying to convince him to stay *out* of Elmhart "

"If you convince him, he can leave." Naomi's tone suggested that she didn't think there was any chance of that.

Harper pointed at the television, which was still showing Rogers's live program. "But he's here in Manhattan now."

Naomi gave him a sad smile, pitying his ignorance. "From the studio he goes to Doubleday on Fifth Avenue. They've been lining up for his book-signing all afternoon. After that, he'll barely have time to limo to the heliport and catch the shuttle to Washington, where he's speaking at a fundraiser. There just isn't any time."

"You really expect me to agree to this? To fly to Elmhart?"

She shrugged. "People have flown in from London to spend five minutes with Speed. From Beijing."

Harper sighed again, more heavily. He looked away from Naomi Glidden and his eyes happened to fall on one of the phones resting on the table. He remembered how he'd been looking forward to calling Laura, telling her he'd delivered the warning and was on his way home.

Only it hadn't worked out that way. It had worked out the way Laura had foreseen, when they'd had that bitter argument in their unpainted dining room. *You're going to find a man who's sitting on a bull's-eye— and join him,* she'd said.

And that was what Harper was going to do. It was the only way to stop the bomber.

He turned back to Naomi.

"See you in Elmhart," he said.

15

Markman got off the highway at the Elmhart Exit. He steered into the parking lot of the C'mon Inn Motel and parked near a sign advertising DYNAMITE PRICES FOR SINGLES. It was an old motel which would readily accept cash in advance. This was why it appealed to him. The office, a separate clapboard structure with a crooked shutter, had a wooden sign over the door declaring that it led to the office. There was a yellowed cardboard VACANCY sign in a front window.

Markman carried his suitcase inside with him. It contained not only his clothes, but a powerful charge of plastic explosives. He didn't like the idea of leaving it outside.

Behind the registration desk stood an old man with a head of bushy white hair. In a chair near the desk sat a small blond girl about nine years old, with long braids. She had a sweet face and smiled up at Markman. Some of her front teeth were missing, but it was a beautiful smile nonetheless.

He told the man behind the desk he'd like a room.

"We got a few available," the man said. Markman had noticed only one other vehicle on the lot when he'd pulled in.

"Toward the back, if you can," Markman said. "I don't like any noise from the road."

"We can do that," the man said. "Give you 9A." He laid a registration card on the desk before Markman.

Markman filled in the card with false information, including an alias. "Cash okay?" he asked.

"Surely is. How many nights?"

"Two. In advance."

"Fine with me," the man said, accepting Markman's money.

The little girl had gotten to her feet.

"Mimi'll take that suitcase for you, mister. That's how she earns her keep around here."

"I'll carry it," Markman said. Then he thought about it. He suppressed a smile as he handed over the suitcase to Mimi, who could barely lift it. Inside was enough explosive to blast her into particles so small they might never be recovered, but she didn't know that.

Markman knew. It gave him a certain pleasure.

"After you," he told Mimi, falling in behind her so he could keep an eye on her. He winked at the man, the two of them conspiring to make a child feel useful. Good Samaritans both.

Never having been to Indiana, Harper had expected it to be flat and featureless. But as he stood outside the gatehouse of Speed Rogers's estate, he could look out over gently rolling hills and copses of tall old trees. He was leaning against a plum tree, which shaded him with a cloud of white blossoms. Spring was much further along here than in the northeast. It was so warm, he'd already taken off his jacket.

The guards at the gatehouse seemed able. They'd verified Harper's identity and searched him, then asked him to wait for Naomi Glidden to come down and drive him to the house. But the well-armed, efficient guards didn't put Harper at ease. Nor did the serene beauty of the estate. He kept being reminded of the day he visited Rod Buckner's equally well-guarded and peaceful estate. The day Jimmy Fahey, Buckner, and five other men were blown to pieces.

Harper massaged his injured right hand with his left. It had been aching all morning. He was tense, and that made him clench his fists without realizing it. That was why the hand hurt. It wasn't an omen. Harper didn't believe in omens.

An open-top yellow Jeep careened around the turn and lurched to a halt beside him. Naomi Glidden smiled at him from behind the wheel. "Hello, Harper. Jump in."

She had tinted lenses clipped on over her old-fashioned glasses. Her long hair was loose around her shoulders and she was wearing a pink top and a short khaki skirt, but still she didn't look any more relaxed in Elmhart than she had in Manhattan. She was checking her watch as he climbed in beside her. She swept the car around in a tight U-turn and roared up the hill. The wind lifted Harper's hair from his head. He figured from now on he could count on Naomi to get him to his appointment on time.

"Have any trouble finding the place?" she shouted over the wind-roar.

"No. Everybody in town seems to know where your boss lives. And they're happy to give directions. And talk about him."

Naomi smiled. "Speed grew up here. I guess you knew that. The Rogers family has been prominent in the area for generations. Moving the show here, renovating the Old Courthouse, building this estate— Speed has been a boon to the local economy and he's very proud of that. His roots mean a lot to him. He's in such a good mood this morning. Happy to be home."

"How long has he been away?"

"Almost three weeks. He took a vacation over Easter and then he had TV shows and personal appearances on the east coast. Three weeks is as long as we ever put the show on hiatus. Why do you ask?"

Harper said slowly, "I was wondering if the bomber is already here. If he's been here awhile, making his preparations. If all he's been waiting for is Rogers to come back."

Harper massaged the aching hand again. Maybe it *was* an omen.

Pushing her hair out of her face, Naomi glanced sideways at him. She looked doubtful and annoyed. "I hope I'm not making a big mistake, letting you see Speed. Just remember, you're down for five minutes, and that's all you get."

"Fine," said Harper. "I don't want to spend any more time around Speed than I have to. Nothing personal, but it's not the safest place to be."

She didn't glance at him again, but threw the car into another sharp turn. Harper grabbed the handle on the dashboard with his good hand

and held on. When he straightened up, he saw that they were approaching the house.

At first sight, it was reassuring. It looked secure. Bunkerlike, in fact. The house was long and low, built right into the brow of the hill. They parked and went in the front door.

The interior was bright, tastefully furnished, and above all spacious— built, Harper supposed, to accommodate Speed Rogers's broad-shouldered figure and booming voice. They descended flights of steps past burbling fountains and stands of green plants with exotic flowers. They had entered the house at the top and were descending, level by level, down the side of the hill. Harper was changing his mind about the security of the place. They kept coming to big windows that looked out on blue sky, rolling green hills, and woods. There were too many places of concealment out there for comfort. And it was all too easy to see into the house.

Naomi reached the bottom of yet another short flight of steps a little ahead of Harper. She said, "Speed? This is Sergeant Harper, formerly of the NYPD."

The talk-show host was sitting in a tan leather armchair, reading a script. He put it aside and stood up. Harper had heard that the TV camera made people look fatter than they really were. It wasn't true in Rogers's case. In real life he looked enormous—bull-necked and barrel-chested. He was smiling. Under the blond brows, his blue eyes twinkled with a boyish happiness.

"Hello there! Nice to see you." He took Harper's hand in a gentle clasp. The missing fingers didn't make him look down in surprise: He'd been briefed and had remembered. "Thanks for coming all this way. Have you eaten? Want to join me for lunch? I've got an order coming from the best burger joint in—"

"Will has only five minutes, Speed," said Naomi.

"Oh. Well, sit down and we'll get down to business. You've got time for a Coke, at least. Diet or regular?"

Harper declined. He found that he wasn't surprised by Speed Rogers's hospitality. Under the bombast and bluster, the talk-show host had always struck him as a friendly man, a man who was eager above all to please. His regular listeners sensed that about him too, Harper speculated. It had as much to do with making them like him as did his ferocious attacks on the people they and he hated.

Harper and Rogers sat down facing each other. Naomi remained standing. She glanced at her watch. Harper began, "I suppose you've been briefed on—"

"Yes, yes. Sounds like you've uncovered another nutcase, even loopier than most."

"You think I'm right, then. That there is a Celebrity Bomber, and he's targeted you."

"Of course. With all the nutcases we've got running around the country these days, why should I doubt you?" But Rogers was smiling as he gazed out the window. Whatever was going on in the country at large, he felt perfectly safe in his own home. "I've got the best security people in the business. There's no reason for you to be concerned."

"Rod Buckner had excellent security too."

"Yes. Poor Rod. I was at his funeral." The light abruptly went out in Rogers's blue eyes. His chubby-cheeked face became solemn. But it lasted only a moment. Then he smiled and turned toward Naomi. "I met Colin Powell there—did I tell you?"

While Rogers related the anecdote to an appreciative Naomi, Harper considered. He thought it was going to be necessary to throw a scare into Speed Rogers, and he was wondering how to do so when someone sneezed behind him.

Stuart, the skinny staffer he'd met yesterday in New York, was coming down the stairs with a big paper bag in his hand.

"Hi, Will," he said pleasantly, and sneezed again.

Rogers chuckled sympathetically. "Poor Stu. Hay fever really gets to you this time of year, doesn't it?"

"I'm all right in New York. But here—" Stuart's face was screwing up with an impending sneeze. He advanced blindly toward Rogers, holding out the bag.

"Ah!" exclaimed Rogers, taking it. "Burgers from Carl's Drive-in in town," he explained to Harper. "Been eating them since I was a teenager, and they're the best I've found anywhere. The ones at the Twenty-One Club in New York don't even come close."

Harper leaned forward alertly. He said to Stuart, "Did you see them put the burgers in that bag?"

Stuart sneezed. He mopped his nose and streaming eyes with a handkerchief. "What? Sure I did."

"Think a minute. Did you actually watch them pack the bag?"

"Harper, this is ridiculous," Naomi said. "There are burgers in the bag. I can smell them from here."

"Something else could be in there too."

"Look, it's just a little drive-in place," Stuart said. "I know the guy. I was talking to him the whole time. I saw everything he did."

"Didn't you have to turn away and sneeze?" Harper asked. "At least once?"

Stuart didn't reply.

Speed Rogers was staring wide-eyed at the bag in his hand. He slowly straightened out his arm, moving the bag away from himself.

"This is ridiculous," Naomi said again. "It's a bag of burgers from Carl's. Anyone can tell that."

"Rod Buckner thought it was a book. Tim Sothern thought it was a box of tennis shoes. How the bomb got into Congresswoman Wylie's suite we still don't know."

"Let's humor Harper, Stuart," Naomi said. "Take the bag down to the gatehouse. They'll know what to do."

Stuart was standing motionless, staring at the bag in Rogers's outstretched hand. He was too preoccupied even to sneeze.

"Stuart!" said Naomi sharply. "You want me to take it?"

Stuart snapped out of it. Taking the bag, he trotted up the stairs.

"It's okay, Speed," said Naomi. "We'll get 'em back, put 'em in the microwave, they'll be good as new."

Rogers sank back in his chair. He gave no sign of having heard her. In fact, he didn't look hungry anymore. He kept glancing up the stairs, and he didn't speak again until he heard the faint sound of the front door closing behind Stuart. Harper had gotten to him.

"Naomi," he said petulantly, "I'm disappointed in you. This is the kind of stuff you usually keep away from me. Why can't you—why can't you work it out among yourselves?"

She drew herself up at the reproof from her boss. She said, "Work it out among ourselves?"

"You know—take Will on down to meet what's his name—the head guard?"

"Jim Clifford."

"Yeah, have Jim give Will a tour of the place. Listen to his suggestions." Rogers turned to Harper. "Just spend an hour with Jim, Will.

He's a good man. He'll convince you I'm safe. Then you report back to me."

"And convince you that you're safe?" Harper shook his head. "I'm sorry, Mr. Rogers. There's only one way for you to be safe, as far as I'm concerned. Get out of Elmhart."

"But this is my home. If I'm not safe here—" Rogers was slowly shaking his massive head.

"Excuse me, Speed?"

Someone else was coming down the stairs. It was another staffer Harper remembered from New York—the Asian guy, Howard. He was wearing a gaudy electric-blue shirt. Harper supposed that being in the provinces relieved him of the necessity of making a fashion statement. But his glasses were still sliding down his nose. He pushed them up with his right hand. His left held a cordless phone, which he offered to his boss.

"This is George. In L.A."

"Oh, sure." Speed extended a hand for the phone.

Harper got to his feet. "Wait," he said, "you recognize the voice?"

Howard looked puzzled. "It's George. Speed's literary agent."

"I don't care who he says he is, do you recognize the voice?"

"What are you talking about now, Harper?" asked Naomi in a bored voice.

"Old Mossad assassination method," Harper replied. "You call your target from a safe distance. When you hear his voice, you send a signal right over the phone line and the plastique charge you've planted earlier in the phone receiver explodes. Takes only a small charge to blow the target's head clean off."

Rogers was staring at Harper open-mouthed. His eyes rolled as he turned his gaze to the phone. He was breathing loudly, raggedly. Abruptly he heaved his bulk from the chair.

"Speed," Naomi said, "give me the phone. I'll verify it's George. Just give me the phone, Speed."

But Rogers was too frightened to understand. He was staring at the phone, paralyzed.

"Speed—" said Naomi again.

Rogers drew his arm back and hurled the phone as hard and as far as he could. It shattered against the wall and its pieces clattered to the floor.

There was a brief silence when only Rogers's heavy breathing could be heard.

"Well, I knew it was George," said Howard. "I talk to him every week."

Rogers didn't seem to hear the muttered remark. A last wild-eyed glance at Harper, and he swung around to face Naomi. "Goddamn it, Naomi. I won't be able to stand this—"

"You don't have to," said Harper. "Just go back to New York."

He gave Harper another quick look, then stepped closer to Naomi. "Can I do that? Leave Elmhart? What'll I say?"

Harper had almost succeeded. Rogers was clearly wavering, looking to Naomi for an out. But she drew herself up. She was smiling and shaking her head. "Now, Speed. Calm down. Get a grip. Where can a man be safer than his own home? What kind of crazy world is it, where you're told to go to New York to be safe? *New York City?*"

"It doesn't have to be New York," Harper started to say, but it was too late. Speed Rogers wasn't listening anymore, he was talking. Naomi had given him the cadence of his own indignant rants, and he'd picked it up like a familiar tune.

"New York City," he intoned. "A place where murder is a popular indoor sport—like bowling is in Elmhart. A place where the police treat homicide as a much less serious matter than—than parking in a loading zone. You park in a loading zone and go in a store for a minute and your car will be *gone*—towed by New York's finest. But you kill somebody, and it's okay. Everybody understands. You come from a deprived background. Society has wronged you, the taxpayers haven't done enough for you, it's not your fault." He gave a grunt of laughter. "Try telling that to the cop in the tow truck as he hauls away your car."

The big man was on the move, pacing the room, gesturing. The twinkle had returned to his blue eyes. Harper knew he'd lost him, but he took one last stab at it. "This bomber is very dangerous. He's never failed that we know of."

"Very dangerous," said Rogers, laying on the sarcasm as only he could. "A master criminal, in fact. How do I know? Because he's waited till I got back to Elmhart to come after me. What a stroke of genius! Someone else, some inferior grade of killer, might have gone after me in New York or Washington, D.C. The murder capitals. Not our man. He waits till I get back to a little town in the cornfields, where the sheriff knows everybody by name, where there hasn't been a murder in five years. Yes, I remember the case, and the man was caught, and he is in jail. Because that's how we treat murderers here in Elmhart."

Rogers swung round on Harper. "And this is a guy you expect me to be scared of? This—this pathetic nutcase? You think I'm going to let him drive me out of my home? I don't think so, Harper. I can get along without your advice. I think you'd better get out of here."

By now he was bellowing. He stalked toward Harper. Being in a confined space with an agitated Speed Rogers was like being in the ring with a sumo wrestler. Harper could almost feel the floor shaking under his feet. Naomi darted across the room and grasped his arm. Her grip was surprisingly strong for such a slight woman. "Come on, Harper," she hissed in his ear.

Rising to his feet, he allowed her to pull him over to the stairs. Rogers was still glaring at him. As they climbed the steps, Harper heard him yell at Howard, "Where are my goddamned burgers?"

Naomi hustled him along so quickly that by the time they reached the top of the stairs, Harper was breathing hard. Only when they were outside the front door did she pause and pull a portable radio out of her pocket.

"This is Ms. Glidden," she said into it. "I'm at the main house. I need someone to give Mr. Harper a ride back to his car. And make sure he gets off the property."

Putting away the radio she said, "That's it, Harper. You heard it from the man himself. Now I want you to leave town. I think I've done enough for you."

"You've done enough, all right. Maybe too much."

She frowned at him, her brows drawing together above her glasses. "What's that supposed to mean?"

"I was getting somewhere with him. I'd almost convinced him to take the threat seriously."

Naomi's brow cleared. She looked away from him, out toward the sunlit fields. "You were scaring him. A scared Speed Rogers is no use."

"No use?" Harper repeated. "No use to you, you mean? Does he work for you, or do you work for him?"

"We both work for the public. For the millions of Speed Rogers fans. We have a show to put on, Harper. And I'm not going to let you get in the way. You won't be allowed within sight of Speed again. So why don't you just head for the airport, and catch the next plane out?"

She turned and went back into the house, without waiting for an answer.

Which was just as well. Because it wouldn't have been the answer she wanted.

Harper had to wait only a few seconds before a Jeep swung around the corner and stopped beside him. The uniformed guard threw open the door. To get here so fast, the guard must have been patrolling in the vicinity. From what Harper'd seen so far, Speed Rogers did seem to have excellent security.

Harper wondered how the bomber was planning to beat it.

16

Twelve miles outside Elmhart lay the old airstrip. It had been abandoned when the county built the new airport on the other side of town. The buildings were gone now and only the long, narrow stretch of concrete remained, cracked and overgrown with weeds. Nobody came out here much anymore, except for the occasional parent giving driving lessons to his sixteen-year-old, or the restless young man itching to open his motorcycle up all the way. On this particular sunny afternoon there was no one around at all.

A dusty pickup truck turned off the road and rolled to a halt on the concrete strip. Markman got out. He was wearing a cap with the name of a fertilizer company on it, a blue pocket T-shirt, jeans, and workboots crusted with dried mud. Keys, a jackknife, and a tape measure hung from his belt. He looked like any other farmer or workman in Elmhart; no one would have given him a second glance.

The tape measure was not just part of his disguise, though. He unhooked it from his belt and went down on one knee. After making a yellow chalk mark on the concrete, he measured off 155 feet down the strip, then stooped and made another chalk mark. At a right angle to the line defined by the two marks, he measured off 52 feet, made another mark, then measured off 27 feet at a right angle to that mark. Then he walked back to his truck.

From the cab, he brought out a toy car and the radio unit that controlled it. He placed the car on the first chalk mark. Straightening up, he glanced at his watch and pressed a button on the remote control. The car rolled along the line he'd walked to the second mark, where he used the control to turn it left and send it to the third mark. Then he turned it right and sent it to the last mark. Each time he stopped the car on a mark, he looked at his watch.

With the course completed, he pressed the button to bring the colorful little car speeding and bumping back to his feet. The cap brim cast a deep shadow over most of Markman's face, but it didn't conceal his thin smile of satisfaction.

He set the car on the mark and ran it through the course again.

And again.

The shadows of trees and fence posts slowly lengthened. As evening drew in, the swallows came to swoop and dart over the level fields. But still Markman continued to run the little car through its simple pattern. He didn't stop until it was too dark to see.

Then he picked up the car and walked along the strip, scuffing out the chalk marks until nothing remained.

On a weekday evening, the liveliest place in Elmhart was the Tahitian Lanes. The bowling alley tried to live up to its name with an orange-and-azure mural of a tropical sunset on the wall above the pins, and a bar that served sweet rum concoctions as well as more serious drinks. The bar was kept as dark as a cave: In this part of southern Indiana, people still preferred to drink in places where they couldn't be seen doing so.

Harper was sitting on a bench behind the lanes, watching the bowlers. There were family groups, with the parents urging on their children, who would stagger to the line and drop the ball with a thud, so that it rolled unerringly into the gutter. There were noisy parties of teenagers, showing off and flirting. And there were pairs of lean men with wizened faces, who kept their cigarettes in their free hands as they smoothly rolled strike after strike. It seemed to Harper they never missed a pin. He wondered why they bothered to go bowling anymore.

Eventually Speed Rogers's staff, conspicuous by their multiethnicity and their loose natural fiber clothing, their ear-studs and sunglasses, came sauntering in. The smell of stale cigarette smoke made them cough and wave their hands around. Harper had been waiting for them. The doings of the Rogers establishment were much discussed in Elmhart, and it was his waitress at the Jolly Porker who'd told him that this was where the young folks from New York liked to come in the evening. Not that they had much choice; it was either the Tahitian Lanes or drive fifteen miles to the Omniplex for a movie they'd seen weeks ago in the city.

They were at the front counter trying on shoes, sniffing them first and making wry faces at each other, when Harper approached.

Courtney spotted him first. The country sunshine agreed with her. The blond hair seemed a shade more golden and there was a light dusting of freckles on her cheeks. She smiled. "Hi, Will! How're you doing?"

The others nodded and smiled. Naomi gave him a sharp, surprised look but said nothing. After returning the greetings of the others, Harper stepped closer to her and said quietly, "Are you going to have the cops run me out of town?"

"Why would I do that? It's a free country." She sat on a ledge and began to put on her bowling shoes. "As long as you stay away from Speed, you're welcome to spend as much time as you want in Elmhart. How do you like it so far?"

Harper sat down beside her. "It's true what the Democrats say; Speed is prone to exaggerate. He exaggerated about Elmhart, for instance."

She gave him a look, but said nothing.

"This afternoon he said the town was so small the sheriff knew everyone by sight. That can't be true. It's a pretty fair sized town. And it's the county seat, so you've got a steady stream of visitors moving through. You've got the airport a few miles north, and the Interstate a few miles south."

"So?"

"So it's not as isolated as it looks. The bomber probably feels quite comfortable operating here."

"You make the same mistake as the Democrats, when they say that Speed exaggerates. He exaggerates only to make a valid point, and the point is that he's perfectly safe."

The other staffers had gotten themselves shod now. They were moving off toward the lanes. Courtney said, "You come too, Will. Show us how it's done." She gave him a brilliant smile before turning to run after the others.

Harper said to Naomi, "Does the staff stay at the house?"

She shook her head. "Speed puts us up at the Holiday Inn. The kids love it. They can lie around their rooms watching C-Span and they only have to take a few steps to jump in the pool."

Harper nodded. "So the only time you're all together—I mean Rogers and the staff—is when he's doing the show?"

"Oh, there are occasional meetings or parties, but basically that's true." She peered at him suspiciously through her tiny glasses. "What are you getting at?"

"I think that's when the bomber's going to make his move. During the show."

She shook her head. "Security's as good at the studio as it is at Speed's home."

"You go on the air tomorrow?"

"Yes. Eleven A.M. Noon eastern time, as usual." Naomi paused for a moment. "So you think this bomber of yours is going to try to blow the rest of us up along with Speed?"

Harper nodded. "That would fit his pattern. He doesn't just hate celebrities; killing them isn't enough for him. He wants to kill the people who make them celebrities. That's why when he killed Sothern the tennis player, he tried to kill his fans along with him. When he killed Congresswoman Wylie, he got her surrounded by her aides and the lobbyists who were paying her way. And he saw to it that Buckner's bodyguards died with him. In this instance, you're the ones who come up with Rogers's bright ideas. You're responsible for his success and fame. The bomber knows that. So you have to go with him."

Naomi didn't reply. They sat in silence for a few moments, watching the staffers. Some of them had already lost interest in the game and were reading magazines and newspapers. A couple were playing with the computerized scoreboard. Stuart was sitting at the back, wheezing into his handkerchief. His hay fever was no better, apparently. But Howard, in a lime-green shirt that clashed violently with the Tahitian mural above him, was getting ready to bowl. He took three gliding steps and went down on one knee to launch the ball. This time his glasses slipped all the way off his nose. They clattered to the polished wood. The ball almost rolled over them. His colleagues applauded appreciatively.

"They're having a great time, aren't they?" Harper said. "They come up with these outrageous ideas for Rogers, and he delivers them on the air, and thousands of people call in. They're as happy as little kids who can do tricks and get the attention of the whole room. Except they get the attention of the whole country. They're having so much fun it doesn't seem quite real to them. But it's real to the bomber."

Howard's place had been taken by Courtney. She hurled the ball and stood watching it tensely, trying to guide it with wiggles of her shoulders and hips.

Naomi looked away from her. Lowering her head, she said, "What do you want me to do, Harper?"

"Let me do a walk-through. That's all I ask. Just let me go around the building with one of your security people, right before the show."

Naomi took off her glasses and rubbed her eyes. Harper watched her anxiously for a long moment. She shook her head.

"Our security people don't need you, Harper. Tell you what I will do. I'll tell them we have reason to fear a bomb, and they'll come in with their equipment. You should see all the stuff they have. If there is a bomb, they'll find it. Now, will that satisfy you?"

He took a deep breath and blew it out. "I suppose it'll have to."

"You're right about that." She got up and walked away from him, toward the lanes.

As Harper got up to leave, one staffer—a muscular black man—was lifting a bowling ball one-handed as if it weighed no more than a basketball, and pretending he was going to toss it to Naomi. The others were laughing and egging him on.

Naomi didn't seem to get the joke.

Markman sat at the desk in his motel room. The motel was located on the Interstate, a few miles out of Elmhart. The ceaseless rush of traffic could be heard in the room, as well as the tinny babble from a television set next door. But Markman gave no sign of hearing. His high forehead deeply furrowed, he was concentrating on his task.

A small box of some light wood lay on the desk in front of him. A lot of work had gone into it already: The smoothness of the corners would have called for careful dovetailing and hours of sanding. Now Markman was painting it. He laid on a coat of medium-blue, so fastidiously that not a brush stroke showed. But evidently the result did not satisfy him. He picked up a piece of stiff, heavy cloth and compared the shade of blue to the one on the box. Then he mixed some gray paint in with the blue, and put another coat on the box. Comparing the box to the swatch of fabric, he found that the shade was now an exact match. He did not smile or give any sign of satisfaction, merely put the tops back on the cans of paint.

Getting up from the desk, he stretched and yawned. The yawn was as noiseless as a cat's. Then he began to tidy up.

The box was left to dry on a sheet of newspaper, but everything else got put away. His large toolbox with its many shelves and compartments was packed up and placed near the door. The shoebox containing the toy car and the remote control went into a suitcase, along with the cheap metal tackle box in which Markman kept his plastic explosive. The paints and brushes he took out to the motel Dumpster. By the time he was finished, the room was neat. Impeccable, in fact. At a moment's notice he could pick up his luggage by the door and walk out, leaving no trace of himself behind.

There was one exception, though—one possession with which he had furnished the impersonal room. It was a color photograph, small but rather expensively framed, which stood on the night table between the telephone and the Gideon Bible.

The photograph was of a woman in her early thirties. The boxiness of the car she was getting out of, and the cut of her elegant black tailor-made suit, suggested that the picture had been taken around 1960. The woman had short blond hair and a lovely, vivacious face. She was smiling up at whoever was holding the car door for her. One high-heeled foot was just touching the curb. Her dress had ridden up above the knee, revealing a long, shapely leg.

Markman didn't glance at the photograph as he moved around the room, tidying up. As he sat down on the bed he almost seemed to be avoiding the blond woman's smiling gaze. He reached in his pocket and carefully unfolded a piece of paper on his lap.

It was his calendar. He drew one of his neat X's across today's date, April 21. The next space was colored in solid red.

Tomorrow was the day.

17

The Old Courthouse had long been the most imposing building in Elmhart. But it had been closed five years before, when the new Government Center opened on Route 17, outside of town. A Wal-Mart also opened on Route 17, and swiftly drove the old downtown stores out of business. Courthouse Square, the center of Elmhart, was in a bad way.

But the Old Courthouse meant a great deal to Speed Rogers. Generations of Rogers men had transacted business and argued cases there. One had even sat as a judge. So when he announced that he was bringing his phenomenally popular radio show back to his hometown, he also announced that he was buying and restoring the courthouse to make it his headquarters.

All this had been told to Harper by various grateful or envious townspeople. There was no question that Rogers had spent freely to restore the building to its former splendor. Harper had had plenty of time to study it. He'd been sitting in his car parked in Courthouse Square since dawn, and it was now quarter to eleven. *The Speed Rogers Show* was about to go on the air.

The courthouse took up half the block and rose six stories. Even today it dominated the town, and its ornate cupolas could be seen across the fields from a long way off. It had been built in the 1880s, when the Romanesque style was popular, and public buildings were made to look as if they could stand up to a long siege. Its walls consisted of massive rough-hewn stones. The figure of Justice, with her scales and sword, loomed over the main doorway.

Rogers's broadcast studio was somewhere in the building. A large disk on the roof, hidden from view by the cupolas, sent the signal to an orbiting satellite, which bounced it back to the hundreds of stations across the country on which it was heard. The offices of his merchandising, investing, and other operations took up most of the rest of the building. Some space was empty, but Rogers was in no hurry to rent it. He hardly needed the money.

Harper had come to see if Naomi would do as she'd promised and order a security sweep of the building. And she was as good as her word. The vans arrived at seven. The name on the doors of the vehicles was one he recognized as that of a top-flight private security firm.

He watched uniformed people unload metal detectors, spectrometers, fluoroscopes, and other high-tech equipment, some of it so new as to be unfamiliar to Harper. As the security people lugged their gear up the steps, another van pulled up. The back doors opened and two German shepherds leaped out, so eager they practically dragged their handlers up the steps.

Harper waited tensely across the street.

An hour and a half later, the doors opened and men, women, and dogs trooped down the steps and back to their vehicles. They looked bored. Even the dogs' tails were drooping. No bomb had been found.

There was no reason for Harper to stay any longer, but somehow he didn't feel like leaving. He got a cup of coffee from the McDonald's around the corner and returned to his car, where he sat and watched the building.

Nothing happened until nine, when a small caravan of vans and station wagons rolled up. Naomi and the rest of the staffers got out and went in the building. A few minutes later, a black limousine stopped at the foot of the steps. A uniformed bodyguard got out first and scanned the street. The man was probably looking for Harper. Harper remembered Naomi's warning that he wasn't to come near her boss. Rogers came into view, gingerly easing his bulk out of the car. The two men climbed the stairs and disappeared into the building.

Harper continued to sit in the parked car, watching people come and go, debating with himself.

He felt very tired. He'd slept badly, tormented by dreams of the blast in which he'd been maimed. It was more vivid in his dreams than in his waking memories: the roaring in his ears, the eerie sensation of whirling through the air as if he were a leaf caught in the wind; then lying there stunned, looking up at the streaks and splatters of his blood on the wall.

He'd given up on sleep at four in the morning. He wanted to call Laura, but what right did he have to ask her for comfort? She'd known somehow where his path was going to lead and warned him against taking the first step on it. He hadn't believed her.

And now here he was.

Rogers's security people weren't good enough to stop the bomber. Harper felt certain of that. But what made him think *he* was good enough? All his training and experience had been in dismantling bombs. He didn't know how to find a bomb that was still lying hidden.

But that was what he was going to have to do. There was no other choice.

He got out of the car, stretched his stiff back, and crossed the sunny, quiet street. It was possible the bomber would try a terrorist-style attack, using a crude but powerful bomb concealed in a vehicle to try to bring down most of the building. But considering the structural integrity of the building, such a bomb would take up a lot of space. The explosive would have to be packed into several large metal drums and to transport them the bomber would have to use a truck or at least a closed van. The cars parked in front of the courthouse were ordinary passenger cars, or pickups with open beds. Harper wasn't surprised. Such a crude method of destruction wasn't the bomber's style.

He turned and walked along the front of the building. There were no openings at street level, only massive rough-cut stone blocks. The first row of windows was a good ten feet above the sidewalk. Squinting, he could see the thin silver wires of the alarm system running through the glass.

He came to the end of the building, where there was a narrow, dim alley. It was a good place to make an unseen entry, Harper thought, and turned in.

Rogers's security experts must have thought so too, because the windows along the alley wall were covered with iron gratings. Harper walked deeper into the alley. Now that he was out of the sun, the sweat felt cool on his brow. He came to a narrow doorway set in the side of the building. It was solid wood. He reached for the knob to make sure that the door was locked.

The knob was yanked from his hand as the door swung open. Harper's heart lurched. He stumbled forward but recovered quickly.

Squinting into the bright light from the interior of the building, he saw Naomi Glidden. She smiled wearily at him.

"Okay, Harper. Enough already."

Harper turned and looked up. Now he could see the small television camera, trained on the door from a high ledge. He said, "How long have you been watching me?"

"Since you parked across the street. I've been getting full reports. You should have more than coffee for breakfast, Harper. It's the most important meal of the day." She glanced at her watch. "I've been patient with you. But the show goes on the air in three minutes, and I don't want any distractions. So you're leaving."

She made a gesture and two fit-looking guards appeared in the doorway beside her. They were smiling, but Harper didn't think it was friendliness. They were looking forward to frog-marching him to his car.

Naomi stepped aside and the guards moved into position, flanking Harper. He said quickly, "The sweep didn't find anything suspicious? Anything at all?"

"Relax. The building's clean, Harper."

"It was clean three hours ago. But what about now?"

"We have a show to do. Good-bye."

Harper felt the guards' hands clamp down on both his arms. He said, "The bomber could've gotten in after the sweep."

"There have been no unauthorized entries to the building. Good-bye, good-bye, good-bye."

The guards were pulling Harper back. Naomi was closing the door. Taking advantage of the light from inside the building while he still had it, Harper glanced quickly around the alley.

It was only five paces away—a hatch with an iron cover, low down on the wall of the building. He shouted, "Naomi, wait!"

She swung the door back open. "Now what?"

Harper couldn't point. The guards were still clutching his arms hard enough to cut off the blood flow. He nodded his head toward the hatch. "What about that?"

She looked at it and back at Harper. "So? It's an old coal chute."

"It's big enough for a man to slide through. Have you got it wired into the alarm system?"

Naomi's eyelids still looked heavy with boredom. She glanced from one guard to the other. The larger of the two spoke up in a rich Kentucky accent. "I kinda doubt it's wired, ma'am. Wouldn't be no point. They stopped burning coal thirty, forty years ago. That door's welded shut."

"Try it," Harper said.

He was looking Naomi straight in the eye. She hesitated, glancing at her watch. Then she stepped out into the alley, walked over to the hatch, bent down to grasp the iron handle in her slim pale hand, and pulled.

The door swung smoothly open.

18

Letting go the handle, Naomi jumped away from the coal chute door. She looked at Harper wide-eyed.

"Not welded shut," he said. "Only painted shut. The bomber finds out things like that. He was probably here weeks ago. Even months ago. Pried the door open with a crowbar. Straightened out the bend. Painted over the chips. Then left it, knowing he'd be able to get in the building when he wanted to. Which was probably this morning."

Naomi pointed at the chute and said to the guards, "Get in there." Then she turned to Harper. "Come with me. We're going to the security desk."

The guards were hesitating, looking at each other. Naomi swung round on them. "Didn't you hear me? I said, get in there."

"Shoot, ma'am," said the Kentuckian. "That's like sticking your arm down a snake hole."

"You've got guns, don't you? So get in there." She strode rapidly toward the street. Harper rushed to catch up with her. As he was about to go around the building, he looked back. The Kentuckian was standing with his gun drawn. The other guard was wriggling head-first down the hatch.

Harper followed Naomi to the main stairs, and up them. She had on flat shoes and a short skirt, and she was running flat-out. She pushed through the doors into an impressive lobby. Their rapid footfalls clattered on the shiny marble floors and brought down echoes from the high ceiling. The guards at the security desk heard. They were rising and turning when Harper and Naomi were still thirty feet away.

"We have an intruder!" she yelled. "Check the screens!"

There was only a moment of startled confusion before the guards turned to their bank of television monitors. An older man with a gray moustache came around the desk toward them. "What's up, Ms. Glidden?"

Harper looked at the man while Naomi explained what they'd found in the alley. He had a ruddy face and his close-cropped hair was as gray as his moustache. He was short and broad-shouldered, and his stomach looked flat as a twenty-year-old's under his tan uniform shirt. There were stripes on his sleeve, so Harper figured he was the Security Chief. The nameplate on his breast pocket said "Clifford." As he listened to Naomi, his mouth set and his face turned a deeper red. Harper sensed that he knew something they didn't know—and the news wasn't good.

"Sir!" It was a young black guard sitting at the console, wearing a headset. He told Clifford, "This is Surtees reporting. They went down the coal chute into the basement. They've looked all over the basement and there's nobody there."

"Maybe they haven't looked long enough," said Naomi testily. "That basement's like a cave. Tell them to keep looking."

"Tell them to come up," said Clifford. He turned his morose face back to Naomi. "I don't think we're going to find anybody in the basement."

"Why not?" said Naomi. "All the doors leading from the basement to the main building are locked and alarmed."

Clifford nodded, blinking his eyes as he did so. "We got a red light on the board a while back. Southwest stairway, basement door. We investigated and found the door locked, no sign of tampering. So we wrote if off as a false alarm." He hesitated, then added, "We wouldn't have done that if we'd known someone had got in the basement."

Naomi was looking at him steadily. Only in her unnatural stillness was there any sign of how frightened she was. She said, "When was this?"

"About half an hour ago. Give me a minute and I'll have the exact time for you." He turned back to the desk.

"Never mind the exact time. I'm going back to the sixth floor." She looked at the guards who were watching the constantly changing images on the bank of television monitors. "Look, have these guys go out and search the building, okay?"

Without waiting for an answer, she headed for the elevator. Harper went after her. "The sixth floor," he said, "that where Rogers is?"

She nodded and stabbed at the elevator call button. She missed it twice. Harper leaned around her shoulder and pushed it. The doors opened. As they stepped in, Clifford came running across the floor toward them. "Wait! Ms. Glidden, what are we looking for—a man, or—"

"No way of knowing," Harper answered. "He could've planted the bomb and gotten away already, or he could still be here. Watch out for suspicious parcels. Have you got metal detectors and fluoroscopes?"

Clifford nodded.

"Bring one of each up to the sixth floor. That's where we'll need them first."

Clifford nodded again and ran back toward the desk. His guards were getting ready to go, strapping on gunbelts, donning flak jackets. The doors slid closed and the elevator started upwards.

"The guy can't be on the sixth floor," Naomi said, in a low, tense voice. "Not near the studio anyway. I would've noticed anybody unfamiliar. Anyway, it's a maze of corridors up there. A stranger wouldn't be able to find his way around. Wouldn't know where to find Speed."

"This guy would know," Harper said.

After that they were silent, watching the number indicators flick on and off.

On the sixth floor, the doors slid open. A guard was sitting at the security desk facing the elevators with a telephone in his hand. He was getting the bad news from downstairs. He looked up at them wide-eyed.

Naomi approached the desk. "Pat, has anybody unauthorized tried to get past you? Have you seen any strangers at all?"

"No, ma'am."

She looked at Harper as if this proved something.

He told her, "This guy won't be using the elevators. Won't be trying to get past security desks." To the guard he said, "Have you got any other security people up here?"

"Four. One on each of the stairway doors, one roaming, and one in the studio with Speed."

"Leave him where he is. Have the other three fan out through the corridors. Stop anyone they don't know. Keep an eye out for suspicious parcels—for anything that doesn't belong here."

The guard looked from Harper to Naomi. She said, "Do it, Pat."

As they started down the corridor, Harper became aware of Speed Rogers's angry, hectoring voice, booming from unseen speakers: "—lost the vote because of so-called moderates who betrayed the people who'd elected them. Weak-kneed, spineless, gutless—"

The corridor was wide and unadorned. It had blue-gray industrial carpeting and white-painted walls. There was nowhere to hide. Naomi led Harper through turn after turn. She was right, the sixth floor *was* a labyrinth. As they came around each corner, Harper expected to see a furtive figure running away or disappearing through a door. The bomber had brought off his previous attacks unscathed. How would he react to an attempt to capture him? Did he carry a gun? Or would he try to use the bomb to bargain his way out? Or would he panic and hit the switch on his detonator? Harper's heart was pounding. His right hand was aching again. Tension had made him clench it into as much of a fist as he could make.

Now he could hear other voices, lower than the amplified bellowing of Speed Rogers. They rounded a corner and came to a lounge area with office doors leading off it. The staffers were gathered here, talking excitedly. It was Howard who spotted them first. He ran toward them, swinging one arm while he held onto his glasses with the other. "Naomi, what's going on?"

"We've got a security problem, but we're handling it," she replied. "How's Speed?"

"He knows something's up. He's giving me looks through the glass in the control room."

"Oh, God. Speed mustn't be distracted, Howard, you understand that? Get back in the control room and—and look calm."

Howard spun and ran across the room to a heavy-looking door. The big, burly guard, whom Harper had seen arriving with Speed earlier that morning, opened it for him.

As Naomi explained to the staffers what was going on, Harper prowled around the lounge and looked into the offices that adjoined it. The tables and sofas were cluttered with books, purses, gym bags, paper sacks from fast-food places. Harper turned back to the group. Raising his voice, he said, "Listen, all of you! I need you to go through these rooms and pick up everything you brought in with you."

"Then what?" said Naomi.

"Then we'll see what's left."

As the young people were scattering to their offices, Clifford, the security chief, came in leading three men who were toting the equipment Harper had requested.

"Where do you want the fluoroscope set up?" Clifford asked.

"We don't need it yet. Let's start with the obvious. Open drawers, look under furniture."

Naomi stepped closer to Harper. "How big would the bomb have to be?"

Harper nodded toward the heavy door. "Rogers is right through there?"

"There's the control room and then the studio, yes."

"Then it wouldn't have to be big. A plastique charge the size of a cigarette pack would take out all these rooms."

"Oh God." She thought it over and gave a small, definite shake of her head. "But I still don't see how he could've gotten this close. There are too many of us running around this area before the show starts. Anyone who didn't belong would be noticed."

Harper nodded. He saw her point. And yet he felt certain that the bomber would want to plant his explosive as close to the studio as possible, to make sure of getting Rogers. He turned to Clifford. "What's above us?"

The security chief was kneeling to look under a couch. He straightened up to answer. Maybe he wasn't as fit as he'd looked downstairs, for he was breathing hard from exertion and tension and his face was now almost beet red. "The roof," he replied. "I've already got a guy up there."

"Then what's below?"

"Nothing. The whole floor's empty."

"Let's go down there," Harper said.

"Nobody can get in. The elevators don't stop and the stairway doors are locked and alarmed."

"He got through a locked and alarmed door in the basement," Harper pointed out.

The chief stood, pulling a jangling row of keys off his belt. "Let's check it out."

They set out through the maze of corridors. Along the way they passed numerous guards running in all directions or pushing through office doors with their guns drawn. One woman was patiently disassembling a drinking fountain. Finally they reached the stairway door. Clifford unlocked it and they went down a flight. When they reached the fifth floor landing, they stopped.

The door was standing open.

Clifford glanced sideways at Harper and drew his revolver. In the other hand, he had a flashlight. He flipped it on and eased cautiously through the doorway.

The fifth floor had no lights. Clifford's beam traveled over bare floors, unpainted walls, empty door frames. The corridor smelled musty, and it was quiet. There were no loudspeakers booming out Speed Rogers's voice. Clifford moved forward, a step at a time, his flashlight scanning the darkness and the barrel of his revolver moving with it.

A noise broke in on the silence. It was a very soft sound and Harper and Clifford had to get closer before they realized what it was.

Breathing.

The labored, broken breathing of someone who was frightened or in great pain.

It was coming from the doorway just ahead. Clifford ran toward it, throwing out his arms, extending the flashlight and pistol together. "Freeze!" he shouted.

The man had his back to them. He didn't do as Clifford ordered, but swung around, lifting up his arms to block the light.

Then he sneezed.

"Stuart," said Harper, recognizing the curly-haired staffer.

"What the hell are you doing down here?" yelled Clifford, lowering the gun but not the flashlight.

"Trying—" Stuart wheezed "—trying to get some air in my lungs. I'm having—an anxiety attack—on top of—an allergy attack." He sneezed again and mopped at his streaming nose and eyes. Then he blinked up at them. "I just wanted some peace and quiet. Okay?"

* * *

When Harper got back to the sixth-floor lounge, he found Naomi leaning in the doorway. He knew at once that her mood had changed. Her thick dark hair had come undone during the morning's exertions, and she was combing it back with her fingers, a barrette clenched between her teeth.

She looked coolly at Harper. Taking the barrette out of her mouth, she said, "No suspicious parcels here. We've accounted for everything down to the last bag of Doritos."

"What about the search of the floor?"

"Nothing so far, and they're almost done."

"Almost isn't good enough. And the search of the building has hardly begun."

She was clipping the bun of hair at the nape of her neck, and paying more attention to the task than she was to Harper.

He said, "The intruder is for real, you know. Somebody did break into the building."

"Yes, and he's gone by now. We do have occasional break-ins. Burglars after computer equipment. Souvenir hunters after Speed's doodle pad. We'll keep looking into it, Harper. We'll mail you a full report."

"When people have a bomb scare, they ordinarily evacuate the building. Call the police."

"We're doing a live radio show, Harper. Do you seriously expect me to pull Speed Rogers off the air?"

"Yes. I think—"

But Naomi wasn't listening anymore.

"Chief Clifford?" she said. "Would you kindly escort Mr. Harper out of the building?"

Surtees, the guard from Kentucky, was sitting at the security desk in the lobby watching the monitors when Chief Clifford walked Harper by.

So they were throwing Harper out at last. Surtees couldn't help smiling. It would have made more sense if Ms. Glidden had allowed him and Tom to escort Harper out half an hour ago. For one thing, it would have spared Surtees from having to slide down that coal chute. That had scared the wits out of him, and he had two scraped knees and a bruised elbow too. And all for nothing. There was no intruder in the building.

Even now the Harper guy wouldn't give up. Clifford was practically pushing him through the front door and he was trying to talk Clifford into overruling Ms. Glidden. No chance of that, Surtees knew. When the show was on the air, Ms. Glidden was in charge.

Suddenly, Surtees leaned forward. He'd seen something on Monitor 6 but he wasn't sure what it was. Monitor 6 was showing a corridor on the sixth floor. He manipulated the controls, panning and zooming the camera.

There it was: a ripple in the blue-gray carpet. He squinted in puzzlement. He could see movement, but he couldn't see *what* was moving. He glanced at the phone, thinking of calling up to the sixth floor. When he looked back, the ripple was gone.

Surtees decided not to call the sixth floor. It was probably some kind of video glitch. Anyway, there'd been enough excitement this morning.

Up on the sixth floor, Stuart and Courtney were walking down the corridor toward the lounge. With his handkerchief pressed to his nose, Stuart was saying, "Who've we got on hold for the next segment?"

"There's a guy who wants to support Speed's stand on the capital gains tax. Let's put him through. Speed loves to talk about the capital gains tax."

Stuart heard a noise and looked down. Something fizzed past his right ankle.

"What the—" said Courtney.

Stuart bent down as the thing raced away from him. It was a box, painted the same blue as the carpet, mounted on blue wheels. It was running out of the corridor and was going to crash into a wall straight ahead. But when it reached the corner it slowed and turned with an eerie precision—almost as if someone was guiding it. Then it disappeared around the corner.

Courtney and Stuart stared at each other. Then she took off running after the thing. Stuart couldn't go with her. He felt another sneeze coming on.

In the lounge, the staffers heard Courtney shouting, "Hey! Watch out!" They rose. They looked around. The guard on the door started forward with one hand on the butt of his holstered pistol. No one saw the little blue box whiz past.

Howard Woo was coming out of the control room. He had spent the last fifteen minutes looking calm and nodding reassuringly whenever Speed glanced through the glass at him. Now he was off duty, because it was a commercial break and Naomi herself was on her way in to talk to the star.

He heard shouts and saw people pouring into the corridor from the lounge. But it was a softer, nearer sound that made him look down, his index finger flying to the bridge of his nose to hold his glasses on.

There was the thing sitting still at his feet, like a puppy he'd called. A small blue box with a stubby antenna sticking up from the top. He thought it must be a prank dreamed up by one of his tirelessly inventive colleagues.

"Get away from it! Get away from it!"

The guard was bounding toward him, waving his pistol excitedly.

The air seemed suddenly charged with electricity, and every hair on Howard Woo's body stirred.

In the studio, Naomi was saying, "Sorry about the ruckus, Speed."

Rogers was rising from his chair, taking off his headphones, smiling at her. In the next instant, the world split apart in brilliant white light.

He saw but would never hear the explosion. By the time the sound wave reached him, he was dead. The glass of the control booth melted away like a drop of water hitting a hot skillet. Naomi didn't have time to turn, but Speed Rogers saw a fiercely bright light expanding and rushing toward them.

The pain was terrible but brief.

19

As Markman drove away from Elmhart, and the rest of its buildings dropped out of sight, he could still look back across the gently rolling hills and see the cupolas atop the Old Courthouse. It had been the tallest building in Elmhart when it was erected, and it had remained so. The view hadn't changed in a century.

Until today, when Markman changed it.

He couldn't resist the temptation to look back. As he pulled his rented pickup over to the side of the road, he thought that surely it was all right to allow himself this one indulgence. It wasn't suspicious behavior. In the last mile or so he'd passed several cars and trucks which had pulled to the side of the road so their occupants could stare open-mouthed toward town.

He parked the truck on the shoulder, got out, and turned. It was even more impressive than he'd expected. One cupola was completely shattered, destroying the ornate symmetry of the rooftop. A pall of smoke drifted slowly away with the east wind. Over the buzz of insects and the trilling of birds in the nearby fields, Markman could hear the wail of sirens.

The massive stone walls of the Courthouse wouldn't burn, of course. It would stand for a long time, a blasted and gutted shell. There wouldn't be anyone to restore it, now that Speed Rogers was gone.

Markman would have liked to roar out his triumph. He might even have pumped his fist and yelled *yesss!* the way the idiots did on television. But his self-restraint was too deeply ingrained. So he just stood there with his arms dangling at his side and his mouth open, like the other stunned hoosiers he'd passed on the roadside.

A thought came to him that made it easier to temper his joy. It was always like that with Markman; he was a perfectionist, a worrier, a slave to compunction. There was always some cloud on the horizon, some unanswered question to nag at him.

Who was the man he'd seen? That was what Markman wondered.

When the time had come to activate the model car, Markman had driven to the far side of Courthouse Square and parked. He noticed the two men standing in the main doorway. The security chief, Clifford, was familiar to him from his long reconnaissance of the building. But he'd never seen the other man before.

The stranger was tall, with broad, sloping shoulders. His beard was gray, his hair a darker shade. The men were clearly arguing. Old Clifford was even redder in the face than usual, and waving his arms around. But the other man stood there like a rock. He looked calm, steady, determined.

It was a trait that Markman had always prided himself on: when other people got excited, he kept calm. For some reason, it bothered Markman to see this trait in the other man.

He'd picked up his remote control, raised the antenna and activated the model car immediately.

Now, as he stood by the roadside looking back at Speed Rogers's smoking edifice, his pleasure in the sight was marred by the knowledge that he hadn't done it perfectly. Hadn't followed his plan. He'd intended to blow Rogers up on the air. Let his millions of listeners hear the bang. That would have been perfect.

But instead, a commercial had been playing on Markman's car radio when he hit the switch. He'd allowed the man on the steps to rush him.

He felt hot with anger at this man whose name he didn't even know. It was a struggle to control his emotion. Anyone who strove for excellence the way Markman did was bound to have a hatred for imperfection. When a device he'd built at his workbench failed to perform up to expectations, he would destroy it, along with the plans and all of the tools he'd used. He'd never leave anything around to remind him of his error, or possibly lead him into making another one.

But this man had been far away from the explosion. He'd escaped it unharmed. And Markman had a premonition that the man was going to interfere with his plans again. Frowning, he climbed back into the truck, started it, and drove away.

His calendar lay open on the seat beside him. He'd thought of rewarding himself for completing the Rogers mission by X'ing off the day, even though it was only just noon. He could celebrate the fact that his last preparatory strike was completed and now he could concentrate on the last one. The grand one. Only twenty-four squares remained on his calendar.

But he picked up the calendar, folded it one-handed, and stuffed it in his pocket. He was no longer in the mood to grant himself this little triumph. It seeemed to him there was now another obstacle between himself and May 15.

He switched on the radio. It would be necessary to monitor the media carefully for information about the man on the steps. Markman needed to know who he was and what had brought him here. Then he'd decide what to do about him.

Markman had no tolerance for mistakes.

Or the people who caused them.

Harper stood by the window, watching the dusk deepen into night.

He was in Indiana State Police Headquarters, a modern building standing on the Interstate, some fifty miles from Elmhart. As he watched, a trio of patrol cars pulled out of the lot and hit their isobars and sirens as they took the entrance ramp to the highway and headed for the stricken town. A helicopter was approaching the building with a buffeting roar, its landing lights blinking. Directly below Harper were several minicam vans from local TV stations. One was raising its rooftop microwave dish for a live remote. The reporter who was about to do his standup stood in a glare of light, smoothing his hair.

A lot was going on out there, but Harper knew little about it. He'd gone from the scene of the bombing to a hospital thirty miles from Elmhart. The nearer hospitals were overwhelmed with serious casualties from the blast, and Harper wasn't a serious casualty. In fact, he hadn't been injured at all. The shock wave had blown out windows not far from where he'd been standing, but the flying glass fragments had missed him. He was lucky, the doctors said, and after his perfunctory examination they released him.

Then he was handed over to the State Police, who brought him to this building and questioned him. For hours. There was a series of interrogators, some sharp, some slow. One was hostile. He kept demanding to know why Harper hadn't come to them with his information before. The Indiana State Police would have taken him seriously. They wouldn't have made the mistake that the FBI had, that Speed Rogers had.

It was easy to say that now, of course.

He'd been allowed one five-minute break soon after he arrived, to use the bathroom and call home. The answering machine picked up. Harper didn't know what the news media were saying about him, so he said haltingly that he was still alive, keeping his voice level to assure Laura that things were well under control.

This was his second break. He'd been shown to a small lounge and given a stale ham sandwich and a soda. He could hear footsteps and voices from the corridor, but he had the lounge to himself.

"Hello! Will!"

Harper got up and turned. Standing in the doorway was Special Agent Frances Wilson of the FBI.

She looked as if she'd just arrived from Washington. Harper realized that she'd probably been the passenger on the helicopter he'd seen landing a few minutes ago. She was wearing gray slacks and a dark-blue jacket over a light-blue blouse. There was a heavy purse slung over her shoulder, a suitbag in her hand. In the other hand she carried a laptop computer. A cellular phone bulged in her jacket pocket. It was chirping, but she was ignoring it.

She came right up to him and bent forward to kiss him on the cheek. It was the same quick peck she'd given Addleman, when they'd met in her office at FBI Headquarters. He supposed it meant she and Harper were old colleagues now. Her appearance had baffled him at first, but now he was beginning to figure out what she was doing here.

"How are you, Will? The reports said you were uninjured, but I wasn't sure."

"I'm uninjured."

"Here, let's sit down. We have to talk."

She unburdened herself of her luggage, then took off her jacket, revealing a 9mm automatic holstered on her right hip. They sat down on facing couches.

"Let me tell you why I'm here," Frances said.

"I think I have an idea. What I have to say to the media could be very embarrassing to the Bureau. Somebody had to come out here and beg me to go easy, and you got stuck with the job."

Agent Wilson crossed her legs and leaned back. She was smiling. "No."

"No?" Harper was genuinely surprised. "You don't mind if I tell the reporters that we came to your office last week and warned you about the bomber?"

"I'm not asking you to take part in a cover-up, Will. The Bureau does learn from its mistakes, contrary to popular belief. Feel free to give the media the facts about your interview with me. And if you want to add any personal comments about my slowness or stupidity—well, I wouldn't think that was fair, but I can't stop you."

Harper studied her for a moment. He said, "You've already talked to the reporters, haven't you? Got out ahead of the curve? Practiced damage control? All that stuff you people in Washington are so good at?"

"There was no reason for me not to talk to the reporters. I have nothing to hide. After our meeting, I followed all the accepted procedures. I promptly reported your concerns to my superiors. I gave them all the information they needed to make a decision."

"And when they sat on their asses, you didn't push them."

"That would have been counterproductive."

Harper nodded slowly, understanding. "Addleman was right, wasn't he? You've got bureaucratic savvy now. You put letters in all the right files. Sent e-mail to the appropriate desktops. And I bet you chose your words with care. If Addleman and I turned out to be crackpots, you wouldn't have been seen as having endorsed us. But when the shit hit the fan this afternoon, your superiors remembered what you'd written and said, Holy Christ, Frances was ahead of us on this one. But not too far ahead, so we can still trust her." Harper was smiling now in sardonic admiration. "They put you in charge of the case, didn't they?"

"Yes," said Frances Wilson. She leaned forward, placing her elbows on her knees. She wasn't wearing perfume, but she smelled clean and fresh. No one would have guessed this was the end of a long day, that she'd traveled hundreds of miles, spent hour after hour in tense meetings in airless rooms. This was the beginning of the big investigation Agent Wilson had been waiting for, and she was ready.

"Everything you and Addleman wanted the Bureau to do is being done right now. The best forensic experts in the world are going over that courthouse. I've got fifteen agents in the area already, with more to come tomorrow. And our analysts at Quantico will be at their computers all night. The Bureau's putting everything it has into this hunt. We'll nail this son of a bitch for you. You can count on that. But I need a little cooperation from you."

Harper said nothing. He waited.

"I told you we won't try to control what you tell the media, and I mean it. But there is one piece of information I'm asking you to keep back. The Aquila pattern."

"You know about the Aquila pattern?"

"I talked to Addleman from the plane."

"I see."

"I explained that we can't let the bomber know we're on to him. Right now we're one step ahead. We know he'll be setting up his next attack in Washington. That gives us the edge."

"And Addleman agreed to cooperate?"

She nodded. "He wants to see this bomber caught. Badly. Don't you?"

Harper thought of the young people who had died today. Stuart. Courtney. Howard. He thought of Jimmy Fahey. Looking down at his hands, he said quietly, "Yes, I want to see him caught."

"Then cooperate with me. Because I'm the one who's going to catch him."

"All right. I won't say anything about the Aquila pattern." Harper felt very tired. He wanted to rest. To go home. He rose to his feet. "I assume I'm free to go."

She smiled up at him. "You were always free to go, Will. We just wanted you to be ready, because those reporters are going to jump all over you as soon as you step out of the building."

"Are they?"

"You'll find out. This case is big, Will. People are going nuts. And you're right in the middle of it. You're a hero again." She stepped closer and dropped her voice. "Let me assure you, by the way, that I'm not going to say anything about the Domenic Fortunato case to any reporter—on or off the record."

Harper felt a stab of tension. In the last few hectic days he hadn't thought about the little boy who'd died in the fireworks accident. Was IAD still leaning on the boy's father, trying to get him to say that it had been Harper who'd sold him the fireworks?

He looked at Agent Wilson's blandly smiling face. He said evenly, "I appreciate that."

"Of course, the reporters are going to be asking a lot of questions about you. That's the downside of fame. So the Fortunato thing may leak. But you'll know it didn't come from us."

She was smooth, Harper thought. Here was the not-too-subtle reminder that the spotlight was a dangerous place for him right now, and he ought to stay out of it as much as possible. Leave the stage to Agent Wilson. He turned away without replying.

Frances Wilson walked with him down the corridor. "When you've finished talking to the media, we'll arrange for a car to take you to the airport."

"Thanks. But I'll have to go back to Elmhart. Check out of my motel."

"That's been taken care of. So has the return of your rental car. Your luggage is downstairs."

"I see."

They'd reached the elevators. Agent Wilson pressed the call button.

"Sounds like you want to get me out of here as quickly as possible," Harper said.

"Frankly, we do. You've done your part. Now it's our turn. You do understand that?" She was smiling, but looking him hard in the eye.

"Yes," Harper said. "I understand."

"Have a good flight home, Will," said Frances Wilson, and turned away.

She'd forgotten to kiss him this time.

20

Laura was hugging him almost before his suitcase had touched the hall floor. He kissed her and felt her trembling, felt the coolness of tears on her cheek against his and then tasted their salt.

"You're crying," he said.

"It's relief," she told him, hugging him close again, burrowing her chin hard into his chest. After a few seconds, she stepped back. She stared up at him, her eyes still moist, the tracks of her tears still wet on her face. "Relief that you're alive."

"Speed Rogers isn't," he said, hearing the bitterness in his voice.

"You did what you could, Will. Rogers was arrogant. Anyone could tell that from his ranting on the radio."

"The funny thing was, in real life he struck me as a likable guy. And the people who worked for him, I got to like them too. They were bright, full of energy." He shook his head. "So tuned in, but so unaware. They wouldn't believe me."

"They only believe what they want to," Laura said. "That kind of thing gets to be a habit."

Harper walked wearily out of the hall and into the living room. He sat down on the sofa and looked around at the rehabbing. There was that small, comma-shaped smear he remembered seeing Laura make when she'd enameled the frame on a stained glass window. The smell of the recently applied paint and of thinner and sealer hung faintly in the air. Home.

Laura sat down next to him. "What about the FBI? I saw that Frances Wilson you told me about on TV."

"I talked to her briefly. She has every confidence."

"But does she have any leads?"

"If and when she does, she won't be sharing them with me. Or Addleman. She doesn't want us getting in her way. This case is a career builder for her."

"She sounds too ambitious."

"As long as her ambition is driving her to catch the bomber, it's fine with me."

They both sat still and listened to what sounded like a street sweeper growling and brushing past outside, taking in the litter that had accumulated at the curb, and then spraying the gutter. It was Laura who spoke when the sound had faded.

"You gave me such a fright, Will."

"I'm sorry. I should have listened to your warning. Would've been better if I'd stayed out of it, for all the good I was able to do."

"You alerted the authorities. They'll catch the bomber now."

Harper said nothing.

"You're perspiring. Do you want a cold beer?"

"No."

"Have you had anything to eat since breakfast?"

Harper wasn't hungry. He shrugged. Laura didn't usually fuss over him like this. If only he could relax and enjoy it. "I can't stop thinking about the bomber. How he beat me. I'd be kidding myself if I tried to put all the blame on Rogers and his staff. I was given one last chance to stop the bomber and I failed. He outsmarted me. His method of concealing and delivering the bomb was one I never would have thought of."

"You had only minutes, Will. You couldn't be expected to—"

Irritably, he waved off the excuses. "We were running around searching hiding places when the bomb wasn't hidden at all—just sitting there on the carpet, invisible. And we thought the bomb would be planted, when it was actually mobile. He was able to move it in range just when he needed to. The guy's a genius."

"He'll be caught. They always are, sooner or later. And the Bureau has time. You told me, he plans and prepares so carefully, the intervals between his attacks are long."

"They were. But they've been getting steadily shorter. I think he's getting impatient as he nears the end."

She frowned in puzzlement. "The end?"

Harper hesitated, then said, "There's something else. Something we know about the bomber that hasn't been made public."

He explained about the Aquila pattern, and how it led them to believe that the bomber's final strike would be on Washington.

Laura sat very still as she listened, her large blue eyes fixed on Harper. When he was finished, she said softly, "Good God—you don't think this nut's going to try to blow up the White House?"

"He's trying to make some kind of statement about fame, but nobody knows enough about how his twisted mind works to tell if the President is going to be his target. There are plenty of famous people in Washington."

"All of them well-guarded," Laura said. "And since the security people are forewarned—there's no way the bomber will be able to get by them."

"I hope not."

"It isn't something you need to think about. You're retired, and the FBI has taken on the case." She edged close to him and hugged him again. "It's their job, their responsibility. You're completely out of it."

Hugging her back, kissing her on the lips, he knew she was wrong.

For the next few days Harper tried not to look at the newspapers or television. Stories about the Celebrity Bomber were everywhere, but it was all speculation. If Frances Wilson's investigation was making any progress, she was keeping quiet about it so far.

So Harper was informed by his own sources in the media, a couple of men on New York papers whom he'd known since his days in the NYPD. They passed information to Harper and he gave them "background." They were the only reporters he talked to.

Not that other reporters weren't trying to talk to him. Harper had given up answering the phone or the doorbell. If he walked to the fruit stand or the hardware store, there was sure to be a reporter or photographer tagging along. But Harper had spoken to the press back in Indiana, and he wasn't going to give any more interviews. He intended to keep his promise to Frances Wilson, not to let slip the Aquila pattern. It was the biggest advantage the investigation had.

The days slipped by, fine spring days of gentle showers and warm breezes. It was the last week of April.

Harper's toolbox wasn't where he'd left it.

If he'd been on his guard, he would have wondered about that, because Laura was always careful to put the box back where he liked to keep it, under his workbench in the basement. But when he found it at the foot of the steps, he merely assumed that she'd been forgetful.

Carrying the heavy metal box, he climbed the steps and went into the front parlor. Laura had painted the room while he'd been away, and she wanted him to hang the mirror they had bought at a country auction last summer.

The mirror, a large, oval glass in an ornate gilt frame, was propped against the wall. Harper hefted it, put its weight at about thirty pounds. He'd want to use a molly bolt to hang it. But first he'd have to find a stud. He walked along the wall, rapping on the plaster.

In the corner of the room, a small, portable TV was playing. He'd turned it on to drown out the incessant ringing of the telephone. Each night before bed he sat down at the answering machine and played back the messages. It could take as much as an hour to get through them, and so far he'd always ended up disappointed. The message he was waiting for wasn't on the tape.

The one from Addleman.

Harper figured it was safe to leave the set on, as long as he remembered to turn it off before the noon newscasts and the latest round of frustrating nonstories about the bomber. Right now he was half-listening to an inane talk show, with a host he didn't recognize. She was a tremendously energetic young woman who dashed from one audience member to another, trying to elicit controversial questions or comments about her guests, two women and a man. The three had apparently done something the audience regarded as shameful and bizarre, but Harper hadn't yet made out what it was. Whatever their transgression, all three seemed proud of it.

Harper located the stud. Now for the delicate task of positioning the mirror and making the mark where he'd want the hole to be. He should have been concentrating on his work. But he couldn't shut out the talk show.

"... told her she shouldn't come around no more," one of the women said.

"So while she was talking to your husband, you blew up her car?" said the host incredulously.

"Didn't blow it up," the woman said, grinning. "Didn't have no dynamite. I poured gas all over it and lit it afire. Went up in a big whoosh." The audience tittered.

"Same thing as blown up!" said the second woman on stage. She was wearing an angry look, but didn't really seem angry. After all, her car had probably been insured, and its destruction meant she was on national television.

"How do *you* feel about what happened, Paul?" the host asked the young man seated between the two women. Paul shrugged, obviously flattered at being such an object of desire that a car had been set afire on his behalf.

"Did you do that to her car because of the Celebrity Bomber?" asked a woman in the audience. "And are you at all sorry now?"

Harper put down the mirror and gave the TV his full attention.

Both women were grinning. Paul shrugged again and looked smugly from one to the other. He was skinny and had bad teeth and didn't look like a man two women would battle to possess.

"Wish'd I woulda had some dynamite," said the car arsonist, and the audience laughed.

Harper reached over to where the remote lay on a chair arm and switched the channel. A man standing on a sunny beach somewhere was explaining in painstaking detail how a fortune could be obtained dealing in real estate.

Better, Harper thought. He called Laura, who was stripping woodwork in the library. She stood in the doorway and directed him to move the mirror up a bit, then down a bit. When she was satisfied, she went back to her own work. Harper made a pencil mark on the wall and put the mirror aside.

Now to drill the hole. He walked over to his toolkit.

Loud, driving music announced the beginning of the twelve o'clock news. He picked up the remote and pointed it at the television to turn it off. But they were talking about the Celebrity Bomber, and he hesitated with his thumb on the power switch.

David Wikerwaith, the new heartthrob who was the star of the TV series *Coastal*, had canceled an interview with network news anchor Brad Philip. Laryngitis had been the official excuse, but Philip let it be known that Wickerwaith, and many other stars, had declined to be interviewed regarding the Celebrity Bomber for fear of drawing his attention to them. Harper thought that was sensible.

Not as sensible was fading star Modessa Swann, who was still attractive after countless birthdays and facial surgeries, and who smiled as the camera moved away from her close-up to reveal her sitting next to Philip behind the news desk. A vulpine blond woman who was probably sixty but looked forty, she was wearing pieces of her personal line of jewelry that she sold regularly on a home shopping network. A gold necklace gleamed above generous cleavage revealed by her low-cut blouse.

"Every star I know, all of us," she said to Philip, "is simply terrified about what's happening. Why, none of us knows if we're going to be here tomorrow or if we're going to be blown up by that madman!"

"You don't seem afraid," Philip observed.

Modessa smiled. "Well, I am, Brad. Only a fool wouldn't be. Even the big brave male action stars are frightened. Some of them won't even leave their estates."

"Rumor has it that many have left the country," Philip said.

"Rumor's correct, Brad." She giggled, reminding Harper of seeing her portraying ingenues in the early films that had made her a star. "I guess they've left it up to us gals to defend show business."

Philip smiled reservedly. "If that's the case, show business is in capable hands. We all applaud your fearlessness."

"If you can't tell I'm afraid, then it's a tribute to my acting ability. But I'm here, even though I know it's dangerous. To some of us, this is part of the show-must-go-on tradition. We can't let anyone scare us away from our first love and livelihoods. This reminds me of my first audition, with all the butterflies in my stomach. It's the very same feeling."

It astounded Harper that she wouldn't know the essential difference. Being ripped limb from limb by an explosion wasn't quite the same thing as failing to land a juicy part in a play or film. *Don't call us, we'll call you* meant that at least there was a future.

"When the time comes to die," Modessa said with practiced flipness, "I'm sure the director will call for my stunt woman."

Harper knew then that she really was terrified, because she *was* acting. Her lines had obviously been written and rehearsed. This was publicity for her. Opportunity. In a way, he had to admire her, and marvel at her enduring appetite for fame. If he was watching, what would the Celebrity Bomber think of her?

Turning off the television, he bent over the toolbox and opened it. Laura might have forgotten to put it back in the right place, but she had left its contents in good order. His electric drill was in its usual drawer. He selected and inserted a bit, then straightened up.

There was an outlet in the baseboard just a few feet from where he wanted the hole. Convenient; he wouldn't need an extension cord. Cradling the drill comfortably in his good hand, he placed the bit against the pencil mark on the wall and pressed the trigger.

It felt as if a bolt of lightning shot through him. The drill seemed to jump from his hand. Gasping with surprise and pain, he staggered back. He looked at his hand to see how badly it was burned.

The drill lay on the floor, sparking and smoking.

Harper sat on the edge of the tub in the downstairs bathroom while Laura applied ointments and Band-Aids to his hand.

"There," she said. "Feel any better?"

"A little. Still pretty tender."

"It will be for a while. The burns aren't serious. But I'm afraid you're finished with carpentry for the day."

Harper raised his left hand and looked at it. The skin was still red, under a glistening coat of burn cream. In the last couple of years, he had learned how to manage with one good hand. For the next few hours he'd have to manage with none. It was an experience that would make a man think. Be grateful for what he had. And what he could still lose.

Which was just the way it was intended to work.

He said quietly, "That was a brand-new drill. Last time I used it, it was fine. There was no reason for it to short out."

"Well, these things happen."

"Laura, did you use my toolbox recently?"

"Recently? I can't exactly remember."

"Yesterday, I mean."

"Oh. No, I didn't. Why?"

"The bomber did this. He rewired the drill."

Laura was packing away her first aid kit. She swung around to stare wide-eyed at him. "What are you saying? The drill just shorted out."

"No."

"Oh God. You mean he was trying to kill—"

"If he'd intended to kill me, I'd be dead. He was just demonstrating how vulnerable I am. Sending me a message, warning me that I'd made enough trouble for him already and I'd better not make anymore."

She sat down on the windowsill. For a moment she was silent. Then she said, "Will, if you're sure, we'd better call the police right away."

He shook his head. "I'm willing to bet that it won't be possible now to tell that the drill was tampered with. So it'll be just my story, and they probably won't take it seriously. They might think it's some kind of post-traumatic reaction to the bombing at Elmhart. Or they might think I'm lying outright—trying to get some attention because I'm pissed off at the way I've been left out of the investigation."

Laura took a deep breath, trying to maintain her composure. "Why did you ask if I'd moved your toolbox?"

"Because it wasn't exactly where I'd left it."

She stood up, raising one hand to her mouth. "You mean he's been—here? In our house? Will, no."

"He's been here."

"But we've got dead bolts on both doors. We've got an alarm system that your friend on the Burglary Squad said was state of the art."

Harper shrugged. "Not a problem for this guy."

Laura walked quickly out of the room. "I left the window open in the back room just now. Oh Lord, of all the stupid—"

"He's long gone," Harper called after her.

She pivoted in the corridor and looked back at him. "But can we be sure he's finished with us? Can we ever feel safe here?"

He shook his head sadly. "No. We can't."

"But where can we go on such short notice? There's—there's my friend Anita. She lives near the hospital. But I don't think she'd have room for you. Maybe we should just go to a hotel."

"Yes, a hotel." Harper looked at his hand. Already the soothing effect of the ointment was wearing off and he could feel the heat. "Look, I'd better tell Addleman what's happened."

While Laura packed their bags, Harper placed the call. Holding the receiver with his fingertips, he explained what the bomber had done.

"Unexpected," said Addleman. "Fascinating. I wouldn't think the bomber would react in such a personal way."

"Do you think we should inform Frances?"

"Assuming we could get through to her? She's a busy woman these days. Anyway she'd only say you're imagining things. If the bomber was going to take this much trouble, he'd have killed you."

"She'd be wrong," Harper said. "At this stage of the game killing me would serve no purpose."

"No. You're out of the action. The bomber's telling you to stay out. He's extending a sort of professional courtesy to you. Saying you're a pro too, but of course you're not in his league, so steer clear. But I gather his warning isn't having the desired effect?"

"No," said Harper coldly. "Just the opposite effect."

"Well, as long as you have to leave home anyway, you'd better come down here. I was about to send you e-mail. I've been working on something."

Harper straightened up. Eagerness made him tighten his grip on the receiver and he winced. "What is it? Something the Bureau doesn't have?"

Addleman hesitated. "Come on down, Harper, and we'll talk."

"See you this evening," Harper said. Putting down the phone, he went to break the news to Laura.

21

It was drizzling that evening when Harper climbed out of a cab in front of Addleman's apartment building and stood on the rain-slick sidewalk. A couple of young men with tattooed arms and bizarre hairdos, lounging across the street and sharing a bottle, eyed him speculatively in the dusk, then turned back to their conversation as they saw something in him that prompted caution.

A few seconds after Harper knocked, locks snicked, chains rattled, and Addleman opened the door and nodded a somber hello. He stood back to let Harper enter the dim apartment. Stale tobacco smoke mingled with the spicy cooking scent that had followed Harper upstairs. He could see down the short hall to the open door to the computer room, where somewhat brighter light spilled out onto the cheap and frayed carpet runner.

Addleman snuffed out his cigarette in an ashtray, then led Harper down the hall and into the room. An elbowed desk lamp was on, but much of the light came from the glow of three computer monitors.

"I've got a crawler working on that one," Addleman explained, motioning with his head toward the computer in the corner. He was wearing dark, wrinkled slacks, and his usual white shirt, with the sleeves rolled to above his elbows. He looked exhausted.

"Crawler?"

"Piece of search software that makes its way through the net, seeking out areas that might give up the information I need. Saves me hours in front of the computer, and it works while I sleep."

"You look as if you should lie down and get some sleep now."

"I should," Addleman said. "I'll lie down when I'm dead."

"While you're alive and it's convenient to ask," Harper said, "why did you have me take the train here from New York?"

Addleman shook a cigarette from the pack. He put it in his mouth, then took it out again without lighting it. "The Bureau's blowing this investigation, Harper."

"How do you know that? They may be making a lot of progress they're not telling the media about."

"I'm not relying on the media for my information. I worked at the Bureau for sixteen years. I still have contacts there. And what they tell me has me worried."

"How so?"

Addleman began to shake his head slowly. A look of deep disgust contorted his features. "Behavioral Sciences—my old department—is working on the significance of the Aquila pattern. They're sure it's astrology."

"I remember you thought the bomber wasn't the type to be interested in astrology."

"Exactly. This guy is a technocrat. Hyperrational. He wouldn't get near astrology. And right now the Bureau has its best brains tied up studying the significance of the Aquila constellation in Greek astrology. Not to mention Arabic, Chinese, and Indian astrology. They're writing horoscopes on this son of a bitch when they ought to be out there trying to catch him."

Addleman was getting himself worked up, emphasizing his points by waving his unlit cigarette around. Harper said, "Easy, Harold. Maybe the astrology thing is a blind alley, but they're chasing a lot of other leads. Something will work out."

But Addleman only began to wag his head more quickly and wave his cigarette in broader arcs. "No! You don't understand. It's the whole bureaucratic mindset that's the problem. Frances and the others have gotten fixated on the Aquila pattern. They're putting plenty of agents into the investigation of the Rogers bombing and the seven previous strikes we gave them. But as to finding any earlier strikes by the bomber, that's low priority. They haven't committed enough people to it and they're not doing it right."

"But I've heard that they're checking out every unsolved bombing case of the last twenty years."

"That's not enough! Sometimes the Bureau isn't the kind of organization that can think about playing the game off the board."

"Meaning?"

"They're not investigating *solved* bombings."

Harper was having trouble keeping up with the enigmatic Addleman. "Why should they?"

"My crawler came up with something on the 'net yesterday. A home page on the World Wide Web that might lead us to the bomber's first job."

"Home page?" Harper had only heard the term, and didn't know exactly what it was.

"It's kind of like a paid advertisement on the Internet. An organization or an individual buys space, and can use it in a variety of ways for a number of causes. Does the name Sam Sugar mean anything to you?"

Harper shook his head no.

"He has a home page, and he's using it to try to get the media interested in righting what he says is a miscarriage of justice. Fifteen years ago he was convicted of sending a mail bomb to a man he owed money to, a rising comedian named Jake Blake."

"Blake was killed?"

"No. That's another reason why this case didn't attract the notice of the Bureau. It's not a homicide, only an attempted murder. Jake Blake lived." Addleman looked down. Suddenly and uncharacteristically, he seemed embarrassed. "His right hand was blown off."

Harper felt an impulse to look down at his own right hand. He resisted it.

Addleman went on. "Sugar served his sentence and was released from prison, but he continues to maintain his innocence."

"That doesn't necessarily mean he's innocent."

Addleman ignored the comment. Putting down his cigarette, he turned to the nearest computer and began to tap keys. His lined, strained features were intent in the soft glow of the monitor. "What Sugar's trying to do now is get the media interested in the crime, get them asking questions that could lead to the reversal of his conviction. He isn't having much success. He's the only one interested in an old, minor crime. And even if he's telling the truth, he wouldn't be the first or last innocent man to do the time without the crime."

"Or the first guilty man to try to scrub away the stain of conviction and incarceration."

"Right. But I happen to believe Sugar. I think he really is innocent and took the rap for the bomber's first strike." He stepped back so Harper could see what was on the monitor—Sam Sugar's home page.

It was a brief, simply written description of the crime, a profession of innocence, and a plea for media coverage so information about the real bomber might surface. Also there was a photograph of Sugar, a thin man with receding hair and a tragic, wistful expression.

"There's audio, too," Addleman said, and worked the keyboard.

Sugar's soft, bitter voice sounded from the computer speakers: "What's written here's all true, and I'm innocent, so help me God. It was my faith that got me through prison, and it's my faith in the Lord that helps me know that someday nobody will think I did that terrible deed. I'm a sinner, like all of mankind, but attempted murder's a sin I never committed. If anyone out there wants to tell me something, or to interview me, just write or call the phone number on the screen, or contact me with my e-mail address. Please help me right this wrong so at last there's some true justice. Thanks, and God bless you." The mailing address was in Solar City, Arizona.

"Isn't there music to go with this?" Harper asked.

Addleman smiled thinly. "It's possible Sugar lays it on a little thick. He needs a writer and a computer graphics expert. Then he might get a few more hits. I was only the sixth person to read his page."

"Why do you think he's innocent, Harold?"

"These." Addleman switched on a lamp and handed Harper some eight-by-ten color photographs. "I talked one of my friends at the Bureau into sending them to me. He didn't so much as ask why I wanted them, which shows you how interested the Bureau is in this case."

Harper was looking at photos of an FBI lab reconstruction of the exploded bomb. It was a thorough reconstruction. Much of the timing mechanism had been recovered. It had been a pipe bomb, and most of the pipe and its caps—that on detonation had become shrapnel— had been found. In one photo the device was lying in pieces on a black background. In another it had all been fitted together like a jigsaw puzzle. The last photo was of Sam Sugar. He looked much older than he had in his home page photo, a man well past middle age, with a thin face and sad, beaten eyes. He had his chin tucked in and was staring up at the camera as if it had just struck him.

"I scanned the reconstruction photos into the computer," Addleman said, "then zoned in on a section of one of them and blew it up digitally."

He worked the keyboard again. The photo of the bomb pieces spread out on black cloth appeared on the monitor. Addleman adroitly played the keys and in a series of quick takes, the lower right section of the photo was enlarged again and again. A tiny bit of shrapnel turned out to be a screw head.

"Look carefully," Addleman instructed.

Harper did, leaning in close to the glowing monitor.

On one side of the slotted screw head was engraved the letter *D*.

He could hear himself breathing faster in the quiet room. "*D*," he said. "The bomber's assembly instructions again."

Addleman looked over at him, amused and triumphant. "So now you're a little more interested, aren't you? Sure that's a *D*?"

"Of course it's a *D*."

"That's what I think too. But others might think it's just a scratch that happens to be shaped like a *D*. We've been through this before, remember?"

"A lot has happened since then. They'd believe us now. We take this to Frances Wilson, Addleman, and she'll order an examination of the original bomb fragments. That'll convince—"

"The bomb fragments are gone."

"Gone?"

"I checked. When the case was closed the fragments were disposed of."

Harper squinted at the *D*. It looked unmistakable to him, but its edges were blurred by the magnification process. "Do any of the other photos show letters?"

"No, and believe me, I've looked." Addleman tapped keys so that the image disappeared. "This one's going to take legwork to check out, Will. One of us should look Sugar in the eye and judge whether he's telling the truth. Either way, I'd also bet he knows where Blake is, which might make finding him easier for us. It's not always easy to track down former comics."

"I hate to bring it up, Harold, but who's going to pay for all this legwork?"

"Don't worry about that," Addleman said. "My house was sold as part of the divorce settlement. I have some money put away, and this is how I want to spend it."

Harper stared at the monitor and said nothing.

"We have to cover all the possibilities," Addleman said. "Frances wouldn't buy our story before. She looked at us and saw a drunk and a corrupt cop. We go to her now, and she'll think we're just resentful because she took the case over from us."

Harper nodded, knowing that she would.

He wondered how his wife would take the news that he was going to Arizona.

He called her from the Philadelphia Airport, where he was planning to doze through what remained of the night in a chair. He didn't want to spend any more of Addleman's money than he had to.

Laura was settled in with her friend Anita, who lived a block away from New York University Hospital, where they both worked. Harper told her the story of Sam Sugar.

She listened in silence. When he was finished, she said, "Well, all right, I can see why you'd want to talk to him."

Her matter-of-fact response was a relief to Harper. He'd been dreading an argument. He said, "I've got an early flight tomorrow. I should be back the day after."

"But you don't know what it could lead to."

"No, I don't."

"Then don't make any promises. Just call me once in a while, let me know where you are and what's going on. Okay?"

She was holding in a lot of tension, Harper realized. He said. "Of course."

"Are you sure you don't want to come back home before you set out?"

"I'd just as soon get the trip over with."

"You won't need any more clothes or anything?"

"I'll be all right."

"What about your identification?"

"You mean, as a retired sergeant, NYPD? I've got that, although I don't think it'll do me much good."

Laura hesitated, then said, "What about your gun?"

The question brought Harper up short. His old service revolver, a .38 Smith & Wesson. was kept at the back of the safe in their pantry. He hadn't thought of it in a long time. He said, "I won't need a gun, Laura. This fellow I'm interviewing may be a jailbird, but he sounds pretty harmless."

"But you don't know where it will lead, you said. Maybe you ought to come back for the gun. You're still permitted to carry one, aren't you?"

"I'm not sure. The truth is, I haven't carried it since I was a patrolman. Once I got on the Bomb Squad—well, you have more pressing things to worry about than keeping up with your target practice. And of course I learned to shoot right-handed. I don't know if I could handle a gun left-handed. I'd probably shoot myself in the foot." He forced a dry chuckle.

Laura tried to laugh too. She said, "Then I guess you're better off without the gun."

"Definitely."

She changed the subject then. They talked about the goings-on at the hospital. But Harper's mind was not on what they were saying. He was thinking about the gun and why Laura would believe that he needed it.

Did she fear that he was going out to hunt the Celebrity Bomber— alone? Did she think that the bomber's nasty little trick with the drill had shaken Harper up so much that he'd lost his objectivity and was turning the case into a personal matter? He wished he could ask her these questions outright. Wished he could promise her he had no illusions about hunting down the killer single-handed. If he found any solid evidence linking the Jake Blake case to the bomber, he'd take it to the Bureau. But Laura had told him she didn't want any promises from him.

So Harper didn't make any. He told her he loved her and hung up the phone.

22

Sugar's address turned out to be several miles west of Phoenix, in the well-to-do retirement community of Solar City.

It struck Harper as he searched for Palm Drive, that while the houses weren't exactly alike, they were so similar that a drunk would have a hard time finding his way home. All of them were pastel, one-story houses with attached garages. Most had screened-in patios. Only a few had lawns instead of layers of colored rocks, usually laid in gentle patterns and partitioned by low black plastic dividers or rows of brick. Many of the houses' front yards featured squat palm trees, some of which were cropped short and had the lower fronds chopped off so the trees resembled huge pineapples. Few cars were parked in the street or driveways because of the fierceness of the glaring sun. Several garage doors were open to reveal golf carts hooked up to chargers.

Neat was the word that kept coming to Harper's mind as he drove along the pale concrete streets. There was little traffic in Solar City—usually expensive, fairly late-model cars. Or older-model, white-haired men or women driving golf carts. Even on the main streets leading into Solar City, Harper had seen people probably too old to be behind the steering wheels of cars driving golf carts; some seemed to be going to the retirement community's golf course, but some obviously used the electric carts for other purposes and destinations.

Sugar's address on Palm Drive belonged to a pale green house with a gray roof and white shutters. In the front yard was a large saguaro cactus, a straight, tall plant that had quilled limbs resembling bent arms. There were green and white canvas awnings over some of the windows, and the garage's white overhead door was closed. As he parked his rental in the driveway, Harper saw a citrus tree in the backyard dotted with bright oranges among its green leaves. This could be a good place to retire to, he thought, if you longed for order and quiet. If your mind was finally at rest.

Maybe someday . . .

He climbed out of the car and felt the heat move in on him as he walked up onto the small concrete porch and rang the doorbell. Chimes sounded faintly from deep inside the house. They played the first eight notes of that song from *Bridge on the River Kwai*, the one whose name Harper could never recall. Jimmy Fahey had once driven a car whose horn sounded those same notes.

A small woman about fifty, with a tan, seamed face and short gray hair opened the door. She looked as if she'd spent her entire life in the sun and was attractive in a way that overwhelmed wrinkles. Her hands were bedecked with half a dozen gaudy rings, most of them silver, and she was wearing a yellow blouse and dark brown shorts. She had very nice legs that were suntanned as dark as her face.

"I was told I could find Sam Sugar here."

She smiled. It deepened the seams in her face, yet somehow made her seem younger. "You look like a cop."

"I was, but I'm not now," Harper said. "I'm surprised it's still so obvious."

"You must never look in the mirror."

"Speaking of which," Harper said, "I understood this is a retirement community. You look too young—"

"Such a smooth talker," she interrupted, still with the smile. "Keep it up, keep it up."

"I mean, isn't there some kind of age requirement to live in a place like this?"

"You have to be fifty," she said. "I'm fifty-eight."

"You don't look it. Really."

"Sure I do. I'm just a good fifty-eight. I eat right and keep myself in condition. You look like you've taken care of yourself, too."

"Not lately," Harper said. "I've been busy."

She dropped her gaze, noticing his bad hand, but showed little change of expression.

The man in the photos Addleman had shown Harper in Philadelphia suddenly appeared just behind her from the dimness of the house's interior. As the exterior glare caught him, Harper saw that he looked even older and thinner than his digitalized photo and had lost most of his light brown hair. He was much paler than the woman, but who wasn't?

"We don't have to worry about the cops anymore, Laverne," he said to her. But he didn't sound so sure.

Laverne almost imperceptibly moved back, so she was touching him. "He says he isn't police," she told him.

"I'm not," Harper said. "My name's Will Harper. I used to be with the Bomb Squad in New York, but I'm retired. I saw your home page on the 'net. I'd like to talk to you about it."

Sugar studied him for a minute with emotionless eyes that hadn't yet realized they weren't still doing time. "Well, well. I was expecting to get my responses by e-mail. Lots of them. Reporters wanting to dig into the case. Public-spirited citizens wanting to express their outrage at the miscarriage of justice."

There was no mistaking the bitter amusement in his tone. "And there hasn't been much e-mail?"

"Not a single message. Instead I get an ex-cop on my doorstep." He shrugged. "Come on in out of the heat."

The interior of the house was quiet and cool. Cream-colored chairs and a sofa were arranged on a pale green carpet. A large, very bad oil painting of a waterfall hung on one wall, and a low, light oak coffee table with a clear glass jar of mints and a *Reader's Digest* and *Newsweek* on it sat in front of the sofa.

Sugar waved a hand for Harper to sit down, which he did, in one of the cream-colored chairs. They had very dark wood arms that didn't match the coffee table.

Sugar sat down on the sofa and crossed his legs, which must have been very thin inside his khaki pants. His white pullover shirt revealed slender but muscular arms. He was wearing tan loafers and white socks. As he crossed his arms, Harper saw what looked like a new gold wristwatch with a brown leather band.

Laverne had remained standing. "Can I get you something to drink, Mr. Harper?"

"Beer, if you have it," Harper said.

"Sam?" she asked.

"Same for me."

She hurried away to what Harper assumed was the kitchen.

Sugar's eyes followed her until she was out of the room. He said quietly to Harper, "Laverne and I wrote to each other when I was in prison. We fell in love. This is her place, but I plan to carry my part of the load. She's been great to me—*for* me. She kept my spirits up when I needed that real bad. And she even arranged a job for me, driving a van and picking up passengers going to and from the airport."

Harper was thinking that Sugar wasn't what he'd expected: a ranting nutcase. There was a sort of dignity about the man. It was possible to believe that he really was innocent, Harper thought. Possible to believe that Addleman's theory might turn out to be correct. He said to Sugar, "Maybe you're lucky, all in all."

"He is," Laverne said, returning with two tall glasses of beer on a tray. There was a third glass containing what looked like lemonade, with ice cubes and lemon wedges in it. It sure looked better than the beer. Harper wished now that he'd asked for lemonade.

She passed around the drinks, then sat down on the sofa next to Sugar. She seemed to want to be near him all the time, to protect him.

"I want to ask you some questions about the Blake bombing," Harper said.

Sugar gave a bitter laugh, almost a bark. "The real police sure as hell aren't interested in finding out who did it."

"You have any ideas?"

"None that hold water."

"I'm not the real police. I don't need a leakproof bucket."

"Jake Blake and I got to be friends when he moved into the apartment next to me in Los Angeles. He was a genuinely nice guy," Sugar said. "In fact, I don't know when I've met a nicer guy. He didn't have any enemies."

"You sure about that?" Harper asked neutrally.

Sugar gave a thin smile. "Yeah, obviously he had one. Guy who sent the bomb. But it couldn't have been anybody in our group in L.A. Everybody who knew Jake liked him. In show business you have lots of temporary friends. People who are using you, I mean. But Jake was a true friend. Especially to me."

"Didn't the police say you two got in a fight?"

Sugar was silent for a moment. He looked stricken at the memory. "Yeah. We had a big argument the week before he got the bomb. It was over some money he thought I owed him, and it was the only argument we ever had. He took a swing at me and broke my nose. I didn't even hit him back. I was too surprised. It was so unlike Jake. But he was starting to get really successful about then, and the assholes and hypocrites were all trying to get a piece of him."

It surprised Harper that Sugar could find any excuses for Jake Blake. "Didn't he testify against you at the trial?"

Again a memory made Sugar wince. He said, "Jake thought I was guilty. He wasn't alone. The fight—such as it was—made me a natural suspect, and my alibi was a married woman who chose to protect her husband and kids instead of me. She lied in court, told them I wasn't with her in San Francisco when the bomb was mailed from some little town in Arkansas, and that was the end of my defense."

"You got a lousy break," Harper said, suddenly feeling a pang of pity for the man.

"That's what Jake Blake told me on the phone, but he was being sarcastic."

"You've talked to Blake recently?"

"Tried to. 'Bout three months ago, right after I got out of the joint. He runs a coffee shop in the Valley. Encino. Been out of show business a long time. In fact, he never did get back into it after his injury. And he was good, too, he could've gone all the way. Guess I can't blame him for not wanting to talk to me."

Sugar was leaning forward, elbows on knees, staring intently at the wall behind Harper's head. His features were contorted with regret.

Suddenly, Harper understood. He said, "It's Blake you want to get square with, isn't it? More than you want to make the Court admit it was wrong. Or clear your name with the public. You want to prove to Blake that you didn't do it."

"I still think of him as my friend," said Sugar. "I can't stand him believing that I maimed him. Ruined his career."

Laverne had moved to stand close to Sugar's chair. He didn't notice her. He was intent on Harper. "Maybe you can help," said Sugar. "Why are you here, anyway? Do you have any idea who could have sent that bomb to Jake?"

Sugar wanted a reason to hope. But Harper had to be careful. If he mentioned the Celebrity Bomber to Sugar, and Sugar let it slip to the media, Harper would be in trouble. He had no authority to be going around the country asking questions—or that would be the way Special Agent Frances Wilson would see it.

Harper said slowly, "I think there might be a link between this case and one I worked on. But I have no idea of the bomber's identity at this point."

Sugar looked disappointed by this statement, but he accepted it. He set down his beer and stood up, with an effort. He looked older than his years. Frail.

Laverne moved closer to him, so that her hip was almost touching his, her nearness offering comfort and protection for Sugar. "Goodbye, Mr. Harper." She made it sound final; maybe she didn't approve of the home page and didn't want anything representing Sugar's old life to intrude into their new life together. That would be impossible, Harper knew, which was sad.

He got up and walked toward the front door. Sugar walked along with him. "You'll let me know how your investigation goes, won't you? Just send me e-mail. Please. It would mean a lot to me."

"All right."

"Where do you go from here?"

Harper didn't think it would do any harm to say. In any case, he felt that Sugar had already guessed. "Encino. To talk to Blake."

Sugar opened the door. He smiled bitterly. "I'd say give him my regards, but he won't want to hear a damn thing about me."

23

Markman had been in show business once. He seldom thought about it, because to remember was to be overwhelmed with disgust for the stupidity of his younger self. But he didn't regret having learned about costume and makeup and playing a role. The skills came in handy sometimes.

As he sat in the waiting room, scanning the headlines in the Washington *Post* the receptionist had given him, he was confident that he looked the part. He'd lavished time and money on today's costume. He'd had to, for he was playing a rich man. The maroon tie was silk, the blue shirt Egyptian cotton. The gray glen plaid suit from Brooks Brothers was a lightweight wool blend. Markman had selected it because he'd expected warm weather in Washington. As usual, his preparations paid off. He'd noticed as he rode around the streets that the cherry blossoms were gone already and summer was almost here. And it wasn't even May yet.

Not quite.

Another thing he'd noticed since his arrival in the capital was that security seemed heavier than usual. There had been long lines at the airport checkpoints, and he'd been just as glad that his own bags held nothing incriminating, that his purpose on this trip was only reconnaissance. At the hotel, the clerks had subjected his fake credit card and driver's license to a long scrutiny. Though he'd prepared this identity carefully and was confident it would stand up, the delay had annoyed him. And everywhere he went around the city he saw armed guards.

It made him worry a bit, made him ask himself if the authorities could somehow have guessed that Washington was the Celebrity Bomber's next target.

Markman was pleased with the name they had given him. He liked the pun: Not only did he target celebrities, he was a celebrity himself, an object of fear and anger, of nervous jokes and unending speculation. Because no one knew anything about him.

Every time he thought it all over, that was the conclusion he reached. The FBI had no leads to his identity, no clue as to where he would strike next. If security in Washington was heavier than usual, it was only because the city was full of pompous windbags who felt that their miserable lives were indispensable to the Republic, and were willing to spend the taxpayers' money to protect themselves.

A woman's voice broke in on his thoughts. "Andrew Marshall?"

Markman stood up at once, smiling and folding his newspaper. He always chose an alias that sounded similar to his own name, in order to eliminate the risk of being suspiciously slow to respond when someone hailed him.

The woman shook his hand and introduced herself. She was Molly Nathan, a little blond with a warm, sincere smile. That smile irritated Markman at once, and he knew he was going to be seeing a lot more of it. He supposed she was typical of the low-level fundraising executives who conducted tours for the sort of wealthy prospective donor he was pretending to be.

"Before we go in, let me give you a little orientation," she said, and launched into a well-honed spiel. "The purpose of Constant Light Children's Hospital is to treat the children of war, innocents who have been wounded in conflicts in which they bore no interest or responsibility. The hospital's patients are from almost every continent and of almost every race and culture. Our work is funded entirely by donations from people like yourself—private individuals of many nationalities who are concerned about the welfare of children. We accept no government funds. Politics stops at the door of Constant Light, and humanity takes over."

It was fulsome stuff, and Markman had to struggle to keep the straight face appropriate to Andrew Marshall. He'd laid the groundwork for this visit carefully, sending letters on expensive, embossed stationary, dropping names judiciously. The identity of Marshall, a wealthy commodities trader from Chicago, was thin, but good enough for the purpose. Institutions tended to check cursorily on people who might give them sizable checks. Pledges might be carried through on, or might not, but each potential donor had to be treated with respect.

As Molly Nathan showed him through the hospital, he didn't pay much attention to the children with missing or permanently damaged limbs, or those whose physical infirmities were eclipsed by the flatness of their voices and expressions and the sad and stunned eyes that still saw, and were deadened to horror. He was really more interested in the building's design and construction, in stress points and load-bearing walls.

He had to remind himself that the usual structural principles would apply, because Constant Light didn't look like the usual hospital. Its floors were carpeted in bright hues, and long multicolored arrows were painted along the corridors to show people the way to various departments. The personnel were just as colorful as the decor. None of the doctors and nurses were wearing white. In their blue, green, or red scrubsuits, with cords knotted around their waists, they looked like kids at a slumber party rather than medical specialists. Still, he noticed that everyone displayed an identity badge. This was a detail he'd have to remember in making his plan.

Molly Nathan broke stride beside him, turning to him with that irritating smile. He realized that he hadn't spoken in a while. Better ask a question.

"I do wonder, Ms. Nathan—is it a wise use of funds to bring these children all the way to Washington for treatment? Wouldn't the money be better spent improving the facilities in their home countries, where they could be looked after by their own families and communities?"

Molly Nathan's bright eyes showed she was ready for that one, but she moderated her voice to project a note of solemnity. "The children of these families have been shattered by war, Mr. Marshall. So have their communities. In some cases, the very countries of which they used to be citizens have been wiped off the map. We are their last hope."

Molly Nathan paused, as a girl of seven or so walked past them. She was wearing the bright flowery pajamas they issued to all patients, and carrying a paper cup. The expression on the small face was purposeful. The smile returned to Molly's face. "Oh, there's Nadia. Come along."

They followed the girl down the corridor and into a room, where another patient was lying on the bed. The figure was so heavily bandaged Markman couldn't guess the age or sex.

Molly was whispering to him. "That's Theresa, Nadia's twin sister. They were asleep in their bedroom in Sarajevo when a mortar shell hit the house. They were only a few feet apart, yet Nadia had only minor injuries, while Theresa—well, you can see."

The girl lying on the bed had no left arm. The left side of her face showed signs of extensive skin-grafting; the incisions had not yet healed. She had a patch covering what was obviously an empty left eye socket and her ear on that side was deformed. It was a cauliflower ear such as boxers get. The explosion had crushed it as precisely as a blow from a fist.

"Fascinating," Markman murmured.

"It is fascinating, the way a child's mind works," said Molly. "I think poor Nadia feels guilty because of her escape. She tries to look after Theresa herself. She imitates the nurses."

The unharmed girl was cradling the other's head, helping her to drink from the paper cup. Molly continued to talk, but Markman wasn't listening. He was speculating on the endlessly complex effects of blast. What an extraordinary explosion this one must have been. That it should hit one person so hard while missing the other almost entirely was unusual, but not unprecedented; Markman had heard of similar cases. But that it had affected only the one side of the one victim's body was unique in his experience. How big had the mortar shell been, he wondered. What was the floor plan of the house? He would have given a lot to see a reconstruction, showing the relative positions of the two girls and the point of impact of the shell. Perhaps a doorway had been placed at just the right angle to admit the force of the blast, allowing it to fall on the left side of the one girl's body. Markman remembered a painting he'd been admiring at the National Gallery that morning, a Vermeer, in which a shaft of light had fallen across a dark interior, illuminating the face and neck and bosom of a lovely girl. The explosion had been like that. Markman marveled at this demonstration of precision and power.

"Fate is so capricious," Molly was saying.

Fate might be, Markman thought, but there was nothing capricious about blast. Blast was predictable. Manageable. A tool in the hands of a master craftsman.

"Would you like to talk to Nadia?" Molly asked. "She knows some English."

Markman turned away and went out into the hall.

"What's down that direction?"

"Beyond that door is the administration wing."

"I'd like to see it."

"But it's just offices."

Markman smiled. "Well, if you don't mind, as long as I'm here I'd like a thorough tour of the building. Including the basement."

"The basement?" She looked puzzled. Perhaps even a shade reluctant.

"Yes. You see, when I make a donation, I make it for a specific purpose. And it's my experience that charitable organizations sometimes neglect their physical plant. If you take me all around I might see something specific I'll want to help you out with."

"We can make the tour as thorough as you wish, Mr. Marshall." The talk about his donation restored Molly's smile, as he'd known it would. She led him down the corridor at a brisk clip. "You know, if you do decide to add your name to our roll of benefactors, you'll be in very distinguished company."

"I'm sure," said Markman.

"Some of the most prominent people in this country and around the world are proud to count themselves as friends of Constant Light Hospital—"

"Yes, yes," muttered Markman, moving a step ahead of her as they went through a set of swinging doors. He found this woman's crude attempt at bribery disgusting. Even though Andrew Marshall was in her view a successful, hard-headed businessman, she thought he could be dazzled by the notion that in handing over his check he was joining a company of famous people. Such was the power of celebrity. It sickened Markman.

Molly hustled after him through the doors. "In fact, the honorary Chairwoman of our Board of Benefactors is—"

That name, of all names. Markman simply had to cut her off before she said it; he'd only just had lunch. "Yes, I know who she is. What's down that way?"

"Secretarial offices," said Molly shortly. Her smile had slipped again; she seemed annoyed by his lack of interest. No doubt it was unusual. The fame of the hospital's Chairwoman could turn even sensible people into awed and giggly fans.

"Did you know that she's going to be here in just two weeks? She's going to tour the hospital and meet with the trustees. Just think— she'll be walking right where we're walking now." Molly looked down at the floor tiles that were about to receive this unparalleled honor.

Now Markman did turn. He was surprised that an employee of the hospital would give out this information so freely. But the visit was no secret, after all. He said, "Really? What's the exact date?"

"May fifteenth," replied Molly.

Markman had only been mildly curious to see if she would give out the date. He wasn't prepared for the impact of hearing it spoken aloud, after he'd been preparing for it, directing all his efforts toward it for so long. He felt a cold pang of excitement deep in his gut.

Molly noticed the change in his expression. She thought she had hooked him at last. Putting on a phony sympathetic smile, she said, "I'm terribly sorry, but there's no way I can promise you an invitation to the reception now. They all went out weeks ago."

"What a shame," Markman said.

"She doesn't visit us as often as we'd like," Molly went on. "People are so excited!"

For the first time, Markman smiled back at Molly Nathan.

"I'm sure the event will even surpass your expectations," he said.

24

Harper caught an overnight bus from Phoenix to Los Angeles, saving both airfare and a hotel bill. He didn't know how far he would have to make Addleman's meager funds stretch. And Harper didn't mind. Once a man had trained himself to doze off in the Duty Room of the NYPD Bomb Squad, he could sleep anywhere.

At the Public Library in downtown L.A. he consulted phonebooks and made calls, trying to locate Jake Blake's coffee shop.

The sixth call accomplished that. Blake wasn't in the shop yet himself, but the woman who answered the phone told Harper he was expected within the hour. Harper thanked her and hung up. He considered taking a cab, but Encino was so far away that he figured renting a car would be cheaper.

Harper waited until ten, when the breakfast crowd would be gone from Midnight Espresso, as the coffee shop was called, before driving to its address on Hobbie Avenue.

On each side of the street were low, stucco buildings containing small retail shops and offices. Everything looked clean and bright in the brilliant morning sun. Midnight Espresso shared a pastel green building with a second-hand clothing shop and a portrait photographer who was promoting a sale on family shots. Half a dozen Brady Bunch-type groupings smiled dazzlingly at Harper as he walked past the show window then took a step up and pushed open the thick, stained oak door to the coffee shop.

It was bright but cool inside. Sunlight poured down from skylights and through the wide windows. The tables were small and round and topped with artificial veined marble. The chairs looked like used wooden schoolroom chairs. There was a stainless steel counter with stools, and behind it a glass case displaying doughnuts and bagels. Off to the right was a rack display of small, hand-labeled paper sacks containing gourmet coffee, next to it a shiny, oversize machine where customers could grind beans to their liking. Midnight Espresso smelled strongly and pleasantly of fresh-brewed coffee.

There were only two customers, an old man in a Dodgers T-shirt, and a bored-looking teenage girl, seated at a table near the fancy grinding machine. A tall Hispanic woman was wiping down tables. Behind the counter stood a wiry man in his mid forties, with vivid blue eyes and wildly curly blond hair that reminded Harper of Harpo Marx. He was wearing a white shirt and a whiter apron. A newspaper he was reading was spread out before him on the counter. As Harper watched, the man adroitly turned a page with a prosthetic right hand.

"Jake Blake," Harper said, smiling and taking a stool at the counter.

Blake looked at him and smiled back. It was a winning smile; Harper could easily believe what Sugar had told him about Blake being a nice guy. "I'm sorry, I don't—have we met?" Blake asked.

"Sam Sugar told me about you," Harper said.

Blake's eyes narrowed with suspicion. "You an attorney?"

"Not hardly."

"Cop?"

"Used to be. On the Bomb Squad. Just a private citizen now."

"I heard about that home page of Sugar's. Don't tell me you got sucked in?" Blake's voice did not sound scornful or indignant. Instead, he seemed to feel a little sorry for Harper.

"Clearing Sugar isn't my main purpose, if that's what you mean. I'm a private citizen looking into long-ago bombings, to see if they might tie in with more recent ones."

Blake considered for a moment, then said, "The Celebrity Bomber?"

Startled, Harper said quickly, "What makes you think that?"

Blake grinned and pointed southward. "Hollywood's just the other side of those mountains. Fella goes around blowing up celebrities, it hits us close to home." He folded the newspaper and slid it aside on the counter. "You aren't thinking what happened to me—my hand— all those years ago has anything to do with the Celebrity Bomber, are you?"

"You're the one who brought up the Celebrity Bomber, Mr. Blake. I haven't said anything."

Blake's amusement deepened. "You don't have to. 'Cause I remember now who you are. I've been following the case. You're that New York cop. Harper."

He leaned over the counter to look pointedly at Harper's maimed hand. Harper wasn't offended. He figured Blake's own injury gave him certain privileges. He said, "I'd appreciate it if you'd keep our discussion private."

"What—you're afraid I'm gonna call some reporter? Try to get my name in the paper? Don't worry. I've had my fifteen minutes of fame. Though it felt like a lot less." A shadow of sadness crossed Blake's face. It was gone almost before Harper saw it.

"Thanks."

"Let's shake on it," Blake said, smiling again.

He held out his prosthetic hand. Harper took it with his maimed one. It felt smooth, dry, and cool.

"Does just about anything a real one would, and I never have to worry about burning it on the stove," Blake said. "Ain't science amazing?"

"I'm envious."

"Don't be." Withdrawing his hand, Blake went on, "Anyway Sugar couldn't be the Celebrity Bomber. He was in prison when most of the bomber's victims died."

"I never thought he was," Harper said.

Blake stared, then shook his head. "Whatever it is you think, if it'll help you any, there isn't any doubt that Sugar sent the bomb to me."

"You two were friends. What makes you so sure he did it?"

"We had a fight."

"Way Sugar tells it, you hit him and he didn't hit back."

"Oh, he was mad all right," said Blake. "Only he let it fester inside. Brooded. Worked out a sneaky way to get back at me, hurt me much worse than I hurt him."

"He still claims he's innocent. Claims it should have been someone else doing that long stretch in prison."

Blake looked uncomfortable. "I guess he's pretty bitter. Maybe I better be careful about opening my mail."

"He doesn't blame you. In fact, what seems to bother him the most is that you believe in his guilt. In a way, he still seems to think of you as a friend."

"Sounds like he convinced you."

"I think he's innocent."

Blake was strongly affected by these words. He was blinking his large blue eyes rapidly and his lips were compressed. After a moment he burst out, "It had to be Sugar. Why would the Celebrity Bomber pick me for a target?"

"You were in show business."

"I was just getting started. A couple appearances on cable TV, that was all—and back then there weren't that many people who had cable."

"That might have been enough."

Blake continued to look intently at Harper. He was thinking fast. Abruptly he straightened up and smiled. "Now, wait. It's coming back to me. Sugar had to be the one who did it. Know why?"

Harper shook his head.

"The bomb came to my unlisted home address. Only people who knew me personally knew that address. It had to be Sugar. Couldn't have been the Celebrity Bomber."

"Even unlisted addresses can be discovered."

"Sure, but I was really careful about telling anyone where I lived. I had this idea at the time that I was on the cusp of stardom and wanted to preserve my privacy as long as possible."

Harper swiveled slightly on his stool, toward the window, and watched the traffic pass out on Hobbie. He didn't want Blake to see how excited he was. Maybe, just maybe, this was the break he and Addleman had been hoping for—a link between the bomber and one of his victims. Suppose the bomber had known Blake personally? Suppose he too was in show business?

Could his deep, abiding hatred of all celebrities have grown out of simple envy for one rival's success?

It was a possibility—but at this stage only a possibility. If the bomber was someone Blake knew, he'd made a bad mistake in sending the package to the unlisted address. The kind of mistake the meticulous planner who'd killed Buckner and Rogers would never have made. But fifteen years ago, when he was young and inexperienced, he might have been capable of such a blunder. He'd been lucky the police had Sugar to fix their suspicions on, and his luck had lasted fifteen years.

Maybe now it was starting to turn on him.

Harper turned back to Blake. This was the crucial question, but he laid no special stress on it. "How many people had your address, Jake?"

Blake shrugged. "Just my agent, my doctor, a few friends. The LAPD checked 'em all out at the time. They were in the clear, except for Sugar."

"What about friends outside of L.A., people you wrote to?"

"Well, there's my mom and dad back in Paducah, but I don't think they sent me the bomb."

Blake gave the line a flawless deadpan delivery. Harper figured he must once have been a pretty good comic. "Paducah? Is that where you were living before you moved to L.A.?"

"No. I had a room in St. Louis, but really I was living in my car. Traveling all over the Midwest, working the clubs. I was at the Crazy Bone in Chicago when I got the call from the coast." Blake's eyes widened. Even now, the memory of getting that call could still excite him.

"Do you remember any of the people who were appearing with you? Did you know them well?"

"Oh, sure. There was a group of us from around St. Louis who often appeared together. We knew a lot of the same booking agents and managers, and whenever one of us got a job, he'd put in a good word for the others. Those were great days. We were great friends."

Blake was showing every tooth he had in a broad smile, and his blue eyes looked a bit misty. Harper was reminded of the famous comics he saw acting warm and wonderful on TV talk shows—except that Jake Blake actually seemed to be sincere.

"How did your friends react when you got that call from the coast?"

"Everybody was happy for me. It was the kind of break we were all praying for. Because it *is* such a rough business, most young performers root for each other."

Harper looked down to hide a skeptical smile. Well, Sam Sugar had told him that Blake was a nice guy. Was it possible that he was himself so free of jealousy and cynicism that he found it hard to believe another human might have resented his lucky break enough to want to kill him for it?

"Who were the other performers at the Crazy Bone?" Harper asked.

"A singer, Belinda Warren. And three other comics: Jackie Davis, Silky Simms, and Darren Snow. We all did standup routines, some improv. We didn't play to sellout crowds, but we did okay."

Harper finished writing the names in his spiral notebook. "Try to remember. How exactly did they react when you told them you were going to Hollywood?"

Jake Blake became somber. "None of them sent me the bomb."

"Just try to remember, Mr. Blake."

Blake looked pained. "I'd hate to accuse anyone . . ."

"Just tell me. Are you sure all of them were happy about your success?"

Blake looked down at the counter. "Maybe not Darren Snow."

"Tell me about him."

"Now don't get me wrong," said Blake hastily. "Darren was perfectly okay to work with. I didn't think he was that talented, but that's just my opinion. He was very professional."

"But—" Harper prodded.

"He was just kinda strange. I never saw him except when we were working. He lived in St. Louis too, but I never knew where. He didn't hang out with the rest of us. We thought he had some kind of problem at home, but he wouldn't talk about it."

"And his reaction to your success?"

"Oh, he patted me on the back, made jokes about smog and sunburn just like everybody else, but I could tell he was dying inside. He was never happy about anybody else's success."

"Why not?"

" 'Cause he thought it ought to be his. He thought he was a lot better comic than he really was." Blake straightened up and shrugged to lighten his thoughts. "But who am I to judge? I don't get half the jokes on *Seinfeld*. Darren was an okay guy."

Harper put away his notebook. He figured he'd better get out of here before the charitable Jake Blake took back everything he'd said. "Thank you for your time. I suppose you wouldn't happen to know where Snow or any of the others are now?"

"We haven't kept in touch. None of them made it big, of course, or I would've heard about it. They're probably long out of show business, like me." An unpleasant thought struck Blake. He said quickly, "Listen, I wouldn't want the cops to come down on Darren or Belinda or any of them because of what I said—"

Blake's niceness was starting to get on Harper's nerves. He interrupted, "Wouldn't you want to see Sam Sugar cleared—if he didn't do it?"

The candid blue eyes opened wide and the blond brows rose toward his hairline. "All these years his guilt's the one thing I've been sure about. But if he's actually innocent, then yes, I want to see him cleared."

Harper got up from his stool. With a nod to Blake, he started to turn away.

"Wait," Blake said. "I don't know much about computers, but my kid's got the modem and the whole setup. Is there any way to—"

"You're thinking of writing to Sugar?"

"Well, maybe. If I can figure out the software."

"I wouldn't let software stand in your way," said Harper, smiling as he turned away.

From a pay phone at the airport, he phoned Addleman in Philadelphia and filled him in on what he'd learned.

There was a long pause after he finished. Then Addleman said, "The bomber a failed comic, motivated by envy? Is that what you think? I don't know if I like the idea, Will."

"That's because it's too simple for you."

Addleman gave his wheezing chuckle. "Lots of people fail in show business. But they don't become killers. There's going to be a lot more to the bomber, even if your theory's right."

"It is just a theory," Harper admitted.

"I'd still put money on us rather than the Bureau," Addleman shot back, in an exasperated tone.

"Been talking to your informant in Behavioral Sciences?"

Addleman sighed. "The FBI is looking for Vedic astrologers."

"Uh-huh. Where do you look for a Vedic astrologer?"

"India. The constellation we call Aquila has an entirely different significance over there. In fact, it has manifold significances. There's a Special Agent on the plane to Calcutta right now."

"Good luck to him," said Harper, "but I think I'll try Chicago. The Crazy Bone comedy club is still listed in the phone book. I'll see what I can find there. You fire up your modem and see if you can collect any information on our four names."

"I'll phone you as soon as I come up with anything, Will."

"I'll phone *you*," Harper said. "From Chicago."

At ten o'clock that evening, Harper was walking into his room at an old hotel west of the Chicago Loop. It was a little seedy, but the price was right. And it did have a bed—the first real bed he had to sleep in since he left home. He sat on it and called Addleman.

Addleman answered on the fifth ring. He sounded tired.

"I've been busy," he said.

"With results?" Harper was weary himself, and would have stretched out on the bed to talk to Addleman if he hadn't been afraid of falling asleep with the receiver pressed to his ear.

"Some. Belinda Warren is deceased. Cancer. 1989."

"What about the other names?"

"Jackie Davis is a heroin addict, in and out of clinics for the past ten years. He still does club comedy, when he isn't in recovery. There's nothing in his past suggesting he'd know how to build a bomb, and at the time of Speed Rogers's death he was in Holy Ghost Rehabilitation, a Catholic center for drug addicts in New Jersey. He couldn't even feed himself, much less construct and plant a bomb."

"So Davis is out," Harper said. "What else do you have?"

"It gets better, Will. Silky Simms is one Sylvester Simms. He got out of show business and into burglary not long after the Jake Blake bombing. He's been in and out of prison; he's out now. And his other free time coincides with the other Celebrity Bombings."

"Hmm. Got an address on Simms?"

"Yeah. He's back in St. Louis." Addleman gave Harper the street and number.

Harper was thinking that it would sadden the affable Jake Blake to find out how badly his old friends had fared in life. He said, "What about Darren Snow?"

"He doesn't seem to exist," Addleman replied.

"That's interesting."

"Frustrating, is what it is. I checked with Actors Equity, figuring it might be a stage name, but Snow isn't in their records. It's as if he never existed except as a performer at the Crazy Bone years ago. I have to admit, I'm stymied."

"Maybe I can find out something at the Crazy Bone."

"We'll see. The really interesting name came up when I got into the old newspaper ads for the Crazy Bone. Seems there was a singer who filled Jake Blake's spot when he went to L.A. Amy Arthur—her real name. She finished the run Blake was supposed to have at the club, then sang there for another month."

"Is she still singing?"

"Nope. That's the interesting thing about her. For the last eleven years she's been doing secretarial work at a quarry near Lakeville, Illinois. I don't have to tell you what they do at quarries, do I, Will?"

"No, you don't. They blast."

"Exactly. Amy has access to explosives. I like Silky Simms for the bomber. Like him very much. But we definitely should look into Amy."

"Maybe there's still a connection between Simms and Amy," Harper said.

"Could be. They're still living in the same area. After you're done there in Chicago, I suggest you fly to St. Louis. And from there you can drive to Lakeville."

Harper didn't want to think about any more traveling right now. He swung his feet up on the bed. Lying down made him even more tired, as he'd feared. He forgot about unpacking.

"Hey, I heard from another friend at the Bureau," Addleman was saying. "He's in the Investigative Support Unit. Seems that the day after the Rogers blast, Frances ordered every Dumpster from every motel within twenty miles of Elmhart brought in. See, they didn't know which motel the bomber was staying in, if any, and they didn't want any garbage that might be his to go away with the regular collection. They figured that once they established which motel he was in, they'd airlift the relevant Dumpster to the FBI labs for examination. Only they still haven't been able to establish which motel it was."

"Why are you telling me this, Harold?"

"Well, you were sounding kind of tired, and I wanted you to know it could be worse. At least you don't have thirty-one full and reeking garbage dumpsters to deal with. You know how warm it was in Indiana today?"

"Thanks, Addleman. I appreciate the thought."

He barely managed to return the phone to its cradle before falling asleep.

25

Three hundred miles to the south, in St. Louis, Markman was spending a quiet evening at home.

He lived in a small brick house, almost indistinguishable from the other modest houses on the block. The architecture was vaguely Gothic, with ornate stonework around the front door, arched brick window openings, and a steeply pitched orange tile roof. Behind the house, at the end of a narrow gravel driveway, was a brick two-car garage whose architecture echoed that of the house.

The living room Markman sat in was small and had stained glass windows on either side of a tiny nonfunctional fireplace. The furniture was traditional and rather austere and uncomfortable. The TV was the exception to the reserved and unimaginative furnishings. It was a newer model, sleek woodtone with a 35-inch screen and built-in stereo speakers. On top of the TV sat a framed photo of a slim, smiling woman with short blond hair. She was seated gracefully before a mirrored vanity lined with cosmetic bottles, wearing only a modest pale slip, and appeared to have been surprised while getting dressed to go out. The amusement in her direct stare, and the high lace bust line of her slip, robbed the photo of any eroticism and lent it a casual innocence.

On the TV screen, the local news had just come on. Markman settled back and watched.

Adroitly finishing each other's sentences, the male and female news anchors described how St. Louis notables were taking precautions against the Celebrity Bomber. The Cardinals' brilliant young shortstop, who was having an all-star season, was under twenty-four-hour guard. A famous overweight actor who'd made it big in Hollywood but still had hometown ties was vacationing in South Africa. Nilly Dames, a comedian who played local clubs and had done some TV talk shows, had invested in an armored sedan once owned by a famous East St. Louis gangster. Markman smiled, thinking that was the only really funny thing Dames had ever done.

Were they truly afraid of him? Markman doubted it. More likely they were just hitching their wagons to his star. Their agents and managers had convinced them that they could get a little more publicity by linking themselves to the Celebrity Bomber.

When he'd been young and stupid, Markman had craved fame so desperately. Now he had it. Everywhere he turned he would see people reacting to his deeds—with fear or outrage, with edgy humor or sneaking admiration. But the paramount emotions were wonder and curiosity. What would the bomber do next?

Just wait, Markman thought, and you'll see.

The female anchor turned to the weatherman and started bantering about the unseasonable heat. So that was the end of the bomber news for tonight. Markman's brow furrowed with annoyance—not because he enjoyed listening to those idiots yammer about him, but because he'd been hoping for something more.

Some mention of Ex-Sergeant William Harper.

He'd been rattled when he first learned the identity of the man he'd glimpsed on the Courthouse steps in Elmhart, just before he set off the bomb. So rattled that he'd taken the trouble to obtain a tape of Harper's appearance before the press, outside Indiana State Police Headquarters. The former New York cop had looked exhausted under the glaring lights. The reporters pressed in close, shouting questions at him. But he still had the quality of calmness, of self-control, that Markman had observed at the Courthouse. He answered the questions concisely, in a firm voice. He'd even used his right hand to point to the next questioner, as if its mutilated state did not shame him.

When Harper explained that his knowledge of bomb-making had led him to link the murders of Sothern, Wylie, and Buckner, Markman listened with mixed emotions. He was badly frightened that he'd been detected, of course. That wasn't in the plan. No one was supposed to know until May 15, when the pattern would be complete. But the odd thing was that he also felt a strange affinity for Harper. It was almost like gratitude. Here at last was someone who understood his handiwork. Who appreciated it.

He and Harper spoke the same language.

What Harper had to say in the rest of the press conference was reassuring to Markman. He didn't know *that* much. What had led him to guess that Rogers was the next target was only a lucky guess—some nonsense about how the talk-show host's abrasive manner might affect an unbalanced criminal personality. The usual pop-psych nonsense that had nothing to do with Markman. Harper didn't know about the Aquila pattern.

Still, after viewing the tape, Markman was convinced that his first instinct about Harper had been right. The ex-cop was potential trouble. He had to be discouraged from interfering any further.

So before going to Washington to visit the Constant Light Hospital, Markman had stopped off in New York. It had taken two full days of surveillance and research before he decided how he would convey his warning to Harper. After that, gaining entry to the house and rewiring the drill had been easy enough.

Markman had to assume that Harper had understood the message. There'd been no mention of him in the media at all, except for a few stale background stories about his career in the NYPD. Having seen what the bomber could do to him, Harper was lying low.

Or was he?

It was always the unknown factor that made Markman nervous. And it was always his work that calmed him. Time to go to work now, he thought.

He switched off the TV and went into the kitchen, where he paused to drink a glass of tap water before going out the back door. It was his seventh, and there would be one more at bedtime. Markman drank eight glasses of water at regular intervals every day, just as the health experts advised.

The night was warm and clear, and the stars seemed as bright and huge as in the Van Gogh paintings Markman had always admired. Insects droned in the nearby shrubbery, signaling that the world was turning in unison with the rest of the universe, and the natural laws of motion and fate were as intact and inevitable as always. Markman had always admired the perfect timeliness and definitiveness of the heavens and was something of an expert amateur in the science of astronomy. The stars and planets in their arrangement and movement were to him like cosmic clockwork, something that could be counted on for eternity. He knew that as long as he acted with the same mathematical precision and certainty as the heavenly bodies in their irresistible, predestined courses, all would be well for him. The result of his intent would be as inevitable as fate. Science as destiny.

The science of explosives.

As he walked along the driveway toward the garage, he fished in his hip pocket for his key ring.

Markman's car was parked in a widened gravel area off to the side of the driveway. He never parked in the garage. In fact, the garage's thick overhead door was bolted and locked permanently on the inside, disconnected from the automatic opener. On the side of the garage was a door whose small framed windows had been painted the same white as the wood. The door was firmly secured with a dead bolt lock, as well as with a thick hasp and large padlock.

After working both locks with the same key, Markman opened the door and stepped into the garage, hitting the light switch.

Bright overhead fluorescent fixtures flickered on. The garage's single window had been painted over like those in the door, and Markman knew that no light escaped. From outside, the garage seemed unoccupied.

Markman relocked the dead bolt and smiled, breathing in deeply, comforted by his secret place, where he used to come to escape from the pressures inflicted on him by the world. Where he could be himself.

Along one wall of the garage was a long wooden workbench equipped with a series of vises and clamps. On the wall itself was a Peg-Board on which hung gleaming precision hand tools. On another wall hung power tools. A second workbench supported an electric band saw with a small lathe attachment, a press drill, a set of steel miter boxes. Both workbenches were equipped with powerful work lights on flexible steel elbows. The lamp on the bench near the hand tools had a built-in magnifier with a universal swivel. There were drawers in the bench containing electricians' tools and supplies, and an engraver for doing delicate close work beneath the magnifier. On shelves beneath the bench were calipers, grinders, soldering guns, and a small welding torch. On the third wall, near the main workbench, was a table on which sat a computer with software programmed by Markman to calculate blast force and angle to a remarkably accurate degree, and to project damage. Markman could direct blast force to ricochet and focus almost with the narrow efficacy of a bullet. At show business he was a failure, but at bomb-making he'd become more than a success—he was an artist.

In the garage that had been converted into a high-tech bomb factory, Markman switched on a small portable radio, tuned it to a station that played hits from the eighties, and sat down at the main workbench. He felt an irrational reluctance to begin work on this project, because it was the last. He would soon be finished with this room, in which he'd spent so many contented hours. He opened a drawer and riffled through some papers, then got out and studied the schematic he'd carefully drafted.

This will do, he told himself. This will more than do.

Planning was of course only the initial stage. But it was the most important. If he planned assiduously, he would always succeed. The confluence of time and effort and desire and destiny would always be more than a match for anyone trying to prevent him from making his kill.

He decided to work late tonight. It was time to begin construction of the final bomb. For this one he'd use all the remaining C-4. Just as well for his stolid South St. Louis neighbors, he thought, that they didn't know that for the last few weeks there had been enough plastic explosive stored in this garage to level the entire block.

He lost himself in his work, as always, ceasing even to be conscious of the music playing on the radio. It was only the voice announcing the midnight newsbreak that got his attention. He got up and went to the other end of the workbench, where his calendar rested. He crossed off today's date, April 30.

At last it was May.

26

Harper spent the morning in his hotel room, watching television. He was waiting for a callback from the Crazy Bone Comedy Club. He'd called them earlier and found out the club had gone through several changes of ownership. The woman who answered the phone said that she didn't know who had been managing the club fifteen years ago, but she'd try to find out and call him back. Harper believed her. On previous visits to Chicago he'd found people to be generally pleasant and helpful. The Second City was a lot friendlier than the First.

While he waited, he called Laura, catching her just as she was coming in from another night shift at the hospital. They didn't talk for long. After he hung up there was nothing to do but sit in the armchair facing the big color television and channel-surf.

He flicked aimlessly until the familiar face of Special Agent Frances Wilson appeared on the screen. She was being interviewed at her desk in the Bureau's Indianapolis Field Office. The reporter was pointing out that she'd closed down virtually the entire town of Elmhart for several days and mobilized the National Guard to collect debris from the explosion. He wanted to know if she'd found out anything to justify the expense and inconvenience.

Frances handled the sharp questioning well. It didn't surprise Harper to see that she was good with the media. When she said she wasn't going to comment—which she did several times—her tone implied that she knew a lot more than she was telling.

But did she?

That was what Harper wondered. Addleman thought the investigation was getting nowhere, but he still had bitter feelings about the Bureau. Harper thought that with all the resources Frances Wilson was able to deploy, she must be making progress. He hoped so, anyway. Because all *he* was doing was chasing a theory.

The phone rang. It was the cooperative woman at the Crazy Bone. She'd made some calls and found out that the manager in the early eighties had been a man named Bill Oates. He hadn't gone far. Oates was currently managing another nightclub in the River North area, within walking distance of Harper's hotel.

After the heat out west, Harper was glad to get back to a part of the country where the beginning of May was still early spring. The sun was shining, but it was chilly in the shadows of the skyscrapers. A strong, gritty wind was blowing in off the lake.

It also felt good—at least to a New York native like Harper—to be walking busy sidewalks again after driving around the barren suburbs of the west. He took Wacker Drive to the Chicago River, a narrow stream that hardly seemed to justify the labor of constructing so many handsome and solid bridges across it. Harper went over one of these and was in River North.

The buildings were older and smaller here. It was an agreeable mix of shops and offices with restaurants and nightclubs. The windows of Bill Oates's club were dark, as was its neon sign, and Harper almost walked right by it. A sign said the club didn't open until six, but the door was unlocked. He went in.

The sun pouring through the windows did a good job of stripping the room of every vestige of showbiz glamour. The chairs had been stacked on the tables, and an elderly black man in overalls, who moved as if he had a sore back, was running a vacuum cleaner over the carpet. The stale smell of last night's spilled beer and cigarette smoke still hung in the air. Without lights, the stage at the far end of the room looked like the mouth of a pit.

The man noticed Harper and switched off his machine. "Help you?"

"Looking for Bill Oates?"

"Upstairs, last door on the right. I wouldn't go up there 'less you really need to see him. Mr. Oates doesn't want to be disturbed today."

"I'll have to fight my way past a secretary to see him, you mean?"

"Mr. Oates don't need a secretary. He can be plenty rude all by himself."

"Thanks for the warning."

As Harper mounted the stairs, the sound of the vacuum cleaner resumed. He saw that the door at the end of the hall was standing open.

Bill Oates had a small, cluttered office. His desk was turned toward the window, probably so he could enjoy the view of Marina Towers. He was sitting with his back to the door, so all Harper could see of him was a head of tousled light-brown hair, broad shoulders in a red golf shirt, and hairy, muscular forearms. He was flipping through a stack of papers and muttering to himself.

"Excuse me, Mr. Oates?"

Oates swiveled the chair around. His face looked twenty years older than his hair, seamed and pouched, with long grooves running from the nostrils to the corners of his mouth. His eyes were cold.

"What is it? Who're you?"

"My name's Will Harper. I just want to ask you a few questions—"

"No time today. One of my acts for tonight just canceled." He turned away, reaching for his phone.

Harper rounded the desk to stand in his line of vision. "This won't take long. I'd appreciate—"

"Son of a bitch cancels eight hours before he's supposed to go on," Oates grumbled as he stabbed at the phone's keypad with his forefinger. "Says his mother's dying. But I know comics. What that really means is he's lined up a better booking."

"How do you know?"

"You kidding? A comic turns down a booking just because his mother's dying? Forget it!" Oates must have gotten a busy signal, because he grimaced and slammed the phone down. "So what do you want?"

"I'm interested in some performers who appeared at the Crazy Bone in the early eighties—"

"The Crazy Bone. The early eighties." Oates rolled his eyes. "I'll save us some time, pal. I don't remember anything about the early eighties, except for my divorce. That I'll never forget. Sorry I can't help you."

"The name Jake Blake doesn't ring a bell? He was a comedian who—"

"Comedians come and go, pal. Only their jokes remain the same."

"Amy Arthur?"

Oates shook his head. He had the receiver in hand and was pecking out another number.

"Sylvester Simms? Silky Simms, he's sometimes called."

Oates started to shake his head, then stopped. He looked up at Harper. "Silky?"

"You remember him?"

"Sure. Crazy son of a bitch writes to me when he's in prison. Asks for stamps. Cigarette money. It builds from there. Some people you can never shake loose. Like parasites, you know?"

"He's out of prison now."

"Good. He doesn't call me when he's out. Too busy doing crimes, I guess. He should stay occupied, leave me alone." Oates's call went through this time. He asked for somebody named Irv, but Irv wasn't there. Oates seemed to take this as a personal affront. He slammed the phone down again, hard enough to make it bounce in its plastic cradle.

Harper said, "Blake and the others were a group of friends from the St. Louis area who often performed together. While they were at the Crazy Bone, Blake got his big break. Went straight out to L.A. to do a TV show."

"How many times do I have to tell you, I don't remember and I don't care. It's history, like the Civil War. Why do you want to know, anyway?"

"In L.A., Blake was injured by a mail bomb. Lost a hand. I'm looking into the case."

"Yeah? And who are you?" Oates looked at Harper's right hand and grinned. "The Avenger from the International Society of Cripples?"

Harper took a step closer to the desk. He stared down at Oates, who stopped smiling. Nothing was said for the next half minute, but Oates turned several shades paler and his Adam's apple bobbed visibly in his throat.

Finally Oates leaned forward in his chair, which gave him an excuse to break eye contact. Harper was left looking down at his luxuriant hair.

"So—uh—you think it was one of the people Blake left behind in the Midwest who sent him the mail bomb?"

"I'm investigating the possibility. You don't recall if Simms was envious of Blake's success?"

"Not specifically, but it's a good bet. This business is awash in envy. What do you expect, when a tiny minority gets fame and fortune while the rest get humiliation and poverty? And they're not the most stable personalities to begin with. Lots of performers crash and burn. Turn to booze. Drugs. End up on the street or in jail, like Simms."

"It's a rough business," Harper said. "It breaks people."

"Don't waste any tears on 'em," Oates replied. "Comics are like nasty children. They'll do anything to get your attention. Work a job like mine long enough, you get real tired of comics and their problems."

Harper figured that Bill Oates probably wasn't interested in the problems of anyone but Bill Oates. He didn't much like this man, with his young hair and old face, his eyes that had no light in them. He thought he wasn't going to get any information out of him, either.

"So you don't remember anything specific about Jake Blake or any of the others?"

"Too long ago, pal, sorry."

Harper nodded. He was just about to thank Oates and leave, when it occurred to him that there was a name he hadn't mentioned.

"Darren Snow?—that ring a bell?"

To Harper's surprise, the question caught Oates's attention. The lines in his face deepened as he frowned with the effort to remember. After a moment he said, "Yeah, I remember Darren Snow."

Harper wondered what it had taken to make a dent in Oates's indifference. "Talented guy?"

"Nah. Just average. If they're really bad they're kind of fun. But Darren Snow got good writers, worked hard on his routine, imitated all the best people, and it came out dull as dishwater." Oates smiled and shook his head. "He was like Bob Newhart without the laughs— button-down collar, high forehead, worried eyes."

"I've heard him described as secretive. And I've had a hard time finding out anything about him."

"Yeah, he was secretive. Darren Snow was a stage name. He wouldn't tell me his real name till I had to fill out a tax form."

"What was his real name?"

"Anthony Markman."

"Anthony Markman," Harper repeated, to set the name in his memory.

"I perked my ears up when I heard that was his name, I can tell you."

"Why?" Harper asked.

"Well, there's a good reason why most comics are trying to earn a living off their hostilities and insecurities—because they haven't got anything else. But the Markmans are a rich old St. Louis family. Own some company. I don't know what they do—some kind of engineering, I think."

"And Anthony Markman used the name Snow because—"

"Maybe he didn't want to embarrass the family. Or he didn't want any special favors because he was rich. I could've told him, Tony, baby, you need all the help you can get."

"So he wasn't getting anywhere in his career, then. Do you happen to remember his reaction when Blake got the call from Hollywood?"

"No. But it wasn't him who sent the mail bomb."

"How can you be sure?"

"Because I know his type. I've had a few others like him working for me over the years. Kids from rich families, with dads offering to pay their way through law school or med school. Or dads who have a job waiting for them in the family business. And they think, oh, it's too safe, too dull. So they go in for standup, or singing, or juggling, or some goddamn thing."

"And they don't last long?"

Oates shook his head. "After a few months in show business, safe and dull starts to look like a real attractive combination. So they go back to school or into the family business."

"You figure that's what happened to Anthony?"

"I guarantee you. He's forgotten all about Jake Blake. These days he thinks only about Btu's. Or whatever the hell engineers think about as they drive their Mercedes to the country club."

"You sound a little envious."

"Hey—there are days when I wish I'd gone into some nice dull business where a guy can make serious money." He looked at his watch again. "And today's one of those days. So listen, uh—whatever your name is, I gotta get back to work."

Harper didn't burden him with the name. "Thanks for your time," he said, and went.

Out on the street, he paused to take out his notebook and write *Anthony Markman* next to *Darren Snow*. From what Oates had said, Anthony didn't sound like a strong suspect.

But as long as Harper was going to be in St. Louis, he might as well check him out.

27

One of the lessons Harper remembered from his years on the NYPD was that if you were trying to catch a scumbag at home, early morning was the best time to do it. So he started off his first day in St. Louis by going to find Sylvester Simms.

He'd flown down from Chicago the night before and checked into a motel near the airport. It seemed to be in the flight path used by approaching planes, whose descending roar rattled the windows at regular intervals.

Harper called Laura, then Addleman, who said he'd see what he could find out about Anthony Markman. Then he set the alarm clock to wake him at six. It took ten minutes to figure out how to do that. Harper, annoyed, remembered a time when you could call the desk of a hotel and ask for a wake-up call. But the campaign to eliminate personal responsibility and human contact from American life seemed to have taken care of the wake-up call. Oh, well, he'd probably be awake most of the night anyway, listening to jet engines.

He was awake only about half the night, and awake when the alarm by the bed began a high-pitched beeping he couldn't figure out how to silence without finally disconnecting the plug.

Harper made breakfast a courtesy coffee and doughnut in the motel lobby, then went out into the gray morning and trudged toward his car. He took I-70 into the city and got off just north of downtown to look for the address Addleman had given him for Simms. This part of the city reminded him of Brooklyn. There were ugly public housing projects, and fine old churches, and block after block of century-old row houses. Most of them were in pretty bad shape, but from time to time he passed a well-kept street where he knew that urban renovators like Laura and himself had been at work. Hope springing eternal.

Silky Simms's street was not one of the better ones. The old redbrick apartment houses were dilapidated, with weathered wood that hadn't been painted in decades and guttering that sagged and dangled where downspouts had been ripped away. Many of the buildings were boarded up. Trash was strewn over the sidewalks, graffiti over the walls. A group of children who'd gotten up early, or maybe had never been put to bed last night, were playing in a garbage Dumpster.

The sun had risen but the sky was still heavily overcast. It would probably start raining soon. Harper drove along slowly, trying to read the addresses on the buildings. He found he'd missed Simms's address.

He parked his car at the curb and walked back. The reason he'd missed the address was that it wasn't there anymore. The building that must once have had the number still stood, an empty shell. It had no roof, windows, or door. Nobody had lived there for years. Harper figured that Simms had never been near here; he'd probably picked the address out of his head at random. Addleman had gotten it from a probation officer's report, and a guy like Simms wouldn't want to make it easy for his PO to find him.

A honk made Harper look up. An old car, fully laden with passengers, chugged to a halt in front of the building next door. The building's door opened and a young man in a crisp McDonald's uniform came out. Keeping his head down, he hurried to the car and jumped in. With a puff of oily exhaust, the car-pool vehicle pulled away.

This was the kind of neighborhood where people who had jobs were furtive about going to them. On the stoop of the next building down, half a dozen homeboys were lolling. Fashionable young men with their baseball caps on backward and their baggy pants pulled down to show their underwear. They were staring contemptuously after the car-pool vehicle. The kid in the McDonald's uniform had moved too fast for them to do anything to him. Now their eyes turned to Harper.

He stood still and gazed expressionlessly back at them. After a while, they all looked away. They'd made him for a cop. Now it was safe for Harper to turn his back and walk to his car. As long as he did it quickly.

Getting into the car, he locked the doors before starting the engine and pulling away from the curb. Large raindrops began to splatter on the windshield. He had to fumble with the unfamiliar controls for a moment before he could turn on the wipers.

He'd only been bluffing with the homeboys, of course. If he were really still a cop, he'd be able to go into the nearest police station, flash his tin, and say he needed some help finding a local hair ball named Simms. But he and Addleman had agreed that he couldn't risk any official contact. If word reached Frances Wilson, either through the media or through the law enforcement grapevine, that Harper was looking for the Celebrity Bomber, she was likely to charge him with interfering in an investigation. She might throw him in jail. Even castration was a possibility, Addleman said.

So Harper was on his own.

It was raining so hard now that he switched the wipers to the fast setting and turned on his headlights. He struggled through the crowded downtown streets until he reached I-64 and headed west. His next stop was Anthony Markman's family firm. He'd found it in the phone book at his motel last night. There were no listings for Markman in the residence pages, which didn't surprise him. You wouldn't expect rich, important people to give their home numbers. But there was a Markman Manufacturing Corp. He was going over there now to see if Anthony Markman was the dull, prosperous middle-aged man whom Bill Oates imagined him to be. If he was, Harper could cross him off the list. Then he might drive over to the Illinois quarry where Amy Arthur worked. Unless he could think of some way to locate Sylvester Simms.

Traffic wasn't heavy going out of downtown at this hour and Harper put on speed. He was pulling out to pass a truck when he saw the giant eagle.

The eagle was outlined in red neon, on a sign above the highway. It was flapping its wings so energetically that the wing tips almost touched at the end of the upstroke and the end of the downstroke. Its whole body quivered with the effort of its muscles. You almost expected it to get somewhere.

As he drew nearer, the flying eagle winked out, to be replaced by a perching eagle which was caged by a giant A, blocked out in rippling white lights. The sign was an advertisement for Anheuser-Busch. Harper remembered that the giant brewery and entertainment conglomerate made its world headquarters in St. Louis. The A went out and the eagle was starting to flap again as he passed under the sign.

He shifted uncomfortably in his seat. The neon eagle had given him a start. It'd been an unnerving sight, especially through the blurs and streaks of a rain-spattered windshield, with the wipers seeming to beat in time with its wing-strokes.

But it had nothing to do with the constellation Aquila. That was too far-fetched to think about. Nor should he think it was some kind of omen, warning him he was getting close, telling him Silky Simms or one of the other two was the bomber.

Harper reminded himself that he didn't believe in omens. Evidence was what interested him. He was a cop.

Used to be a cop.

Still was.

Sort of.

28

The address of Markman Manufacturing was on Macklind Avenue, which turned out to be in an industrial area on the city line. Harper's car bounced over railroad crossings and splashed through dips and potholes. Macklind Avenue was in bad shape, probably because most of the traffic consisted of heavy trucks. The street was lined with warehouses and factories. Thick power lines ran overhead. With the rain letting up, he was able to hear machinery whining, clattering, and pounding. Everything about Macklind Avenue spoke of honest toil. It wasn't a pretty place, but it made a welcome change from the slum he'd just visited.

Markman Manufacturing was headquartered in an old brick building completely devoid of frills. But family pride was evident in the gold-on-black sign which spelled out the name and the legend, SINCE 1907.

Harper parked in a gravel lot surrounded by a chain-link fence. On the way to the door he passed a gleaming black Mercedes-Benz. The very car Bill Oates had pictured Anthony Markman driving.

A young blond receptionist smiled mechanically at him as he came in. "Can I help you, sir?"

"Yes, I'd like to see Mr. Markman."

The receptionist frowned. Her mouth dropped half open, revealing a wad of green chewing gum on her tongue. "Mr. Markman?"

"The owner of the company?" Harper pointed at the sign bearing the company name, on the wall behind the receptionist's head.

She actually turned to look at it. When she swung back to face him, the puzzled frown was gone and she looked alert and even wary, as if she thought he was trying to put something over on her.

"Sir, the owner of the company is Alexon Industries. There's nobody named Markman here."

"Really?" Harper considered for a moment. "Maybe you could find someone senior for me to talk to?"

"Someone senior?" she repeated.

"Anyone who's been here a long time and might remember the Markmans."

"All right," she said doubtfully. "Please have a seat, sir."

He thanked her and turned away. Markman Manufacturing didn't go out of its way to impress visitors. There was a well-worn sofa facing a table with a few magazines on it. These were all issues of a trade journal called *Canning and Bottling*. The room smelled of machine oil, and coffee that had been sitting on the burner too long. When he looked back, the receptionist was on her feet, talking to an older woman. They kept glancing surreptitiously at Harper. Then the older woman went through a door that was mostly frosted glass. There had been black lettering on the glass long ago, but too much of it was worn away to be legible now. The sound of machinery was louder while the door was open.

Harper sat down to wait, wondering what kind of story he was about to hear. Probably the Markmans had sold out to a conglomerate, and Anthony was leading a life of leisure someplace like Santa Fe or Cape Cod. Which meant that finding him and eliminating him from the list of suspects would take longer and cause Harper more trouble.

The older receptionist came back through the door. There was a gray-haired man with her. She pointed Harper out to him and he approached, frowning.

"You're the guy who's asking about the Markmans?"

"Yes. About Anthony Markman, to be exact."

The man reacted to the name as if he'd taken a sip of milk and found it sour. For a moment, he seemed too disgusted to speak. Then he asked, "Who are you, and why do you want to know?"

The tricky questions. Harper was leery about telling anyone else, particularly someone who appeared to be as hostile as this man was, that he was hunting for the Celebrity Bomber. So he said only that he was a retired policeman looking into an old crime, an assault on an acquaintance of Anthony Markman's.

The man grunted. "This guy—he's some showbiz type?"

"Yes. A comedian." Harper was relieved that he didn't want to know anything more about the case. "I just want to locate Mr. Markman so I can ask him a few background questions."

"Can't help you. Don't know where he is. Don't know if he's alive or dead."

His tone made it clear that he preferred the second possibility. Interesting. Harper relaxed a little. It was always easy to get people talking about someone they disliked. He said, "I'd appreciate a few minutes of your time, Mr.—?"

"Hayden. Chuck Hayden." He reached in his shirt pocket for a pack of cigarettes. The shirt was an odd one. It would look like a white dress shirt when he had his coat on, but it had two flapped pockets and epaulets. Harper guessed that Hayden had been in the service once and still liked the military style. His gray hair was crew-cut. His gruff voice came up from deep in his chest. It was a voice that had barked a lot of orders in its time. But Hayden had a puzzled, melancholy air that suggested to Harper that people weren't snapping to attention for the old man anymore.

Shaking out a cigarette, he said, "I don't mind answering your questions, but I've got to have my morning butt at the same time. Can't spend too much time away from my desk. Those bastards at Alexon probably have my chair wired. They know when I'm not there."

"Sure."

They went out into the parking lot. Hayden looked at the building as he lit up. "This used to be a good place to work. Lucas Markman, Tony's father, was a fine man."

"What do you do here?"

"We make machines that put caps and labels on bottles, put the bottles in six-packs. That kind of thing. You didn't impress people at cocktail parties telling 'em what you did, but it was interesting work. Now it's all changing. Computerization. Robotics. Alexon keeps sending us memos, talking about cyber-this and cyber-that. I'm just trying to make it to retirement before they replace me with somebody younger.

Or an android." Hayden gave a bark of laughter, then his expression sobered. "In the old days, when men retired, Mr. Markman used to give a dinner for them. In his own home. He'd make a speech. Present a gold watch. A man would feel like he'd done something worthwhile with his life. Now that's all changed. Thanks to that little fucker Tony Markman."

Harper smiled. "Seems like you're putting an awful lot on him. It isn't any one guy's fault that times change."

"No, but Mr. Markman never would've sold us to a conglomerate if he could've passed the company on to his son. But the only son he had was Tony."

"And Tony wasn't interested in engineering?"

"That's the really sad part. Tony was a genius at engineering. A natural. From the time he was a teenager his father was bringing in gadgets he'd made. Tony had imagination. More important, he had persistence. Persistence you wouldn't believe. He'd stick with something, keep trying till he solved the problem. And the solution would be something nobody else would've thought of."

Harper felt a prickle at the back of his neck. For the first time it crossed his mind that Anthony Markman might—just might—be the bomber.

Hayden went on, "Tony was pulling straight A's at the Washington University engineering school. But he dropped out. He'd been bitten by the showbiz bug. That's what Mr. Markman used to say. Like it wasn't Tony's fault. It was some kind of virus that had infected him and eventually he'd get over it."

"So his father didn't oppose his trying to become a comic?"

Hayden lit a fresh cigarette. "Not at first. He told Tony to take a year and try to make a go of it. What could be more reasonable than that? But the year ended and Tony didn't have anything to show for it, and he still wouldn't come back to work. That was when Mr. Markman started to get mad. See, the way Tony was acting—it reminded Mr. Markman of Tony's mother."

"His mother?"

"Yeah. She was long gone by then, of course. Dragged Mr. Markman through a messy divorce, then went off and got herself killed in a drunk driving accident. Tony was their only child, and she spoiled him rotten. I remember how Mr. Markman used to come in complaining how the night before he'd gone off to bed alone, leaving the two of them together watching Johnny Carson. They were always watching TV together. That's probably how this damned showbiz craziness got hold of Tony in the first place."

"What happened when Tony said he wanted to keep on working at comedy?"

"Mr. Markman simply wouldn't stand for it. He told Tony to come back to the business or he'd cut him off without a cent."

"That's pretty harsh."

"Mr. Markman didn't have much choice. He was getting older. His health was failing. There wasn't much time to bring Tony into the business. Tony had to snap out of this showbiz dream right away."

"The ultimatum didn't work, did it?"

"Nope. Tony sent a postcard from North Carolina. He was appearing at stock car races. Things were starting to happen for him." Hayden flicked away his cigarette. He didn't light another. "That was the last Mr. Markman heard from him. Later, when Alexon Industries made an offer to buy the company, Mr. Markman accepted."

The story seemed to have reached its tragic end, as far as Hayden was concerned. After a moment, Harper prompted, "What happened then?"

"Mr. Markman retired to Florida. Didn't get to enjoy it for long before he died of a heart attack. The rest of the family has moved away or lost touch over the years. I guess they're okay. Mr. Markman negotiated a good deal with Alexon."

"And Tony didn't get any of the money?"

"Hell, no. He didn't even come to the funeral. Never contacted the lawyers. I guess he had some sense of shame after all. Look, I gotta get back to my desk."

"Couple of quick questions. Was Tony interested in astronomy?"

"I wouldn't know," answered Hayden. Now that he'd vented his anger against Tony Markman, he seemed to be losing interest.

"How about eagles?"

"I wouldn't know," Hayden said again. "So long. Good luck finding Tony. No need to let me know if you do."

Squaring his epauleted shoulders, the old soldier marched back into the building.

*   *   *

On the way back to the Interstate, Harper stopped off at a Bob Evans for a late breakfast. While he was there, he thought he might as well use the pay phone in the restaurant's vestibule to check in with Addleman.

"We're going to have to do some more digging on Simms," he told the profiler. "That address was no good."

"Okay," Addleman said, "I'll see what I can find. How are you doing with Arthur and Markman?"

Harper related what Hayden had told him. Addleman listened in silence.

When Harper was finished, Addleman said, "Grudge against celebrities. Mechanical ability. This guy would fit the profile."

"So would a lot of other people, I'll bet. Anyway, a profile isn't proof. We have nothing to take to Frances yet."

"No. But do me a favor, Will, and keep after this Markman guy."

"It won't be easy to locate him. After all he's been through, I'd expect to find out he's a wino living on the streets of L.A."

"Why would he do that, when he owns a house in St. Louis?"

Harper could tell from the sound of the voice that Addleman was smiling, pleased with this surprise he'd sprung on Harper. And it *was* a surprise. Harper said, "St. Louis is the last place I'd expect him to be living. He had nothing to come back to here."

"Well, I can't be sure where he lives, but his credit report indicates he's been paying a mortgage to Mercantile Bank for the last eight years, secured by a property in St. Louis."

"You can get peoples' credit reports, Addleman? I thought they were confidential."

"Harper, grow up. You want the address?"

Getting out his notebook, Harper took it down. "What else did you find out about him?"

"His credit rating is good. He has no criminal record. There's not much else. Guy seems to lead a quiet life. But after what you've told me, I'm going to dig deeper."

"Don't forget Simms. He *does* have a criminal record."

"I'm disappointed in you, Will. That's conventional cop thinking."

"Conventional cops are the people we have to convince," Harper said. "In fact, the sooner we get some conventional cops into this, the happier I'll be."

Addleman was quiet for a moment. "You okay, Will? You sound a little jumpy."

"I guess I am. Something kind of strange happened this morning. I've been thinking about it ever since."

"Something strange?"

"I saw a giant neon eagle." He described the advertising sign to Addleman.

"You don't really think the Aquila pattern comes from a beer ad, do you?" Addleman asked.

"No. But what bothers me is, we don't have any idea where it does come from. We think the Bureau's wrong with the astrology angles they're trying, but we don't have any other ideas."

Addleman was silent for a long moment. Harper imagined his lined, worn face in the soft glow of the computer screen. Addleman didn't use a telephone anymore. Too old-fashioned, and holding the receiver was a nuisance. Harper had seen him taking calls right on his computer.

He said at length, "When I say it's not astrology, Will, what I mean is that I don't think there's any mystical significance to it. He doesn't believe that following the Aquila pattern brings him luck or anything like that. This guy is too cold, too rational, for that."

"So what significance do you think it has for him? If it has any?"

"Oh, it's significant all right," Addleman said. "I think it's his signature."

"His signature?"

"Remember, the bomber's original plan called for him to go undetected until he made his last strike on Washington, completing the pattern. At that point, he's finished. Whether he's intending to commit suicide or simply disappear I don't know. But he wants the investigators who'll be picking up the pieces to be able to figure out who he was, how he did it, what message he wanted to send to the world. I think Aquila is his way of putting his signature on his handiwork. It means something to him, all right. But there's no telling what the meaning is."

"Maybe it's a joke."

"A joke?"

"Assuming for the moment that the bomber is Markman or Simms. Both of them are failed comics. The world didn't appreciate them. They get the last laugh on the world."

"Interesting, Will. Very interesting."

"But not very useful."

"No. Sorry. Call me again this evening. I may have something more for you. Maybe even a good address for Simms. What'll you do in the meantime?"

"I was planning to drive over to that quarry where Amy Arthur works."

"Do me a favor, Will. Go by Anthony Markman's house first. The guy intrigues me."

Harper looked at the slip of paper on which he'd written the address. The house probably wasn't very far away. Closer than the quarry, for sure.

"Okay," he told Addleman. "Markman first."

29

In South St. Louis, they take literally the saying that a man's home is his castle. Or so it seemed to Harper, as he drove around looking for Anthony Markman's address.

The houses were small, but their architects had dreamed big, furnishing them with crenellations, turrets, bartizans. They were built of brick or stone and most had heavy tile roofs. First-floor windows were usually covered with bars or grilles. A few houses were surrounded by wrought-iron fences with tops like spearheads. Harper wasn't sure they were ornamental. He wondered who was supposed to be kept out by all these fortifications. To him this seemed a quiet, safe, middle-class neighborhood, unlikely to be invaded by barbarians.

Markman's house had no fence, but otherwise it looked much like its neighbors. Harper parked in front of it and climbed out of the car to take a better look. The house would be about fifty years old, he judged, and it was well kept up. No paint was peeling, no bricks needed tuck-pointing. Markman's lawn was even, dense, and weedless as Astroturf. He had no shrubs or flowers, though. All along the block, the daffodils were blooming, and the forsythia and dogwood were in bud, but this house had only a green carpet out front. Maybe Markman was one of those fastidious householders who didn't want nature making a mess on his property.

A narrow drainage channel with sloping concrete walls and a chain-link fence ran along the edge of the property. The driveway ran next to it. No car was parked in the drive. There was a garage, though, and its overhead door was closed. No telling if anyone was home.

Harper began to walk up the drive, looking at the windows of the house. It would have been interesting to see a telescope in one of them, but he didn't. Now that the rain had stopped, the day had turned muggy, but all the windows were closed. The central air-conditioning unit at the side of the house was silent. Harper was willing to bet that there was no one here. He decided to do a little poking around.

First, the garage. It was a sturdy brick structure in the same style as the house. The windows in the overhead door had a heavy coat of paint on them. Curious, he thought. He bent and gave an experimental tug to the door handle. It wouldn't budge. He got the feeling the door was permanently sealed shut. This was even odder.

He walked around to the side of the garage. There was another door here. He was grasping the knob when he heard a car approaching, far down the quiet street. He moved closer to the wall of the building, where he wouldn't be seen. He'd wait until the car went by before he went in.

But the car didn't go by. It turned into the drive.

Harper snatched his hand away from the knob as if it had suddenly become hot. *Oh, great!* he thought. There was no hope of getting back to the sidewalk unseen. And this looked like the kind of neighborhood where the householders treated trespassing as a capital offense. What would he do if Mr. Markman called the police? Run for it? Try to make up some explanation that wouldn't get him in as much trouble as the truth? In any case, delay would only make matters worse.

With an uneasy smile on his face, Harper walked around to the front of the garage.

Markman was getting out of his car. His head was turned as he looked at the unfamiliar car parked in front of his house. He was tall, about Harper's height, but slender and narrow-shouldered. Hearing Harper's footsteps on the driveway, he swung around.

"Mr. Markman?" said Harper quickly. "I was just looking for you. Do you have a minute?"

Markman didn't answer. His gaze had passed right over Harper's face to fasten on his crippled hand. For a long moment, Markman stood frozen, wide-eyed, staring at that hand.

Harper had to fight against an impulse to put his hand in his pocket. He'd gotten such reactions before, usually from children, but sometimes from adults. He tried not to let them bother him.

"My name's Will Harper, Mr. Markman. I'd like to ask you a few questions, if you have a moment." Still smiling, Harper walked closer to the man.

Markman kept silent.

Suddenly Harper became suspicious. The other man's reaction wasn't just surprise or disgust. There was fear in his eyes. Maybe he wasn't staring at Harper's hand because cripples revolted him, but because he recognized Harper. He'd seen him on television or in the newspapers. He was terrified to find Harper here. *Because he was the bomber.*

But the next moment, Markman recovered. He blinked and shifted his gaze to meet Harper's. There was no fear in his eyes now. In fact, his expression was perfectly bland. Harper remembered Bill Oates's description of Markman as an unfunny Bob Newhart. It was apt. Markman had the high forehead, the ingenuous blue eyes, the thin, pursed lips.

"What do you want to ask me about?"

There was no alarm or hostility in the voice, only mild curiosity. But Harper did not relax. He didn't know what to make of this man yet, and he intended to be as cautious and alert as he'd ever been while disarming a live bomb. He said, "Jake Blake. Remember him?"

Markman looked blank for a moment. Then he smiled and said, "Jake. Of course. Have you seen him? How's he doing?"

No sign of a guilty start there, Harper thought. If Markman was acting, he was very good. "Could we go inside?" Harper asked. "This'll only take a few minutes."

"All right," said Markman, with every appearance of casualness.

As they walked across the front yard, he continued, "Are you a friend of Jake's, Mr. Harper?"

"I'm a retired policeman, looking into the attack on Jake."

"The mail bombing, you mean? That was a terrible thing. But I thought they'd caught the guy."

"I don't think it was the right guy." Harper looked sideways at

Markman. His heavy eyebrows were raised. He seemed to be intrigued, but nothing more than that.

After unlocking the front door, he led Harper into a rather cramped living room dominated by a huge television set. There was an armchair facing the screen that looked moderately comfortable, but guests would have to perch on a hard banquette off to the side. Harper guessed that there were seldom any guests in this house. Anthony Markman lived very much alone.

Or maybe not entirely alone, Harper thought the next moment, as he spotted a framed photograph on top of the television set. It showed a woman, a pretty blond, whom he judged to be a good deal younger than Markman. A girlfriend? A niece? Maybe just a favorite TV actress.

"Have a seat," Markman said, indicating the banquette. "And tell me about Jake. We haven't seen each other in a long time."

The tone was so natural that again Harper doubted his earlier suspicion. Maybe Anthony's fearful expression had only been what you would expect from a solitary man who led a quiet life.

"Jake's doing okay," Harper said as he perched on the banquette. "Runs a coffee shop in Encino."

"I'm glad to hear that. Jake and I used to be good friends, when we were both in the business."

"Would you say that you and he were rivals, Mr. Markman?"

"Oh yes. For girls and for jobs. It was a pretty wild life we were living. But always friendly rivals."

"Jake had the impression you were envious when he got his big break."

Markman blinked in surprise, as if this hurt his feelings. "No, I was happy for him. Figured I'd be joining him in L.A. before long. Jake's memory is at fault there. It was a long time ago, after all."

Harper wasn't getting anywhere. He decided to change the subject. "Well, Jake's made a pretty good life for himself, even though he didn't make it in show business. And I guess the same could be said for you, Mr. Markman."

Markman made no answer. He simply looked at Harper. There was something disturbing in his gaze, but maybe it was just the contrast between his dark, heavy brows and his pallid eyes. Harper had thought outside that they were blue. Now he'd have said hazel, or gray. Really they had hardly any color at all.

"You've got a nice house here. Nice, safe neighborhood," Harper went on, with a wave of his hand. "What line of work are you in?"

Markman hesitated, then said, "I'm an independent investor."

"Nice work if you can get it," replied Harper, smiling. If this was true, he was wondering where Markman had gotten his start-up capital. He hadn't made it doing comedy, and his family hadn't given it to him. But Harper didn't ask the question. He didn't want to tell Markman about his visit to the former family business. At least, not yet.

"It takes a lot more time than you would think to do the research," Markman was saying. "I don't live a life of leisure by any means."

Harper nodded. "And I expect an old house like this requires a lot of upkeep. You do the work yourself?"

"Yes," Markman said. "I'm good with my hands."

Harper figured he'd given himself a good enough excuse to poke around a bit. "I'm involved in rehabbing a house even older than this one," he said, rising and walking into the front hall, glancing up the stairs. If only he could get up to the second floor, see if there was a telescope or a star chart lying around.

He wandered back into the living room. Markman's pale eyes followed him as he went over to the front window, which was framed with stained glass panels in a grapes-and-leaves motif.

"I've got a stained glass window in my house," Harper said. This happened to be true. "It's in bad shape, and I really don't know what to do with it. Did you do your own work on this one?"

"Yes," Markman said. "It needed a fair amount of restoration."

Harper pointed. "Are these panes replacements? The color's a very good match. Well-mounted too. You must be good at soldering."

Markman sounded quietly pleased with the compliments. "It's just a matter of having the right equipment."

"Really? I'd appreciate it if you'd show me."

"What?"

Harper turned to look at him. "Could you show me your workshop? It's in the garage, isn't it?"

The pale eyes met Harper's calmly. "I'm sorry. The garage isn't really fit to be seen. I've got my current project spread out all over the place."

"Really? What's your current project?"

Markman said, "I'm repairing my lawn mower engine. It's in pieces all over the floor. Sorry."

The two men continued to gaze at each other. If Markman was rattled by the talk about his workshop, he gave no sign of it. In fact, he seemed perfectly relaxed, as if he was pleased to have Harper here. Maybe he was just what he appeared to be, a lonely, somewhat eccentric man who'd been battered by life. Harper's interruption of his quiet routines had thrown him at first, but now he was enjoying it.

Harper decided to make one last effort to shake Markman. "You know how I found you?" he said. "I went over to Markman Manufacturing."

Markman remained silent. He continued to look at Harper. But there was a quaver in his cheeks as he set his jaw. After hesitating a long moment he said, "Who did you talk to there?"

"Man called Hayden."

Markman's eyes widened and he blurted out, "Mr. Hayden! He's still there?"

"Yes. Hanging on by his fingernails, apparently. The new owners—"

"Does he know I'm here?" Markman interrupted. "Back in St. Louis, I mean?"

"No. I think he'd be surprised if he found out."

Markman nodded slowly. He wasn't looking at Harper any more. His attention had turned inward. "There's no reason I should've stayed away," he murmured. "St. Louis is as good a place as any for me."

"Does anyone know you came home?" Harper asked.

Markman's lips twisted into a bitter smile. "Fundraisers."

"Fundraisers?"

"Once you've given an institution money you can never shake them. I still get calls and letters. From Country Day, where the Markmans used to prep, and Washington University, where we went to college. From the Symphony and Barnes Hospital and the Episcopal Church of St. Michael and St. George. They all say the building that has our name on it needs repairs. Or the trust fund we established could do with a new infusion of cash."

"What do you tell them?"

"That they've got the wrong Markman. I'm not related." He looked up at Harper again, his eyes full of apprehension. "What did Mr. Hayden say about me?"

"He told me the whole story. He's still angry at you."

"I'll bet." Markman gave Harper a sharp look, as if he knew Harper was taunting him, trying to get a reaction out of him. He blew out his breath and shrugged his shoulders. It was an effort to lighten his thoughts, and it seemed to work. He sounded amused as he said, "Did you enjoy the Tony Markman story, Mr. Harper?"

Harper matched his irony. "Very dramatic. Just like a TV movie."

"Not quite. In a movie, I'd have become a star."

"You're right."

"Of course I'm right. It was movies that seduced me. The movies guaranteed there would be a happy ending to my struggle, just so long as I didn't quit." Markman made a small movement of his head. "I should've quit, of course."

"You must be bitter about it."

"What's to be bitter about? Lots of people don't make it."

"Few of them lose as much as you did by trying."

"I have only myself to blame," Markman said, in the same mild tone. "I let myself be seduced."

It was the second time he'd used the word. "Who do you think seduced you?"

Markman inclined his head. Harper thought at first that he was indicating the girl in the photograph, but he meant the television set. "All the voices coming out of that box. Whatever else they disagree on, they all agree on this one point, don't they?"

"What point?"

"Hang on to your dream and it'll come true." Markman smiled ruefully. "The preachers who tell you Christ will make you euphorically happy. The pitchmen who say you can easily be worth a million bucks. The gurus who tell you you're up for a much nicer reincarnation next time. The Democrats who promise the government can help you and the Republicans who promise it will get out of your way. And of course the stars, who make you think you can be like them, that you're special inside. Everybody on that box wants you to keep on dreaming."

Harper had to admit that Markman had a point.

Still smiling, Markman turned to Harper. "But let's talk about the way things are in real life. What do you think, Mr. Harper? Do you expect a happy ending?"

His gaze dropped to Harper's maimed hand. Harper looked down at it too. His thoughts went back to that quiet corridor in the Queens high school. He'd been so sure, in that last moment, that everything was going to turn out all right. He was going to get rid of that stick of gelignite safely. Already he was thinking about going home that night, about Laura.

Then the stick exploded.

No, there had been no happy ending to his career at the NYPD. Instead there'd been a brief period of agony, followed by a long period of tedium and frustration as he struggled to recover, knowing all along that he'd never be as good as new. Then there'd been the humiliation of being forced out of the Department by Captain Brand.

Harper put the thoughts away. He realized that Markman had diverted him, placed him on the defensive. A devious tactician sensing weakness and seizing the initiative. He looked up, to see that Markman was waiting for an answer. "No," Harper said, "I don't expect a happy ending anymore. The best I can do is hope for one."

Markman nodded. He seemed keenly interested, but he didn't ask any more questions. Instead he rose and walked over to where Harper was standing.

"I'm afraid I'm out of time," he said. "But good luck, Mr. Harper." And he held out his hand.

Harper took it with his maimed hand, watching Markman's eyes.

Two maimed men, he found himself thinking.

30

After shutting his front door behind Harper, Markman ran to the bathroom and vomited. The spasms went on racking him until his stomach was empty. Pale and trembling, he sank down on the edge of the tub. He didn't know how he'd gotten through the last fifteen minutes. Never in his life had such a supreme effort of self-control been required of him.

When he'd first seen Harper coming toward him from the garage, he'd been unable to believe it. Only when he looked at the crippled hand did he grasp that this really was the man he'd seen on the televised press conference, the night of Speed Rogers's death. Somehow Will Harper had tracked him down.

In that first moment, Markman assumed it was all over. Harper had been in the garage and knew everything. In a split second, cops and FBI agents would burst from concealment, surround him, hurl him to the ground. They would carry him off to interrogation, imprisonment, even execution. But Markman hadn't been thinking of his future. He'd thought only that he had failed. The pattern would go uncompleted. His statement to the world would never be made. *She* would make her visit to the Constant Light Hospital and would depart unharmed.

These thoughts passed through his mind in a second. But as Harper got closer to him, Markman realized that he was smiling, speaking politely. He even seemed a little embarrassed. Markman grasped that Harper didn't know everything. Not yet.

So now it was imperative to deceive Harper—and find out just how much he *did* know. Markman would have to push his fear deep down inside himself. It would be necessary to control his emotions more completely than he had ever done.

Now, sitting on the edge of the tub, he reviewed his performance. It had been a good one. He'd learned it was the Jake Blake mail bomb that had led Harper to him. This wasn't really a surprise. It had been Markman's first strike, and he'd been brooding about it ever since. Not that he regretted crippling Blake—the conceited bastard had it coming. But he'd made so many mistakes, acted without his emotions completely in check. It was sheer luck that he'd gotten away with the bombing at the time.

He'd been an amateur then, unable to spend the time and money to do the thing right, gripped by feelings over which he had no control. That was before the great change in his life, before the setting of the goal, the establishment of the pattern. Before Aquila.

Just as he'd been beginning to relax a little, even to enjoy the game of question and answer, Harper had dropped the casual announcement that he'd been down to the old plant. Talked to Hayden. So he knew all about Markman.

Markman knew now that this should have put him on his guard. But at the time, it'd had the opposite effect. He'd felt relief. And not only the much talked about relief of the guilty man finally able to confess at least part of his crime. What had affected him so was the realization that he and Harper were much the same sort of person, sharing many qualities, and it relaxed him to think that Harper knew his story and understood him. Markman couldn't resist the impulse to talk to the man. It was a long time since he'd talked to anybody.

Markman dug his fingernails into his palms and glared at his reflection in the bathroom mirror. "Stupid shithead," he muttered. Will Harper wasn't his friend. Wasn't his goddamn shrink. He was a cop, trying every trick he could think of to provoke Markman into a fatal mistake.

But *had* Markman made such a mistake? He went over what he'd said to Harper. It humiliated him that he'd spoken so carelessly, revealed so many of his thoughts. But his tone had been that of a defeated man, a helpless victim. He must have fooled Harper.

Maybe.

Maybe not.

Markman ran up the stairs to the second floor, stood on tiptoe to grasp the pull for the hatch, and brought down the ladder that led to his attic. It was warm and musty up there. And the wood floor was mostly bare, since he had little to store. His telescope stood on its tripod near the north-facing dormer window. He moved it forward and leveled it to scan the horizon.

It was only after he moved the telescope to the east window that he spotted Harper. His car was parked on the edge of the public park, just a block down the street. He must be waiting for Markman to make a move—probably to jump into his car and roar away in a desperate attempt to escape.

Markman straightened up from the telescope. So Harper was suspicious. But he wasn't sure. He was hoping Markman would panic and make up his mind for him.

Well, that wasn't going to happen.

Ducking beneath the angles of the roof, Markman moved the telescope from window to window, continuing to scan the horizon. He saw no helicopters, no snipers on rooftops, no police cars, no TV minicam trucks. There were no watchful men sitting alone in parked cars—except for Harper. He had no official support, then. He was as alone as Markman.

Returning to the east window, Markman focused the telescope on Harper's broad-browed, gray-bearded face. He was quite still, gazing steadily down the street. He looked as patient and calm as a fisherman on a shady riverbank. He wasn't going anywhere for a while.

Eventually, of course, he'd decide that Markman wouldn't be making a run for it. Then he'd go talk to the police about his suspicions, or continue poking around St. Louis, delving into Markman's past. He wasn't going to give up.

Which meant he'd have to die.

Markman straightened up and slapped the telescope so that it swung away from him. He wasn't happy about this decision. The Aquila pattern did not call for Harper's death. In fact, it would have been a good thing for him to be alive after May 15, to help explain Markman's intentions to the world. But he had to be killed, and right away. So there was no point in debating or thinking any more about the decision—the death sentence.

Markman brushed the attic dust off him and went down the ladder and then down the stairs. He would take no chances on Harper seeing him leaving the house. He went out the dining room window, on the side of the house away from Harper. It bothered him, having to leave the screen up. Insects would get in. Using the house to block him from Harper's vantage point, he ran to the garage. His heart was beating fast and he was breathing hard from his exertions. His hands trembled a little, so that he had trouble fitting the key in the lock.

But he knew from experience he would calm down as soon as he was seated at his workbench, with his familiar tools in his hands. The workshop had always been his place of sanctuary, where with a calm mind and steady hand he devised the answers to his problems.

Today's bomb would be a very simple one.

31

Harper's heart was pounding and he felt light-headed with excitement. He felt certain that Markman was the bomber. But he didn't know why.

As he sat in his car looking down the street, he kept imagining himself talking to Special Agent Frances Wilson, making the case against Markman. There was no case, though. Markman hadn't said anything that could be considered incriminating.

Yet Harper's instincts told him Anthony Markman had killed thirty-three people. And was laying plans to kill many more.

Harper stared through his windshield down the quiet suburban street. Markman had known who he was; Harper was as sure of that as he was of Markman's guilt. But he didn't know if his visit had alarmed Markman. Someone like the Celebrity Bomber would be driven by raging ego and a smug superiority that brushed morality and law and compassion out of the way. Possibly the killer was supremely confident and thought he was in no danger. He certainly wasn't making any attempt to flee.

What Harper wanted most was to get into that garage. One minute in the workshop and he'd know for sure that Markman was the bomber—and be able to prove it.

But he couldn't get near the garage as long as Markman was home. So he'd decided to wait and watch. If Markman drove away, he wouldn't follow, but would grab his chance to break into the garage. If Markman stayed put, he would wait until nightfall. Under cover of darkness, he might be able to reach the garage unseen. It would all depend on where Markman had put his yard lights.

For the rest of the afternoon, Harper waited, watched the empty street, and pondered the drawbacks of his plan. One possibility was that Markman had booby-trapped the garage. He certainly had the expertise to set an undetectable trap, if he was the Celebrity Bomber. It was also possible that Harper's instincts were wrong and he wasn't the bomber—in which case, Harper might end up spending tonight in jail on a charge of breaking and entering.

Harper pushed away his excitement and apprehension and settled down in the seat behind the steering wheel, conserving his energy, gathering his strength and his nerve for what was to come.

The small public park behind Harper was empty and quiet until four. Then a group of skinny teenage boys in baggy shorts rode up on skateboards. For the next two hours, they practiced riding the boards down a short flight of concrete steps into the parking lot. The ceaseless banging and clattering got on Harper's nerves, but he figured listening to it wasn't as bad as doing it. None of the boys managed to reach the bottom of the steps without falling off, not even once. It looked unbearably tedious and frustrating. Not to mention painful.

Finally it got too dark for the boys. They put their skateboards under their arms and started limping for home across the softball field. Watching them go, Harper noticed a sort of small pavilion near the field. It had a Coke machine and a pay phone inside it.

Harper remembered his promise to call Addleman. He was overdue, and besides, Addleman might have something for him. He rose stiffly from the car and walked toward the pavilion.

From his hiding place in a thicket at the side of the road, Markman watched Harper walk away from his car. This was what he'd been waiting for, but Markman never let impatience get the better of him. He was going to stay put until he could no longer see Harper through the thickening dusk—until there was no chance of Harper seeing him.

It had been a long wait. Markman had finished his work in the garage quickly, then gone over his back fence and crossed his neighbor's yard to the street, to work his way around behind Harper. None of the drivers who'd passed him had looked twice at the man walking along the sidewalk, with a shoebox tucked under his arm.

He'd only used a car bomb once before, back in Oklahoma ten years ago, to get that idiotic weather girl. That had been a fairly complex bomb, with the explosive mounted under the hood against the firewall, and the priming charge wired to the ignition. This bomb was much simpler: just four sticks of dynamite and a blasting cap, wired to a simple radio receiver and its small battery. After planting it, Markman was going to return to his hiding place, wait for Harper to return to the car, and detonate the bomb. It wasn't that he wanted to watch Harper die. Nothing like that.

He simply had to be sure.

Harper was no longer in sight. Markman waited for a car to pass on the street, then got up and walked quickly over to Harper's car. The best place for the bomb was under the seat. Markman tried the door and found it locked. He could have opened it, but there was no need to waste time. Placed under the car, the four sticks of dynamite would still do the job.

He waited until another car passed, then went down on one knee. From the shoebox he took the bomb and a roll of duct tape, which he was going to use to strap the bomb to the undercarriage. Before handling the tape, he put on latex gloves. Tape took fingerprints extremely well. Markman had read once of a terrorist who'd been caught because a one-inch square of tape that happened to have his thumbprint on it had survived the blast and been found by the police.

They weren't going to get Markman that way.

As he was about to plant the bomb, he heard another car approaching. Unhurriedly, he got to his feet, holding the bomb close to his chest so the passing driver wouldn't be able to see it, but not so close that the tape could pick up fibers from his shirt. He turned away from the road.

The car went by without slowing. But Markman remained standing, staring across the dark softball field to the little pavilion. There was no light inside, but there was one of those vending machines whose whole front was a glowing red Coke label. In front of it, Markman could see the silhouette of a man. He squinted. It was Harper, using the telephone.

This was unexpected. He'd have to think about this.

Markman backed away from the car, stepping on the shoebox and almost tripping. He bent to scoop it up along with the roll of tape. Then he walked quickly away. His heart was hammering and there was bitter taste beneath his tongue. There was nothing he hated more than a last-minute hitch that forced him to change his plan.

He'd seen no police around, and assumed that Harper was working alone. That had been a mistake. Harper was talking to someone and it was possible—no, probable—that he was reporting about Markman.

So killing Harper wouldn't make Markman safe. Instead, it would bring the cops down on him even more quickly.

Bending forward, Markman walked quickly away into the darkness. He didn't know where he was going or what his next move would be. Sweat broke out on his brow and he mopped it with his sleeve. It humiliated him to think about how stupid he'd been, how close he'd come to making a fatal mistake.

He'd felt secure in his home base for so long. He'd become wedded to his timetable and his fastidiously laid plans. Harper's appearance had changed all that. Markman had been slow to understand that. He'd reacted instinctively, thinking he could take Harper out and carry on with the plan as before.

He'd been stupid. Panicky. Markman burned with humiliation when he thought of how he'd let his emotions run away with him. Blowing up Will Harper, only a block from Markman's own home. *Christ*! He might just as well have called the FBI and turned himself in!

At least he could see the realities coldly and clearly now. He was going to lose his home base. The old timetable would have to be scrapped, the plan he'd labored over for so many months would have to be thrown out. He'd have to lay out a new and entirely different route that would take him to the Constant Light Hospital on May 15. And he'd have to do it fast.

Markman walked on, deep in thought, until he came to the house that backed on his own. He ran lightly up the drive and jumped over the fence.

He was going home for the last time.

32

When Harper had arrived at the pavilion, he'd been annoyed that there was no light. At least he got a dial tone when he lifted the receiver. Squinting at the keypad in the rosy glow from the Coke machine, he tapped out Addleman's number.

"Hello!"

Addleman gasped out the word. Harper would've thought he'd had to run to catch the phone, if he hadn't known that Addleman never went anywhere. So it had to be excitement.

"What's up, Harold?"

"Harper! Where the hell have you been?"

"I've—"

"Never mind. I found something on Markman. He's our guy for sure."

"For sure?" Harper repeated. He felt the rush of exhilaration again. A combination of satisfaction and apprehension that came with the knowledge that at last they were closing on their quarry. Had men felt this since the hunt had begun aeons ago?

"I've been downloading stuff from the local paper out there, the *Post-Dispatch*. Found a story about our friend, from eleven years ago."

"A story about Markman? What did he do?"

"Bear with me for a minute. You have to understand the time frame.

This is after his father died, after Markman Manufacturing was sold, with not one red cent going to our Tony. He's given up on his comedy career, and he's back in St. Louis working at a Six Flags amusement park."

Harper nodded to himself. Amusement parks were a traditional employer for young people on the way up in the entertainment business. Or not-so-young people on the way down.

"This story was about the decision in his lawsuit against the park," Addleman said. "He fell from the platform of the roller coaster. Claimed he hurt his back. The park had its doubts and it sounded like so did the *Post-Dispatch*. But Markman had a sharp lawyer. He won four hundred grand. Probably got to keep half."

"I see," said Harper. "So that was where he got the money he invested."

"Yes. It was perfect timing. This was the mid eighties. He probably put the money into junk bonds and saw it double, triple, within months."

"I see."

"What a difference that money made. Now he had the leisure and the means to act on the scheme that must have been festering in his head all the time he was working as an underpaid drudge. He'd gotten some twisted satisfaction out of mutilating Jake Blake. Now he was ready to undertake his life's mission."

Yes, Harper thought—his mission to demolish the celebrity mystique and show the world what life is really like. Now Markman could buy equipment, conduct experiments, travel. The accident made it all possible. He said, "How does this tie in with Aquila?"

"That's my favorite part. You were on to something when you said it would turn out to be a joke. It is—a very bitter, sardonic one. Our boy Tony has a lot of buried guilt and anger and resentment. The fame and fortune as a comedian that he felt he'd earned, he never got. The family fortune he should have inherited was taken away from him. Then finally he does get a small fortune—thanks to luck, legal trickery, and the jurors' pity for what a loser he was. You can see how the absurdity appealed to him. I can't wait to talk to this guy, Harper, what a mind he has."

Addleman didn't have to remind Harper of Markman's twisted and brilliant mind. Harper tried again. "Harold, where does the Aquila come in?"

"Oh, didn't I tell you? The roller coaster at Six Flags—the one Markman fell off—was called the Screaming Eagle."

"The Screaming Eagle . . ." Harper smiled thinly. Aquila, the eagle constellation. So a roller coaster was what had made Markman choose his pattern of vengeance and death—his paean to the luck that had set him free from the workaday world and placed him above the rest of humanity, where he belonged.

Addleman gave his wheezing cackle. "This is going to be a blow to Frances, after she sent all those agents over to Calcutta and Hong Kong to consult astrologers, but I think I'd better call her."

"It's too late for that," Harper said. "I approached Markman. I'm afraid I alarmed him."

"There's a flight risk?"

"Yes. Look, I'm going to call the St. Louis police right now. Then I'll go back to his house and watch it till they get there."

"The St. Louis police! What are you gonna tell them?"

"I don't know. But they'll get here faster than if we have to go through Frances, in Indiana or Washington or wherever the hell she is. I'm breaking the connection now, Harold, we have to get this son of a bitch before he slips away."

"You be careful, Will!"

Harper didn't take the time to answer. He hung up on Addleman and called 911.

33

arper slowed the car and doused its lights as he approached Markman's house five minutes later. He was hoping the bomber was still in there, and he didn't want to scare him. Just let him stay put a little while longer! Harper prayed over and over to the God that raced in cops' veins at crunch time.

As he slid to a stop across the street, he noticed with relief that Markman's Honda was still parked in the drive. There were lights on in the front hall and in an upstairs room. The shade wasn't drawn and Harper gazed at the rectangle of light for a long moment, hoping he'd catch a glimpse of Markman moving around the room. But he didn't.

His gaze shifted to the garage at the back of the property. A light mounted on the side of the house made it possible for him to see the sturdy redbrick structure with its white overhead door. But if a light was on inside the garage, it wouldn't show through the painted-over windows. Markman could be in there, in what Harper was sure was his personal bomb factory, devising God only knew what kind of hellish device.

Mopping the sweat off his brow with his sleeve, he glanced at his watch. What was keeping the police? He'd known it would be pointless to go into long explanations as to who he was and why he needed them, so he'd said something cryptic about a crime in progress and given the address. He'd explain when the cops got there. All he wanted them to do was take Markman into custody. If they took him into custody too, that was all right.

And there it was at last: the distant whine of a siren.

Almost as soon as he heard it, as if it were a prearranged signal, Harper saw the front door of the house thrown open. Markman burst through it. He ran to his car, jerked the door open, and piled inside. The sound of the motor turning over came to Harper.

Harper started his own engine. As Markman began backing down his drive, Harper stamped on the accelerator and veered sharply across the street to block the entrance. Instead of stopping, Markman tried to maneuver around him.

But there wasn't room. The rear end of the Honda slammed into the chain-link fence along the drainage ditch. Harper saw the front wheels spinning. There was a scream of rubber and white smoke billowed from the wheel well as Markman tried to escape, but the car was stuck fast. Throwing open the door, Markman jumped out and started running.

Harper leaped from his car and ran at Markman. Markman saw him coming and tried to dodge. But Harper closed in. He wasn't trying to do anything fancy—just catch Markman up in a bear hug, lift his feet off the ground, and fall on top of him. He didn't want to risk harming the bomber, wanted only to hold him until the police could arrive to arrest him.

Spreading his arms, he hurled himself at Markman. His right shoulder made solid contact. The two men grunted at the impact. Markman staggered backward and almost went down. But Harper couldn't manage to lock his arms around Markman's body. Markman was thin, but stronger than he looked. Twisting and turning, he managed to break out of Harper's hold.

While Harper was still trying to regain his balance, Markman pivoted and punched him in the face. Harper's head snapped back. He was dazed. In a world that had begun to tilt and spin, he blinked, trying to focus on Markman.

Markman was moving in. His right fist shot forward and another flash of pain went off in Harper's head. Again he staggered backward. But the sirens were louder now, and behind Markman he could see the spinning red and blue lights of a police car as it rounded the corner at the end of the block.

He lunged at Markman, making another effort to get hold of him, but he was slower this time. Markman dropped to a crouch, ducking under Harper's encircling arms. Then he drove his shoulder into Harper's stomach.

Harper grunted with pain. He fell over backward. His back hit something which gave way under him. It was the chain-link fence, he realized. It had buckled under the impact of Markman's car, and it couldn't stop Harper from falling into the drainage ditch.

He landed hard on the sloping concrete wall and went sliding and scraping to the bottom, where he came to rest on a thin carpet of damp leaves.

Harper struggled to his knees. The blow from Markman's shoulder had knocked the wind from him and he gasped and wheezed as he tried to get it back. The palms of his hands were on fire where the concrete had scraped the skin off. He got one foot under him and rose shakily to a standing position.

Now he could see over the top of the ditch. Markman was climbing into Harper's car. But he was hesitating, half in and half out, turning to look up the street. The police car, its siren whooping and lights flashing, was closing in fast.

Suddenly Markman jumped away from the car. He must have decided he couldn't escape on wheels. He dashed back up his driveway with speed that surprised Harper.

Harper assumed he was going to try to escape through the neighbor's yard. But when Markman reached his garage, he stopped. Harper could see him fumbling with the key for a moment, then he went inside.

Suddenly Harper knew what was going to happen. Guessed which way out Tony Markman had chosen.

And there was nothing Harper could do about it but drop down to the bottom of the drainage ditch and cover his head with his arms.

A split second later the explosion came. Even through his closed eyelids the light was dazzling. The roar deafened him. Being in the ditch, he was protected from the shock wave. But not from the heat. He felt as if his skin were blistering, as if he were breathing fire. Instinctively he began to crawl away on hands and knees. He was coughing and gasping.

Something hit him hard in the shoulder. He looked up in time to see a crumpled steel mailbox fall to the ground in front of him. It was only the beginning of a hail of debris—pieces of wood, chunks of metal, bricks. Harper couldn't think clearly anymore, but he knew that safety lay in the culvert that took the drainage ditch under the road, which he could see ahead of him. He started to crawl toward it, grunting in pain as more objects fell on him.

He didn't make it. Something hit him in the head. He saw a flash of pain that was almost as bright as the explosion.

Then darkness, blacker and blacker . . .

34

Nothing quite like this had ever happened in St. Louis before. The TV anchorpersons, searching for phrases to narrate the footage their helicopter-mounted cameras had shot of Anthony Markman's block, kept coming back to the same words: *It looks as if a tornado hit*.

They were right. A twister, touching down on a single spot then lifting off to resume its capricious flight, would have wreaked exactly this kind of concentrated and terrible destruction.

Markman's garage was gone, its place marked by a deep crater. The back of his house had been cleaved open to reveal the rooms within, so that it looked like a doll's house. The back fence had been blown down and two tall oak trees pulled up by the roots. The near side of the closest neighbor's house was a tumbled ruin.

But that was all. The rest of the surrounding structures still stood, although most of their windows had been blown out and they'd taken minor damage from falling debris. Many people had suffered injuries from the same sources, but no one had been killed in the blast except the man who'd set it off.

Assuming, of course, that Markman really was dead.

Will Harper was in St. Anthony's Hospital in St. Louis County. His hearing had come back. His cuts and scrapes had been bandaged. But his doctors were keeping him under observation, to see if he developed aftereffects from the concussion he'd suffered. They were also searching for the kind of blast injuries that were difficult to detect but potentially serious: burst blood vessels, twisted joints, torn muscles or ligaments.

They were just bringing him back to his room from a CAT scan when Special Agent Frances Wilson came to visit.

"Will! How are you?"

Harper raised his head so that he could see the figure in the doorway. He was feeling dizzy and a little nauseated from the fluids they'd made him drink before the tests. It took him a while to bring Agent Wilson into focus. She was wearing a rather elegant spring suit in a black and white houndstooth check, and was heavily burdened as usual with purse, briefcase, and laptop computer. The accoutrements of her trade, in addition to her gun. She had a concerned smile on her face. Walking over to his bedside, she took his left hand in both of hers.

"Now, you're taking good care of him, aren't you?" she said to the orderlies who were standing by the gurney.

"Yes, ma'am," he heard an orderly reply in a bored tone. "Now if you'll just get out of the way we'll put him back in bed."

As they maneuvered the gurney next to the bed and manhandled Harper from one to the other, he tried to figure out why Frances was being so nice to him. He'd interfered in an ongoing investigation and heaped embarrassment on the Bureau and Agent Wilson herself. Harper hadn't expected anything from the Feds other than a long, angry debriefing and threats of prosecution.

Instead, here was Frances gazing down at him with a face full of gravity and sweetness. She said, "Laura should be arriving soon."

"She's coming here?" Harper blurted out, surprised and pleased.

"Yes. On a government jet. If she came by regular plane, the reporters would hector her to death. You're the man of the hour, you know, Will."

Harper grunted. Maybe Frances was paying him compliments so the orderlies would overhear and report her graciousness to the media types who were probably hanging around the public areas of the hospital right now.

She was shaking her head with rueful amusement. "But I have to tell you, Laura and I would both like to sock you one for what you put us through. And it was completely unnecessary."

"It was?" asked Harper thickly. He was having a hard time talking. What was that stuff they'd given him? His tongue felt like an ironing board.

"If you and Harold had brought us this Sam Sugar thing right at the beginning, we would have taken it from there."

"You would have believed us?"

"Of course. No reason not to. Some of my people were working on the same approach themselves."

"They'd found the Sugar case?"

"Not exactly. But they were working on the same approach. You know, old bombing cases. They would've found Sugar eventually."

Sure, Harper thought. Along with a hundred other old cases. And the Bureau would've taken years to follow up on it.

The orderlies were leaving. If Frances was counting on them to carry the word to the media, she was in for a disappointment, Harper judged. They didn't appear to be paying any attention. She waited while they wheeled the clattering gurney through the doorway Then she sat down by his bedside, bringing her face close to his. He could see the lines of fatigue and anxiety in the fine, dark skin around her eyes. It had been a long time since Agent Wilson had enjoyed a good night's sleep.

"Listen, Will. I hope you can pull yourself together. You're going to have to face the reporters soon. They're all over this hospital. I had to run a gauntlet to get in here. They act like it's my fault they can't see you—as if I'm keeping you under wraps or something."

"Frances," Harper said. "I'm not interested in making you look bad in front of the media."

Her smile of relief revealed the depth of her anxiety for the first time. "That's good to hear."

"All I want in return is some information."

Her face became serious. She looked around the room, making sure they were alone. "What kind of information?"

"Have you found any trace of Markman's remains?"

Frances didn't hesitate to reply, but she dropped her voice. "No. And our scientists tell me it's possible we won't. That was a terrific explosion and he was right at the center of it. He could've been vaporized. Blown to atoms."

Harper raised himself on an elbow despite the dizziness so he could look her levelly in the eyes. As distinctly as he could, he said, "Don't count on it."

She met his gaze and held it. "We're not. We have cops as well as our own people combing the area. Every law enforcement agency in the area is on the alert. And, Will, the guy's face is plastered all over TV. If he did get away, he's bound to have been injured. And he was on foot." She shook her head decisively. "If by a quirk of fate he is still alive and somehow mobile, he won't get away."

"Okay," said Harper, and sank back against the pillows.

For the moment, there was nothing he could do but hope she was right. Undoubtedly she knew more than she was telling him. But he still wasn't as sure of Markman's death as Frances was, because he knew something she didn't know.

He knew Tony Markman.

35

Markman sat slumped on one of the hard wooden benches in the bus station in Wayling, West Virginia. There were a few dozen other people in the waiting room, some of them killing time until the bus from Norfolk arrived, then continued west. Markman was killing time waiting for the next eastbound bus.

He was wearing a toupee and dark-framed glasses with tinted lenses. The only other change he'd made in his appearance was to shave the hairs over the bridge of his nose, cleanly separating his eyebrows. He was confident that he was unrecognizable, though. The high forehead, the beetle brow, the almost colorless eyes were his only distinctive features. Otherwise his appearance was bland and forgettable. He'd been told that often enough when he'd been trying to get jobs as a performer.

Markman smiled thinly. There was no danger of anyone recognizing him as the Celebrity Bomber—especially now that the bomber was believed dead.

He glanced at the Clarksburg newspaper lying on the bench next to him. As a rule he wasted little time or money on the products of the news media. He had no use for these peddlers of sensation and celebrity, and ordinarily he wouldn't have changed his opinions just because they happened to be covering *him*. But he'd made an exception for today's newspaper when he saw the headline announcing he was dead.

It was a great relief, being dead. It was going to make everything easier for him. Today was May 9. Six days to go.

It had taken Special Agent Frances Wilson of the FBI a week to conclude that Markman had died in the garage explosion. He figured that a certain amount of bureaucratic frustration had entered into the decision. They'd been searching so hard for him, expending so much manpower and money. And after an entire week, they'd still found no trace. The Feds were ripe and ready to fall—and fall they had, for Markman's carefully prepared trick.

The newspaper story laid it all out. A piece of wood splashed with blood had been found in a yard fifty feet from the blast site. This wasn't significant in itself. Debris from the explosion was strewn over the whole block. And, since so many people had been injured by flying glass, a good deal of blood had been spilled in the area too. But laborious checking of all the hardware stores in the area and exhaustive lab analysis of the woodgrain had established that this piece of wood came from Markman's workbench. Then DNA analysis had proved beyond doubt that the blood was Markman's.

All this was quite true. While waiting for Harper to close in on him, Markman had broken off a piece of his workbench. Then he'd drawn a syringe of blood from his arm and poured it onto the piece of wood. Finally he'd planted it in the neighbor's yard. Markman had long known the time might come when he'd want to fake his death in such an explosion. He'd had preparations, a plan. As he planned for everything.

And of course his pursuers had been fooled. Markman had turned their own science against them. DNA had become their religion, and if DNA evidence suggested Tony Markman was dead, in the minds of the FBI, he was dead.

Wrong. He was very much alive—but he couldn't say undamaged. His ears had never stopped ringing from the explosion, and he suffered from bad headaches. Some heavy piece of debris—maybe a brick—had fallen on his arm. The pain had been so excruciating that he'd feared the bone was broken. But it was now just a bruise.

Markman had taken only two items with him. One was the block of C-4. He'd used dynamite to blow up the garage, because he had other plans for the hard-to-obtain plastic explosive. The other was a wallet containing driver's license, social security card, and Visa card in the name of Jim Monninger. Monninger was a solid and carefully prepared identity, which he'd been intending to use for his getaway after May 15. But thanks to Will Harper, all plans had to be changed.

The bus from Norfolk came rumbling and hissing into the station. Some of the people slouching in the wooden benches stood up and moved toward the glass doors leading out to the arrival and departure area. Within minutes, passengers began streaming into the terminal, lugging or rolling suitcases. The damp outside air and diesel fumes came into the station with them, along with the steady, rhythmic thrumming of the idling bus engine. A weary-looking woman trailing two preschool-age girls straggled past, trying to catch up with the husband hurrying toward the exit to the parking lot. He seemed angry about something, and the woman kept begging him to tell her what was wrong. One of the little girls was complaining about having to use the bathroom, but the procession didn't slow as it left the terminal. It seemed suddenly quiet without the clamor of the two kids and their imploring mother.

Markman glanced over at the kiosk where newspapers and magazines were sold. He could see half of one of the displayed headlines: ER KILLED IN BLAST. When he'd been young, and had craved fame, it used to make him almost sick with excitement to see his name in print—usually very small print, in the entertainment ads at the back of a newspaper. Now a pleasant tingling sensation grew deep inside him. He was famous at last. What he'd done had made everyone sit up and take notice. And they only *thought* they'd seen the last act.

He didn't want to, but he couldn't resist. He had to get a closer look at the papers and news magazines, maybe buy one. His name would be in the headlines, surely. The headlines!

He stood up, leaving his cheap, scuffed suitcase on the bench, and wandered over to the kiosk.

Feigning casualness, he stared at a *Newsweek* cover of the ruins of the garage under the heading DEMISE OF A BOMBER. There was an inset in the upper right corner, a photo of Will Harper looking noble, the hero of the moment. Markman smiled but didn't reach for the magazine. He picked up instead a newspaper with his photograph on the front page. DEAD IN FIERY BLAST read the caption. A warm rush of well-being flooded through Markman. Then something else.

Disgust.

With himself, his momentary loss of self-control. He'd thought he was beyond feeling the lure and narcotic of fame. Above it. And he *was*! He *was* above it!

He hurled the newspaper into a nearby trash receptacle, then immediately realized he hadn't paid for it. The old man seated on a stool near the kiosk was staring at him.

Markman smiled and shrugged, then dug in his pocket and placed two quarters on top of the stack of papers. "Lost a political bet," he explained, his own words muted by the ringing inside his head.

The old man gave him a look, then returned to reading the folded racing form in his lap.

Markman slunk back to the wooden bench and sat down next to the scuffed attaché case. He shivered slightly. The ringing in his ears grew louder, more shrill. His shame at his temporary lapse of control made him all the more determined to carry out his mission.

To strike his deadliest blow at the cult of celebrity.

Three days later, May 12, Markman was in Wilmington, Delaware. It was his last stop before Washington. He was staying in a suburban motel located on a busy highway lined with shopping malls. He was buying tools and materials to replace what had been lost in the blast, taking his time about it. Resting up.

It was odd, but the nearer he came to May 15, the calmer he felt. He put it down to the soothing knowledge that now *she* had only three days to live. And for only three more days would she be loved and admired. In a single blow, Markman would end her life and extinguish her fame. No one would mourn her.

As he was walking from the parking lot into Wal-Mart, he passed a newspaper vending machine. Ever since that moment of weakness in the West Virginia bus station he'd managed to avoid newspapers and television. But when he glanced through the clear plastic of the vending machine, he saw something that froze him in mid step.

The Aquila pattern. Drawn on a map of North America with bold, straight, blood-red lines.

Markman felt naked and defenseless. He looked dazedly around at the shoppers hurrying past him into the store. No one gave him a second glance. He forced himself to step closer to the vending machine so he could see the paper better.

The headline read: CHILLING NEW LOOK INTO BOMBER'S MIND. On the map, the name of each of his victims was superimposed over the name of each city where he'd struck.

So they knew Washington, D.C. was to have been the next city. They just didn't know who was the target. Instead of a victim's name, there was a question mark.

Markman's thoughts were whirling. With trembling fingers, he fumbled a few coins into the slots and took out a newspaper. Then he returned to his rented car and sat down to read the story.

When he finished it, he felt better. There was no threat here to his mission. No one quoted in the story had any doubt that Markman was dead. The fact that this story had come out only indicated how confident the authorities were that there was nothing to be feared from the Celebrity Bomber anymore.

Still, it was unsettling to Markman to read that they'd known about the Aquila pattern for some time. This leak had come from someone in the White House, who said that the Secret Service had been on the highest level of alert ever since the death of Speed Rogers, and was only now relaxing its vigilance. Special Agent Frances Wilson was quoted as confirming the report. She suggested, without quite saying so, that the FBI had figured out the pattern. The reporter seemed to think it was really Will Harper who had figured it out, but Harper couldn't be reached for comment. The last paragraph of the story mentioned a former FBI profiler named Harold Addleman, whose connection with the case was only now emerging.

Markman folded the paper and stowed it under the car seat. As long as they thought he was dead, none of this mattered, he told himself. But the new information was jarring all the same, and he decided that from now on he'd have to monitor the news media more carefully.

Being dead didn't mean he could relax.

36

That evening, when his errands were done and his purchases packed away, Markman lay down on the bed in his motel room and reached for the remote.

Stories about the Aquila pattern featured prominently in all the network newscasts, but there was nothing more than he'd read in the paper. It was even more comforting to Markman that the tone was the same: Everyone assumed that the bomber was dead, the danger was past, and it was safe to indulge in a tasteless guessing game about who the last victim was to have been.

He'd intended to switch off the set as soon as the network newscasts ended. Instead he pressed the up-button on the remote and began to flick idly through the higher-numbered cable channels. The sight of a familiar face stopped him.

It was a middle-aged man with a paunch and a head of frizzy blond hair. Markman struggled to put a name to the face. Another man, a thin, stoop-shouldered man, came into the shot. He looked familiar too. The two were beaming at each other. They embraced.

Markman turned up the sound. A female reporter with a well-practiced throb of sincerity in her voice was explaining that this was the reunion of Jake Blake, the Celebrity Bomber's first victim, with his once and future friend Sam Sugar, who'd been wrongly convicted of the crime. Almost choking up herself, the reporter called the reunion a "heartwarming sidelight on this bloody tale of the late Tony Markman, a man twisted by hate and envy."

Jolted, Markman pulled himself upright on the bed. The last time he'd allowed himself to watch television, he'd been the unknown and fearsome Celebrity Bomber. Now he was only the late Tony Markman. Of course the media were going to trivialize him. He should switch the set off now.

But he felt a curiosity that was both nauseating and irresistible. He couldn't help continuing to flick through the channels, stopping whenever he saw a familiar face.

The journalists had been busy. They'd found comedians he'd performed with, to testify to his lack of talent. They'd found people from his childhood who he'd assumed were dead—teachers, servants, relatives. These people said the most shameless and infuriating things about him. Markman found himself wincing, muttering sarcastic replies. A housemaid's comments about how his mother had spoiled him brought him to his feet, shouting at the screen.

That was it. He'd watch no more. He could not permit such a humiliating loss of self-control. He muted the sound and turned away from the screen to pace in the narrow space along the bed.

He was near despair. It seemed to him that he'd lost his struggle with the celebrity-glorifying media. They'd made him out to be a spoiled rich kid, a sore loser, determined to tear down those wonderful, talented people who had achieved what he couldn't. Instead of exposing the celebrity cult, he was contributing to the greater glory of celebrities.

He glanced up. *The Tonight Show* was coming on. He'd wasted an entire evening watching television. He picked up the remote to switch it off.

Jay Leno walked onstage. He was carrying a bomb.

It was a big, round bomb with a wick sticking out, the kind of bomb cartoon characters throw. Markman brought up the volume. The audience was whooping with delight. Leno handed the bomb to his bandleader and went into his monologue. Whenever a joke fell flat, he'd go over and get the bomb and threaten to throw it at the audience.

The audience was roaring with laughter when Markman switched channels—to Letterman, who was doing the Top Ten Reasons Not To Heckle Tony Markman.

Markman hit the off switch. He sank down on the bed and buried his face in his arms. This was the worst yet. He'd become a national joke. Why had he allowed himself to look at *Tonight*, of all programs?

He hadn't watched it in almost twenty years. The show brought back memories he usually tried to keep out of his mind. Now he couldn't help it. He was a boy again, sitting on the couch with his mother watching Johnny Carson. His father, having made the usual complaints about it being way past Tony's bedtime, had gone to bed. Now it was just the two of them, laughing at Johnny. His mother was whispering to him that one day he'd be a famous comic too. The whole world was going to love him just as much as she loved him.

Now Markman opened his eyes. The remote was still grasped in his fist. He drew back his arm to hurl it at the blank television screen.

But at the last moment, he managed to get control of himself. It was a long time since he'd allowed those memories to upset him. Shoving them into a back corner of his mind, he lowered his arm and dropped the remote on the bed.

This was no time for emotional self-indulgence. This was a time for cold, clear thinking. He was an engineer like his father, and he'd reexamine his plan as if it were a malfunctioning machine. Find a way to repair it.

The problem, he decided, was that his identity had become known before he had a chance to complete the pattern with his final strike. The other bombings were only preparation. It was the final strike that would have spelled out his message to the world in a form that could not be trivialized or ignored. The final strike would have shown people that the celebrities on whom they lavished so much adoration didn't care about them at all. People would have seen through the false allure of celebrities. They never would have allowed themselves to be seduced and used again. If they hadn't discovered Markman's identity until the pattern was complete, they would have looked at him with awe, as someone who'd taught them a hard but necessary lesson.

It all would have happened according to plan—but for Harper.

Markman's hands curled into fists. His nails dug into his flesh. He could have killed Harper back in St. Louis—and he wished he'd done it.

He gave in to the anger, but only for a moment. It was another emotion he couldn't allow himself. He reasserted his control.

He sat up straight, opened his fists, and put his hands flat on his thighs, so that the sweat would be absorbed by the cloth of his trousers. He breathed deeply and evenly until he was calm.

This whole evening had been a waste of time, he decided. That was what always happened when he allowed his emotions to get the better of him. What did it matter if people were laughing at Tony Markman now? The laughter would cease on May 15. His plan was still on track. The pattern would be completed. *She* would die.

There was no reason to be angry at Harper, either. Markman had spared him in order to use him—and he'd proven useful. The plan had worked.

It crossed Markman's mind that he couldn't be certain Harper himself had fallen for the trick. Among the major figures in the case, Harper was conspicuous by his silence. Several of the newscasts had reported that he and the other guy, Addleman, were going to be in Washington tomorrow, in their capacity as consultants to the FBI.

Here was the only potential threat to his plan, Markman thought. Harper. He shouldn't have allowed all the media coverage to distract him. He should have been thinking about Harper.

Markman got up from the bed and sat down at the narrow desk against the wall. For the next few hours he sat there motionless, his gaze abstracted, just as he used to do at his workbench in the garage.

Weighing possibilities.

Laying plans.

Markman could think of several ways he might use Harper. Some of these plans involved his destruction. But Markman felt no hatred for the man. In fact, he felt an admiration for Harper, who in some ways was not unlike himself. He didn't seek vengeance on Harper for the media humiliation Markman had just gone through. No, Harper was just a tool. If he died, it would be for a useful purpose. Nothing personal.

Markman smiled. He hoped Will Harper would appreciate the distinction, but he probably wouldn't have time.

37

The plane landed at Washington's Dulles airport on time at 8:10 A.M. Neither Harper nor Addleman had checked-in luggage, so they headed for the rental car counters.

Rounding another turn in the long, crowded concourse, they saw a phalanx of journalists coming toward them. Neither man was surprised. Most were print journalists, but Harper saw at least two shoulder-mounted Minicams with TV news logos on them.

"What are you going to tell the FBI at your meeting today?" asked the woman in the lead, wielding a microphone like a gun. Addleman stared at Harper.

"Sorry, no comment," Harper said, shifting his garment bag strap to his other shoulder.

"Who really figured out the Aquila pattern? It was you, wasn't it, Mr. Addleman?" a man asked. The lens of a Minicam was peering over his right shoulder like the huge, intent eye of a giant insect.

"I—I really can't say." Addleman was blinking rapidly, looking straight ahead, trying to keep moving.

The crowd of reporters had attracted onlookers. They stared and pointed and asked who it was. This happened to Harper whenever he went out in public. He'd learned how to lip-read his name.

"Do you have any comment on the FBI's handling of the case?" asked the woman with the wireless microphone.

"No," Harper snapped.

"Oh, come on, Will, you've got to give me something," said the woman, as if they'd known each other for years. In fact, he'd never seen her before.

Another reporter jostled forward to get in Harper's face. "Do you concur with the Bureau's conclusion that Markman is dead?"

"Let's get out of here," Harper muttered to Addleman.

A reporter stuck the toe of his wingtip shoe in front of a wheel of Addleman's rolling suitcase to slow them down. Several of the media people were forging ahead to circle around in front of them, to trap them.

"Faster," Harper whispered to Addleman.

"They'll be on us at the car rental counter," Addleman said, gazing around with disbelief at the mass of media and onlookers.

"Forget about the car," Harper said, picking up speed and causing Addleman to struggle to keep up. "We can rent one at the hotel. Let's get a cab."

They pushed their way through the crowd at the carousels, then ran out of the terminal to a cab stand. A cab was letting someone out about a hundred feet beyond the lead taxi in line. Harper and Addleman reached the vehicle just as the driver was closing the trunk lid.

"Sorry, fellas," she said, "I gotta get in line behind the other cabs."

Harper fished out his wallet and removed a twenty. "Not this time, all right?"

The cabbie, a wizened, elderly woman with hard eyes and frizzy blond hair, glanced beyond them at the crowd of media types. She unlocked and opened the trunk lid again. "We can make an exception. Been makin' 'em all my life."

Harper and Addleman tossed their luggage inside, then quickly piled into the back of the taxi. The driver was in before they were. Harper heard the doors lock automatically from up front. Just in time, as a frenetic journalist with half-rim glasses and a red beard tried to open one of the cab doors. He apparently hurt his hand, because he backed away and stood bent over clutching it and making a face. Someone tapped loudly on Harper's window with a microphone, inches from his ear, as the cab pulled away.

"Persistent bastards, ain't they?" the driver commented, with a glance in the rearview mirror.

"Their job," Addleman said. "But I wish they'd do it someplace else."

Harper grinned as Addleman pulled out a handkerchief and mopped his flushed and perspiring face. As always, it had been a struggle to extricate the profiler from his hermitage in South Philadelphia. Even though he, like Harper, had been personally invited down by the FBI Director to consult on the bomber case, he was as reluctant as ever to visit the J. Edgar Hoover building.

Now that they were free of the media, Harper leaned back in the cab's soft upholstery. It was so much easier to relax in a cab when you were on expense account.

"How about that guy asking if Markman was really dead?" Addleman said. "That's a question I haven't been asked in a while. It's like that guy had some doubt."

Harper nodded. "A minority view."

They exchanged a look, but said nothing. Harper gave the driver the address of the hotel the FBI had booked them into.

The Omnium was a new hotel, with a lobby that was as busy, utilitarian, and charmless as the airport concourse they'd just left. They checked in and Addleman went up to their suite while Harper asked the clerk where he could rent a car. The clerk smilingly assured him that it wouldn't be necessary. An official limo would be pulling up outside at ten sharp to take Mr. Harper and Mr. Addleman to the Hoover Building.

Harper thanked him and turned away. Alarm bells would have been going off in his head if he'd been running security for a celebrity. He would've been asking how many people knew about the schedule, and how long had they known?

But he wasn't running security. He was the celebrity himself. He hadn't gotten used to it. In fact, he wondered how anyone got used to it. People seemed to know so much about him. They wanted to do things for him. And, of course, they wanted him to do things for them.

A few days before, Laura had been interviewed on television. She'd answered questions about their plans to restore their old brownstone, sell it, and retire on the proceeds. The interview brought a barrage of calls from TV producers. They wanted to know how Harper had managed to do the repair work. They wanted to videotape him driving screws and hammering nails. Harper refused, but that didn't stop the craziness. Gifts of power tools began arriving in the mail. A lawyer called to say his client wanted to buy their house when they were finished with it, for half a million dollars. Ten minutes later another lawyer offered to buy the place immediately, for three-quarters of a million.

The phone rang all the time these days. Security consulting firms offered him jobs. Charities for disabled people and retired cops offered him seats on their boards. Print journalists and TV producers demanded endless interviews. Literary agents and publishers told him he ought to be writing the story himself. Plastic surgeons wanted to try out radical new procedures on his hand.

At night, Harper and Laura would unplug the phone and go to bed, and remind one another that this strong wind that was roaring around their ears and unsettling everything in their lives would eventually blow itself out.

But there was no sign of that yet.

He was walking toward the elevators when he heard his name called. He turned—and froze in astonishment.

Striding toward him across the lobby was Captain Brand, his old boss on the Bomb Squad. The man who'd maneuvered Harper out of his job and then implicated him in the IAD probe. Now Brand was bearing down on him, smiling with hand extended. He was wearing his NYPD dress uniform. Hurrying to catch up with him were a young woman carrying a bulky carton, and a man with a couple of cameras slung over his shoulders. *Great!* Harper thought. *More media types.*

"Will, terrific to see you!" Brand boomed in the hearty voice Harper remembered far too well.

"Hello, Captain," Harper said. He'd gotten over his first surprise and was curious to see if it would bother Brand to shake hands with him. It didn't.

"Call me Nathan, please, Will."

The Captain went on beaming at him. Harper smiled back. He couldn't help it; he was genuinely amused. Brand was one of the most dedicated and energetic headline-chasers in the NYPD. Now here he was courting Harper. It was an accolade, of sorts.

"Listen, Captain, I'm a little pressed for time." Harper couldn't deny that it was a pleasure to say that to Brand, after all the times Brand had said it to him.

"Sure, Will, I understand. There'll be more than enough time to reminisce later. We'll just do the presentation now."

"Presentation?" echoed Harper, bewildered.

Brand turned to the young woman. She was a tall, beautiful redhead in a short skirt. Brand had always liked having a lovely aide at his side. She bestowed a melting smile on Harper as she handed the bulky box she'd been carrying to Brand.

The cameraman moved into position in front of them. People all over the lobby were stopping and staring. Captain Brand commanded the stage on occasions like this, Harper had to give that to him. "Will," he said, "the men and women on the Squad asked me to give you this. We all hope you'll never need one again, but if you do, we want you to have the best."

He opened the carton. Inside it was a blast-protection suit. Brand held it up for the camera. The flash went off. Then he handed the box to Harper.

It surprised Harper how light the box was. The suit was a new model, unlike the kind he'd worn during his days on duty. It was brown, and on the sleeve was the stencil NYPD.

"It's the latest technology," Brand said proudly. "More protection and less weight. You can move around like a cat in it, despite its bulk. It's even vented so you won't sweat like a pig in it, and its shatterproof visor is a special material that won't fog and obscure your vision."

"Impressive," Harper said, staring at the bomb suit.

"When the Feds let you go, the Squad would like to invite you to come back to Rodman's Neck," Brand said. "We'd be honored if you'd lecture at the training school."

"Even though I'm a subject of an IAD probe?"

Brand shrugged. "I happen to know that's never going to go anywhere. Besides, real cops will think you're more of a hero than ever for having been investigated by those bastards in IAD."

Harper didn't have the time to think it over, but he knew what conclusion he'd reach. Brand was obviously self-serving, but Harper did want to go back and talk to the Squad again. "I'll be there," he said.

Brand grasped his hand again and turned to grin at the camera. Harper knew it was naive of him to think that anything Captain Brand said could be true, yet he hoped that it really had been the men and women on the Squad who'd sent the bomb suit to him. A few months ago, Brand had told him they wanted nothing to do with him because he was a hard-luck guy. That had hurt him deeply. Deep down, he'd always believed he was still one of them.

One last handshake and photo, and Brand let him go. Tucking the box under his arm, Harper made for the elevators. He had to hurry and change into his suit if he was going to be ready when the government limo arrived to take him to FBI Headquarters. Not that it would matter that much if he was late. He'd noticed that these days people expected him to be late. They knew how busy he was. They were willing to wait.

Frances Wilson would be especially willing to wait. Now that he and Addleman had become media darlings, Wilson and the FBI were courting them no less ardently than Captain Brand. They were completely vindicated. They had triumphed. If Harper had any doubts about that, all he had to do was look at the television.

As the elevator ascended, he couldn't resist opening the box to look at the bomb suit again. He ran his fingers over the NYPD stencil. It was pleasant to anticipate his return to the Bomb Squad. He thought of familiar faces he hadn't seen in a long time. Imagined the admiring gazes of the new recruits.

Back in St. Louis, in that odd, brief meeting that Harper couldn't get out of his head, Anthony Markman had told him that all the happy endings were on the screen. There were no happy endings in real life.

But now it seemed that old injustices were going to be put right, old grievances forgotten, and there was going to be a happy ending to his career at the NYPD. What would Markman say about that?

Harper closed the box and straightened up. His reflection in the mirrored wall of the elevator looked grim. He knew what Markman would say.

That it wasn't over yet.

38

At first, Harper thought they were being taken to Frances's office, but instead they were ushered into a conference room. It had a view of Pennsylvania Avenue, and in the distance the Washington Monument. The white spire was more visible than on Harper and Addleman's first visit, when the day had been overcast.

The room itself was large, with a wide, hexagonal table of oak with an inset slate center. Brown, leather-backed chairs were arranged around the table. There was a smell of astringently scented air freshener. As in Frances's office, the walls were hung with portraits of the President, the Attorney General, and the FBI director. No J. Edgar Hoover portrait here, either. The Bureau was always trying to live down something. It was a fine organization, but with too many Frances Wilsons.

"Get you some coffee? Anything?" asked the agent who'd shown them in. He was a clean-cut young man with hair so short his scalp showed through. The knot in his tie was the size of a pea.

Harper and Addleman declined. The agent padded across the soft carpet to the door and left them alone in the quiet room.

They didn't have long to wait.

Frances Wilson burst through the door smiling broadly. She was wearing a light-gray suit with a rather long jacket and a rather short skirt, and carrying a leather briefcase. In her wake trailed a short, slender, gray-haired man. Harper, who noticed hands, saw that this man's were manicured and as delicate as a woman's.

"Special Agent Ralph Dexter of Investigative Support," Frances said. There were handshakes all around.

"Please make yourselves comfortable," Frances invited. Pulling out one of the leather-backed chairs, she sat, showing a lot of leg.

Agent Dexter waited until everyone was seated, then chose his chair carefully, as if to complete some sort of symmetry. He didn't look comfortable.

"I've asked Agent Dexter to sit in because he'll be taking over the day-to-day running of the Markman investigation," Frances said.

Addleman raised his eyebrows. "You're moving on to other things, Frances?"

"Other cases are pressing, yes."

"We called this meeting to get your input," Dexter said. "Loose ends need to be tied up and questions need to be answered. Even though we have no trial to prepare for, the media pressure is intense, so we want to wrap up this investigation as soon as possible. Do you think we have to worry about caches of explosives the bomber may have left behind?"

Addleman glanced at Harper. Harper said, "I don't think he had explosives cached. But I think he may have taken some with him."

Agent Dexter squinted at Harper. "I don't get—when—"

"When he escaped from the garage," said Addleman.

Sighing, Dexter turned to Frances. "Well, here we go," he muttered. "Supermarket tabloid time." He was obviously cut from the same bolt as Frances.

"We haven't said anything to the media about this," protested Addleman. He was unwrapping one of the candies he chewed when he wasn't able to smoke. He popped it in his mouth and bit down on it. "But we think you ought to conduct this investigation on the assumption that the bomber is still out there—at least until stronger evidence of his death surfaces."

Dexter was shaking his head disgustedly. He started to speak, but Frances held up a hand. "Let me say first off, we appreciate your coming to us rather than the media. We'll give your views a full hearing."

She smiled at them, with what appeared to be genuine gratitude. Harper thought she had more gray hairs now than when they had met in this building just a few weeks ago, and that her eyes seemed more hooded. Sleeplessness, pressure, and frustration would do it to a person. The Markman case had not been kind to Agent Wilson.

Dexter said, "The bloodstained piece of workbench isn't good enough evidence for you that he's dead? Its DNA matches Markman's DNA. We took several organic samples inside his house. Hair from the bed, samples taken from used tissues, mouthwash, a razor. Do you think our lab guys made a mistake?"

"No. It's Markman's DNA," said Harper. "I bet he cut himself deliberately, then smeared the blood onto the piece of wood. Then he planted it."

"That's some devious thinking, on the spur of the moment," Dexter said.

"It was preparation," Harper said. "An adaptable plan. Markman never does anything on the spur of the moment."

"If he had time to do all this, how come he didn't just make a run for it?"

"He saw the advantages of being thought dead. Chief among them, the advantage of surprise. Once again he has the freedom of operation he used to enjoy when nobody knew about him," said Addleman.

Frances stared at Harper. "Do you actually think that's possible, Will?"

"Of course it's possible. And it worked. You and Dexter are convinced Markman's dead."

"I'm convinced Elvis is dead, too," Dexter said.

Frances raised her hand again to silence him. "How did he get out of the garage without being seen?"

"There was another door at the back. The neighbor told the police that."

"But if he was that close, and out in the open trying to run away, the explosion would have killed him."

"He knows how to direct blast. Remember the Buckner killing? He brought that building down exactly the way he wanted to, and he did the same with the garage."

Dexter could contain himself no longer. "You saw him run into the garage, you saw it blow up. How can you of all people—"

"I'd alarmed him when I talked to him," Harper said. "Given him too much time to prepare. When the cops arrived, he was ready. Knocked me into the drainage ditch where I'd be able to witness the show he was putting on."

"Harper's appearance was a serious threat to him," Addleman said. "But he figured out how to turn it into an opportunity, like a master chess player. That's Markman's profile. We know this guy, Frances."

Dexter said, in a bored and dismissive tone, "Tell us where you think Markman went."

"He's not far away from us right now," Addleman replied, glancing out at the Washington Monument.

"Why wouldn't he leave the country, if he's such a careful planner? Go where he's safest?"

"Safest?" Harper said. "He didn't fake his death to be safe. He did it so he could complete the pattern. He has one more strike to make. The big one."

Addleman nodded vigorously. His face was turning red with excitement. "Frances, come on. Markman's still out there, more dangerous than ever. You can't close the case just because you want to get it over with."

Frances straightened up. Her heavy lids lifted from her dark eyes and she glared at Addleman. Then she got control of herself. "I admit this investigation's been an embarrassment for the Bureau. And for me personally."

"Which is why you want it closed and forgotten as soon as possible," Addleman said.

She remained calm, which impressed Harper. "There are other considerations, Harold, which you and Will have the luxury of not worrying about."

"Political considerations, I'm sure," scoffed Addleman.

"Of course they're political. This is Washington. When the Aquila pattern was leaked, it shook people up, and they haven't calmed down yet. If we now announce that the bomber might still be alive, a lot of senators and congresspeople are going to get seriously worried that they might be the next targets. And these are the people who vote on our budget. Cabinet members—even the Attorney General herself—would get worried too. You can't imagine the kind of pressure we'd bring on ourselves if we waffled on the question of Markman being dead."

"Waffled," muttered Addleman, and shook his head.

"You know how many people in this building have been going without sleep for the last few weeks, working on this case? And it's the same with the Secret Service. They were at the highest level of alert until we announced Markman was dead. Can you imagine how they'll react if we go back to them and say we're not sure?"

Addleman made a sweeping gesture. "None of this matters, Frances! Will you forget all the bureaucratic bullshit and listen to your gut instinct? Deep down, do you feel sure Markman is dead?"

Frances looked him in the eye and said, promptly and tonelessly, "Yes, I know he's dead."

Addleman laughed harshly. "Hey, you've learned to say the official line as if you mean it. That would be enough if this was a press conference. But it's not. We're all cops here." He glanced sideways at Dexter. "Except I don't know about this guy."

Dexter set his jaw. "Well, I know about you, you old drunk. I've read your file and—"

"Ralph, stop right there, please," said Frances crisply, and Dexter did stop. She laid her hand on his arm and smiled at him. "Listen, I have to apologize. I brought you into the process too soon. I didn't realize how much still had to be ironed out with Will and Hal. If you'd just give the three of us a little time together—"

Dexter, tight-lipped, nodded to her and left the room.

"I appreciate this, Ralph, thank you," she called after him. Harper had to admire the firm yet gracious way she'd stopped the shouting match and gotten rid of Dexter. She knew how to run a meeting. If that was all there was to it, she'd be a great investigator.

"Before we continue with the discussion, I'd like you to review these." Frances rose. Taking two slim manila folders from her briefcase, she passed them to Harper and Addleman.

"What is this?" asked Addleman, frowning.

"Your contracts as independent consultants. Your compensation is discussed in paragraph eleven. And Hal, there are some changes in your pension and health insurance that should interest you."

Harper and Addleman glanced at each other. They didn't open the folders. Frances continued as pleasantly as ever.

"While you review those, I'm going to call the Director's office. If he has a minute free I'll take you up."

"A handshake and a photo," said Addleman. "Something to show our grandchildren."

"When is the press conference, Frances?" Harper asked.

"Press conference?"

"That's the idea, isn't it? You want us to get with the team in delivering the message. Markman's dead. Everybody can relax."

"It's not true, Frances," Addleman said. He pushed the folder back across the table toward her.

Frances stopped smiling. She sat down and looked at Harper, then at Addleman. "Hal, you've already allowed self-destructive behavior to destroy your career once. Now you've got a second chance. Don't blow it. The Bureau wants you on the inside. We value your input."

"No, you don't," said Addleman wearily. "You're not the Bureau, Frances. You're out for yourself. You're misusing the Bureau."

She turned to Harper. He shrugged and looked away.

"Okay, fine. If that's the way you want it." Her tone was cold now. "What you are going to do now—and I mean now—is leave Washington. You will tell the media that we had a full and frank discussion. You will not say one word about your theory that Markman is alive."

"Or you'll do what?" Addleman taunted. "We know you can bribe, now let's see how you threaten."

"Shut up, Hal. I've taken enough crap from you today." Again her eyes moved from Addleman's face to Harper's. "You guys are pretty full of yourselves. You like being media heroes, don't you? Then you'd better understand that the only reason you became heroes is that the Bureau allowed it to happen."

"By handling the investigation incompetently, you mean?" asked Harper.

Frances went on as if she hadn't heard him. "We let it happen, and we can turn it around. You guys are outsiders. Amateurs. The Bureau has long-standing relationships with powerful people in the media. When we choose to spin a story, we can do it."

"How do you intend to spin this one?"

"If you two don't sew your lips shut, you'll start to see TV reports about how the Bureau was a lot closer to tracking down Markman in St. Louis than anyone knew before. A lot more receptive to your suggestions. We could have brought him in alive. People will believe that; the Bureau has been building a reputation for resolving confrontations peacefully. And what happened instead? You rushed in alone, Markman blew himself up, and scores of innocent people were injured, thousands of dollars in property damage was done. All because Will Harper is a headline-grabber, a hot dog, a loose cannon. You like those names, Harper? They're what you're going to be hearing."

"I'm sour on the Bureau," Addleman said, "but I know it's better than that."

"In this case, I *am* the Bureau," Frances said. "I can use it the way it uses me." Folding her arms, she leaned back in her chair. She watched the two men and waited. Neither said anything. After a moment, Agent Wilson was satisfied. She picked up her briefcase and rose.

From the door she said, "Security will be here in a minute to escort you out. Go straight home, and we won't have any problems."

Turning, she disappeared into the corridor. The room seemed suddenly very quiet. Harper turned to Addleman. He was looking at the portraits on the wall.

"Know something?" he said. "They ought to have a picture of Hoover in here after all."

39

The "escort" Frances sent was not a special agent but a uniformed member of the FBI Police—the Bureau's own internal police force. The unsmiling man showed Harper and Addleman out by a side door. No reporters or photographers were waiting for them. It was as if Frances Wilson were giving them an early demonstration of her power.

No official car was waiting for them either, of course. So Harper and Addleman began to walk down Pennsylvania Avenue and look for a cab.

Although it was only May 14, the weather was summery, hot and humid. The tourist season already seemed to be in full swing. There was plenty of traffic. Buses lumbered past on the way to the Mall museums. Families lined up on the curbs, to be photographed against the backdrop of the Washington Monument. A long line snaked around the Hoover Building itself, waiting to get into the FBI Museum.

"We could go public of course," said Addleman abruptly.

"Yes, we could."

"All we'd have to do would be schedule a press conference. Hundreds of reporters would show up. We might even be live on C-Span."

"Or the networks."

A motorcade—two limousines, flanked by police motorcycles—rounded the corner with sirens wailing and lights flashing. Tourists turned to watch as the long black vehicles with little flagpoles on their fenders swept by. Harper could see the inquisitive smiles on people's faces as they wondered who was behind the darkly tinted windows. A Cabinet member? A foreign dignitary?

"There's no question the media would jump on the story," Harper said. "But as to whether any effective action would come out of it, who knows?"

Addleman shoved his hands into his pockets and bowed his head in thought. Harper would have expected that being out on the crowded street would make the reclusive profiler nervous, but he seemed too preoccupied to notice what was going on around him. Harper stopped looking for a cab. There was no hurry, after all: They didn't have any idea where to go or what to do next.

The shrill warble of sirens made him turn. The two black limos and their motorcycle escort swung around the corner again. Were they lost, Harper wondered, or circling the block because the VIP was early for his appointment? But of course it could be a different motorcade. At any given moment there must be a number of important people on the move around Washington. Once again, pedestrians all around them were turning to watch the limousines go by and speculate about who was inside.

How Anthony Markman would hate this little scene, Harper thought as he walked along. It would enrage him to see the excited smiles on the faces of these people, as they tried in vain to peer in the tinted windows of a passing limo. Markman, bitter and ingenious as he was, had made it his task to reverse the powerful attraction of fame and fortune, to bring everyone down to his level—or below. Looking around at the intrigued expressions and curious gazes, Harper could see that Markman hadn't made any progress yet.

But he wasn't finished, of course.

"Harold?" Harper said. "Do you think we can anticipate him again? Figure out his next move?"

Addleman was lighting a cigarette. Harper noticed that there were other puffers around. In the Federal city, the street was just about the only place where smoking was allowed. Addleman didn't speak until he'd had that first drag. "We know where. But we don't know when, and we don't know who."

"His trajectory is upward. Always has been. This will be the most ingenious bomb. The highest death toll. The biggest celebrity."

"There are a lot of people in Washington who are more famous than Speed Rogers," Addleman said. "Far too many."

"But won't Markman want to go after the most famous person in the country?" Harper said. "Maybe we should buy a *Washington Post,* see if the President has any public events scheduled any time soon."

"I'm sure we'll find out that he does, but so what?" Addleman blew out smoke. "It's more likely to be the First Lady. That's only a guess, of course."

Harper stared at him. "Why do you say that?"

"Look at the bomber's other victims. Markman's never gone after people who had real power. It's fame that draws him. He likes to destroy people who have a certain kind of allure, a certain capacity to make people admire and envy them, independent of how much power or wealth they have. Perhaps famous people who don't deserve to *be* famous. I can't explain it any further."

They'd reached another corner. The signal was against them and they had to wait while Washington's heavy traffic rolled past. Exhaust fumes were thick. The sun was hot on Harper's head. He loosened his collar and peeled off his jacket.

"There must be a way we can use what you've figured out," he said.

Addleman threw away his cigarette. He shook his head in frustration. "I've been trying. I've been thinking about nothing else. But it's all too damned vague. It doesn't cut down on the possibilities."

The light changed. They crossed the street in a throng of pedestrians.

"I'll tell you something else useless," Addleman said.

"What?"

"I think it may be personal this time."

"Personal?"

"He started out by attacking Blake, someone he knew and bore a grudge against. I think he may be coming full circle in his last strike."

"You mean the target may be someone he knows?"

Addleman laughed dryly. "I was up all night reading everything we know about Markman, and I couldn't find any instance of his meeting anybody famous—or knowing anybody who later became famous."

They walked on. Up ahead, Harper saw a tall iron fence, and beyond it, trees. They were nearing the grounds of the White House. Since the last time he'd been here, this stretch of Pennsylvania Avenue had been closed to traffic as a precaution against car bombs. The resulting pedestrian mall was a lively place on this sunny day, with vendors and entertainers working the large crowds of tourists and office workers on their lunch hour.

Harper became aware of a new sound underlying the hubbub of the crowd. It rose to a buffeting roar. Looking toward the White House grounds, he saw a blue Marine helicopter rising above the tops of the trees. It rose a little higher, then nosed down slightly and moved swiftly northward, passing directly overhead.

As the shadow flitted over him, Harper looked around. The office workers had stopped eating. The musicians had stopped playing. The juggler was holding onto his wooden pins. A nearby vendor had frozen with a hot dog in one hand, a ladle of sauerkraut in the other. He and his customer were watching the helicopter. Everybody was watching the helicopter.

A chill passed through Harper as he imagined that Markman was nearby, observing this scene. As the helicopter roared away in the distance, he turned to Addleman.

"Maybe we'd better call the Secret Service. Warn them the First Lady might be a target."

Addleman frowned. "That would be rash. Probably counterproductive. Anyway, it's only a guess."

"Then maybe we ought to schedule that press conference. Tell them Markman's still alive."

"That would be rash too. But I see your point." Addleman smiled sourly. "Let's go back to the hotel, see if we can think of an effective course of action."

"And if we can't?"

Addleman shrugged. "Then we'll do something rash."

Harper couldn't think of a better idea, even though he knew rash behavior and bombs could be a deadly combination.

40

The suite at the Omnium had two bedrooms, each with its own bath, opening on a large living room. The windows overlooked Connecticut Avenue and a row of chic storefronts and restaurants in which only lobbyists could afford to dine. Fresh flowers and a bowl of fruit were laid out on the rosewood coffee table. The tan suede couch offered ample room for Addleman to sprawl full-length, and Harper had twelve feet of Persian carpet to pace over.

They'd come a long way since their last brainstorming session in Addleman's South Philadelphia tenement.

Only the frustration was the same.

They didn't know who or when. All they knew was that Washington was the place, and that wasn't enough. Addleman had plugged in his laptop and modem and started hitting government Web sites and downloading schedules and announcements of appearances. Looking them over, Harper realized that Washington was a feast spread out before the Celebrity Bomber. In addition to the First Family, he could choose for his victim among the Vice President and his family, the members of both Houses of Congress, and the justices of the Supreme Court.

Even if Addleman was right about the bomber preferring a glamorous person to a truly powerful one, he still had plenty of choices. A vain

TV correspondent who always tried to outshine the events she was covering was holding a book-signing in Georgetown. A movie star turned activist was testifying before Congress about an environmental issue. A basketball player was leading a delegation of ghetto youth to the White House. There were too many possibilities.

By mid afternoon, Harper needed a break. Leaving Addleman smoking and muttering to himself, he went down to the lobby newsstand to pick up the latest editions of the *Post* and the *Times*. The desk clerk flagged him down on his way back to the elevators. He and Addleman hadn't been answering the phone, and there were a lot of messages for them.

Back at the suite, he gave the newspapers to Addleman, then emptied the pink message slips from his pockets into an unused ice bucket. He sat down and put the bucket on the coffee table in front of him and drew a slip at random.

"Here's one from the accounting section of the Bureau," he said, "notifying us they're not going to pay our hotel bill. And here's one from Frances herself. All it says is 'go home.'"

"Don't waste your time with that stuff, Will. Help me with the papers. Here, you take the Metro section."

"In a minute," Harper said.

Addleman stifled a yawn. "Look, if you're expecting a call from Laura, why don't you just go ahead and call her first? Don't waste your time going through all those messages."

"It's not Laura I'm expecting a call from," said Harper, as he scanned another slip and put it down.

"Who then?"

"Markman."

Lowering his paper, Addleman stared at Harper. "Markman's not one of your sicko sex killers who calls up cops and reporters, practically begging to get caught. That doesn't fit his profile."

"No, but he seems to think he has some kind of . . . I don't know, some special relationship with me. He might have sent a message, and it may tell us something."

"You're wasting your time," said Addleman, and returned to the *Post*.

Harper riffled through the messages and found to his annoyance that Addleman was right. There was nothing from the bomber. Most of the messages were from reporters, with the usual sprinkling of con artists and publicity-seekers. But there was one slip that Harper returned to.

"Harold?" he said. "A guy named Aaron P. Sherman called. Says he has information that may be important to us."

"A fruitcake. Toss it." Addleman was scanning the columns of the newspaper and didn't bother to look up.

"He left his work number. It's at Carlson & Wolper. Aren't they one of those big D.C. law firms you read about—the ones where senators go to work when they're out of office?"

"They are. What would somebody at a firm like that know that could help us?"

"I don't know, but he's probably not a fruitcake. I'll call him."

"Suit yourself."

A mellow-voiced receptionist answered at the law firm. Mr. Sherman was unavailable, so Harper left his number. Then he picked up the *Times* and started to go through it.

Twenty-five minutes later, Sherman called back. He was using the hotel's house phone from the lobby. Harper raised his eyebrows to Addleman as he asked Sherman to come up. Whatever information the lawyer had, he was certainly anxious to unburden himself.

Aaron P. Sherman turned out to be as imposing a figure as Harper had expected. He was about sixty, and he united the advantages of dignity and vigor. His blue eyes had heavy bags under them, but were still clear, his swept-back silver hair thick. He had a lean physique and very broad shoulders; either he was out rowing his scull on the Potomac every morning, or the man who'd tailored his dark-blue pinstriped suit had done an exceptionally skillful job.

It was strange to see a man like this looking so nervous and undecided. Sherman gave each of them a firm handshake, but he couldn't quite look them in the eye. Perching on the edge of the sofa, he put his leather briefcase in his lap, then laid it on the floor. Now he didn't seem to know what to do with his hands. He said, "I—uh—I have to ask you a few questions."

Addleman smiled. He was taking an interest in their visitor now. He said, "I thought it was the other way around. You had information for us."

"I do. But I don't know if it's important. It may not matter at all. You have to tell me—is Markman dead?"

Harper and Addleman exchanged a glance. Before either of them could respond, Sherman started talking again.

"I'm not sure I'm doing the right thing," he said. "I didn't want to go to the police. You see, in a way it could be said that I'm violating a confidence. And—and I don't really know if the information I have is of the slightest importance."

"But you couldn't just keep quiet about it. You didn't feel right about that either," said Addleman, in a soothing tone that surprised Harper. He sounded like a shrink who treated Upper East Side neurotics rather than a criminal psychologist who dealt with psychotic killers.

Sherman nodded. "This isn't hot information, believe me. It all happened a long time ago. In a way, I hate to bring it up again, certainly not with the police, who'd be sure to leak it to the media. I'm paid to keep secrets, gentlemen. If my clients saw my name in the papers, read about what I'd told—"

He broke off, swallowing nervously. "I've been following the investigation, waiting for proof of Markman's death to surface. Because then there'd be no reason to bring up this old story. And the FBI says he's dead; everybody says so, but you, Mr. Harper—you've kept silent. When I heard that you were in Washington, I—"

"You're not off the hook, Mr. Sherman," said Addleman. "Sorry."

"Markman is alive," said Harper. "He's probably in Washington right now, setting up his next bombing."

Sherman looked down and sighed heavily. But he wouldn't have been a Washington lawyer if he hadn't known how to handle bad news. So after a moment he began to tell his story.

"Thirty years ago, I was an associate at Wyland Nave, the leading law firm in St. Louis. Markman Manufacturing was one of our clients. And—well, to make a long story short, I ended up handling the divorce of Lucas Markman. Anthony's father."

"Did you?" said Harper, with keen interest. He remembered Hayden, in St. Louis, talking about the divorce.

"Yes. We were a corporate law firm. We didn't do marital work as a general rule. But the Markmans had been clients for years, so—" He shrugged.

He seemed to have stalled, so Harper prompted him. "It was a bitter divorce, I understand."

"Very. In my career, I've handled much more important matters. Billion-dollar cases. But there's not one I remember as clearly as this one." His eyes narrowed and his lips set. Harper thought he was going to dry up again, but after a moment he went on.

"The wife, Joanna, was a good deal younger than Lucas Markman, and from—well, from a very different background. But she was beautiful and he was infatuated with her. It went very much the way you would expect. By the time of the divorce, they hated each other. She intended to make him pay—literally. She wanted the house, and a large cut of the family fortune, including an ownership stake in the firm. They were absurd demands, but I think Lucas would have accepted them, if she hadn't demanded custody of Tony, who was twelve at the time."

Sherman paused, looked down, got going again. This was getting harder for him. "Joanna's lawyer was greedy and unprincipled. It was impossible for me to deal with him. That was why I had to resort to—why I did what I did."

"You threatened to accuse her of sexually abusing her son," said Addleman. Harper looked over at him in surprise.

Sherman looked down again. In the course of this meeting they'd seen as much of his silver hair as of his face. In a long drawn-out sigh he said, "Yes. And It wasn't an empty threat, or one I would have made lightly. Lucas was quite sure of what was going on. I will always remember the day he told me, how bitter and ashamed he was. I only wish I'd been more understanding. It seemed shocking to me. Monstrous. You have to remember, this was thirty years ago. Incest was still the darkest and deepest of secrets."

"And the threat worked," Harper said.

"Oh, yes. She gave up all claims on Tony—in fact, she never saw or spoke to him again. We paid her off and she left town. A few years later she was killed in a car wreck." Abruptly Sherman got to his feet. They looked up at him. "This is one case in my legal career that I'm not proud of," he said. "If it's not important, I trust you won't make it public."

"It's important," said Harper.

Addleman looked at him. But Sherman didn't seem to have heard. He picked up his slim leather briefcase and got out of the room as quickly as he could. It was as if he believed he had rid himself of this unpleasant memory once and for all. Now he was eager to return to his posh law office and his comparatively sanitary billion-dollar cases.

As soon as the door closed on him, Harper said, "We need a picture of Joanna Markman."

Addleman didn't ask why. He picked up a manila folder bulging with printouts and clippings that was resting on the coffee table and began to leaf through it.

"You already knew he'd been abused," said Harper.

Addleman replied without looking up. "No. But with this kind of personality disorder, you're always alert for the possibility of some kind of mother complex."

"You didn't mention the possibility to me."

"You seem to have limited patience for psychological speculation unbolstered by evidence. Here we go."

He held up a page clipped from last week's issue of *Time*. Under the caption A PRIVILEGED CHILDHOOD were several photos of Markman as a boy. In one, he was an infant in his mother's arms. She was lovely, as Sherman had said, compact, and smiling in a way that dared. She had a dancer's tight, shapely body.

"Yes," Harper said.

"You've seen this picture before?"

"No. I've seen another one. At Markman's house. Framed, on the television."

"He probably has pictures of her everywhere," said Addleman. "He's probably in denial about the incest. Has deep and conflicted feelings about her. Anger. Guilt. A sense of betrayal he doesn't understand. A sense of loss, too."

Harper was up and pacing, returning in his mind to that strange meeting with the killer in his living room. "He kept talking about how celebrities seduce people. How they win people's trust and then use them."

"He's really talking about his mother, of course. Why didn't you tell me about this picture before, Will?"

"I guess I forgot. I didn't think it was important. It wasn't the sort of picture a guy usually keeps of his mother."

"It was sexual?"

"I guess, in a way. I thought at first it might be a picture of a girlfriend. She was young in the shot, in her early thirties. She was seated at a dressing table and was smiling, and she was wearing lingerie, something silky and white that showed a little cleavage."

"Lingerie? Blond, with a dancer's body?" A strange, intent look came into Addleman's eyes. Then he was up, grabbing the *Washington Post* he'd been perusing before Sherman came in.

"What is it?"

But Addleman paid no attention. He tore through the pages until he found the one he wanted. Folding the paper, he thrust it in front of Harper.

He recognized the woman in the picture immediately. It was, after all, one of the most famous faces in the world. This picture, like many of the ones he'd seen of her, showed her with her hands on her hips, grinning beautifully and defiantly. She wasn't wearing lingerie in this shot, but she had in plenty of others. The caption said she had arrived from Buenos Aires that day at Washington's Dulles Airport.

"I don't see—" Harper started to say.

Then he did see.

It was the very familiarity of the person that had prevented him from seeing the resemblance at first, but there it was: the blond hair, the compact, dancer's figure, the erotic challenge in her grin and her stance. She was no doubt the most famous and recognizable woman in the world. And perhaps the ultimate celebrity.

"She's going to be his last victim," Addleman said.

Harper nodded. It had to be.

Delilah! Singer, dancer, actress, self-promoter and rock star turned cultural icon.

And mother.

41

Harper hadn't been in a helicopter in many years. The pilot seemed to be flying very fast and low. As they went over the Mall, they were level with the top of the Washington Monument. He could distinctly see the people walking on the grass below, trailing long shadows from the setting sun.

The helicopter soared over Fourteenth Street, which was clogged with rush hour traffic. The Potomac flashed like a mirror as they crossed it. Harper had a glimpse of Arlington Cemetery—green lawns and long, orderly rows of white crosses—and then there was only suburban sprawl that seemed as if it would never end.

It did end, though, and they were flying over woods and fields toward the Blue Ridge Mountains. Occasionally Harper glimpsed the roof of a big house, or a cluster of horses grazing on a sun-streaked greensward. This was Virginia's fox-hunting country, where many members of the capital's elite had their weekend places. Delilah and her entourage were staying at a rented estate here.

It wasn't the sort of place he associated with the rock star. Not at all. But throughout her long career there'd been a New Delilah every couple of years. The latest transformation was the most complete. She'd become a mother a year or so ago, and ever since she'd been staying out of the spotlight as much as a superstar could. Some said it was just an extended maternity leave, and she was going to be back soon, just as outrageous as ever. But others insisted that she was going to abandon the whole rock scene to become a serious movie actress, and still others said she was going to quit show business entirely. Her visit to the Washington area had naturally stirred rumors that she was becoming interested in politics. These rumors, absurd as they seemed, had brought fulminations from the Christian Coalition.

Harper had rented a helicopter for this trip not only because it was the fastest way to get to the country but because he wanted to make an impressive arrival. He doubted, now, that anybody'd be impressed. There were numerous helicopters in the air around him: homeward-bound Washington power brokers, for whom the helicopter was a commuting vehicle.

The pilot was talking on the radio. Harper couldn't hear, but he must be obtaining permission to land. They were slowing and descending. They passed over a mansion on a hilltop, and Harper saw a columned portico and a vast slate roof with a long row of dormers and numerous chimneys. Then they began to drop toward a helipad.

Abruptly the descent ceased. The craft hovered. Leaning toward Harper, the pilot shouted over the racket, "They won't let us land. Sorry. You want me to set down at the nearest airport, or go back to D.C.?"

"Go ahead and land," shouted Harper. "I'll take the responsibility."

"Sorry, sir. I could lose my license."

"Just set it down!"

The pilot shook his head. The helicopter pitched and went into a wide turn, picking up speed and altitude.

Leaving Delilah behind.

Harper pounded his thigh in frustration and yelled at the pilot, but it was no use.

By the time Harper made his way back to the estate it was dark. A taxi dropped him at the front gate, and he pleaded his case into the grille of an intercom, under the beady eye of a videocamera and the bright beam of a halogen light. The voice on the intercom told him to wait.

It was a long wait. He spent the time thinking about what he'd say if they let him in. Harper knew no important person who'd be willing to make a call for him. He had no credentials to show. All he had was a copy of *People* magazine he'd bought at the newsstand in the county airport where the helicopter had dropped him off. It had him on the cover.

He remembered what Addleman had said that afternoon, about glitzy celebrities who had fame but no real power. That was Harper. He'd become one of those people for whom Anthony Markman felt the deepest contempt. He shoved the *People* into the pocket of his suitcoat.

The night was very quiet and he heard the car coming down the drive a long time before he saw it. Headlights dazzled him as it approached.

The car stopped and a tall man climbed out. Harper'd been expecting a rent-a-cop in uniform, but this man was wearing faded jeans and a black T-shirt that swelled over his gut. His shoulders were broad and his bare arms bulged with muscle. A tattoo of a snake wound around his left bicep. His graying hair was pulled back in a ponytail. The blunt-featured, deeply-lined face wasn't friendly.

He didn't open the gates but walked up to talk to Harper through the bars.

"Now what are you on about, mate?" The voice was deep, the accent British, or possibly Australian.

Harper said, "I have to talk to Delilah."

"Not a chance."

"Do you believe I'm who I say I am?"

"Oh yes, Mr. Harper. I believe that. I already called the FBI about you. They say you're barmy."

"You ought to consider the consequences if the FBI's wrong."

The big man folded his arms and rocked back on his heels. He smiled with what appeared to be genuine amusement. "Next you'll tell me that the person who has my job on Speed Rogers's staff is still kicking himself because he didn't listen to you."

"No, she isn't," said Harper. "She's dead."

The man stopped smiling. He didn't say anything, but after a moment he took a remote control out of his pocket and clicked it. The gates swung open.

Five minutes later, Harper was following the security chief down a hallway on the second floor of the house. They passed a few people who glared at Harper and said hello to Bobs the big security chief.

"How come they call you Bobs?" Harper asked, trying to gain a little trust from the man.

"Name's really Bob, but I'm big enough for two so I'm plural."

"Got a last name?"

"Nope. Just Bobs, is who I am."

"You work for Delilah a long time?" Harper asked.

"Off and on for three years. My regular employer's Lord Melroy. He owns this place, but he's out of the country so he's lending it, and me, to Delilah."

"His name's familiar. Is he British nobility?"

Bobs grinned. "He's not what you'd call a real lord, except with his group, Lord Melroy and the Mad Plaid. You saying you never heard of them?"

Now Harper did recall the Mad Plaid, and Lord Melroy. The Plaid, as they came to be known, were one of the more successful British rock groups that invaded the U.S. in the seventies. "I've heard of them," he assured Bobs. "There must be a lot of money in rock music."

Bobs rolled his eyes. "Great riches, you might say."

Lord Melroy had taste not usually associated with middle-aged men who'd screamed lyrics and set fire to their guitars on stage. The effects of great riches, Harper assumed. The hall had wainscotted walls and was hung with oil paintings of hunting scenes and impressionist land-scapes. It ended in an ornately pedimented double doorway. Delilah would be just the other side of those doors.

Harper found himself thinking about his wife. Laura, being a nurse, was careful to eat a healthy diet and take regular exercise. She neither smoked nor drank. She had only one vice and that was Delilah. In the supermarket she would choose the longest checkout line so as to have ample time to peruse the latest magazine articles about the ever-evolving rock star.

In fact Laura had been a fan from the beginning and still had her copy of Delilah's first hit record, "Maidenhead." That had been in 1983. A string of outrageous hit songs had followed; what little the lyrics left to the imagination was shown in the videos. Then Laura'd had to suffer through Delilah's flop movie, and her flop marriage to her co-star. Only a couple of years later, though, the singer made a big comeback with her Blonde on the Run World Tour. In Canada the police had almost stopped the show and arrested her. In Italy the Pope had denounced her. Then the documentary movie had come out, revealing that the goings-on back-stage had been even hotter than the show itself.

Last year Laura had stayed up late watching the Oscar show, because Delilah was up for Best Actress. But she didn't win, and some cynics said that it was disappointment and not motherhood that had led to the current hiatus in her career. The curious fact was that she'd become even more of an object of facination since she'd gone into relative seclusion.

Harper had to admit to himself that he was nervous. Now that he was about to meet Delilah, he was glad he'd never seen her naked. It hadn't been easy to avoid the sight of her bare body over the last decade or so, but he'd managed.

Bobs threw open the double doors and stepped back. He was going to wait in the hall, apparently. Harper went in.

It was a small sitting room with high-backed armchairs ranged around a coffee table. A bowl of brilliant azalea blossoms stood in the fireplace. There appeared to be no one in the room except a child, a little girl not much more than a year old. She was working her way around the coffee table hand over hand. It took concentration; she didn't have this walking business down yet. She looked up at Harper with large, solemn eyes.

This must be Fatima, Delilah's child. He smiled and said, "Hello, there."

A blond head came into view over the chairback. The woman had been slouching there, invisible to Harper. She turned to look at him, but even then he wasn't sure she was Delilah. He'd been expecting the masque of her stage makeup: the platinum mane, pale face, heavy black brows and blood-red lips. This was a good-looking woman with golden-brown hair, big blue eyes, and a light suntan. Her brows weren't particularly heavy and her lips weren't particularly full. If he'd passed her on the street, he would have turned to look at her but wouldn't have guessed who she was.

She got up and came toward him. She was wearing a baggy T-shirt and long, tight lycra shorts of the kind European bicycle-racers wore. She had the legs of a bike-racer too, Harper thought—thin and hard-muscled, with bony knees. She didn't say anything, just put out her hand. Harper took it.

Then she did something no one else had ever done. Continuing to hold his hand, she turned it over and looked down at it.

"I read about how you hurt your hand. Scary story. Does it still hurt?"

She seemed to want a real answer, so he said, "In cold weather. Or when I'm tired or tense."

She was still studying the hand. "Must've taken a lot of surgery."

He hesitated, but no one had ever called Delilah squeamish, so he told her briefly about his treatment in the hospital. He was aware of other people coming into the room behind him, but she paid no attention to them. She was concentrating on Harper.

"Wow," she said when he was finished. "It must've been hell."

"Delilah," said a chiding voice. It was that of a slender, dark-haired young woman, who was sitting down in an armchair and drawing the child to her.

"What?" said Delilah. "You mean *hell* counts too?"

The woman nodded.

Delilah raised her hands. There was a rubber band around her left wrist. She pulled it out and let it snap back. It had to sting. "That's to remind me to watch my language. For my kid's sake," she explained.

He smiled. He was warming to Delilah. Her interest in his wounded hand touched him. Of course, he was aware that charming strangers was merely a trick celebrities were good at, just as Harper was good at finding parking spaces in midtown. Still, he found himself liking Delilah.

Enough to want to save her life.

She returned to the chair she'd been sitting in and waved him to one on the opposite side of the coffee table. Another woman sat down on the love seat near the fireplace. She was brunette and plump. Her face had a calm, alert expression. Harper recognized her from pictures as Nancy Kinsolving, Delilah's oldest friend and most trusted advisor. Bobs, the big security man, had also come into the room. He didn't sit down. Instead he paced noisily behind Harper's chair.

He said, "Delilah, if you really want to hear this man out, okay. But I think we oughta wait till Agent Wilson gets here."

"Agent Wilson?" said Harper.

Bobs came around the chair to look down at him. "That's who I talked to at the FBI. She's on her way out here by helicopter now." He turned back to Delilah. "She wants to explain to us why everything this guy says is bullshit."

"Bobs, watch your language," said Delilah, looking at her daughter in the nurse's lap.

Bobs shut his eyes and struggled with his temper. "Sorry."

Harper said, "You might as well hear me out. It won't take me long to make my case."

It better not take him long, he thought. Once Frances Wilson got here he wouldn't be doing any more talking. She'd see to that.

He leaned forward and told the rock star as briefly and forcefully as he could that the Bureau was wrong. Anthony Markman was still alive and even now preparing to strike his final victim. Harper summarized the reasoning that had led Addleman and him to conclude that the victim was Delilah.

While he spoke, Bobs paced heavily behind him, moving with precise, measured steps, like a large animal in a smalll cage, giving occasional grunts of disbelief or amusement. Nancy Kinsolving gazed steadily at her friend.

The star listened with lowered eyes. For a full minute after Harper finished she continued to look at the floor. Then she looked up at him.

One eyebrow rose, the upper lip curled, and suddenly she looked like Delilah. Her face was full of disdain, bravado, sexual challenge. Until now she'd been speaking softly, with a singer's crisp enunciation. But this time she spoke in the taunting, raucous voice that had been heard from concert stages all over the world.

"So—trying to scare me, huh?"

Harper held her eye and nodded.

Bracing her feet on the edge of the coffee table she slumped in her chair, so deeply that she was looking at him from between her bony knees. "What's your advice, then? What do I have to do to be safe from this guy?"

"Harper wants you to hole up here, of course," said Bobs. "Never leave the estate. Hide out from a man the FBI knows is dead."

"Shit," said Delilah. Then she frowned and snapped her rubber band.

Harper said, "Even that wouldn't be enough. We have no way of knowing when and where he'll strike. A public appearance might seem to offer him the best chance, but he got his last two victims when they were in private, seemingly secure areas. The only way for you to be safe is to get far away from Washington, D.C. I advise you to go straight home."

"Back to LA," said Delilah. Her lip curled again. "This is really depressing. You know why I came here in the first place?"

"I've heard a lot of theories."

"I was house-hunting. I want Fatima to grow up in the country. Someplace where there are clear streams and horses. And nobody's in show business. You know, someplace normal. *Normal.* And this sh—, *this* happens. Nancy, what do I do?"

"I have no way of knowing if he's right about the Bomber, but I'll tell you one thing." Kinsolving pointed her finger at Harper. Her eyes were hard with dislike. "When that man goes back to Washington and tells the reporters about this meeting, we'll get some very bad press."

"I won't be talking to reporters," said Harper.

No one paid any attention to him. Delilah put her feet down and straightened up. "Bad press? Why? 'Cause some nut is out to kill me? They gonna make that out to be my fault, like they do everything else?"

"I won't be talking to reporters," Harper repeated.

"Aw, cut the shit, Harper. Everybody who talks to me talks to reporters afterwards." She snapped her rubber band and leaned back in the chair.

"And another thing," Nancy said, "Those politicians and media types who said they'd throw parties or luncheons in your honor—they're all going to back out as soon as word gets around."

Delilah gave another of her stage expressions, a girlish moue of disappointment. "Even Senator Standling? But he said he was willing to defy the Christian Coalition to invite me to his home."

"The Christian Coalition doesn't blow people up," said Harper.

Delilah's expression sobered. "You really think this Markman guy is alive? And out to get me? You're sure?"

Harper nodded. Behind him, Bobs muttered irritably.

"I keep telling you, it doesn't matter if he's right or not, we have to leave before the story surfaces." Nancy leaned toward Delilah. "Otherwise the media will be saying it's not true you've been fulfilled by motherhood. That you'll still do anything to grab a headline, even at the risk of making your child an orphan."

Delilah looked at Fatima, dozing in the nurse's lap. She smiled.

"All right, Harper. You win."

Harper let out the breath he hadn't realized he'd been holding.

Nancy reached for the phone on the end table. "I'll make the arrangements. You want to go first thing tomorrow morning?"

"No. The afternoon. There is one thing I gotta do."

Nancy frowned, thinking. "Constant Light?"

"Yeah."

Harper looked questioningly at Nancy, who explained, "It's a hospital for war orphans. Delilah's their main patron. She's scheduled for a tour and a fundraising luncheon tomorrow."

Harper turned to Delilah. "I advise you not to go."

"Yeah, well, you can just blow me, Harper." She paused to snap her rubber band. She was going to have a very sore wrist by the end of the evening. "I don't have to look at houses. I don't mind missing out on a bunch of Georgetown cocktail parties. But those kids have been expecting me for months. I'm not going to stand them up."

Harper said, "It's your life we're talking about. The Bomber is just as likely to be targeting you at this hospital as he is at any other time during your visit."

"And if this leaks we'll get raked over the coals on the morning news shows, even if you leave in the afternoon." Nancy had the phone in her lap but hadn't lifted the receiver. "Remember your responsibilities, they'll all be saying. Remember your child."

Delilah's face was drawn. "I do. But I also gotta remember the children who aren't as lucky as mine."

"But—"

The star held up her hand, palm out. "Look, when the hospital asked me to sit on their board and I agreed, I wasn't doing it for the publicity. You know that, Nancy. I was thinking about those children. It cheers them up to have me visit. I can see it in their eyes. There's more to the job than hitting up my friends for contributions. I'm going to visit those kids tomorrow."

She looked at each of them in turn. No one said anything. Delilah rose from her chair. "Then it's settled. Everybody up."

Bobs stepped forward. Nancy stood. So did Harper, confused. They formed a circle and their hands met in the middle. Now he remembered. Laura had told him that Delilah always led her dancers in a prayer before they went onstage. He decided to go along with it, even though he hadn't taken part in a ritual like this since the basketball final in his senior year at high school. They'd lost that game, if he remembered right.

"Oh Lord, I know you want me to do this," she said. "I'm plenty scared but I'm hoping you'll watch over me, and you won't let me or anyone else get hurt, okay? Amen."

There was a pause as they lowered their hands. The buffeting roar of an approaching jet helicopter could be clearly heard. Frances Wilson was arriving. Not that it mattered; he doubted he'd be able to change Delilah's mind, even if he had more time.

He'd done his best. He'd have to live with the star's visit to the hospital.

And hope she could do the same.

42

Harper reported the evening's events to Addleman from a prone position.

It was long after midnight by the time he'd made it back to the hotel. He was exhausted. It seemed years ago, rather than this morning, that he and Addleman had arrived at National Airport. Things hadn't gone well since.

So when Harper finally stumbled into the suite, he'd gone straight to his bedroom, where he took off his shoes and jacket and flopped on the bed. He didn't even bother to switch on a light before he began relating the events of the evening while Addleman sat in a chair by the door and heard him out.

Harper told it straight through, finishing with the scene with Frances Wilson. He tried to make her insults and threats sound funnier than they had been in actuality. But Addleman wasn't laughing. In fact Harper had the sense that he wasn't even listening anymore.

He propped himself up on an elbow. Addleman was sitting there hunched and still, almost as if he were simply another shadow in the dim room. In the faint light, Harper couldn't see his face.

"It's the hospital, Will."

"What?"

"Markman's planning to blow up that hospital tomorrow. He wants the children to die with Delilah."

"You can't be sure of that," Harper said, though his own thoughts had run in the same direction. "Maybe we're just thinking that way because the hospital's the one obligation Delilah has vowed to meet."

"No, it isn't that. It's the obvious target for Markman. This is the culmination, the coming together of his childhood trauma and his obsession with celebrities. He identifies Delilah with his mother, who used him sexually. The way he sees it, she's is using the children in that hospital. People admire her for helping to rescue and heal these children, and Markman can't stand that. He's going to 'prove' that she's false and selfish like his own mother. He's going to kill those children—and make sure Delilah will be blamed for their deaths."

That all sounded reasonable to Harper except for the last part. "Why should *she* be blamed?" he asked.

Addleman hesitated, then said, "Because of you, Will. You warned her tonight. But she chose to ignore you. Sure, she thought she was being brave and generous. But after tomorrow, after the disaster, people will say that by going to the hospital despite knowing the risk, she endangered the children along with herself. The bomber hates her. He doesn't just want her dead. He's going to make sure no one mourns her. He'll make her *infamous*. And you've made that possible, Will."

Harper's mind reeled with shock and outrage. He lurched to his feet and began to pace across the carpet in stocking feet. "That's crazy, Harold. Markman couldn't know in advance that lawyer would come to see us, that we'd stumble onto who the next target was, that the Bureau would cut us loose. The guy can't see into the future."

"No. But he can plan for contingencies, and better than any bomber or any other kind of criminal I've profiled. Remember, Will, when you went to his house in St. Louis? That could've been a disaster for him. He could've panicked. But he didn't. He figured out a plan that put you to good use. He's still a step ahead of us. He's still using you. You're his Cassandra. Your role is to predict what's going to happen and not be believed."

Addleman sighed and leaned back in his chair. He looked as wasted as Harper felt.

Harper pressed his hands to his temples as he continued to pace.

Had they come so far only to fail in the end? And this was worse than failure. He'd become Markman's unwilling accessory. His pawn.

He spoke loudly and raggedly, "There's nothing more I can do! She's determined to go to the hospital. Anyway, I can't talk to her again. Frances Wilson saw to that."

"Then you'll have to go to the hospital tomorrow."

"Frances made it clear that I'd be arrested if I tried to get near Delilah again. And there'll be security people all over the place."

"Not enough to protect her."

"There's nothing I can do."

"Helpless," Addleman said in a tired, hoarse voice. "Like Cassandra."

Harper sank back down on the bed. He sighed heavily.

"I'll go to the hospital," he said.

43

The Constant Light Children's Hospital was located across the river, in suburban Virginia. Delilah's visit was scheduled to begin at 10:30 A.M., and Harper didn't want to arrive much earlier than that. There was no point. He wasn't going to waste time arguing with officials and staffers. Frances Wilson would have given them solid bureaucratic reasons why they shouldn't listen to that nutcase and loose cannon Will Harper. Only Delilah herself, whose life was on the line, would have any inclination to believe him. His only chance was to get to her.

He turned off a busy suburban street onto an access road that looped around a parking garage to the main entrance of the hospital. It would have been a difficult area to lock down completely, and the cops hadn't tried to do so. Harper noted a heavy security presence but people were coming and going freely.

He slid his rental car into a space below a sign that said RESERVED FOR R. PATEL, M.D. Looking across the drive, he could see that the hospital's reception committee was already standing on the front steps. There was the usual crowd of well-wishers and gawkers, being held back by yellow sawhorses and local police and private security people. On the other side of the steps a group of reporters and photographers were milling around casually. Just another day on the celebrity beat; nobody seemed to expect any trouble.

Harper scanned every face in the crowd, but he didn't really expect Markman to be this close to the scene. He wasn't a man to take unnecessary risks. He would have found some remote vantage point from which he could watch what was going on. Or maybe he wasn't even here. He could have set the timer and planted the bomb hours ago. Maybe he was in some hotel room, watching TV and waiting.

Harper glanced at his watch. Delilah was late, but he expected her to arrive soon. He began to roll his head, to hunch and relax his shoulders—all the tension-easing tricks he'd learned on the Bomb Squad.

You had to learn how to wait. That was what the old pros had told him, when he'd first arrived at the Rodman's Neck Range of the NYPD as a recruit. In your whole career, the amount of time you'd spend actually disarming bombs could be measured in minutes. But you would spend hours, days, even weeks, waiting to go out on a job. If you didn't learn how to wait, nervousness would sap your powers of concentration and wear down your confidence. You wouldn't be ready when the call came.

So Harper had learned how to wait. And he'd survived longer on the Squad than most. He'd almost made it to retirement. Almost.

The crowd was stirring now. The cops were striding around purposefully, yammering to each other on their portable radios. The microwave dish atop a TV van began its ascent. The reporters were snuffing out their cigarettes and throwing away their coffee cups. The photographers were moving up to the barriers, jostling each other for position.

Harper turned to look down the access road. He could see a police car approaching with flashing lights. Behind it was Delilah's limousine. They were driving very slowly.

Harper got out of the car and began walking slowly toward the entrance to the hospital, intending to arrive just as the limo did.

He was still a dozen paces away when he saw a young black uniformed cop turn, glance at him, then give him a second look. The kid was on the ball, Harper thought. He'd been listening when word had come down from the FBI to be on the lookout for Harper. He quickened his pace. The kid got the attention of another uniform and pointed at Harper. The two moved to intercept him, closing in to cut off his angle of escape.

Harper knew that if he started running, they would too. So he just kept walking through the crowd that grew thicker the closer he got to the hospital entrance. He began to weave around people, hoping the cops would lose sight of him.

They didn't. He was still half a dozen steps from the barriers when they closed in.

"William Harper?" the young black cop said. It was an official voice, but friendly, as if his next words might be to ask Harper for his autograph.

"No, not me," Harper replied with a smile, trying to step past him.

But the older cop blocked his way. "Mr. Harper, you have to leave this area immediately or you'll be placed under arrest."

"Isn't that a bit harsh?" Harper asked.

The young cop shrugged. "You know how it works, Mr. Harper. Orders."

"Yeah, orders."

Looking between the two cops and over the heads of the crowd, Harper could see the limousine drawing to a halt at the hospital entrance. This was his best chance; he wouldn't get a better one.

"I'll stand right here, but I want to talk to your sergeant," he said.

In unison, the two cops shook their heads. Negotiations seemed to have reached an impasse.

Harper dropped into a football linesman's crouch and tried to drive right through them.

The older cop grunted and gave way but the younger one wrapped his arms around Harper and held on. Harper staggered on another pace before dropping to his knees. The older cop jumped on top of him and all three went down.

As he rolled and wriggled and strained to get to his feet, Harper could hear the gasps and exclamations of the people around him. There were shouts and the pounding of feet as more cops and guards converged on them. Harper struggled on, but it was no use. Within moments he was belly-down on the asphalt. His arms were pulled up onto his back and he felt the metal rings slide onto his wrists and heard the snick of the locks.

The weight on his back lessened. Several pairs of hands lifted him and set him on his feet. As his head came up, he saw the glassy eyes of dozens of lenses pointed at him, and heard the ratcheting of camera motor drives. The reporters had arrived. He'd never been so glad to see them.

"Hey—that's Harper!" someone shouted.

"What are you doing to Harper?"

"Who ordered Harper's arrest?"

"Harper—do you believe there's a bomb—"

A man loomed up between Harper and the reporters. In a low and urgent voice, he said to the cops who were holding Harper's arms, "Get him in the car—right now."

The man stayed right next to Harper as they hustled him along. The blue suit and the grim expression on the clean-cut features tipped him off even before he saw the FBI creds dangling from the man's neck. This guy had been sent by Frances to prevent Harper from embarrassing her. He'd get Harper off the scene or die trying.

Harper tried dragging his feet. No use: He was lifted up and carried. Out of the corner of his eye he could see the photographers and reporters still keeping pace. Everyone seemed to be shouting at once.

"What's the charge against this man, Officer?"

"Harper, what'd you do?"

"Is there a bomb in the hospital?"

"Is Delilah the target?"

Harper turned his head and said to the FBI man, "I want to talk to Delilah."

The agent gave a tight smile of disgust. "No chance."

"Then I'll start talking to these guys."

"Don't try it, asshole."

"You take me to Delilah or you're gonna have a panic on your hands."

The agent's hand darted under his coat and came out holding a can of pepper spray. He pointed the nozzle at Harper's face. Harper clenched his eyes shut and tried to turn away, knowing it was hopeless, knowing that in a split second the spray was going to render him mute and helpless.

"You can't do that!" shouted a new voice. "Not in front of the cameras!"

He opened his eyes to see a chunky woman in a police sergeant's uniform. She was standing in front of him, her hand grasping the arm of the FBI agent. He was cursing at her. By now the media people had closed the ring in front of them. Camera lenses covered every angle. Shouted questions were coming from all sides.

Abruptly a tall bald man appeared in front of Harper. It was Bobs. He said, with great aplomb, "Delilah will see Mr. Harper."

"No, she won't," said the FBI man.

"I talk to her or I talk to them," Harper said, nodding toward the reporters.

"Take him to the limo," the sergeant ordered, tucking her thumbs in her belt.

Harper's feet were allowed to settle on the ground. The hands that had been holding his biceps in a viselike grip let go. The party began to make its way back through the crowd to the limousine. The reporters continued to shout questions. They'd started calling Harper *Will*, now, as if that would make a difference. The agent, in a soft, bitter voice, was telling the sergeant she was making a big mistake and that this was the end of her career. The sergeant seemed unperturbed.

A security man opened the limo's rear door as they approached. Bowing his head the way he'd seen so many suspects do, Harper clambered in. The door slammed shut behind him. He found a jump seat to perch on and turned to face Delilah.

She was alone on the spacious backseat. She was wearing a tailored suit that was a bright yet delicate shade of pink which he'd seen before only in azalea blossoms. Every hair was in place. There seemed to be four or five different shades of makeup on her upper eyelids. Harper had never seen anyone in real life look so perfect. He stared at her as if she were a holograph.

She said, "You asshole, Harper."

He sat blinking at her. The tone of voice left no doubt that she was furious at him, but there was no sign of it in her face. She looked calm and composed. Only now did Harper realize that the photographers were moving to surround the car. Camera lenses peered in at every window. He didn't know how much they could get through the tinted glass, but they weren't going to get a closeup of Delilah raging at Harper. She'd been playing the game for years and was too smart for them.

"You set out to ruin my visit, didn't you?" she went on. "You think there's nothing for it now but for me to turn around and go home."

"No, I—"

"Well, I won't let you stop me. The children are waiting and I won't disappoint them. I'm going in there."

"There is a bomb in the hospital."

She gazed at him expressionlessly. "Agent Wilson spent two hours with us after you left, Harper. She explained to us all about the DNA evidence. She had charts. Markman is dead."

"Wilson is wrong, he's alive."

"And she explained why we shouldn't listen to you. Bobs was convinced. And Nancy."

"And you?" said Harper. "Were you convinced—completely convinced?"

She hesitated, but only for an instant. "There's no reason why I shouldn't go into that hospital."

"No, there isn't," Harper retorted. "Assuming you're as crazy as the tabloids say. Assuming you've decided that being assassinated would be a good career move."

The facade cracked. Delilah's lips tightened and she glared at him. "How dare you say that to me?"

"If you want to die, fine. But for God's sake don't take all those children with you. You care about them—I know you do."

Delilah looked down at her hands, which had remained demurely clasped in her pink lap throughout the interview. Harper held his breath. This was the moment. Either she was going to order him out or she was going to listen to him.

Excited shouting and the faint whirring of automatic-wind cameras came to them from beyond the bulletproof windows. The car rocked as a photographer tried to climb on the trunk and was dragged off by cops.

Delilah raised her eyes and met Harper's. She smiled, the familiar wry half smile. "For your information, Harper, I don't have a death wish."

"Oh?"

"I hope to live a long time. I intend to be old, ugly, and beloved by everyone."

Harper smiled back at her. Delilah, he thought, could teach the members of the NYPD Bomb Squad a thing or two about how to wait.

The moment passed. Delilah became grave. "I don't know what to do. Of course I don't want to put those children at risk, but I have no reason to believe you. The security experts have gone all over the hospital. I've been assured that there is no bomb."

Harper said, "Let me go in there, Delilah. Wait here while I look around. If I don't find anything, then you go ahead with your visit."

Delilah locked gazes with him for another long moment. Then she nodded slightly.

"All right, Harper. It's your show."

44

When Harper got out of Delilah's limo, the crowd seemed twice as large as when he'd gotten in. Looking over people's heads, he could see up the access road to a traffic jam of police cars and minicam vans which were trying to get to the scene. A helicopter came in low, heading for the landing pad on the hospital's roof. A new patient, Harper wondered—or Agent Frances Wilson, arriving to take personal charge of the situation?

Better get on with the search.

He fell in behind Bobs, ignoring the reporters who shouted his name and grabbed at him. Six cops in full riot gear had to link arms and form a wedge to push through the crowd and deliver them to the front steps of the hospital.

Two men were waiting for them near the front doors of the building. One was a small man with a lined brow, a neatly trimmed goatee, and a double-breasted suit. Bobs introduced him as Dr. Rosen, director of the hospital. He looked annoyed at having to talk to Harper, while the other man looked bored. This was Captain Alberghetti, a tall, narrow-shouldered man with coarse-pored skin, a receding chin, and salt-and-pepper hair, wearing the green fatigues of the U.S. Army. It was Alberghetti who'd run the search of the building, but Harper turned to Rosen first.

"Doctor, how difficult is it for an unauthorized person to gain entry?"

Rosen's mouth was so tight he looked like a wooden marionette. "Not difficult enough to satisfy you, I'm sure."

Bobs put in smoothly, "Doctor, if you would please cooperate with Mr. Harper—"

"We've been over this before," grumbled Rosen. "There's only so far I can go for you people. I can't allow security to interfere with the running of my hospital."

Harper figured he'd save further questions and assume that Markman would have had no trouble smuggling the bomb in and planting it wherever he wanted to. He turned to Alberghetti.

"Captain—"

"The building's clean, Mr. Harper. I just finished my sweep."

He seemed to think Harper ought to be satisfied with that. He was striking a John Wayne pose, with hands on his web belt and head tilted, for the cameras that were clicking behind Harper. It crossed Harper's mind that Captain Alberghetti might be a lot like Captain Brand. He felt more skeptical about this sweep.

"How did you proceed, exactly?"

Alberghetti blinked and shrugged to indicate that he was bored rather than offended by the question. "We went over Delilah's whole route. There is no bomb."

"What technology did you use?"

"Everything in the truck," said the Captain, jabbing his thumb over his shoulder. At the side of the steps, soldiers in green were loading metal cases into the back of a truck. A German shepherd sat patiently next to his handler's leg.

"This will go more quickly if you'll answer Mr. Harper," said Fox.

Alberghetti didn't glance at Fox. "We used a fluoroscope and metal detector."

Harper said, "Neither of those pick up plastic explosive, which our guy used on his last job."

"We also used an Arleigh B-19 scanner."

Harper had heard of this scanner. It picked up on materials of very high density and thus was able to detect plastic explosives. But the device was new and had some shortcomings.

"Those scanners are real heavy," he said. "Have they developed a portable version I haven't heard about?"

Alberghetti looked uneasily over Harper's left shoulder, then his right. "This model has limited portability. We took it up in the elevator. Whatever object we wanted scanned, we brought to it."

"How about objects that couldn't be moved?"

"In that case we did visual inspection."

"You looked at them, you mean. Suppose there was a plastique bomb concealed behind a wall, under a floor? You wouldn't have found it."

"Duke would have," said Alberghetti, nodding at the German shepherd.

Harper nodded. He had a lot of respect for the nose of a well-trained explosive-sniffing dog. He looked at the German shepherd sitting beside his trainer at the bottom of the steps, patiently waiting to board the truck. "You took the dog all along the route?"

There was a pause before Alberghetti spoke that made Harper look back at him. He said, "Through all the public rooms, yes." And then he looked at Rosen.

The little doctor threw his shoulders back and clasped his hands behind him. "Obviously I couldn't permit a dog to be taken to the third-floor wards. We have very sick children up there. Very delicate equipment. A dog would be disruptive and unsanitary."

Harper turned to Alberghetti. "Get Duke. We're going to the third-floor wards."

"Now, wait—" Rosen began.

"Sorry, Doctor," Harper said. "We have to assume the bomber found out about your decision and exploited it."

Alberghetti was walking down the steps toward his men. Duke had heard his name. He was already on his feet, his long tail swinging in slow arcs behind him. Harper wished Alberghetti and Rosen had had the same spirit of cooperation.

Rosen was arguing loudly. Harper decided to leave him to Bobs. He turned to look around. He'd sent somebody back to his car and hoped the person had returned.

She had. A Bethesda policewoman was standing just behind him with a box under her arm. She offered it to him. "Here you go, sir."

"Thanks."

Harper lifted the lid and pulled out the NYPD blast protection suit Brand had given him. As he put it on, he found that what Brand had said was true. This was a big improvement over earlier models. The last time Harper had put on a bomb suit was in the silent corridor of that Queens high school, with Jimmy Fahey at his side. Harper pushed the thought away.

Fastening the Velcro closure at his neck, he tucked the helmet under his arm and turned. Dr. Rosen was still arguing with Bobs. The veins in his temples stood out like cords. Alberghetti was coming up the steps along with the dog and his handler. "Let's go," he said to Harper. He said it loudly enough for the reporters to hear. He wanted them to assume he was in charge.

"You may want to put on some protection, Captain," said Harper. "And bring along your tools."

"I'll call my people in—*if* we find anything," Alberghetti said, with a hard, skeptical look. Harper figured that like Captain Brand, Alberghetti believed working on live bombs was a chore better left to his inferiors.

They pushed through the glass doors. Guards and receptionists and most of the clerical staff of the hospital were crowded around the front desk. Wide-eyed and unspeaking, they stared at the men and the dog as they walked past to the elevators. It was quiet enough to hear Duke's toenails clicking on the tile floor.

They stepped into the elevator and Alberghetti pressed 3. Duke sat down. His brown eyes were shining with eagerness, but he wasn't panting or wagging his tail. A well-trained dog, Harper thought. His handler, a freckle-faced corporal, looked much more excited.

The doors slid open, and they stepped out onto the most cheerfully decorated hospital ward Harper had ever seen, with a bright-blue carpet and long, multicolored arrowed stripes along the walls. The figures in scrub suits at the nurses' stations looked up from their clipboards and computer screens with bleary eyes. It must be late in their shift, thought Harper. They looked as tired as Laura did when she got home. Evidently Bobs had persuaded Dr. Rosen to make a call, because no one questioned Harper and the others as they walked past.

"Let's just walk Delilah's route, slowly," Harper said.

The corporal bent to murmur a command in the dog's ear. He barely had time to grasp Duke's harness before he was off down the corridor.

Harper dropped back until he was trailing the party. His mouth was dry, his heartbeat rapid. He scanned every inch of the corridor, but he knew he wasn't going to spot anything. Markman hadn't gotten this far by being careless. It was up to Duke.

Harper had read somewhere that a German shepherd's sense of smell was a million times stronger than a man's. A good thing, he thought, because he couldn't smell anything but the faint tang of disinfectant.

Duke was moving in a purposeful zigzag across the corridor, nose to the carpet, when an olive-skinned, dark-eyed child appeared in a doorway. His head was shaved and he had a tracery of healing scars on his face and neck. He burst into a grin when he saw the dog and shouted something in a language Harper didn't understand. Then he ran over to Duke and threw his arms around his neck.

The three men looked at each other helplessly. Even in the circumstances, it was more than any of them could do to separate boy and dog.

More children were appearing in other doorways. Confused, Duke sat down. Harper thought he should have been paying more attention when Rosen warned of the disruption Duke would cause. How long had it been since any of these kids had seen a dog?

The corridor was now full of pajama-clad children of all ages. It seemed that every patient on the floor who could walk—and a few who were in wheelchairs—was surrounding the dog, jostling to get closer, talking excitedly in a mélange of languages. Many small hands, some of them missing fingers, stroked Duke's luxuriant fur.

"We better break up the party, Captain," the handler said, "or this dog won't be fit for sniffing nothing."

Already nurses and doctors were wading into the corridor to restore order. There were tears and wails as they were herded back to their rooms. An Indian doctor, wearing a white lab coat and a blue turban, approached Harper to upbraid him for the disruption. Harper listened and placated, all the time thinking of Delilah, trapped in her limousine downstairs and no doubt rapidly losing patience. And of Special Agent Wilson, who was surely on her way to the scene by the fastest means available.

And of the bomb.

Finally the corridor was cleared and Duke went back to work. His tongue was still hanging out, but he seemed to have recovered his concentration. He padded briskly along, quartering the corridor.

"Is Delilah supposed to tour the whole floor?" Harper asked.

"No," Alberghetti replied. "She's going to this lounge area around the corner. They're planning to gather the children around her there."

Harper nodded. "We'll have to go over the lounge carefully. That could be the place."

"Whatever you say," said Alberghetti casually. He still thought this search was pointless, and nothing had happened so far to shake his aplomb.

They turned the corner onto another corridor with doors standing open on patients' rooms to either side. In one doorway stood a cardiac monitor, angled so that doctors and nurses passing in the corridor could check the heartbeat of the patient at a glance. The soft, regular beeping of the monitor was the only noise. At the end of the corridor, through open glass doors, was the lounge, a cheerful place with children's paintings on the walls. There were colored pillows, books, and toys scattered on the floor.

A place the bomber might have turned into a death trap. Harper swallowed and started toward it.

He'd only taken one stride before Duke surged past him, dragging his handler. He went straight to the cardiac monitor, stopping only when his nose touched the metal doors of the cabinet that supported the screen. He sat down. The three men froze. Duke turned to look up at their faces, confused because they failed to understand that here was what they sought.

Harper's throat closed up. His heart was pounding adrenaline into his bloodstream. It was the fight-or-flight reflex that a Bomb Disposer had to learn to ignore. He swallowed and said, "Better get your EOD team up here, Captain. And give orders to clear the—"

But Alberghetti wasn't listening. Dropping into a crouch in front of the heart monitor he opened the metal doors. Harper's heart lurched. It was a stupid risk to take when there was a possibility of a booby trap.

But they were in luck: nothing happened.

The cabinet was bigger than it needed to be to contain the tubes and circuits of the monitor.

There was plenty of room on its metal floor for the bomb—a simple detonator apparatus and a hunk of C-4 the size of a brick.

"Jesus Christ!" said Alberghetti. "That's enough to take out this whole side of the floor. And the floors above and below."

"Get your people up here, Captain," Harper said. "Tell them to bring their equipment. This'll need to be disarmed in place."

Alberghetti pulled a portable radio out of his pocket.

This time Harper was ready. His left hand darted out to grasp the arm that held the radio. "Let's not take chances, okay?" he said levelly. "This is a radio-controlled detonator. Use the phone at the nurses' station."

Alberghetti didn't argue. He was happy to have an excuse to get away from the bomb. Another Captain Brand, all right.

Duke whined and butted his handler in the thigh. Having done his job, he wanted his Milk-Bone.

Harper said to the corporal, "Maybe you ought to get the dog away from here. Go to the head of the corridor. Keep people back."

"Yes, sir!"

The corporal trotted off, the triumphant dog beside him.

Duke was wagging his tail again.

45

Now Harper was alone with the bomb. Again his mind flashed back to that other quiet corridor in the Queens high school, and again he pushed the thought, the crippling emotions, away from him.

He had to clear his mind. Think what to do.

The helmet was still under his arm. He started to put it on, but changed his mind. The bomb suit was no protection. Standing this close to an explosive so powerful, he might as well be wearing Bermuda shorts.

It would go off whenever Markman pushed the button on his radio transmitter. And he could do that anytime.

But would he?

If he was close enough to observe the scene, or if he was watching television in a hotel, he'd know Delilah was still waiting in her limo. So Markman would wait too. He wouldn't panic and push the button. That wasn't his style. So Harper told himself.

If he was right, they were safe for the moment and all they had to do was wait for the EOD team to get here. And there was no reason for Harper to wait where he was. He could turn and walk away, join Alberghetti at the nurses' station.

He turned his head and looked into the room, where a blond girl of five or so lay unconscious on the bed, an IV in one arm. She wouldn't be going anywhere. Nor would the patients in all the rooms up and down the corridor.

Harper found that he couldn't walk away. It was partly a reluctance to abandon the children, even though he couldn't do anything for them. But more than that, it was irresistible curiosity. In his long pursuit of Tony Markman, this was the first time he'd come face to face with one of Markman's bombs. He couldn't resist the temptation to examine the Celebrity Bomber's handiwork.

He went down on his knees and looked closely at the device lying on the floor of the metal cabinet. It was a clean, simple job—what was needed for the purpose and no more: block of C-4, detonator, radio receiver, and battery. He noticed that the coating with the maker's name had been painstakingly scraped off the battery, leaving the metal casing bare and gleaming. Even on his last job, when it didn't matter anymore, Markman kept to his fastidious habits, eliminating any potential clue. Every piece of plastic and metal looked new and clean, and the wires were no longer than they had to be. No untidy loops. This was a labor of love, like all of Markman's bombs.

Harper frowned. His eyes narrowed. There was one wire too many. Odd. It led off into a corner of the cabinet which Harper couldn't see because Captain Alberghetti hadn't opened the left-hand door all the way.

Instinct told Harper not to pull the door open. Instead he moved closer, being careful to touch nothing, and peered around the edge.

Yes, there it was. The wire ended in exposed copper next to the hinge of the door. Another wire came out of a battery fastened to the inside of the door. The ends of the two wires were half an inch apart. If Alberghetti had opened the door all the way, the two ends would have met, completing the circuit.

Exploding the bomb.

They'd escaped by half an inch.

Harper put out his hand. His first reaction was to shut the door, separating the wire ends still farther, putting everything back the way it had been before Alberghetti disturbed it. But how did he know there wasn't some other booby trap he couldn't see and might trigger?

He withdrew his hand and slowly stood up. Harper knew a lot about fear. It went with his work, just the way fatigue went with nursing.

Laura had told him she knew when she was simply too tired to go on. Right now Harper was too scared to go on.

Time to walk away, he thought. This wasn't his problem. Alberghetti's team was coming. They had the best tools and the most exhaustive training. They had five fingers on each hand. And they had their nerve because they didn't know what it was like when a bomb went off and threw you around like scrap paper and splashed your blood on the walls.

Harper started backing slowly away.

"Hey!"

He turned to see a bespectacled black doctor striding toward him. "Are you in charge here? This man says there's a bomb—"

He jabbed a thumb over his shoulder at the corporal, who was peering nervously around the corner.

"There is," Harper said. "Stay back."

The doctor halted. Light glinted off his glasses and Harper couldn't see his eyes.

More people in white coats or multicolored scrubs were coming around the corner—nurses, orderlies, other doctors. Harper stood in front of the bomb and spread his arms. "Please, everyone stay back!" he shouted. "A team will be here soon to disarm the bomb. Right now we have to be very careful we don't disturb it."

"You mean it could go off anytime?" asked the black doctor, dubiously yet with the faintest hint of alarm.

"It could."

The medical people stayed stock-still for a moment, exchanging startled looks. Then, without a word, they moved.

But they didn't retreat around the corner, as Harper hoped. They broke in all directions, heading into the rooms.

"No!" Harper yelled. "You can't evacuate the patients now! You've got to—"

He broke off, seeing that it was pointless. No one was paying attention to him.

A nurse ran by him, passing within a foot of the cardiac monitor. All it would take was one brush, one jar, and the door would swing all the way open and the bomb would explode.

A nurse and a big red-headed guy in what looked like a paramedic uniform brushed past Harper as they went into the room of the girl who was hooked up to the cardiac monitor. They began to unhook the IV and raise the railings. They were planning to roll the whole bed out.

Only there wasn't room with the heart monitor in the doorway.

Harper looked down the hall. Already medical people were emerging from the rooms, some of them carrying children in their arms, others pushing wheelchairs. One orderly was pushing a chair with each hand, taking up almost the full width of the corridor.

Harper looked down at the metal door hanging precariously half open on its hinges, and decided.

He stepped into the room, where the paramedic was locking the railings of the bed in place. He'd noticed the gleaming handle of a pair of small scissors in a sort of holster on the man's belt. "I need your scissors," he said.

"These are for cutting stitches—nothing else," the man replied irritably. He was in a hurry and didn't glance at Harper.

Harper blinked slowly, trying to control himself. Long ago Jimmy Fahey had said admiringly that Harper had a tone of voice that made people do what he said. He could only hope he still had it.

"Give me the scissors now," he said.

The paramedic froze for a second, then his hand went to his belt and he handed the scissors over.

Harper swung around and went down on one knee before the metal cabinet. He couldn't use the scissors with his crippled hand so it would have to be the left. Since the accident, Harper must have regretted ten thousand times that he was right-handed. He'd never regretted it more keenly than now.

He had to lean far to the right and twist his entire body to angle his arm into the cabinet the way it had to go, and look over his left shoulder to watch what he was doing. His elbow was uncomfortably close to the edge of the booby-trapped door. The stiff, heavy sleeve of the bomb suit was another hindrance.

With his right middle finger he lifted the wire that led from the transmitter to the detonator. He couldn't grasp it because he didn't have enough fingers. He needed the forefinger and thumb to pinch the booby trap wire and lift it so he could cut it. This was like some hellish game of cat's cradle.

There was tumult all around him, shouts and the rattling of gurneys and wheelchairs and the crying of children. He shut it all out.

Nothing mattered but the booby trap wire. His finger and thumb reached for it and he could feel the strain throughout his awkwardly twisted body, feel the weight shifting and the soles of his shoes starting to pivot on the floor. Too far and he'd topple over, taking the cabinet with him.

There! He had the wire. He lifted it and fitted it between the jaws of the scissors. He squeezed and felt the blades cut through the plastic casing.

But not the copper wire itself.

Christ! Harper thought—these were made for cutting stitches, what if they wouldn't cut through metal? Flexing every muscle from his shoulder down he squeezed on the scissors.

The wire parted.

Even over all the noise in the corridor Harper could hear his own sigh of relief. He looked at the detonator wire draped over his middle finger and thought a little giddily, why not? He snipped that one too.

Then he sat back on his haunches, staring at the block of C-4. A moment ago, a minute pulse of electricity reaching it would have released the destructive force of a tornado and a forest fire.

Now it was merely a lump of Silly Putty.

46

Markman was in the parking garage opposite the hospital. Crouching in the narrow open area between two parked cars, he peered over the concrete parapet at the hospital entrance below. In one hand he held the transmitter he'd intended to use to trigger the bomb, in the other a radio that scanned police frequencies.

What he was hearing was a confused jumble of static and excited voices, but it was clear that the bomb he'd placed in the cardiac monitor had been found and disarmed.

By Harper.

Markman was almost overwhelmed by anger and dejection. He wanted to scream, to beat the useless transmitter against the concrete until the plastic shattered into a thousand pieces.

But, as always, he managed to control himself. With a slow, deliberate movement, he placed the transmitter on the gritty, oil-stained floor.

Then he reached in his pocket and took out the other transmitter.

For the other bomb.

The drive in front of the hospital was now even more tightly packed with people, but the police and security guards were getting the scene under control. A stir of excitement in the crowd made him look down. They were taking Delilah out of the limousine and conducting her into the hospital. They figured it was safe now. Wrongly.

Even from up here Markman could hear the sigh of the crowd as the door of the limo opened and she stood up. There was jostling and straining all along the police barricades. Idiots, he thought. How badly they needed to learn the lesson he had to teach. His backup plan wouldn't spell out his message as clearly as the original plan would have, but it would do the job. Markman could rest satisfied.

He looked down at the blond head, the slim figure clad elegantly in pink. Oh, she was beautiful, he had to admit that. He had to stifle an urge to pick up his binoculars for one last look at her. It crossed his mind that if the high-powered rifle had been his weapon—

But it wasn't. He had a very different weapon. Slower than a bullet, but just as sure.

Delilah and her cordon of guards went up the steps and into the hospital. Through the glass doors he could see her moving to the left. They were taking her to the waiting room off the entrance lobby, where Markman himself had waited before his own tour of the hospital two weeks ago.

Picking up the binoculars, he trained them on the window of the waiting room.

He couldn't see Delilah herself. The room was filling up with the usual celebrity parasites—harried-looking people in suits and uniforms, milling around and talking on their portable phones and radios.

Markman could hear some of them on his scanner. It was a jumble of voices and static, but one word kept coming through: *Harper.* He was the man of the hour. The celebrity. Everybody wanted to talk to him, though Delilah, of course, took precedence. Even now Harper was being brought to her, straight from the third floor. They wouldn't even give him time to change out of that stiff and ugly brown bomb suit Markman had watched him put on.

A knight in not-so-shining armor, being brought before the princess he'd served. A touching scene. A perfect photo-op. Anyone who'd studied Delilah the way Markman had would have known that this was what she would do.

Markman smiled bleakly and focused his binoculars on the glass doors of the hospital. He couldn't see all the way to the bank of elevators, but he could see the crowd around the reception desk, and he'd know from their reaction when the hero arrived.

He was vaguely conscious of noises coming from the parking levels below him. The radio messages had made it clear that the police were finally recovering from the initial confusion and were setting about securing the area. They'd sealed off the entrances to the garage, and a SWAT team was working its way up, searching each level. It didn't matter. Markman had no interest in getting away.

A few more minutes were all he needed. Time enough to complete his mission and his life.

He continued to gaze steadily through the binoculars, and in a moment his patience was rewarded. Harper had to be stepping off the elevator now. The signs were unmistakable. The glare of Minicam lights, the shimmer of still photographer's flashes, could be seen through the glass doors. The jostling of the crowd intensified. Some people in back were actually jumping up and down to get a glimpse of the great man.

Markman switched off the scanner, then shut his ears to the shouts of the searching cops below him. He concentrated on watching the crowd through the thick glass doors. He ought to be able to see Harper for a moment as he passed them. Markman would start counting then. After Harper disappeared from view, Markman would give him three minutes to be conducted into the waiting room and up to Delilah. Then—

His finger poised over the detonate button.

When the doors of the elevator slid open on the lobby, Harper was bathed in light—the flicker of flashbulbs and the steady glare of the halogens the TV people used. Laura had commented that when he appeared in the papers Harper was usually wincing and blinking, and it would probably happen again. Everyone was shouting questions at him, but he couldn't make them out, didn't care to answer. He was in no mood for dealing with questions.

When the scissors blades had bitten through the wire, Harper had gone into a sort of happy daze. He'd experienced the strange mood before. It was as if the intense concentration of disarming the bomb demanded a release of tension once the danger was past. Harper's attention was scattered. He was only vaguely aware of the people surrounding him, talking to him, ushering him to Delilah. Mostly he was thinking about seeing Laura again. Reflecting on the wonderful prospect of years of being able to go on breathing. He'd never take that activity for granted again.

They were coming to a doorway. Beyond it he could see a smaller room, just as crowded as the lobby. He caught a glimpse of the superstar, sitting in the middle of the room and looking expectantly his way.

His wayward thoughts turned to Anthony Markman. Here was one of those happy endings the bomber so despised, of whose falsity he was so determined to convince the world. A true Hollywood fade-out, with the little people warming themselves before the glow of the stars, one of whom, incredibly enough, was Harper.

The feeling of happiness and ease drained away as Harper's mind came alert. Markman was still at large—why should Harper assume he was through? Harper still sensed his nearness, just as he'd been sensing it ever since he came to Washington. The first time had been in the hotel lobby, the morning he'd arrived, and Captain Brand had presented him with the bomb suit—

Harper stopped dead. His sweat ran cold under the bulky body armor. What if his instincts had been right? The lobby had been crowded, so that the bomber would have had plenty of cover from which to watch the little presentation ceremony. And Harper had left the suit in his room all morning, giving Markman plenty of time—

To plant a second bomb, just in case the first failed.

In the bomb suit!

Harper was bringing Delilah the fiery death she'd just avoided. And he'd die with her.

"No!" he shouted.

He struggled to free himself from the hands that were pushing him toward Delilah. People didn't understand why their hero was behaving this way. They continued to grin at him though their eyes were puzzled.

"What is it, you need to take a leak?" someone asked jokingly.

"He's gonna barf, they always do that after they work on a bomb," said a woman reporter in knowledgeable tones.

A voice started sputtering, "Delilah—Delilah—"

Harper had no time to explain. He didn't want to yell *Bomb!* and cause a panic which might make it even more difficult for him to reach an exit. Shaking off the hands that grabbed at him, he wriggled and shoved through the confused, protesting crowd, heading for an EXIT sign he could see above their heads.

At last he reached it, and threw it open to find a flight of concrete steps leading to the basement. He hurtled down them. Behind him the door flew open. They were still pursuing him, shouting questions. Harper turned and yelled, "I'm the bomb! Markman planted explosives on me! Stay back!"

That did it. The people scrambled backward up the steps and the door slammed shut.

Harper was alone in a dank, narrow basement corridor. He patted at the stiff fabric of the suit. It had no pockets. The plastique must be sewn right into the material. It was so thick you wouldn't be able to feel a small, flat charge—but up against his skin, it would eviscerate him. There would be a detonator the size of a thimble and a miniature timer—or transmitter. Which? No time to think about it. All that mattered was shedding the suit and getting away from it.

A man with two good hands could get it off in seconds. But for Harper it was a struggle. He tore open the Velcro straps at the wrists and neck. Then he yanked the zipper so that the groin-protecting flap fell heavily between his legs.

Crossing his arms, he pulled the top-piece up over his head. Now he was in darkness. The stiff, heavy garment wouldn't come off. He wriggled and pulled. The sound of his trapped, panting breath filled his ears. Finally, with a desperate tug that made him grunt with effort, he got the top free of one shoulder. It was taking his sweat-soaked shirt with it. He could feel cool air on his bare back. He shrugged off the top and shirt and let them fall to the floor. Then he looked down at his pants.

And realized that to take them off, he would first have to take off his shoes.

Should he get the whole suit off, or run for it right now? One last time Harper tried to put himself in Markman's mind. The thicker padding was in the top—easier to hide the bomb there and it'd be closer to his vital organs. Harper looked at the top lying on the floor.

Then turned and ran.

He sprinted down the dim, narrow corridor, gasping for breath. He could only hope he was leaving the bomb behind, rather than taking it with him.

He saw a turning ahead of him and ran at it full tilt, trying to get around the corner before the bomb—

A roaring filled his ears and the floor seemed to fall away from his feet. The blast picked him up and slammed him against the wall.

The next thing he knew, he was lying in a heap on the cool concrete floor. His ears were ringing painfully. Lifting his head, he looked down at his bare chest, his legs, his feet.

Still in one piece. Thank God!

He'd guessed right. The bomb had been in the top.

His entire body began to tremble. He lay quietly and let it, knowing that eventually the quaking would stop of its own accord.

And after that—he'd have the rest of his life!

Markman raised his head above the parapet and stared incredulously at the hospital. He'd just pushed the button. He should have heard the explosion. Seen the windows blown out, the crowd in the drive screaming and ducking. What could have happened?

What had gone wrong?

"Freeze!" yelled a voice behind him. Exactly like an actor on a bad TV show, Markman couldn't help but notice.

So the cops searching the garage had found him at last. It meant hardly anything to Markman, compared to his sense of failure, to the crushing realization that he'd left the pattern uncompleted, his life's mission unfulfilled, his message to the world undelivered.

Maybe he ought to allow his capture. Use his trial as a public forum, a platform to speak to the world about the big lie of celebrity.

No. It wouldn't work. In captivity he would be a circus animal, to be gawked at and laughed at but not taken seriously. TV psychologists would explain him.

No. That would never do.

So Markman didn't freeze. He turned and straightened up.

He never expected to complete the movement. He expected the bullets to hit. A moment's heat and pain, and then oblivion.

But the cop didn't shoot. His face was young and scared, eyes wide and mouth open under the SWAT team helmet and visor. The gun, though braced in both outstretched hands, was still shaking as he pointed it at Markman.

"Freeze!" he shouted again.

Markman smiled and stepped toward him.

The cop didn't shoot. *Christ*, Markman thought, what was it going to take?

"Drop the weapon!" the cop shouted.

He meant the transmitter, which Markman was still holding in his left hand. Some weapon. Just a useless piece of plastic.

"Drop it! *Now!*"

Markman smiled. Maybe it wasn't useless after all. Maybe it would bring him the only thing he sought.

He swung the transmitter up and pointed it at the young cop.

That was what it took.

EPILOGUE

Away from the brilliant TV lights, and the cameras, recorders, flashes, and microphones, Harper lay with Laura in the bedroom of the Brooklyn brownstone with its smells of fresh paint and raw wood and tacky varnish. It was a quiet night. Only the sounds of sparse but rushing traffic and an occasional faraway siren or high jet aircraft found their way into the dark bedroom.

Harper listened to those sounds and to the rise-and-fall sighing of Laura's breathing and stared at the shadowed ceiling, feeling the past release its grip.

Markman was unmistakably and finally and forever dead. Like Jimmy Fahey.

Frances Wilson had been reassigned by the Bureau to the New York office Bank Robbery Division. Addleman told Harper this meant that teamwork and not supervision would be her life in the Bureau for the foreseeable future. Her career was stalled.

Addleman himself had been the subject of media speculation, had been offered a book contract, employment with private security firms. He'd turned everything down to do consultant work from his apartment in Philadelphia. Now that it was his choice, he'd told Harper, he was content precisely where he was.

Harper knew what Addleman meant, because he'd turned down the same kinds of offers himself. Most of them, anyway.

He had agreed to the book, to working with a writer an agency and his publisher had recommended. The contract wasn't enough to make him and Laura fabulously rich, but it was a sum Harper wouldn't have dreamed of a few months ago. Money wouldn't be a problem ever again, if he played his investments right. And Laura would have whatever within reason she wanted, and could quit work at the hospital.

If she wanted to quit. Maybe she'd be like Addleman, and decide she'd rather continue doing what she'd been doing. That would be okay with Harper, who would go to Rodman's Neck whenever he was invited.

Because now Harper was content in retirement, beside Laura, in the brownstone that was home.